PRAISE FOR *THE PREY OF GODS*

**Winner of the Compton Crook Award and
the RT Reviewers' Choice Award (Science Fiction)**

"Fans of Nnedi Okorafor, Lauren Beukes and Neil Gaiman better add *The Prey of Gods* to their reading lists! This addicting new novel combines all the best elements of science fiction and fantasy."

—RT Book Reviews, "June 2017 Seal of Excellence—Best of the Month"

"This dense and imaginative debut is . . . a book like no other, with a diverse cast that crosses the spectrum of genders and races, and a new idea (or four) in every chapter."

—B&N Sci-Fi and Fantasy Blog, "The Best Science Fiction & Fantasy Books of 2017 So Far"

"Drayden's delivery of all this is subtly poignant and slap-in-the-face deadpan—perfect for this novel-length thought exercise about what kinds of gods a cynical, self-absorbed postmodern society really deserves. Lots of fun."

—New York Times Book Review

"Thanks to a rip-roaring story and Drayden's expansive imagination, it all coheres into the most fun you can have in 2017."

—Book Riot

"One of the biggest pleasures of this book is the plurality of its voices and story lines, and the way Nicky Drayden skips and weaves between them. . . . It's a book full of energy and momentum, strange wit and sensitivity. It is a LOT. And it is wonderful."

—Vulture, "The 10 Best Fantasy Books of 2017"

PRAISE FOR *TEMPER*

**A *Publishers Weekly* Best Book of 2018 and a
Vulture Best Sci-Fi and Fantasy Book of 2018**

"Drayden . . . crafts a tangled, fantastical African society as the setting for her spellbinding sophomore novel. . . . Drayden takes speculative fiction in an exciting direction with a harrowing and impressive tale of twisted prophecy, identity, and cataclysmic change."

—*Publishers Weekly* (starred review)

"[Drayden] excels at making every twist and turn of the plot meaningful to the story. Moreover, the world-building is deliciously lush and complex."

—*Booklist* (starred review)

"Drayden is an amazing writer and deft plotter. The twists are unexpected and never feel contrived, just as the novel explores real-world issues without sounding preachy."

—*Library Journal*

ESCAPING
EXODUS

ALSO BY NICKY DRAYDEN

The Prey of Gods
Temper

ESCAPING EXODUS

A NOVEL

NICKY DRAYDEN

HARPER Voyager

An Imprint of HarperCollins*Publishers*

ESCAPING EXODUS. Copyright © 2019 by Nicole Duson. Excerpt from THE PREY OF GODS © 2017 by Nicole Duson. Excerpt from TEMPER © 2018 by Nicole Duson. All rights reserved. Printed in the United States of America. No part of this book may be used or reproduced in any manner whatsoever without written permission except in the case of brief quotations embodied in critical articles and reviews. For information, address HarperCollins Publishers, 195 Broadway, New York, NY 10007.

HarperCollins books may be purchased for educational, business, or sales promotional use. For information, please email the Special Markets Department at SPsales@harpercollins.com.

Harper Voyager and design are trademarks of HarperCollins Publishers LLC.

FIRST EDITION

Designed by Paula Russell Szafranski

Frontispiece and interior art © Fernando Cortes / Shutterstock

Library of Congress Cataloging-in-Publication Data has been applied for.

ISBN 978-0-06-286773-5

19 20 21 22 23 LSC 10 9 8 7 6 5 4 3 2 1

To Katie and Laika,
across all space and time

contents

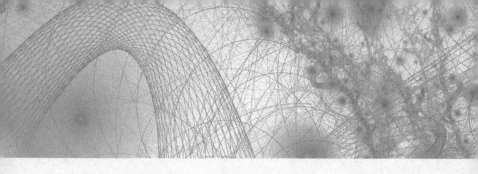

ESCAPING
EXODUS

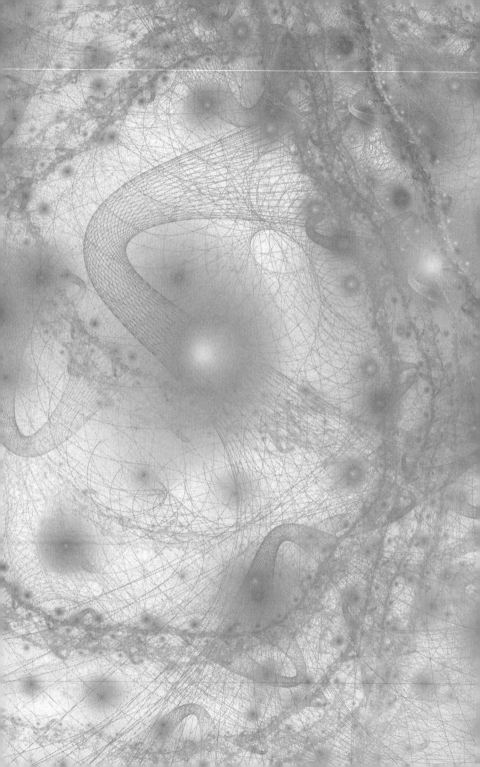

part I

excavation

Our histories lie in rubble, buried upon a dead
rock spinning under a forgotten sky. Our futures
lie in waiting, buried within this magnificent beast
traversing the stars we now call home.

—MATRIS OTOASA,
438 YEARS AFTER EXODUS

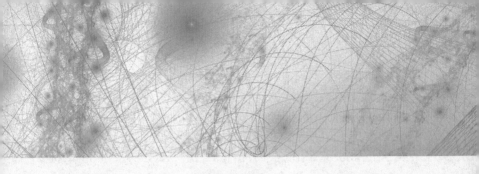

SESKE

Of Old Friends and New Awakenings

Our family's stasis pod seems impenetrable as I rub my hand over the inner surface, looking for the exit seam. I'd underestimated the depth of the darkness that would saturate the pod, and without vision, without hearing—and with my mouth and lungs and stomach filled with sleep balm—touch is the only tool to help me escape.

I feel the flesh of my mothers and fathers beneath me, bodies limp and near lifeless as they await the construction of our new world. Me, I am not that patient. This is my first excavation, and I don't intend to miss it. Matris, my head-mother and our clan's matriarch, had been raised from our pod well before my sedatives wore out, probably as soon as the herd was in sight. My fingers twitch, imagining Matris as she took aim and dealt the crippling final blow to the spacefaring beast. At our next exodus, Matris promised that she would let me drive the helm, but that is still some twelve years off.

I can't wait a moment longer, though, knowing all that is going on around me.

Beneath my desperate hands, the soft nap of the stasis pod goes to partially healed scar tissue, smooth and thin. I pull the bone shard I'd smuggled in here, my laugh a silent jiggle of liquid-filled lungs. If Matris knew her accountancy guards had missed it during their oh-so-thorough inspection, she'd have them strung up by their thumbs for a week.

The incision I make is slow and precise, matching the original hair for hair. I can't leave any evidence of my excursion. A gentle blue light seeps through the cut. I push apart the layers and press my head through. Air hits my face, and the instinct to cough catches me by surprise. Sleep balm spews from my mouth and my nose, as sweet air fills them, quickly washing away a metallic aftertaste.

"Daidi's bells," I curse upon the memory of every heart-father there ever was. I quickly recoil, covering my mouth with balm-slick hands. I'd imagined my first words on this new world would be something more profound, something graceful and fitting of the clan's future matriarch.

The cargo hold feels more like a crypt, half-full oblong sacks just large enough to house the families who opted to sleep through the construction. In a few months, they'll wake up to a perfect replica of their former homes, detailed down to every chip in their countertops, every scuff upon their sickle-scaled floors, right on down to the creak of the boneboards beneath. Matris says they have forgotten that we are nomads and that it is for the best. It is better for them to focus their efforts on infusing the economy and advancing technology than worrying over the droll trivialities of beastwork . . .

Beastwork. The promise of seeing our new beast before the excavation work begins thrills me to my core. I don't know why anyone would opt to sleep this time away when they could be witnessing the workers sinking their siphons into the first artery. I'd practically begged Matris to be woken early, but she insisted that this was a delicate time for her, and she didn't need the distraction of family as critical decisions were being made.

I hope I'm not too late. I hurry, pulling my body through the incision that I now realize is too narrow for my hips. I twist, trying to finesse my way through. My feet find purchase on the familiar ripple of my bapa's abdomen and the indistinguishable arm crook of one of my mothers. The delicate seam tears, running jagged this way and that. I ignore the pit in my stomach. It is still early. Maybe it will heal in time. Maybe I can bribe the accountancy guards to look the other way instead of tattling to Matris.

"Psst, Seske!" comes a voice from inside the hold. Adalla's voice for sure, but I don't see her.

"Where are you?" I whisper.

"Here," Adalla says. She peeks out from a stack of deflated pods and smiles at me, her hands and face already darkened by the beast's blue-green ichor.

I clench up, my stomach raw and sore with disappointment. "I've missed the first letting."

She shrugs. "You slept two days too long." Adalla looks around the cargo hold.

She approaches along the wall, slipping in and out of shadows until she's upon me. She frowns at the seam rip and the steady burble of sleep balm wasting over the edges. Then, with a beastworker's strength and grace, she hoists me up and out of the pod like my bones are made from mad vapors.

"Why didn't you wake me?" I ask Adalla.

"This beast has spirit. Your Matris called all hands to steady it. But it'll last us fourteen years, the Senate agrees already, and you know how often they agree."

"Great," I grumble. That's two extra years I have to wait to see the next first letting.

"Don't be mad."

Adalla pulls a stiff roll of fabric from her pack, the iridescent blue of a beastworker's suit. The natural creases of beast hide still run through it. She hands it to me, and I slip out of my nakedness and into my disguise.

"We've got two hours before we need to get this back. And *you* back. Lash counters are on edge. My amas say they've never seen them so flighty, especially during excavation."

I bite my lip. Adalla's amas—may the ancestors soothe their sweet little hearts—are older than anyone I know and have been through seven beast cycles. Two of her amas had begun their courtship as teens but didn't take on their third until they were well past their childbearing years. They bucked convention, and some had even dared to call them a "couple," though they fervently denied it, claiming they were just taking their time searching for the exact right woman. They were every bit as sharp as they were eccentric, though, and if the amas say something is amiss, then something is amiss.

"Don't pout," says Adalla, tugging me forth. "I've got something even more exciting to show you." She offers me her re-breather, but I push it away. The air is still thin, but they're boiling ichor as we speak, filling the beast's insides with breathable atmosphere and all the scents of home. I'll be fine.

"What is it?" I ask, pressing my hand in hers, and in an instant, I've forgotten all about the late wake-up call. "Are we going to the gills?"

"Seske, are you crazy? Do you know what Your Matris would do to me if she found out I'd gotten you gaffed on mad vapors? She'd have it out on my hide, and my mothers would be sure to tear up any pieces she overlooked! This is way better anyway." Adalla reaches into her work satchel and retrieves her knife—sharp, long, and *metal*. A family heirloom, three hundred years old, or so Adalla claims.

"Beastwork?" I grunt. This had better be good. I didn't risk being raised from my stasis pod early to get stuck boring holes in the beast's body. I want to see something exciting. The more reckless, the better.

"Nuh-uh. This," she says, raising her knife, "is for protection."

I perk up. "Protection? From what?"

"Some of the workers think this beast is full of spirits," Adalla whispers.

"Of course it is. Matris took great care to bring the spirit wall—"

"No, not *those* kinds of spirits. The kind that torment people. Like Quiet Medla. She'll steal your voice if you skip your prayers. Or Halli the Mangler, who'll turn a girl babe into a boy if you don't braid her hair before she cuts her first tooth. Or Ol' Baxi Batzi, who'll smother you in your sleep, unless you . . ." Her brow tightens. "What?" she asks me.

I must be making a face. "Nothing," I say. "Go on . . ."

"You don't believe in them," she says, not a question.

"I . . . uh . . . I don't *not* believe in them. It's just a lot to take in all at once."

"And how many times has your family dragged you to the spirit wall? How many times have you left offerings for your ancestors?"

Too many times. And I see her point. Who am I to say whose spirits are real and whose aren't?

"So, what do we do if we see one of these spirits?" I ask.

"Well, I've got a plan," Adalla says, slipping her knife back into her satchel and pulling out a small ley light, some candles, a jar of brown grease, a length of twine soaked in something that smells sickly sweet, and a shiny copper disk, just like the one she keeps next to her bed. Or maybe it's one and the same. Adalla shakes the ley light, the chemical solution inside filling the space between us with a warm red glow. She starts explaining how each of her spirit wards work, but my mind gets lost, just enjoying the cadence of her words, as I think about all the adventures we'd had on the old beast. But when the light hits Adalla just right, and those old memories fizzle out of my head, I notice how she's filling out her beastworker's suit; where she used to be long and lean, now she's got muscles straining the fabric.

I could kick myself when I realize why. She's been training hard in hopes of getting promoted from the ichor vats. Ideally, to the beast's primary heart, but any major organ would do. Or so she said. The heart is the only place Adalla belongs, and we both know it.

But just as I open my mouth to ask her how her training is going, we hear the steadfast footsteps of an accountancy guard echoing through the hold. Adalla stuffs her spirit wards in her satchel, grabs the ley light, then nudges me behind a pile of flattened stasis pods, our bodies caught between it and the wall.

My lips are upon Adalla's ear. "Maybe she won't notice the rip," I murmur.

"You must have already taken a sip of mad vapors, Seske. You know lash counters notice *everything*."

I do know. The members of the Accountancy Guard, or lash counters as the beastworkers call them, are renowned for their heightened senses, which have landed me in trouble more times than I'd like to admit. They'd noticed the mere sip of blood wine I snuck from Matris's bone chalice during the first inhumation ceremony I'd attended. They'd noticed the faintest bruise I'd left upon Sisterkin's arm the time we'd fought—*really* fought—over whom Matris loved most. And most recently, they'd tattled to Pai, my head-father, that I hadn't actually memorized the Lines of Matriarchy but instead had written all 118 names in the teeniest of scripts up and down my arm with brown ink a half shade darker than my skin, which maybe was true, but that accountancy guard should have had the decency to bring my shame upon Matris and not my poor trodden pai, who'd wept for a straight month.

This would be much worse.

Folklore has it that back in the day, under Matris Otoasa's rule, every gram mattered during exodus . . . when our whole clan crams into our original ship, leaving behind the exhausted carcass of our beast in search of a new one. They say space aboard the ship was so precious that Matris Otoasa's accountancy guards could count the exact number of lashes on your eyelids within a fraction of a second, and if you had too many, you were pulled out of line to receive a proper grooming. I don't know if it's entirely true, but it's true enough. So we're as good as caught. For me, I'm used to dealing with Matris's wrath. She'll scold me and tell me how disappointed she is. Tell me how I should behave more like a matriarch in training. How I should be more like Sisterkin.

But Adalla . . . she's got much more to lose. A demotion to boneworks, if she's lucky. A thumb hanging, if she's not. I can't let *either* happen.

"Stay here. Stay quiet," I say, wriggling my body back out into the openness of the hold.

"Where are you going?"

"Turning myself in. No use in both of us being caught."

"My hero." Adalla giggles, then catches herself. "You don't have to do that. I'll stand by you. Proudly. Besides, I've got strong thumbs. I could hang for days."

My stomach cramps up at the thought of Adalla suffering through that punishment. I mean really cramps up, worse than it ever has before. A moan escapes my lips.

"Are you okay?" Adalla asks. "Please, allow me to come with you."

Finally, the ache subsides. "No—stay here," I tell her. "Consider that an order from your future matriarch."

She sighs, rolling her eyes at me as I gather myself and prepare to face the bane of my existence. The accountancy guard's footsteps are already headed my way, and when I turn to face her, my jaw drops.

It's worse than I feared. Way worse.

"Wheytt," I say with a pained exhale as my eyes stick to the sculpted flesh beneath the sensory-dampening layers of his uniform. Matris's new male accountancy guard—mothers' mercy—looks down upon me through bone-rimmed goggles. I cannot see his eyes through the darkened lenses, but his scowl line is more than obvious. Accountancy guards are bad in general, but Wheytt is the worst, out to prove to himself and to Matris that he's more than capable of working outside the family unit. Because of his insecurities, he tattles like his livelihood depends on it. And that means that there's no talking my way out of this one. Matris already knows.

"Matriling Kaleigh," Wheytt says to me with due respects, though it is a sloppy wave of obligation and not the stiff salute of reverence he gives to my head-mother.

"Call me Seske," I grate at him. "Better yet, don't call me anything at all."

"Mmm," he says dismissively. "Matris wishes to speak to you. And your beastworker friend can come along too."

My gut shifts yet again. "There's no one else here. I escaped on my own," I say, willing my eyes not to dart in the direction of Adalla's hiding spot.

"I smell ichor," Wheytt says.

"Perhaps one of your fellow accountancy guards tracked it through here, too busy prying into everyone else's business to watch where they're stepping." I cross my arms over my chest.

"Perhaps," he says, unconvinced. "But I heard whispers. A conversation."

"I like to talk to myself. Is that a crime?"

"We can keep playing these games if you like, Matriling Kaleigh—on our way to see Matris Paletoba." Wheytt lays one of his pristine white gloves around my wrist, the finest beast hide I have felt upon my skin, even more luxurious than Matris's raiment. We both look at his hand upon me, and he snatches it away but does not apologize for the offense. "Beast-worker Adalla," he shouts into the hold. "In the name of Matris Paletoba, reveal yourself."

Adalla slinks out and stands beside me, fingers clasped, tumbling her thumbs over and over each other.

I cringe, admitting defeat. "How did you know it was her?" Best to know my enemy's strengths, so maybe next time we won't get caught.

"Your naxshi," Wheytt says. "They always brighten two and a half shades when you share her company."

I touch my cheeks, feeling the warmth budding where my ancestral tattoos sit. The heat-sensitive pigments in the naxshi ink have betrayed me. "You think you know me so well?" I hiss, though I can feel my tattoos brighten even further from a new kind of heat brewing within me.

"I know that you have ripened and you are ready for womanhood. I have sent word of this ahead to Your Matris as well." Wheytt bends down on one knee, wipes his gloved index finger upon the floor, then turns it up so I can see. A small dollop of blood stains the tip of the glove, and the undeniable smirk of menses envy sits upon his lips.

The cramping. The taste of iron in our sleep balm. All at once, my emotions cram up into my throat. The pride I should feel for *finally* catching up to my peers is squelched cold by the fact that Wheytt had discovered my first menses before I'd even known myself. As if I needed one more reason to hate him.

From a pocket in his uniform, he pulls out the little black ledger that has haunted me since my early childhood and apparently will follow me right into womanhood. He presses the blood drop upon the ledger's sensor, then types something onto the keypad.

"Take me to my mother!" I yell at him, the archaic term more of a cuss than generic maternal designation, though there's definitely no need for me to specify *which* mother.

We're done for.

WHEYTT LEADS THE WAY AS THE THREE OF US FILE THROUGH the belly of the beast. I leave footprints upon the ground where it's soft and still moist, not the paved walkways I am used to. I'd wanted to see excavation, and I'm seeing it. The beast's stomach is still a wide expanse of wild frontier, full of the untamed life native to the beast's gut, an ecosystem that nourishes the beast during its journey through the void.

Soon it will nourish us. This is where we will live, big, beautiful ceiling of flesh lofting over us. Incisions are cut here and there as workers pull resources from other parts of the beast. Slivers of rib are used for scaffolding and building materials, harvested and carved up by boneworkers. The hide is thick and is cut for work leathers and boots, while silks are harvested from gall worms—big lumbering beasts the size of two full-grown women. It'll take a ton of work to get this place habitable, but unlike our cramped ship that now clings to the beast's hide like a wart, there is room for us to expand here, to live here. To thrive. But right now, it feels so cavernous and empty without structures climbing up the walls, and so hollow without the wild calls of vendors, the laughter of my cohort, and all the scents and textures of the meticulously manicured gardens in which I often find myself lost, both in thought and body.

My stomach still cramps, but it's from dread now and not my menses. What I thought would be a ten-minute journey upon walkways cobbled with pearlescent stones has turned into a thirty-minute slog through a hostile, overgrown marsh—and we are only halfway to Matris's throne room.

Now that I've had the time to think clearly, I realize the real trouble we are facing. Maybe Adalla can tolerate the thumb hanging, but even if she can, she'd be left with a criminal record. She'd end up a boneworker with ornate scars covering her whole body, bone chips in her hair, probably in a gang. Or worse, she'd be sent to swab the beast's bowels right as she is starting her years of courtship. What kind of wives and husbands would she find there among the refuse? Other criminals serving their time instead of respectable beastworkers? My heart weeps, thinking about the little bowel-swabbing child her family unit would share, a daughter most likely, her hair brittle from a nutrient-deficient diet, unable to hold the braids or twists or knots of her family line.

And then I am actually weeping, over the nonexistent future of a nonexistent child. Adalla lays her hand upon my shoulder. "Are you okay, Seske?" she whispers into my ear. Wheytt walks several feet ahead of us, but I am certain he is listening.

There's not much I can do to deter my punishment, but Matris is expecting only me. If I can get Adalla free, it will be my word against Wheytt's, and whose word would Matris believe? I cringe. Wheytt's probably, but he'd have no physical proof and Adalla would be spared.

I take Adalla's hands in mine and draw the Vvanescript symbol for *we*. Adalla looks at me, confused. But then I cup my ear and nod at Wheytt to indicate that he might be eavesdropping, wink at her, and start the inscription again. *We* . . . Adalla's eyebrows crinkle as she looks at the strokes I made. Adalla's still learning, but she's sharp, and I'm not a bad teacher either. Yet when I retrace the script once more, slowly, she shakes her head.

"I don't remember," she whispers. How can she not remember? We've been practicing her Vvanescript for four months straight! We'd just had a session last night, right before—

Exodus.

I bite my lip. For me, it feels like hours ago, but for Adalla, it's been nearly half a year. Once our old beast's resources had waned beyond the point of being sustainable, Matris had ordered all nonessential Contour class family units into their stasis pods, while the Accountancy Guard began the meticulous task of taking stock of everything that would need to be re-created, and then beastworkers condensed or dismantled or eviscerated the insides until every last usable scrap from the beast had been harvested.

Daidi's bells. Why can't I ever catch a break? "Do you trust me?" I say to Adalla, more than a whisper, because there's no use trying to hide.

"Of course," Adalla says.

"Then give me your ley light and follow my lead."

Wheytt stops and turns around and approaches me. "What are you plotting, Matriling Kaleigh?" His brow is doing that patronizing thing again. It fires me up inside. And then I realize why. It's the same look Matris gives me when she's too disappointed for words. It is a flimsy imitation, though, and I refuse to be intimidated by it. I'll show him and his stupid heightened senses. Behind my back, Adalla's ley light sits coldly in my hand. I grab the goggles from Wheytt's face. Immediately, he winces and brings his hands to his temples.

The color of his eyes strikes me—his irises so pale, they're nearly white, and the pupils are like a burst of black ink, spilling out in all directions. I blink, stunned by their odd beauty . . .

Adalla tugs my arm. "I'm supposed to be following your lead . . ."

Ah. The ley light. I shake it vigorously, until the solution inflames and then shoots out a bright red light. I shove it right in Wheytt's face. His howl echoes through the cavernous, not-yet city of our beast. His hands go to his eyes and he falls to the ground. "You've blinded me!" he calls out.

"Only temporarily," I yell back, as Adalla and I make our way to the large knotted twist of a woodward canopy, more of a cave than a tree. We duck inside, but instead of the familiar neat paths I'm used to strolling upon, there is a thick tangle of reeds resting in a swamp of putrid burbling juices. Carnivorous plants snap at us, and thorny vines cling to the ceiling, scratching at our skin as we pass under them. I look back, and Wheytt is stumbling around, eyes clenched shut and hands outstretched. Then his nose sniffs at the air and he turns and starts walking right toward us. I've knocked out one of his senses, but he's still more than capable of tracking us down. Plus now, he's *really* mad.

I take a step and the spongy ground swallows my leg up to my calf. "Come on. We can hide in here. He won't be able to track us. Not with this smell."

"Seske," Adalla says to me in a way that makes me stop and look back at her. I'd asked her to trust me, but I can see in her eyes that it is taking everything in her being to do so. "Are you sure we're not just making things worse?"

I shake my head adamantly. "Your child is not going to be a brittle-haired bowel-worker with criminal parents!"

"My *what*?"

I don't answer, just tug her deeper into the canopy, carving my way through the native flora and fauna and those things caught between. I feel something slither past my ankles, and suddenly, one of those things caught between catches me. A tentacled frond spirals up and around my thigh and tightens until my circulation is choked off and my leg throbs like my veins are about to burst. I shriek. Adalla shrieks, caught by the tentacles as well. I pull my bone shard and cut like mad, freeing myself, then freeing Adalla.

Wheytt shrieks, a blood-curdling cry that makes all the critters in the canopy go silent. Shadows twist in the murderous red glow coming from the ley light, and this place gets a whole lot creepier. Thoughts of Adalla's torturous spirits run through my mind, and just for a moment, I worry that one has gotten to Wheytt and that we'll be next, but when I look back, Wheytt's battling a crib worm, of all things, its latch bored right into the exposed skin on his neck.

It's cute, as far as crib worms go: big, fat circular mouth, pudgy grayish-purple body, and stubby little tail. Their venom is harmless, and in fact, it's soothing. I'd slept with one until I was nearly twelve years old, though I won't admit it to anyone, not even Adalla. They draw blood, but not much, and their latch tickles more than anything, but on Wheytt's hypersensitive skin, it's probably agonizing. He shrieks again.

I sigh. "I suppose I should save him," I say to Adalla. "Go back home, and if anyone asks where you were, deny everything. I'll cover for you."

"Is that an order from my future matriarch?" she says with a grin.

"It's a request from your best friend. This is all my stupid idea. You don't need to suffer for it." I give her a quick hug, her arms as tight around me as that tentacle frond had been. I feel the heat rise in my cheeks, knowing my tattoos have brightened two and a half shades.

And then Adalla is off, and I'm left with boy wonder here.

"Be still," I say to him, his eyes still clenched. Removing a crib worm this big can be a tricky maneuver. Luckily, I've had a ton of practice. I examine it from all angles, looking for the darkest of the dark spots beneath its chins. Carefully, I plunge my finger into the soft divot and wiggle around until I feel the nodule beneath. I rub at it a few times until the crib worm begins to purr, and the suction breaks with an audible gasp. I cradle it in my arms, tickle its underside. For a moment, I am a young girl again, not one teetering on the responsibilities of womanhood.

"This is all going into my ledger," Wheytt scolds me, rubbing at the purple hickey on his neck. His eyes are just barely slits now. I bid myself not to look directly into them. "I could have died, you know."

"What?" I'm suddenly filled with hope. "You could have died? So you're saying I saved your life?"

"No, but—"

"I just saved your life, and as such, you're bound by Fate's Accounts. And while you're at it, I think a thank-you is in order." I smile to myself. Wheytt owes me one. Adalla will be spared.

"*Thank you?*" Wheytt tries to give me my mother's scowl, but he can't. There's something else sitting on his brow now. Not quite respect . . . more like restrained derision, but I'll take it.

"This may all be a joke to you," he continues, "but another minute of that, and I could have gone into sensory overload, and you would have been charged with deadly assault. Not even your pedigree would save you from that."

"For giving you a hickey? You mean neither of your wives ever laid one on you?"

He flinches. I've made him uncomfortable. He's obnoxious, yes, and probably deserves it, but I'd never ask something like that from one of my mother's female guards.

"Sorry," I say to him. I hand Wheytt his goggles and watch those exotic eyes disappear behind them. "Sometimes my mouth says things before I get the chance to think them through." The silence stirs between us, and I dig my foot into the murk, kicking up black grit from the bottom. It swirls in pleasing patterns.

"You know this place hasn't been neutralized yet," Wheytt finally says. Behind the dark lenses of his goggles, I feel his eyes smiling at me, even though his lips deny it. "We're basically slowly digesting in this beast's stomach acids."

"Eh," I say. "There are worse fates." Like the one currently awaiting me in the throne room.

❖

NEAR THE HEAD OF THE BEAST, THINGS START TO LOOK MORE normal. Behind the scaffolding, boneworkers have already completed the framework for our family dwelling and those of twelve of the thirty-seven Senators. Walls are starting to go up, and nerve lines are being rerouted to fill our rooms with a pulsing pale-blue light.

Then I feel a foreign movement beneath my feet. The ground lurches. My eyes flick to Wheytt. He's as startled as I am, which brings me no comfort.

"It's just a little tremor," he says, jotting something in his ledger. "We've been having them all day." His head pricks up from his book. His body tenses, his mouth opens slightly, and I get the feeling that his mind has floated off to somewhere not quite here—

Wheytt shoves me forward, into a naturally occurring canal, then shields my body with his. Right when I begin to protest about being handled so roughly, the ground bucks again, harder this time. Someone barks out instructions, and the boneworkers react, helping one another down to safety in five seconds flat. Just as the last worker reaches the ground, the scaffolding she'd been perched on buckles, and the framework collapses. Debris rains down around us, and a stack of it falls exactly where Wheytt and I had been standing.

It takes me a moment to catch my breath, but as soon as I have it I thank him, still caught between his firm body and the soft, waxy moss lining the canal. "How did you know that was going to happen?" I ask.

"Smelled it. Tasted it. Felt it." He shakes his head. "It's too hard to explain."

"Try," I say. "Or is it some lash counter secret?"

He flinches. "We don't like being called that. And it's not a secret. Just honed senses."

"How many fingers am I holding up behind my back?" I ask.

"Three," he says without pause.

"How'd you know that?"

"Not telling."

"How about now?"

"Five."

Right again, I think. "What color am I thinking of?"

"Doesn't work like that." Wheytt peels back from me and dusts himself off. "Look, Matriling Kaleigh, I'm just accountable for getting you to Matris. Then you're her responsibility."

We start walking again, and I can't help but notice how Wheytt walks next to me now. He's quiet. Focused. Tuned in to the world in the way only an accountancy guard can be, noticing *everything*. Me, I'm busy worrying if another quake is going to knock me senseless, if the ground is going to open up and swallow me. Maybe I should have just slept through the excavation phase, all the gritty hard work, taming this wild into something civilized, or at least less deadly. Right now, I could be curled up with the rest of my family, my bapa and my pai, and all my mothers, and Sisterkin, too, I guess, who has a small stasis pod of her own, right next to ours. Then we'd awake with the rest of the Contour class to celebrate the first day of the expansion phase. Safe. No chance of getting brained by falling scaffolding.

"We're even now, you realize," Wheytt says, interrupting my thoughts. "All of Fate's Accounts are balanced."

Mothers' mercy. He's right. I saved his life, and now he's saved mine. Our debts cancel out, and now he owes me nothing, and he's going to tattle on Adalla. I shoot him a tight scowl. Balanced forever, too. Even if I saved his sorry self a hundred more times, we'd still be even. Not that I'd lift a finger if he were in need of saving again.

"After you, Matriling Kaleigh."

"How many fingers am I holding up behind my back now?" I say.

"One," he says with a sigh. "And it's most inappropriate."

MATRIS GREETS ME, ARMS SPREAD OPEN, ENVELOPING ME INTO the folds of her raiment. I wriggle and fuss, like any daughter my age would, but to be honest, I savor the affection. I'm swaddled in layer upon layer of silks and overwhelmed by the scent of her musk, a cloying perfume made from the rare white blooms of agile clover found upon the ceilings of woodward canopies. Mother pulls back and looks me over, ignoring my fetid and dampened beastworker's suit and the flecks of builder's bone in my hair. "It's so good to see you, Seske." She smiles, but her eyes don't quite meet mine. "Oh, I cannot believe you've finally ripened. This is a proud moment for me."

Something is definitely wrong. Ripening or not, Matris should have me by the thumbs by now, her tongue lashing out and chastising me and threatening to raise my will-father so I'd have to deal with his disappointment as well. I'm so confused by her display of affection that I find myself groveling, knowing that if she turns . . . *when* she turns . . . her mood swing will be brutal.

"I'm so sorry, Matris. I should have never—"

"Seske," Matris coos into my ear. "Your curiosities do not catch me by surprise anymore. But you shouldn't be about. You've seen how ornery this beast is. It's too dangerous for a young girl." She turns to Wheytt. "She wasn't any trouble, was she?"

"Not a once, Matris Paletoba," Wheytt says with a full flourish of respects, including a double arm roll and a bow down on his knee. I gasp. Is he really going to lie to Matris?

"Don't be modest. You delivered my daughter with such diligence and haste, despite these awful tremors." Matris can be charming when she feels like it, and her voice comes out smoother than the silk of her raiment. But I know how fast it can turn.

I wrinkle my nose, and while I'd like to think that saving my life would entail such high recognition, there's no mistaking that Matris wants something from him.

"What is your rank, Patriline Wheytt Housley?" she asks.

"Audit clerk, Matris."

"Clerk? Someone of your quick action and accountability should be serving as a tactician already," Matris says, an alluring lilt in her voice.

This reeks of manipulation.

"Matris," I plead. "Let him return to his duties. I'm sure he's had more than enough excitement when he saved me from falling—" I cinch my lips. I shouldn't have said that. If she thinks she's indebted to him, I'll never hear the end of it. "But you don't owe him anything! I saved his life already, so we're even," I explain, hoping that'll stave off any questions, but my tongue keeps going. "See, what happened was, on our way here, we got stuck in a bog. Things were crawling all over us, and then Adalla and I—"

"Adalla," Matris says in her familiar condescending tone. I welcome it, feeling relieved that we are once again on normal terms. "You're not creating mischief with that scoundrel again, are you? Is she, audit clerk?" she asks, this time from Wheytt.

Wheytt's mouth opens.

Please don't tell on us. Please don't.

I fear for the worst, what with my mother practically dangling a promotion right in front of him. Who could turn that down? I know her better than to think this is some sort of gift on her part, though. What Matris's reign needs most right now is a distraction, and what better way to get people's minds off her wretched selection of a beast than to promote the first male accountancy guard?

But I've got a distraction of my own. My mother called him "Patriline," the title for an unmarried man. And as of today, I am wholly a woman. If I lay intentions upon him, by the Laws of Lineage, he won't be able to speak against me.

I cringe, then pull him close and seal my lips around his. I don't know who's caught more by surprise. My first kiss . . . never in my wildest dreams would I have thought it to be with a man.

"Seske!" Matris squeals.

I peel back, my lips tacky with saliva. "Wheytt and I are declaring intentions, Matris."

"I was wrong," she says, shaking her head. "You do continue to surprise me." And disappoint her, but she is too noble to say that in mixed company.

"There's no need to worry yourself, Matris," Wheytt says flatly, body stiff, like he wishes he were anywhere but here. "Matriling Kaleigh and I have not, in fact, declared intentions."

This time I'm the one who is shocked. What kind of man is this who would deny a chance to sit by the throne? I cringe, suddenly realizing I am no better than my mother. I've embarrassed him, and myself too.

This has all gone sideways.

"Is that so, Patriline Housley?" Matris is ever the diplomat, but even she cannot hold in the sigh of relief that comes next. "I'd like to know exactly what happened out there. Every detail."

"Yes, Matris Paletoba." Wheytt relays the events marked in his ledger, accounting every detail down to the exact shade of my menses, the precise measure of luminosity of the ley light, even the pitch of his scream when I pulled the crib worm from his neck. But there is one thing he's omitted.

"And what of Beastworker Adalla?" Matris says.

"Beastworker Adalla was not with us. Matriling Kaleigh's *lips* must have *slipped*," Wheytt says to my mother. Or maybe to me. "It was only her and I the entire time." His lie is bold and not very good. But I can tell by the resolve in his voice that he is willing to stand by it.

"Indeed," Matris says, clearly not believing him. And with that, Wheytt's chance at a promotion slips from him just as fast as it came. Matris can hold a grudge with the best of them, and if a male is ever to make it to tactician, I can tell you now, it will *not* be Wheytt.

And now it is I who owes him.

"Thank you," I whisper to him, so softly, I know only his sensitive ears can hear me. I'll find a way to repay him for sparing Adalla. But as I look at him, I notice he's gone stiff again, all his senses on full alert. I wait for a tremble, but nothing comes. Something else is making him nervous. "What's wrong?" I ask him.

"Nothing," he says, turning to face Matris. *Awful, awful liar.* But something's transpired between them. I quiet my mind, still my breathing. Listening.

Then I hear it, the ruffling of silks coming from behind the throne. My heart drops. My eyes cut at Matris. I never knew she could hurt me this deeply. Before the exodus from our old beast, I'd asked, *begged,* for Matris to allow me to work by her side as she got the new beast up and running. She said I was too young, but that I could do it next time. Too young, she'd said, again and again, each time I'd asked. And so I'd hatched a plan with Adalla to get out on my own, to prove to myself that I wasn't too young . . . but age had nothing to do with it after all.

"Sisterkin!" I call out. "Come out, I know you're in here."

"Seske," Matris says, extending her arms, and the betrayal becomes too much for me to bear. "I know what you're thinking, and it's not like that at all—"

"I am the next in line! Not her!" Tears streak down my cheeks, hot and heavy. So many, I can't see straight.

Footsteps echo, filling the room with ripples of movement. Through my blurred vision, I see my sister, a visage caught somewhere in between a shadow and a reflection upon a pool of water. The hush of her silks, regal and fluid, and the tinker of gemstones knocking into themselves.

"Seske . . ." Sisterkin says, drawing my name out in an exaggerated lilt that makes it seem like she's about to break out into song and dance. Her speech is practiced and dignified, as though her hair doesn't sit in an unbraided puff on top of her head. Her raiment, though its silk is not spun from the family lot, is hand-dyed and frilled and just as regal as mine, maybe even more so. She is everything that I should be. Yet Sisterkin is *not* the future matriarch and never will be. She'd missed that opportunity by four and a half days.

Sisterkin had been carried in Matris's womb, and at the same time, I was being carried by my will-mother. It was a delicate situation, two mothers in the same family unit, pregnant at once, knowing only one child could be allowed to live. Sisterkin was conceived first and should have been born first, but patience has never been my virtue. I'd entered the world nearly four months ahead of schedule, too small to tolerate even the smallest of crib worms, but first nevertheless. I was so weak and frail, no one expected me to live. And for the first and last time in her life, Matris thought with her heart instead of her head and chose not to end her own pregnancy. By the time they realized my will to live, Sisterkin was here, and Matris twisted each and every one of the ancestors' rules and regulations to allow Sisterkin to remain with us.

That's how I ended up with the only sibling in our whole clan. Lucky me.

"Matris only raised me first so that I could be of better assistance to you," Sisterkin says, her voice at just that certain pitch that it sends ice coursing down my spine. "You know that I would never do anything to hurt you, my dearest sister."

The touch of her silks against my skin is enough to drive me to madness, but it is the false silk in her voice that pushes me even further. I'm burning up, like my skin is on fire from the inside, and I can't hold in my anger anymore.

Matris goes out of her way to include Sisterkin in all manners of her life, but I will draw the line at including her in my future rule. "No!" I say to Matris. "She will not advise me. Maybe if you focused more on your true daughter, I would have turned out more to your liking."

"Seske!" Matris says. "Please watch your tone." She turns to Wheytt, that embarrassed look on her face she always has when I'm about. "Patriline Housley," Matris says, "thank you for your services. You may return to your former duties.

"Despite what you think," Matris says to me once our company has departed, "a little blood between your legs does not make you a woman. You need to earn that title. The truth is, I didn't raise you because you aren't ready. I worry for our matriline, Seske, with you at the helm someday." Matris sighs at the thought. "I'll forfeit the throne before the Senate rather than have you run our name into nothingness, but it doesn't have to come to that."

Sisterkin steps between us. "I can guide you, Seske. I know all the ways of the Matriarchy, all the Lines." She smiles, though the gesture is more like the baring of teeth, the too-white teeth that haunt children's dreams. Though she was born of Matris's blood, she is not a part of our family and has no claim to our lines. As per the tenets of our ancestors, she cannot partake of our family teas, so she sips hot water from her dainty cups instead. Our head-father is not permitted to teach her, so Matris hires private tutors. Sisterkin is not allowed at our table, so Mother had an archipelago built where Sisterkin can dine with us without dining *with* us. Her hair grows freely upon her head, like a boundless sunburst, not the carefully braided knots of our line. Sisterkin has been given nothing, not even a true name. Sisterkin was Matris's first abomination, and now there's this surly beast she's chosen. It is not my competence Matris should be questioning but her own.

"This isn't fair. You should have taken her to the spirit wall. The minute I was born, you should have taken her!" I don't really wish my sister dead. I just want an apology from Matris and for her to profess that she is *my* mother, and mine alone, and the blood that she and Sisterkin share means nothing to her. But the way her eyes dart between my sister and me, I know it isn't nothing.

"Seske," she says, finally wrapping me in her silks. "Of course, you are right." She blathers on, apologizes, but it is too late. Yes, she'd chosen me, here and now, but there should have been no deliberation.

At least I know now where I stand. I'll show her. There are several beast cycles left in her reign, but I will use my every waking moment to study hard and prove her wrong.

ADALLA

Of Solid Heartbeats and Dented Pans

That girl's going to break your heart, betcha girl," Ama Morova sasses at me as she adds another amber bead to my hair. She is not gentle. My neck strains as she twists my head this way and that. She tugs so hard at my roots as she braids a sloping, curving line tight against my scalp. I've got tears in the corners of my eyes, but truth is, I'd be crying anyway, and any heart-mother worth her ichor can tell the difference between tears of pain and those of sorrow. "Best not get tangled up with those sorts, 'less you end up like Ol' Baxi Batzi."

My lips purse. I dare not sass my mother back, but I want to, betcha. Comparing me with Our Lady Baxi Batzi? Two hundred years her bones have been drifting through space, given a charlatan's burial for consorting with Matris Borgall's daughter—shot straight through the beast's anal sphincter with all that thrice-recycled sludge, which is just a polite way of saying "third-ass shits." Your mother comparing you with

Baxi Batzi and third-ass shits is never a good thing, 'specially when she's got a good hold of your hair.

"Seske and I are just friends," I tell my ama. "My heart is in the job and my job is in the heart."

"Betcha," Ama says, snatching my head back so hard, the skin at my throat goes tight. I struggle to swallow, and the tears I'd mostly contained start flowing. "You don't know all I've gone through to get you this promotion. This family has climbed to the top of the pile, child. It's nice up here, but you go walking around with a headful of dizzy thoughts, the fall won't be kind. For any of us."

The snots. The snots are coming now. I snort 'em back up best I can and try to compose myself. I try to forget what I'd heard that lash counter say, that Seske's always flushing around me, because I know my face always gets hot around her, and maybe my humble bits, too, but until my ama said it out loud, I never even considered my heart being caught up in a tangle. I'm a beastworker. She's in line to be our next matriarch. Us being friends is enough to cause this beast's bowels to roll.

Ama's fingers are like fire twisting the second braid down my back. She ties it off with a stretchy strip of cartilage. When she's done, she dips her hand in a jar of yonatti oil, fragrant and fresh and flowery, just gathered from the blooms in the beast's stomach. Ama says the yonatti blooms are always the first to be completely culled, but while we've got them, their oil will make your hair shiny and strong as beastie's backbone. Maybe it'll make me look like I'm deserving of this promotion. She smooths down my edges with a bit of ichor, then turns me around, looks me up and down, and ichors my eyelashes as well, so they look longer, fuller. A big *fuck you* to the lash counters.

"There," she says, patting my cheeks, pleased with her work. "You'll fit right in, sure is sure is sure. Come, we can't be late."

She tugs me up, yanks me forward with those hard hands that could crush bone, and I'm suddenly on my feet. Numb feet. I've been sitting so long, brooding so long, trying not to be mad. It's not so uncommon for people to forget things right out of stasis. Seske would have remembered to ask about my promotion, if she'd been given another minute or two before that lash counter interrupted us.

"Dizzy head, this way, girl," my mother calls.

I look up and she's practically to the next living pod. My feet are steady now. My heart . . . my heart is another matter. I catch up, not wanting to get lost. I still haven't figured out the layout of our new pod yet. It's not neat and nice like the Contour class gets, every piece put back how it was before. Here we get new neighborhoods, new neighbors, new problems. Like we've got high ceilings now, which is great for Sonovan's hunch, but that means we have trouble keeping heat when we sleep, and we burn nearly twice as many parchment rolls to keep our toes from freezing. Freezing toes used to not be a problem for any of us, high ceilings or not. We had pet murmurs, back on our old beast. Four of them. Bepok was mine. She was the runt, wingspan barely able to cover me up to my shins, and she was as thin as an old sheet, but, girl, did she purr like the thickest of them. Not having her at night leaves me with a whole 'nother kind of coldness, betcha.

Ama leads us through our neighbors' living pods, our eyes cast down when the ley lights are dimmed or off, stopping a moment to chat when they're burning brightly. It's what passes for privacy. Truth be truth, I never thought anything of it before I happened into Seske. But the first time I had her over, she couldn't stop staring at our neighbors, like the ley lights meant nothing to her. Old Man Saym, he'd gotten mixed up with some bad, bad favors—his wrecked-out will-mother put a curse on him, sure is sure, and he'd be on his dent pan, trying and trying and trying to take a shit, and Seske just stood there and stared and pointed, like she could *see* him, and kept asking why he didn't just go somewhere with more privacy, and I said, "I'm not sure what you're talking about, silly girl, there's nothing there but the ley of our home," even though I also saw Old Man Saym, squatting, thighs shaking, eyes quivering, lips cursing that mad jealous wife of his.

Dent pan got filled eventually, and my nose ignored that too.

"Damn dizzy-headed girl!" my ama screams. I've rolled up on her. Knocked her down, nearly. Old Man Saym has caught her, his hands out, his face flushing.

"So sorry, Morova," he apologizes repeatedly, like it's all his fault. He's a lot more careful about throwing his glances around these days, but hugging up on a woman, 'specially a heart-mother, would have him squatting on the dent pan for a month straight if his wife caught him.

"It's this one's fault," my ama says, a thumb and index knuckle pressing the life out of my earlobe. I dare not make a peep. If I was dizzy before, I'm not now. Embarrassing your ama, now that's just not something you do. But that's not it. Ama Morova, old as she is, she's solid as a brick of builder's bone. I've seen her stop a runaway cart filled to the brim with core wax, head-on, and not even flinch. Nothing can topple her. 'Specially not the likes of me.

At least not the wispy girl I *used* to be. I glance at the bulge of my biceps, feel the strength in my core, flex thighs solid as gall casings. Working in the ichor pits has molded me into something presentable, and for the first time, I feel like my body is ready to take on the physical challenges of organ work. My only hope is my mind is ready too.

"Ama, you sure I'm ready for this?" I ask her, real quiet, once we're back on the move. "Aren't there some kind of tips you can give me?"

"You're ready for this," Ama says. She smiles, but it looks more like she's holding back a mouthful of sick. "Sure is sure."

The missing "is sure" doesn't go unnoticed. With beast-workers, "sure" is akin to a very soft "maybe." "Sure is sure is sure" means you'd stake your life on it. And "sure is sure" . . . well, that's something drenched in doubt. Not a hard no, but about as close as you can ride up on it without it biting your head clean off. I want to pry, wondering if it's just a general nervousness she's feeling or if it's something I need to be worrying about. I spend a few minutes trying to think up a way to question my ama without my earlobe ending up in another of her vise grips, but then the ground starts trembling before me. I brace myself up against the side of the wall, nervous about another of those tremors we've been having, and oh, blessed mothers, Ama laughs at me so hard, she's got tears in her eyes.

I'm about to grab Ama's hand to try to save her life, despite how small she makes me feel, but then she says, "That's no tremor, girl. It's the beat. The heartbeat of the beast. Once every three minutes and forty-seven and a half seconds. Remember that. Remember it better than your own name. How's that, girl?"

"The beast's heart beats once every three minutes forty-seven and a half seconds," I report back, serious from the tips of my braids to the toes in my boots. I've been begging my ama to take me to visit the heart since forever, but she kept that side of her a secret from me, and now look at me—so, so close. I go to set my watch, to show her I'm being proactive about keeping proper time, but Ama takes one look and her face goes blank.

"Who gave you that? Was it Matris's girl? That kind of gadget will get you killed up here faster than a murmur sucked up the valve."

"Sonovan," I say with a shake of the head. My tin uncle, adopted father, whatever you want to call him. My headmothers' almost-but-not-quite husband after my pai died. "He made it for me, out of a bunch of discarded parts. Didn't cost him anything, if that's what you're worried about."

I've got a sore spot for Sonovan, sure is sure is sure, and that must have come out in my tone, because now Ama's cold, open hand is speeding toward my cheek, and I've got about three-eighths of a second before the slap lands, and I can decide to take it, and have that be over and done, or I make this into a *thing*.

A thing. It's going to be a thing, betcha. I pull back, just out of her reach, and Ama goes swirling. I reach out, catch her in my arms right as she loses her balance.

"Now don't go cursing my tin uncle, Ama. He didn't mean any harm in this. Just thought it would give me a hand up. He knows how important this is to me—to us." I set my ama firm on her feet, and oh, the smolder in her eyes; I can feel the heat from them where I'm standing.

"Girl," she says. One word, but she drags it out into at least three syllables, and I'm holding back all my urges to protect my soft spots. She keeps staring. For so long. Not letting up. Finally, she says, "Beat."

Half a second later, the ground trembles again.

"Three minutes and forty-seven and a half seconds is not something you can time on your wrist. It's something that needs to be timed in your soul. Sonovan, bless his fathers nine and nine generations back, is a good man. He's great at fixing things and mending things and doing men's work. But he knows *nothing* about the heart. How are you going to waste time, glancing up and down at a gadget, when there's a hundred different checks and balances needing to be done between each beat? Or sweat gets in your eye and you misread the dial and miss sealing a valve or you nick an artery, and all of a sudden, we're all dead. Get me, girl?"

"Betcha, Ama," I say, slipping the watch off my wrist and into my pocket.

"Feel it, girl. Every time, a second before, I want you to scream out 'beat.' Be more than five seconds early and you line up for lashes at the end of the day. One for each violation."

"And if I'm late?"

"*Never* be late. You're late, and we're as good as dead, sure is sure is sure."

AMA HERDS ME ALONG WITH A HANDFUL OF RECRUITS through the dank, dark twists of rerouted arteries. It smells heavily of ichor in here, the floor still slick with its oily blue-green residue. I mind the countdown timer entwined with my soul, trying to step with a steady rhythm.

"Beat!" one of the other recruits yells, a whole fifteen seconds early, so early she nearly throws me off my own count. She's nervous now. We all are. Three beats ago, another of the recruits had been late. The heart-mothers had held the girl down, and one by one, they cut the girl's braids from her scalp. I'd stood there, watching in horror as her identity was ripped from her, her history erased. For hundreds of years, that same pattern had been braided upon her ancestors' heads, representing the constellations we'd drawn in the sky, our people traveling freely among the stars. All these centuries later, our sky has changed, but those braided patterns hadn't, and now it would stop with her. The girl's own ama had sobbed and wept, watching her family line come to an end. The weight of such shame for such a minor infraction seemed so cruel. I wanted to comfort the girl, comfort the ama, too, but we left them where they were.

"Beat!" scream two more recruits. Still a tad early. Then several more sound off. My own heart is beating fiercely, waiting for that five-second mark and not a moment later, when finally, I gather everything and scream out, "Beat!"

Then I count the seconds.

One.

Two.

Three.

Four.

Thunder rumbles all around us. We stand sure-footed as the amas have taught us and wait for the trembles to subside. For the few seconds that follow, everyone is quiet, no one breathes, and all is sacred, feeling the connection we all share with the beast. Then we're on the move again, like it never happened. Some of the other amas glance at me, impressed that I've never been more than five seconds early, but not my ama. She acts like she hasn't even noticed, just yells that I'm walking too slow or gawking too much or breathing too loud.

Some of the other recruits start yelling "beat" right after me, like I'm their crutch. The amas are quick to catch on, though, and the recruits get scolded. No promise of a lashing, but, girl, if tongues could sting like a strap of fresh beast leather, they'll be feeling those words for days to come.

We continue trudging through the maze for four more beats, knives always at the ready, one of the few sets of instructions they've given us. Not for protection, but if we get caught by the ichor's current, we are to press the blade deep into our stomachs. They show us just where, marking an X on our dresses. Death would be swift, they promise. And it would make the knife easier to retrieve later. The metal is more precious than our lives, though I've known that since before I could count. The artery butts up against a bone-carved door inset into the flesh of the beast. We wait there, call out the beat—half of us on time, the others early but not obscenely so. The beat comes, and then two of the amas twist the door open with their wiry muscled arms, herding us quickly through as ichor dribbles over the door's eave.

We cough as the sweet stink of copper overwhelms our lungs, and we tear up at the acrid sting in the air. The amas stand and stare at us knowingly, waiting for us to come to our senses. It takes a full minute for most of us, but the one called Tanika is wheezing so hard, I think she's going to pass out. None of the amas seems concerned enough to even ask if she's okay, but I catch the slight tremble of Tanika's ama's lip. I don't want to let another of us fail, another name added to the list of the shamed, so I slide over to her, wrap my arm around her, breathe hard in and out, setting a rhythm for her to follow. She follows along with me, and soon her eyes become less glassy, her cheeks a less blanched shade of brown. She nods me away when she's okay.

Suddenly something grips me, like I've been holding my breath too long, and I yell out, "Beat!" The others frantically follow, and the beat comes not a second later.

"You let yourself get distracted, girl," my ama says to me immediately after. "Only one heartbeat matters, and that's the beast's. If we start mourning our dead where they lie, there will be no one left to mourn us."

I bristle all over. I try to bite my tongue, oh blessed mothers, I try. "You're saying I should have just stood by and watched her die?"

"There are always one or two who can't adjust quickly enough to the scent of ichor. Better to root them out when the stakes are low. Speak out of turn again, girl, and I'll lay shame to our family line just as fast."

We continue on at a brisk pace through another set of doors, trudging through knee-deep ichor. The amas are all behind us, herding us forward. Rage burns in my heart. I thought I'd grown resistant against Ama's cold, cruel demeanor, but turns out, I'd fully underestimated it. Tanika brushes my elbow, and I look back at her. She dips her head at me, a silent thank-you, then she smiles. If nothing else, at least I've mattered to her. That calms me some, betcha, which is good, because then I notice the ichor that had once flowed along with us has suddenly ebbed, lowered from shin-high to ankle-deep in the course of seconds, and is streaming back against us. Unlike the last artery, this one is tacky all over—the walls, the ceiling. It's active, and whatever it does when the beat comes, it's about to do it.

I glance behind me to get direction from the amas, and they're all a ways back, cutting deep gouges into the wall. "Beat!" I yell out, a whole twenty seconds too early, but it's the only way to warn the others without shaming my family out of existence. The others startle, then notice everything I've noticed, and we all take our knives and start cutting. I copy my ama's movements, best I can, two deep arcs into the flesh, then a cut behind them to form a handhold. I slip my arms in and hold on for dear life.

The thunder comes, and for a brief moment, the ichor on the floor is only inches deep. Then a wave rushes past us. Instinctually, I hold my breath, as we had done so many times during practice, though from the gasping all around me, not everyone has been so thoughtful. The oily flow grips at me, bids me to get washed away. I hug that little strip of flesh like it's my closest friend, hoping my cut holds just a few seconds longer. But in all my fear, all my dread, something springs forth in my heart . . . a feeling that I'm in a place I've belonged all my life. Suddenly, I'm not clinging on for life, because my life is not so significant a thing to cling to. Life is what is flowing all around me . . . I feel it as it moves past me. So, so much of it, and I'm blessed enough to have had so many generations come before me, sacrificing everything for me to have this very moment.

And yet it is over all too soon. I will have other moments, many other moments, like this one, but there will never be another first.

The flow of ichor is at my shins again. I unlatch myself from the wall, facing the amas. My ama sees me, sees the light in my eyes. And somehow, I understand her now. Her face is still covered in ichor, but I see her brow bunch. Then everything in her face loosens and she's running to me, wrapping me up in a hug so tight, so warm, I don't know what to do with myself. "You felt it?" she whispers into my ear.

I nod. I don't know what *it* is, but I definitely felt something. Something I can't wait to feel again. She turns to the amas and they all stand looking at me, dumbstruck.

"She felt it!" she screams at them. "On the first day. In the first *hour.*"

I turn to accept the praise of my cohort, but of the eight of us, only five remain. Tanika and two others are nowhere to be seen. Some time ago, maybe as short as thirty minutes ago, I would have cried out about such a cruelty, wondering why they hadn't better prepared us before throwing us to this murderous organ. But now I understand. Once you've become one with the heart's beat, there is no going back to how life was before. It's hard to explain, but it changes you. It becomes a part of your soul, and to be turned away from the heart after feeling its all-encompassing grace would be the biggest cruelty of all.

THE AMAS, THEY TALK ABOUT ME LIKE I'M NOT STANDING FIVE feet away from them. They examine the cleanness of the cut I'd made into the beast's flesh like three of their daughters hadn't just been washed away. They argue that I'm a prodigy, that what I did was a fluke, that I'm ready, that I'm too inexperienced. That I'm lucky, that I'm blessed. That maybe I'm all those things, and that none of them matters, because in the end, I'm just wasting my time here when I could be doing something useful, like helping to save everyone's lives.

They're yelling over one another, and I'm not even sure where my own ama stands on the issue, but it's all over in two minutes, and Ama is rushing me away from my cohort, through a bone door and out of the artery, before the next beat comes.

She's huffy, out of breath, irritated, and a little proud.

"Did I do something wrong?" I whisper to her. It seems safe here, away from the rest of the group.

"No, girl. You did something exceptional." The way she says it, though, doesn't quite sound like a compliment. "We've lost entire cohorts before. Probably would have happened today if you hadn't spoken up. Maybe that'll make your lashes more bearable this evening."

"Beat." I say it calmly now, and the world stops for a moment. I savor the tremble. Yearn for it. It's become a part of me already, involuntary, easy as breathing. Then: "Lashes? I was only early that once."

"The day is still young, child. I can't tell you much, but cling to your instincts. There is much for you to learn, but good instincts, that's just something that can't be taught."

Those girls, the ones who had been washed away, Ama doesn't even mention them, doesn't shed a single tear. They were too slow on their feet, too slow with a knife, too slow in their reactions . . . the kind of slowness that could mean death for us all if they'd been allowed to advance in rank. It was a kindness, really. But then I start wondering at those who had successfully heeded my warning. "Ama, the others. Will they be good enough? I shouldn't have warned them, should I?"

Ama sighs. "It would be good for you to stop thinking of death as something permanent and final. What we take from the beast, we give back eventually. One or two would have caught on before the beat came. The others would have enriched the beast's blood, making the beat stronger for us all. Does this bother you, girl? Or will we be able to count you among our rank?"

I swallow back my sick, wondering how many beats would pass before arms, legs, hair, or teeth were reduced to bits indistinguishable from the ichor. I wonder how many pieces of lives now drip from my skin in viscous clumps. It bothers me, but truth is, I can see it is also necessary. "You can count upon me, Ama."

Ama squeezes my hand, then pulls me along. The artery we're standing upon dips, down, down, down, opening into a cavernous expanse of arteries and veins, alive, undulating at the flow of the beat. And at the center of the network stands the heart.

Ama touches my chin and I close my gaping jaw. The heart, it's massive. I mean, I knew it was going to be massive, but I just hadn't fathomed the girth, the complexities of all those chambers. Must be a thousand ley lights strung up all around it, each as big as a speck from down here, but all together, they cast a soft light upon this glistening gray-brown node, wibbling, wobbling, growing slowly larger. And then . . .

"Beat," I say, right as the contraction starts, a ripple of muscle that sends millions and millions of gallons of ichor coursing through the arteries of a beast the size of a small moon. I take in the breadth of the massive organ as the tremor shakes nearly every thought from my head. I forget how to blink. Or maybe I just don't want to miss a single thing.

"Ama," I gasp.

"I know, girl. I know."

She lets me gawk a little longer—to enjoy the view, I think, but Ama has never let me enjoy anything, so I realize it's not that. She's waiting for me to say something, to notice something. I squint, looking at how all the muscle and tissue comes together, then see little black specks crawling in and out and all around. People. Those are people.

"We're going up there, Ama? Way up there?"

"Betcha, girl. How?"

I look all over, studying the structure. My eyes track the ripples and undulations, the dozens of entry and exit valves to the chambers. The flow soon forms a map in my mind, and then I point. "There," I say, gesturing at the access door directly across from us. The vein is the shortest and has a gentler slope compared with the others. We'd be going with the flow, and we could make it in and out within two heartbeats if we hurried.

"Mmm. Not the best way, but acceptable." We cross the expanse, wait for the beat, then rush inside. The vein is steeper than I expected, and I immediately start to wonder if I've made a mistake. Ama just pushes me forward. I'm looking up, trying to figure out how we'll climb all the way to the valve, when instinct tells me to brace myself. I steady my stance, and suddenly, there's a tremendous suck. The valve flaps open and Ama and I are sucked right in along with the tide of ichor.

I'm drowning, not sure what's up and what's down. I've got seconds to act. Soon, we'll be expelled. I right myself the best I can, swim up. Ama's already clutching at one of the tendons connected to the valve. I grab one as well and hoist myself up, high as I can, until my cheek's pressed up against the ceiling.

I'm in the heart. Blessed mothers, I'm inside the beast's heart. The chamber clears, and we drop down to the floor. Doors open, and workers come rushing in, see my ama and me, and a heated exchange follows while I catch my breath and thoughts. The arguments here are concise and very pointed. No time to waste beating around the bush. My ama's words hold clout, but still no one believes.

"You," a woman says to me, the naxshi patterns on her face so dark that they must be newly set with ichor from this beast, not like the faded ones we all wear. Her uniform is special, too, made not from the beast's hide but from tender inner flesh—maybe made from heart leather itself. "Let's see what you can do with this." She tosses me a knife, a metal one like my own, but three times as big. Worth more than my life many times over. The hilt is heavy and cold in my hand, carved with symbols of tribes long forgotten. The blade gleams, impossibly sharp and waiting. "You want a spot in the heart? Claim it."

She points me to a calcified pillar of flesh, unpliable, the wall and floor around it looking aggravated and angry. I know instantly that it doesn't belong here. As I get closer, the smell becomes chalky and putrid—a sickly-sweet fragrance I can taste in the back of my throat. An impish girl comes shuffling up behind me, eyes cast down, holding a bucket.

I've got a minute and forty-five seconds left, but still I eat up several moments deciding where it'd be best to cut. I touch the blade to the calcification, getting a feel for the texture, examining how deep it penetrates the healthy flesh. I can feel the anxiety growing behind me. Rushing me. But this is not something that can be rushed. I take note of the four nearby capillaries, one of them compromised, and then plunge the knife an inch below with the force of my entire body. I ignore the collective gasp and slice downward in a clean motion, flaying one side of the tumor away. I take a second cut, wedging my way deeper into the structure, then do the same from the other direction. I prop up the massive growth with my off hand and my hip, like I'm carrying a child. The angles are odd from this direction, but I've cut so deeply, only a few nicks are needed to pull the tumor completely off, all except where the bad capillary sits. I leave a little tumor there, serving as a protective cap, and then I hand the large tumor—nearly half as big as I am—to the girl with the bucket too small to contain even one of Old Man Saym's shits. She drops her bucket and holds the tumor up with both hands as two other girls come running to help.

I don't waste a second and rush back to the capillary. Take two more precise slices, until only the thinnest layer of bad flesh remains. It doesn't look quite right, but what to do next falls far beyond my instinct. "What do you do now? Have some sort of surgeon repair this?" I ask.

When no one answers, I turn around, noticing the crowd I've attracted. The woman in heart leather comes and examines my cuts. "Hail a surgeon immediately!" she shouts, then whispers to me, "I meant only for you to cut a few chunks from the calcification. Not the entire tumor."

"With all respect, why? That would take hours!"

"Why? Because if you would have nicked here, or here, or here, we'd all be dead right now." She scoffs, but her eyes are wide with wonder as she turns to my mother. "We will take her *provisionally*. She will work directly under me."

"Thank you, Uridan," my ama says to the woman. Then she looks at me and nods once. From her, it's like a celebration with favors and food and family. For maybe the first time in my life, I've impressed my ama.

I wish so much to savor this moment, to allow myself to live in it, but we're nearing in on thirty seconds, and this tumor needs to be cleared away. I hack at it, breaking it down into five chunks, so it can easily be carried out. My head is still dizzy, and when I toss a tumor chunk toward the bucket being held by one of the waifish girls, I miss. I'm so embarrassed, I quickly go fetch the tumor before anyone notices. She stoops at the same time, and we grab the piece together. Our eyes meet.

She has my pai's eyes, blessed mothers.

Same eyes I have, a pale reddish brown, and everyone's always going on about how unique they are. She has my pai's jawline also, his brow. Might as well be looking into some sort of funny mirror, one that reflected a different reality. I've nearly forgotten the word for it—a word that's become more of a cuss than anything useful—but then it comes rushing back.

Sister. This girl could be my sister.

"Hello," I say timidly.

She nods, then scurries off with the tumor chunk. I run

off after her. It's time to get going, after all, before a million tons of ichor come crashing down on my head. But my earlobe screams out in pain, and I'm yanked back, caught in my ama's grip.

"Don't you *ever* talk to her again," Ama says. "Do you understand me?"

I squirm. We've got twelve seconds left. Everyone else has already evacuated, but she holds me firm.

"Do you understand?"

"But, Ama! We need to go. Now!"

"Understand me, girl?"

"Yes!" I scream. "Yes! I won't talk to her again."

Then we're running. *"Beat!"* I scream as we duck through the doorway and seal it behind us. I'm still pressed up against it as my entire world continues to shake, and it has nothing to do with the beat of the beast's heart.

SESKE

Of Lost Lines and Found Texts

Think harder, Seske," Pai says, his brows arched and eyes peeled wide, as if he's trying to project the quiz answer directly into my mind.

My thoughts tumble past me, all the names of the Lines, but for the life of me, I can't grab on to the one I need. Hamish, Inikodo, and Semirami are, of course, the first three, but then it gets fuzzy until Crown Safran, who decreed that every family would always be allowed one child, despite the additional strain on resources. But then years later, when it became evident that our generation ship would not be able to accommodate such a population, he stealthily defined a family as a man and two women. The men rejoiced, of course, but little did they know that this move would be the downfall of man. The Lines of Matriarchy were born under Crown Safran's rule, both literally and figuratively, with Matris Abinaya, who when she came of age had taken the Crown by coup and took Crown

Safran to the spirit wall. Well, his head at least. She'd pressed it into the wall, and the beast's secretions covered it, where it stood, slowly digested by enzymes until there was merely a calcified husk left. They say Abinaya was such a cruel matriarch that when her own body was taken to the wall, she'd tainted it in such a way that enzymes no longer secreted from where her body had been inhumed.

"Matris Abinaya," I answer my pai. It is the wrong answer to his question, I know, but at least he will think I made an effort.

"Oh, Seske." He stands and dusts his hands on his thighs. "You're off by over two hundred years. Trying to put knowledge into your brain is like trying to shove a fist through a wall of bone. Matris Tendasha is the answer. Matris Tendasha made the old Rule of Tens that helped to counteract the population explosion after the Great Mending. Ten fingers." Pai opens his hands and wriggles his long, slender fingers, patinaed with the deepest shade of orange. "Ten persons in the family unit. Three men, six women, and a child shared between them all. *Ten* for *Ten*dasha."

I wrinkle my nose at my head-father. "I may be slow at the Lines, Pai, but I *can* count."

He looks at me, skeptical. "Maybe we should save the rest for another day. Why don't you run along and play?"

Before I was a woman, two days ago to be exact, I used to impatiently wait for Pai to release me from the torture of his lessons with those very words, but now play is the last thing on my mind. "I don't have time to waste. I need you to teach me everything there is to being a proper matriarch."

Pai looks at me and smiles warmly. "Seske, despite the many gray hairs as you've put upon her head, Matris is still very young. There will be time. It is better not to force such things."

My pai looks at me with kindness and admiration. In his eyes, I am his only child, and he has never let me forget that, despite that it is his blood running through Sisterkin's veins and not mine. I am his only daughter, and he is my favorite father, not that I would ever tell my bapa that, though I am of his blood. It is tacky to make such distinctions either way, but every child has their favorite parent. And least favorite.

"Matris thinks I'm a lost cause. I need to prove her wrong, *now*, not twenty years from now. I'll be twice the matriarch she ever was and ever will be."

"Now, Seske, your head-mother has made mistakes—"

"In birthing Sisterkin, you mean?"

Pai winces at the name. "Mistakes in general. We all make mistakes. Even you make mistakes . . ." He lets the words hang and peels his eyes open again. With Wheytt, he means. Or perhaps any one of the hundreds of other mistakes that I've made recently. I can't read his favor-barren mind. But I get the gist. "You need to go easy on Matris," he says. "Forgive. Forget. It will eat you up on the inside if you don't." Pai smiles, but it is a smile of remorse.

If my will-father had told me such a thing, I would have dismissed it as his normal blather, but coming from Pai, his head as firm upon his shoulders as a man ever had, perhaps I should at least consider it. "Yes, Pai," I say. He squeezes me, then lets go.

"We'll start again tomorrow?"

"I'm off to go study right now," I tell him. "You'll be so proud . . ."

"I'm already proud of you, Seske. But you're sure you're okay with the Texts? Alone?"

"I won't eat or drink near them, I promise."

"Or fall asleep on them?"

Again, Pai wants to add, but he is the matriarch's husband a thousand times over, and decorum is his middle name.

"No drool on the pages, I promise." I swaddle the tome in my arms. It is heavy with the weight of our people, heavy with years of dust, of sweat, of everything that we've lived through during the past several centuries. It is the oldest relic we have, and besides our technology, it is one of the few items we allow upon our ship during exodus. Our world can be re-created, replicated, and refabricated just so, but our past is fragile, irreplaceable.

I'm still beaming inside when I sit down with the Texts. I run my fingers over the Lines, saying them through aloud, once, twice, again. Vvanescript blurs. My head tilts, and suddenly the cool paper is upon my cheek. I press myself up, slap my face. I am awake. I quiz myself on the first twenty but make it only halfway through before my mind fails me. Then a familiar smell sets my mind alight. Kettleworm tea. Figures Bapa would have some brewing, even before we have walls up in the kitchen. Carefully, I close the Texts and slip the tome into its cover, old brittle skin from one of the first beasts we'd brought down from the days when we merely harvested their resources to store aboard our ship.

Bapa greets me, a steaming cup of kettleworm tea already extended my way. I breathe in the vapors. Bapa makes the tea extra strong for me, with lots of pulp to help me keep my thoughts organized. Tiny bits of kettleworm dance and wriggle in the heat, trying to latch on to each other to form a larger organism, but I stir them all apart with my finger, suck it clean, and watch their dance begin again. The kettleworms themselves are a deep purple, but their excretions are a vibrant and fierce orange that stains your mouth. They are extremophiles, but when the temperature shifts too suddenly, they release their savory enzymes. Bapa has the brewing process down to a secret science, and his fame has spread well beyond the walls of our family unit. If Matris would allow men to own such things, he'd likely have a thriving business, but as progressive as she seems to the outside world, she'd never let such a thing happen in her own home, under her rule.

"I hear you've kissed a boy," Bapa says, stirring his own tea, unwilling to look me in the eye. "Is this an urgent need, or can it wait until your amas are raised from sleep?"

Lust is a matter of will for Bapa to deal with, while love is a matter for my amas, and as for the technical mechanics of the physical act, well, that falls upon my head-father and -mothers. I've had the sex talk eight times. So far. Each time more excruciating than the last. And favors forbid I actually have a question. I get routed and rerouted, bounced between parents, until I get so frustrated that I give up. My head-father refuses to talk about the mechanics of sex between women, my amas can only speculate what it's like to love a man, and my will-mothers are useless on any matter that doesn't involve the Five Chronicles of Willpower, and Bapa just gets nervous and falls into senseless allegories. And Matris . . .

"My will is strong, Bapa. It was a foolish mistake, that's all."

"Good." He sighs. "There are times when a woman's needs become burdens, like the loads of water wax the beastworkers carry upon their backs. And when it comes time for the burdens to be laid down—"

Mothers spur his wonderful will, I really don't have time for this. "Excuse me, Bapa, my studies await," I say, taking my cup with me. I dodge boneworkers who are busy putting the detailed touches on our home, consulting their ledgers. One worker gouges the pristine surface of our dining table with her agile chisel. I cringe, remembering how mad Matris had been when I'd practiced my Vvanescript right there on a single sheet of parchment, my sharp quill leaving etchings of ill-drawn words forever in the table's finish. But then an involuntary smirk leaves my lips. Matris could have ordered the new tabletop to be left unblemished if she'd wanted. For better or worse, it is a part of our family unit's history and a part of our future.

In the relative seclusion of my room, I carefully set my cup next to the Texts and open the book yet again. My eyes dart back to my cup. I'd promised Pai, hadn't I? No eating or drinking near the Texts? Suddenly, my hands tremble as I ease the cup away from my study area. Kettleworm stains are nearly impossible to get rid of, and the last thing I want to do is explain to Pai why our sacred texts are blood orange. With a cool sense of relief, I set the cup upon the sill overlooking the scaffolding of the cityscape beyond. Despite my better judgment, I crack open the window. I'm flooded by the sweet sting of newly let ichor, and bone dust tickles my nose. The echo of all the simultaneous construction is deafening and unrelenting. Work continues on at all hours. I shut the window. There will be months of this yet. I can see why Matris keeps the Contour class in stasis during excavation.

The vapors go straight to my head. I sit down at my desk. The boneworkers have yet to detail my room, and my fingers run over the empty spot where I'd carved Adalla's name and mine, on the side facing the wall so that no one would see. I take a pen and carve it again, deeper this time. And neater. My cheeks flush and my insides clench; a new and odd feeling pulses pleasure all through me. The hairs on my arms stiffen, as well as those at the nape of my neck.

"Focus, Seske," I tell myself, and I pull the Texts in front of me, staring down at all those names. Of the 118 matriarchs, only four of them had been will-mothers, and none of them had been heart-mothers. If I want to prove my potential, I'll have to keep my head about me, not be distracted by the imminent conclusion of what was an innocent childhood crush.

We haven't much time left if there's anything to come of it. Matris is probably already arranging my coming out party, and as soon as the rest of my cohort is raised, I'll be expected to choose a suitor. Female preferably, to fortify the matrilines, but at this point, Matris would settle for my interest in any suitable mate. No matter what, all possibilities between Adalla and me will be over. In fact, I should probably put her out of my mind now and save us both some heartache. But that thought causes a sob to surface, and I fight to snag it in my throat. I catch a tear upon my fingertip before it lands upon the page. My nose runs as well. I sit back, clean myself up, wipe the bleariness from my eyes. Adalla's thumbs will be safer with me out of her life. I nod to myself, willing my mind to accept that it is for the best, then look down again at the page.

My heart stops. My nose was not running. It was bleeding. I stare at the glistening dome of the red drop perched upon the page. *Don't panic, Seske.* I grab a towel and, with the slightest of movements, let the blood droplet wick up into the fabric. *Better,* I think. Just a pale-red splotch. I dampen the towel with my saliva and begin to gently rub. The spot fades to near nothing, but some of the ink has come up as well. I pull my ink and quill from my drawer and, with a steady hand, touch up the lettering. There. Perfect. Well, an accountancy guard would notice, but it will be enough to escape the notice of my headfather and -mothers.

As I sit back, smug in my chair, the inkwell rattles upon my desk. The whole of my room begins to shudder. Another beastquake. They've become less common and less forceful, but this one is still enough to topple my ink. A black slick moves across the surface of my desk, bleeding into the back cover of the Texts. I swipe the book up, clench it to my chest as the tremor eases, but it is too late. I hold the mess in front of me in horror, wondering if I'll be the first addition to this beast's spirit wall.

I can think of only one person who's skilled enough to fix this.

Sonovan.

I MAKE MY WAY THROUGH THE IDES, THE TEXTS BUNDLED UP IN suede wrappings and clutched close to my chest. The beast-workers' homes rise up and around me in unfamiliar clusters of warty domes. Artisans stir vats of water wax, preparing to mold furniture, utensils, and other necessities. Unlike the Contour class, where luxuries abound, in the Ides, they make use of what is given. Though the layout of each of the beast's warts is as unique as a fingerprint, it is fairly easy to navigate, since the family units try to approximate the same location. I come to the cluster that I think belongs to Adalla's family.

I step through the doorway, into the living quarters of one of Adalla's neighbors, a young unit all in their teens, with a baby boy being tossed between his fathers. The child giggles hysterically before being shushed. Eli is the boy's name, as I've picked up from my many trips through their home to Adalla's, but it is custom to turn your eyes and ears away from their goings, giving privacy in the mental realm where none exists in the physical. There is much I pretend not to see. Adalla's cluster is a large one, and she's close to the center, so I have to pass through four units to get to hers. I don't see the amorous triad—a tangle of limbs upon a standard-issue water wax bed—don't hear the angry cusses of fighting wives, don't smell the man loosing his bowels into an old, dented pot, nor do I apologize when I accidentally kick over his soiled rag bucket as I try to scurry past. At last, I reach Adalla's home. Her ama smiles as she sees me coming.

"Who is this strange woman before me?" she asks, beaming. This is Purah, the last to join their triad. She pinches at the sides of my breasts, then knocks me in the hips with her fists. "Very sturdy. Oh, how your amas must have hoisted you!"

"My amas haven't been raised from stasis yet," I say bashfully. "Just Matris and my fathers. We will celebrate when—"

Purah's eyes go wide, her wrinkled hands go to my hips, and all at once, she thrusts me into the air. She is retired from beastwork, but her body has not forgotten its strength. I tense through my core, trying not to tip over. "The cut of mothers, the cut of wives, the cut of leaders, she bleeds from inside! Rejoice the flow, so red and bright! A girl this morning, a woman tonight!" Purah chants, then starts again, another voice joining her this time, more hands beneath my hips. Another set. All of Adalla's amas hoist me, tossing me higher and higher. But they are not through. The pretense of privacy is lost, and every heart-mother within hearing comes cramming into Adalla's living room, twenty of them at least, all tossing me, all beaming at me as if I were their daughter. I allow myself a moment of joy, pushing aside all the trouble I'm in to savor their cheers. I love my own amas with all my heart, but their celebration will be one of planning and diligence, with everything prim and proper. I will sit on a hoisted throne, high above their heads. Poems will be read, lengthy and droll. A soothsayer will agonize over spotting patterns upon my first rags and consult the ancestor spirits about what my life holds. It will be well and fine and—I'm sure—very expensive, but it will not compare to this.

"Enough! Enough!" I protest, though inside, I yearn for just a little more. But the Texts are being jostled, too, and I can't afford to tear a page on top of the stain that continues to set. The crowd gently lowers me, then dissipates. I look around for Adalla, but she must be off working her shift. I take a deep breath, then say, "I need to speak to Sonovan. Please, is he here?"

The amas huddle together and their eyes dart about in a silent conversation that I am left out of. There are hushed squeals and giggles. "Aye, he is. Is that bundle you have there for him?"

"Yes," I admit. There is more squealing, worse than the wheeze of the gills of our last beast right before exodus was declared. I know the amas are known for their eccentricity, but this is odd, even for them. I can't help but wonder what they're so giddy about.

"I'll fetch him straightaway," says Purah, leaving me with Doram and Morova. Their wrinkled hands catch in each other's, and they both lean into me.

"This must be an urgent matter," Ama Morova says, eyes wide. The inks above her brows have long since faded, but even in this time of scarcity, she's made the effort to pencil them in around the edges. Her hair is up in a gray twist of three celestial knots, each representing a principal star from her line, and the parts between them are painstakingly straight. Adalla had taught them to me many years ago, and I knew the tales of her ancestral mothers just as well as I knew my own. Probably better.

"It is urgent," I say, swallowing saliva. Matris's name cannot bear to be tarnished a third time. The Senate would pressure her to concede the throne. If Sonovan can't help me, then I'm ruined.

Sonovan is Adalla's tin uncle. Her real head-father died when she was just a young child, in a hull breach two exoduses ago that took the lives of thirty-eight souls. Though he has no real family authority under law, Sonovan has been a good pai to Adalla, a worthy husband to her head-mothers, and the whole family unit has benefited from his keen householding. In all my years visiting Adalla's home, I've never seen so much as a crumb on the floor or a chair askew. Under my grandmatris's rule, he had been hanged for adultery of the worst sort, lying with the wife of his will-husband. He was strung up for ten weeks for the offense, one week for each of the lives he'd ruined and shamed, and afterward he had been shunned and left to fend for himself. These amas had offered him sanctuary when no one else would. There was drama, of course—there always is with Adalla's amas. But the scandal blew over, and people forgot, and Sonovan worked his way into the lonely bed of the head-wives. The amas' hearts are just as big as their mouths are crude, so I'd heard their remarks about his waymaker being just as impressively long as his thumbs. Not information that I particularly wanted to know, but if gossip were grapes, Adalla's amas could feed their entire village.

"We are humbled to have you," Morova says, her hand upon my knee. Of all the amas, she is the one I fear most, with that thin smile always set upon her face. "But if you break our daughter's heart, Matris help you . . ." She leaves her threat open, her smile parting to reveal teeth stained a deep gray.

"Morova!" Doram says, tugging her wife back. "That's no way to treat our future law daughter."

"Law daughter!" I choke on the words, then look down at the bundle in my arm and then into the archway now occupied by Sonovan. Despite his transgressions, time has been nothing but kind to him. The whites of his eyes stand bright against the ink upon his face. Not a single patch of skin has been left bare, so that from afar, it looks to be a wash of solid purple. Then he nears, and I see the tale of love and loss and redemption. No one knows more about ink than Sonovan, and I am sure he can salvage the Texts, but I fear I have made a horrible transgression of my own.

In my haste and desperation, I forgot that I am no longer a child and must now call upon Sonovan through the Lines. I should have addressed his head-wives first, or Adalla. There is only one exception to this, and that is when asking for a woman's hand in marriage, where it is custom to offer a—

"On behalf of my husband and wives, I accept this dowry with joy and gratitude," Sonovan says, beaming at me as he attempts to take my bundled Texts from me. His long, limp thumbs flop over the sides as he tugs it. I do not release my grip. "Matriling Kaleigh, we are humbled to accept you into our fold."

"But—" I shout. I fumble to explain myself. "What I meant . . . What I came here for . . . Please, forgive me if I've misstepped . . ."

"Burning lakes of ichor!" Sonovan exclaims. I realize I've let loose my grip, and the tome now stands unwrapped in his hands. "We could not possibly accept this . . ." He turns the Texts over and sees the giant stain. His eyes widen. "Morova, please fetch my tin oil and flashing cloth. Doram, a bucket of twice-laid soap. Purah, a full stretch of quarter claim from the market."

The amas protest at being ordered around in such a manner, but Sonovan stands firm, and the room clears.

Then his mouth cinches, and I can tell he's put together all the pieces of this misunderstanding. He looks at me. I wince, then nod, confirming that I am not here to woo his daughter. He bids me forward with an arched brow. "I'm afraid you've made everyone terribly excited. You know how the amas get. This will be news about the whole of the Ides before the next work shift."

"I know," I say, wishing the floor would swallow me up whole. "How mad do you think Adalla will be?"

"If you tell her before anyone else gets the chance, that should soften the blow. She should be home soon, if you want to wait."

"How is she? Did she tell you about the trouble we almost got into?" I know this answer. Adalla tells Sonovan *everything*. It's annoying, but in turn, he's come to be a confidant to me as well.

"With the lash counter, yes. I told her it was a bad plan, but the girl never listens. Maybe this position in the heart will be good for her. Teach her some discipline."

I sit bolt upright. So she *had* gotten the promotion. I feel like a terrible friend, missing out on something so important. What do you get to celebrate something like that? I could pick her some flowers from the woodward canopies. Nice bloated ones that would dribble fluorescent ooze for days.

"I'll be back in a bit, okay?" I say, standing up to leave.

"Mmm," he says, already studying the stain, then dabbing the oils laid out beside him.

I make my way out of their home and run into Adalla standing in the archway, not dressed in the beastworker's suit that's become indistinguishable from her own skin, but in a bright orange heartworker's dress. I'm almost glad that I've come empty-handed, because the most beautiful blooms would palc in comparison to her new look.

My heart leaps and knocks against my rib cage. "Adalla! Congratulations!"

I go to hug her, but she cringes away from me, wincing. She's mad at me. I get it.

"I should have said something earlier. I should have remembered. I'm sorry."

"No, it's not that," she says. "And thanks." She turns, and I see several strips of blood soaking through her clothes.

"Sonovan!" I yell out. He comes running and sees the blood marks across her back.

"I'm fine," Adalla says as he lifts her dress to inspect the damage. Twenty-seven welts, I count them all.

"What happened?" I ask.

"The secrets of heartwork." She grins hard at me. "I did it, Seske. I made it to the heart."

Sonovan stands there, looking between Adalla and me. "Tend to her first," I tell him. "The Texts can wait."

Sonovan scuttles out of the room, then returns with clean cloths and ointments. He applies them gently and efficiently, and in no time, Adalla is nearly good as new. He leaves us alone to return the Texts back to their pristine form. Hopefully.

"You really can't tell me anything?" I ask Adalla.

"I'm sworn to secrecy in all things heart-related. But there was one thing that was . . . odd."

"What?" I lean in. "Did you see Quiet Medla?"

"No. No spirits. But I saw someone. A helper. Seske, she looked just like *me*. Or close enough to it. We worked together some today. She didn't speak a word. But I don't know, there was just something about her. I feel like I'm missing a limb I never even knew I had. I have to find out more. Who she is. Where she lives."

There's something that Adalla isn't quite saying: a word that's practically sacrilege. I don't hold back, though. "You think she's your sister? That your parents have a secret child out there that they never told you about? Plenty of people look alike, Adalla. And trust me, if she is your sister, you don't want anything to do with her. They're nothing but trouble."

"Maybe," she says. "But since when have you been known to turn down a chance to get into trouble?"

She's got me there. I smile.

"You'll come with me then?" She pulls my hand.

"*Now?* But your back."

"It's fine. Apparently twenty-seven lashes is the record for a heartworker's first day on the job."

"Yeah, okay. That's like me bragging that I only ruined *one* volume of the ancient Texts today."

Adalla sticks her tongue at me. "That's the lowest number, Seske. The previous record was fifty-five."

"This is sounding like a pretty awful job. And aren't you supposed to be all hush-hush with heartwork secrets?"

"Well, tell me a secret and we'll be even." She leans in close, her earlobe next to my lips.

"I carved our names into my desk." A small secret. Harmless. Maybe.

"That's not a secret. You told me about that years ago."

"Well, I did it again. Today. I didn't want any random boneworker re-creating it. I wanted to carve it myself. Again."

"Did you at least spell my name right this time?"

"Daidi's bells," I cuss. Adalla pinches my cheek, then leads me out and through the Ides. We run fast and hard, but she notices the stares we're getting.

"Why is everyone grinning at us like that?" she asks.

Oh. I forgot to tell her. "I might have accidentally asked Sonovan for your hand in marriage."

"You *what?*"

"I didn't mean to. It was a big misunderstanding. Unfortunately, I didn't get to tell your amas that before they ran off."

"All of the Ides knows by now, then. They can't possibly take it seriously, though. You. Me. Really?"

"Yeah, it's ridiculous," I grumble. A beastworker marrying someone in the Contour class is scandal enough, but the heir to the throne? Only I don't know why it should matter. Not saying that I do want to marry her for sure, but I know the idea of not being with her is awful. It pains me that we won't be able to enjoy each other's company like this anymore. At least we'll have this one last adventure together, and I intend to make the most of it.

"It'll blow over soon enough," Adalla says. "Gossip is the one thing we're never in short supply of, betcha."

"Mmm." I hope she's right.

She leads us farther and farther away from the Ides, into a section of the beast I've never been in. The air thickens, almost to the point of being suffocating, the sweet smell of home replaced by something danker and more sinister. "The bowels?" I ask. "You're sure about this?"

"No. I asked around, but no one knew where she went after shift, or else they just wouldn't tell me. But there are hundreds of waifs, Seske, maybe thousands, helping out, filling in when needed. People treat them like shit, like they don't matter. I just kinda thought . . . if they're not in the Ides, where do they go? This seems . . . right. Where else would you put a bunch of people you want to pretend don't exist?"

Anywhere but here is what I'm thinking. "Seems right by me too" is what I say. I inch closer to the pond of cool, debris-ridden slime that rims the sphincter. It pulses, back and forth, back and forth, a putrid-looking pucker of flesh. Adalla sticks both of her hands in the hole and pulls hard, her muscles rippling and bulging. The rim tries to hold tight, even looks like it's tugging against her, but eventually it gives, and the hole widens just enough for a person to slip through. I hesitate, but not just because of the lewd pucker of flesh in front of me. I've spent so much of my life wishing I didn't have a sister, and I can't imagine wanting to go through all of this to find one on purpose.

"After you . . ." Adalla says, nodding me forward.

My face is a knot, but I work my way through the sludge, put a foot on her outstretched knee for a boost, and then wiggle my way over. I try to catch myself on the other side, but it's so slippery, so slimy, my every attempt at gaining purchase results in empty fists, and then I'm welcomed face-first into the swamp of putridity. Wet debris clings to my eyelashes, blankets my skin, and creeps in the corners of my mouth no matter how tightly I keep it shut. As Adalla slips through the hole, the sphincter shuts behind her, and the light from the other side vanishes, leaving us completely in the dark.

Adalla lands besides me, then seconds later, a small blip of candlelight casts the entire room in a soft, warm glow. She lights another candle for me. I ask Adalla why we just don't use a ley light, but apparently these scented candles are meant to ward away spirits. I'm not about to question her on it now. Shadows dance, flickering across walls. If there's anything haunted in this beast, this is where it resides. With my free hand, I try to wipe my face of muck, but fail miserably. And when I realize it's *crawling* over me, fuzzy little worms, I focus all my energy on not screaming.

"There, let's follow the path and see where this thing takes us," Adalla says, somehow unfazed by the worms.

"I know where it leads . . . a long stretch of filth then another sphincter, and then the final one that drops us off in the dead of space."

"We won't have to go that far," she says, but she can tell this is bugging me. "Four hundred steps. That's it. We don't see anything, we come back. Okay?"

"Okay," I say.

We make our way around polyps and fissures spewing bubbles into the grimy puddles of water at our feet. It's warm and dank in here, and smells like a backed-up drain, and I can't even imagine how many baths I'll have to take to get all the stink off. The walls undulate around us, and long, gristly strings hang from the ceiling, occasionally slapping against our foreheads. Then the candlelight hits them just right, and I realize they have *teeth*.

My hand slips into Adalla's, and I try to put on a brave front, but inside, I'm counting down the steps until we can turn back and declare this adventure over and done. Just fifty more now.

But then, 387 steps in, we see it. Signs of civilization. Giant polyps erupt from the walls of the beast, narrow at the base, but widening toward the top, big enough to house two or three people. Dim lights shine from inside, and we see silhouettes. Eating, playing, working. Dancing. But the entire camp is quiet. Dead quiet.

"Quiet Medla was here," Adalla says, nodding to herself. "I told you spirits are real. The waifs must have skipped prayers, sure is sure is sure." She reaches into her satchel, pulls out sweet-scented twine, breaks a piece off, then hands it to me. "Here. Chew on this. Just in case she's still wandering about."

I take the piece, unsure of how it's supposed to protect me, but still chewing the heck out of it. Adalla and I creep closer. I glance over my shoulder at the puckered sphincter leading back to the first bowel. It's not too late to abort our mission.

In the center of the village, frothy liquid bubbles up from a fissure. A few dozen waif girls gather around it, collecting pieces of debris and putting them into baskets. Their hands and arms move about excitedly.

"This is eerie," I whisper. "Too eerie. I want to go back." But even my whisper carries like normal speech in this place. Damn near a scream. The silhouettes all stop. All turn toward me. One by one, they slide down the polyps, exiting through a little flap of skin at the base. They see us, and Adalla and I, we run so fast, our feet splatting through shallow puddles. They're gaining on us, silent, but they might as well be cussing us for encroaching on their land. We've gone too far. Adalla grabs my elbow, pulls me sideways into a flap of flesh; she takes her knife and cuts until there's room enough for us to tuck fully inside. On the outside, footsteps press past us, then it's quiet, but neither one of us is ready to move.

Her chest rises and falls. My breath huffs so hard I knock out my candlelight.

"Daidi's bells!" I mumble.

"It's not out, not completely," she says. "Watch this." Adalla holds her candle flame several inches above my extinguished wick. A tiny bead of light works its way down, until it hits my wick and it bursts once again into a flame.

My breath catches as the candlelight hits her face just right. Sure, it's covered in living, crawling moss. And sure, we both smell like the deep end of a latrine. But that's the thing about Adalla: I can be anywhere with her, *anywhere*, and all that other stuff melts away, like we're two souls, floating out in the void—stars at our backs, and stars in our eyes. I could kick myself for wasting my first kiss on Wheytt, when it could have been here . . . Adalla and me, in the worst of situations. In the best of situations.

"Cool trick," I say. "Can I try?"

"Sure," whispers Adalla. Then she blows her candle out.

Then I blow my candle out.

In the dark, covered in moss, slime, and dozens of other substances I don't even want to think about, I lean forward until I feel Adalla's breath upon my face. We are close. So close.

"Seske?" comes her voice, soft, timid. Nothing like the confident girl I've known since forever.

"Yes, Adalla," I say, the tension throbbing inside me causing my voice to crack.

"How much longer do we have? You know, until thoughts of me kissing you will get me killed?"

I pause, frowning. A few months, likely. But I could delay, find excuses to feed Matris. Avoid declaring a suitor for years. Adalla and I could sneak away just like this . . . well, not *just* like this, but we could sneak away to private spots, spend our moments skin to skin, all the burdens of life left behind. "We've got all the time in the world," I tell her, trying to believe it myself. "I'll give up being heir if I have to. I won't be any good at it anyway."

"Seske, you are not giving up your claim to the throne, for me or for anyone. You are more deserving of it than any woman who's sat on it before you. And you'll be better than all of them too."

I wish I believed in me the way Adalla believes in me. "I'll forgo suitors then," I declare. "Matris will be upset, but she'll have all the problems of this favorless beast to deal with. And then, when *I'm* Matris . . ."

My chest tightens, thinking of her ama's threat—*if you break our daughter's heart* . . . But I would never do such a thing.

"What, Seske?" she asks. I can taste the hope on her breath. She wants to know if this will ever be more than a secret affair, if she'll ever be allowed upon my arm in public.

"I can promise you my reign will be full of scandals, and you, Adalla, will be my first one."

Our noses touch. All the tension between us melts away. And then with a furious force, I am upon her, but not in the way I'd hoped. We are knocking together, and our foreheads become weapons, limbs butting against each other, her elbow in my eye, and I'm thinking something's definitely wrong, because it's not supposed to be this shaky, this *loud*. We grip each other, holding tight against the tremors shaking us senseless. I am screaming, but the wail of the beast swallows all. Finally, after what seems like an eternity, the quake subsides, followed by a gentle pulsing of flesh pressed all around us.

Adalla and I clutch each other, wordless, breathless, for a long, long time. I realize my arms are against the welts on her back, so I loosen my grip.

"No," Adalla says. "Don't let go."

I hug her tighter, and she does likewise. And I get it. At the end of this embrace, our worlds will be changed. That quake was big, much too big. Lives were lost, most certainly. Matris would be blamed. She'd need to calm things down, get us back to normal as fast as she could. She'd need to shift her focus. A distraction. A perfect distraction. And there was nothing more distracting than the pomp and circumstance that went behind an heir declaring her suitors. I didn't have years. I barely have months.

As soon as excavation is over, and the rest of the Contour class is woken up from stasis, I'll have to name a wife, or at least a husband. I would have to set the course for the future of the people, a strong one that would make them forget how awful this beast would be to us for the next decade.

From now on, I will have to be the perfect daughter. Not the daughter who steals off to sneak kisses with beastworkers. This moment—this is the only moment we'll ever get.

Suddenly, I see a glint in Adalla's eyes, her lips parted, chest rising and falling against mine. It takes me a moment to realize the light is coming from the opening behind us. Someone's wedged their arm inside and has got a grip on Adalla.

"Don't worry. Help's coming," I hear a voice say. And the body who belongs to that voice is tugging and tugging, and Adalla is getting farther and farther away. It's like I'm stuck in a nightmare, and I can't get her back. Our only moment stolen away from us.

Our fingers touch, and then her knife is sitting in my hand. Her eyes implore me. We can't be caught together, not like this. Not now. For her sake, and for Matris's.

I watch her as she's drawn out of the fissure. My lips ache so hard for hers, an ache that makes itself known through every tender part of my body, but then she mouths, *Go*, to me, and I'm cutting deeper and deeper into the flesh of the beast, hoping to find another way out.

I FIND MYSELF IN A THIN PASSAGEWAY, KNIFE GRIPPED TO MY side for protection now. I walk a tightrope of firm tendon, surrounded by gorges of fatty tissue deep enough to swallow a woman whole. If another tremor happens, I'll fall and die for sure. The walls flex and bend, like there are hands pushing through from the other side, trying to escape. An eerie hiss has become the background noise to my panicked thoughts.

It's too late to turn back. No way would I find the entry wound I'd made into this cavity, so I keep pressing forward, hoping for the best. Finally, I spot a colony of crib worms, mouths plastered to the flesh of the cavity wall. I tickle a small one until it unlatches and cradle it in my arms. Its mouth finds my biceps, and it latches on to me. It takes only moments for its soothing toxins to calm my mind, to ease my heartache.

Funny how easy it is to turn back to such childish things. But when childhood makes more sense than adulthood, who can blame me? A little blood stains my pants, and all of a sudden, walls are erected where lines were once drawn. I'm given choices as wide as this passageway. All I can do is mourn for a relationship lost, for a friendship Matris will press for me to forget.

But I will never forget.

I slow down when I hear voices from the other side of the wall. Spirits, I can't help but think at first, maybe Ol' Baxi Batzi herself, come to seek revenge. Adalla says that she walks between walls, from home to home, calling out the names of people who are on her list to torment next, but if you keep a small bit of polished copper next to your bed, she'll get distracted by her reflection and forget all about smothering you in your sleep. Old beastworker superstitions, is what I think. But maybe I better make sure she's not calling my name. Just in case.

I tickle a few large crib worms away from their grips and arrange them on the wall in a line, so they form a ledge. I step over the fatty gulf, onto my makeshift shelf, then press my ear against the flesh, listening. Not Ol' Baxi Batzi, for sure. Just some people arguing. And it's heated. Sounds like they're arguing about the beast. They know something's wrong, and it's not spirits. Curiosity gets the best of me, so I take Adalla's knife and carefully make a small slit, just enough for me to peek through. I nearly gag as the smell of burned flesh wafts back at me. Sure enough, there are beastworkers there, huddled around an enormous dome in the center of a room the color of pus. They're taking readings with devices, then yelling and arguing some more.

The beastworker with the full, flush face is the leader, I gather. She's barking orders at the others, pointing at a purplish scar running along the dome. Then there's a flash beneath the surface of the dome, a dark shadow swimming past, big as twenty women and then some. The shadow is long, sleek, and oblong, its movement graceful yet intimidating. The purple scar bulges, leaks some, and a faint tremor echoes through the room. My mind is still churning slowly from the crib worm, but I know what that is. It couldn't be anything else. I'd seen that shape in the Texts many a time, only on a scale a million times bigger. It's a baby beast. And this is the womb.

My heart sinks to my stomach. Our beast is pregnant. I'm not even sure what that means, but it can't possibly be a good thing. That baby beast is sucking up resources for sure. Resources we need to live. How many years would it cut off the viability of this beast? Two? Five? Maybe this beast isn't viable at all. Maybe that's why we're having these quakes.

"We can try a higher setting," the leader is saying. "A longer duration."

"We need more time to study it," says another worker. "To scout out weaknesses. To find an entry point."

"We have no time," the leader says. "We promised Matris it would be dead and disposed of by now. We haven't even cracked the surface. Full power. We need to give it everything we've got."

"We can't afford any more quakes."

"Then up the sedatives again."

"But the beast's heart will strain further—"

"Up the sedatives!" the leader screams. The other worker nods, then takes off into another room. A few minutes later, she returns. All around me, I feel the flesh of the beast loosen. Tension recedes.

"It's done," she says. "We're ready to try again."

Three other workers move a pole toward the dome, right where the purple scar oozes. They shove the tip of the stick in, press some dials, and the rod comes to life, flickering with blue arcs of electricity. The womb convulses, fluids inside swishing side to side. The white-pus surface clenches, solidifies into a black web of fibrous tissue. It looks impenetrable.

There's a small quake, barely a rumble.

"More power!" the leader shouts.

Arcs jump all over the place, fizzling out as they hit the crusted shell.

"More!"

"That's all we have, ma'am. It's just not working."

The leader grabs the stick herself, shoves it farther in the scar with all her might, but nothing else happens. Finally, she gives up and throws the stick to the ground. "For will-mothers' sakes, if the power capacity isn't doubled by tomorrow, then I'll have all your backs burned by the Ancestor's lace!"

I cringe at the severity of the threat, a punishment deemed cruel and unusual a hundred years ago. The leader leaves, and the others duck into the adjoining room. For a long while, it is quiet. Slowly, the black web of the womb softens, returning to pus-colored flesh. The purple scar is larger now, and the leak has worsened, the womb's contents slowly dribbling to the floor.

I don't know if it's my curiosity or loss of inhibitions from my crib worm high, but I widen the slit just until it's big enough for me to slip through. My feet hit the floor quietly, and I sneak over and look up at this thing plaguing our new home. It is massive. I run my hand along the lumps at the base of the womb. The dark shadow passes by me once, twice. I ignore it. Try not to look directly at it. Try not to notice the translucent spots in the womb, where I catch glimpses of its skin, its tentacled mouth. Its big, bulging, wanting eyes. I knock on a translucent spot with my fist, and it clouds over with pus.

But it's still watching me. It purrs at me, a low tremble that I feel more than hear. It's clear what it's saying, though. It's pleading for its life.

Of course, I'm most certainly projecting. Giving human traits to a soulless beast that's only good for drifting through space, big open maw filtering out bits of stardust from young nebulas. It's certainly not following me out of curiosity now. A section of pus pulses translucent three times, and I step back. Then the entire womb goes crystal clear, revealing the beast's whole body. Its face stares right at me.

It's beautiful. And ghastly. Ghastly beautiful. Blue, pink, and teal lights run all along its skin, with curtains of thin tendrils running underneath. Its eyes blink at me, slowly.

My mouth gapes. Its mouth gapes. A mouth that could swallow me whole and still be left wanting. Footsteps slosh through the womb water on the floor. The beast vanishes behind a thick wall of pus. I step as quietly as I can, rounding the womb, keeping on the far side and hoping no one else comes back in. I'd be caught for sure. I keep my back pressed up against the womb and hold as still as I can.

I hear the *click*, then smell the bite of electricity in the air. There's a quaver in the womb, and giant arcs of light fill the room. The jolt travels through the womb, through me, ripping away my very thoughts. I want to scream out, to tell them to stop—that they're hurting me—but my mouth is held tight against my will, teeth clenching so hard together I think they might shatter. I can smell my skin smoking. My cheek presses up against the womb. My vision skips in and out, but next to me, a small swath of the womb goes translucent, then thins completely until there's a wet emptiness touching my skin. Neon tendrils wrap around my head, my torso, and next thing I know, I'm being pulled *inside* the womb. It closes up behind me and knits together an impenetrable black web, separating me from everything I know.

I'm surrounded by a liquid that's maybe closer to air, tendrils all around me, swaddling me. The electricity burns through here, but not as bad. I can think now, which gives me enough time to panic. I struggle to free myself, but the tendrils hold tight, trying to drown me. Am I its hostage? Is it trying to negotiate its freedom? Or just plain revenge? A life for a life?

Nonsense. It's just a beast—not much different from a crib worm, though on a much larger scale—a combination of flesh and bone and ichor meant to be someone's home for a while.

"Help!" I yell out, my words a spray of thin bubbles.

The beast startles like it's heard me. Like it's surprised I said something. It purrs back at me. The womb water sizzles, and from somewhere between my ears and my brain, I hear my word repeated back to me in a voice that sounds more like a painfully slow cough. "Help!"

I hold my breath until my lungs are pounding in my chest. I'm going to drown. I'll be mourned for sure. Nobody would dare speak ill of Matris, bereaved. And then Sisterkin would find some two-hundred-year-old loophole in the Texts that would let her take my place. The people would rejoice to have such a fine heir. Such a perfect heir. The heir that should have been all along if I hadn't prematurely escaped the confines of the womb that once held me. Sisterkin's suitors would bring stability to the throne, to our matriline, and we would go on and on for generations, culling all the best beasts, surviving, thriving, forever and ever.

Maybe me dying in here would be what's best for my people.

I let loose my breath, let the cool liquid air leak into my lungs, and wait to suffocate. I cough violently, expelling that sticky wetness only to take on more. Gradually, though, my coughing eases. I wait for my vision to fade to black, but it doesn't. Tendrils jostle me, moving until I'm eye to giant eye with the baby beast.

I can breathe whatever this stuff is. It stings going in and out with each breath, and I strain like I'm sipping malt through a too-thin straw, but I can breathe it well enough. And finally, the electric shocks subside, and we both untense—this baby beast that more than likely saved my life, and me.

My mouth hangs open in disbelief, but I quickly regret this as a tendril slips inside, fishes around, brushes against my teeth, then glides down my throat. I gag, coughing up a stomach full of kettleworm tea into the womb water, but the baby beast doesn't look concerned. It whips the tendril back out, then dips the tendril into its own mouth, sucking it clean. Other thinner tendrils pull bits of kettleworm from the water, and it swallows those as well.

The tendril comes for my mouth again. This time, I clamp down hard. A thinner tendril edges for the corner of my eye. I struggle, kick. Finally, my foot lands square in the baby beast's eye. It cries out, then pushes me away. It's sulking, I think. Like I hurt its feelings. I realize that it's just a child. An unborn child that learns through touching, tasting. And here I am, a grown woman kicking babies. An apology almost escapes my lips, but then I catch myself thinking those thoughts again. It's a baby, yes, but still a beast.

But the baby beast claims vengeance anyway and pushes me toward the edge of the womb. The skin thins to nothing, then with a hard punch to the chest, I'm kicked out.

I land on the floor, body splayed out, ear-deep in a puddle of womb water. If I breathe now, I know I'll cough and draw attention if I managed not to do so already. So I turn my face into the water and expel slowly, readying my lungs to transition back to air. I lift my head. Listen. The room is quiet. I look back up at the womb, the baby beast staring at me through the window, like it wants to tell me something. I shake my head. It's foolish of me to try to pretend it's more than a beast... that it has feelings, and wants, and ... *fears.*

I can't deal with that. Not now. I can't grow attached to something Matris aims to kill. I take one last mournful look at the beast, then put it out of my mind as I cross the room and hope upon the memory of all heart-fathers that I can slip out of here undetected.

"MY DEAR SESKE," MY MOTHER SAYS TO ME, MUCH LATER THAT day. There may be a major crisis outside the walls of the throne room, but when Matris wishes to receive you as her audience, your finery must be flawless. I fidget with the frill of several layers of petticoats and itch at all the spots where my braids strain against my scalp.

"Yes, Matris?" I say. "May I ask why you have called me here today?" Did someone see Adalla and me together? Did someone see me in the hallway leading from the womb? Does she know I know about the baby beast?

"I've been waiting for this day, my dearest daughter. A day I can speak to you of the ways of love."

My face falls into my hands. My ninth and final sex talk. Here it is. I was fidgeting before, but I'm squirming now. "My fathers and other mothers have talked to me plenty. I think I'm good."

"Dear, they haven't even scratched the surface. Sex is much more than the throbbing of your genitals and dopey chemicals surging through your brain."

Okay, can I be swallowed up by the floor now? Big fissure, just open up below me. Any second now. Any second . . .

"Sex is about power. About position. About securing a future for our matriline. Sex is an intimate contract mooring together families. For every hole you fill, for every hole you let be filled, there is an exchange of trust, a building of bridges, a fortifying of lines. When you lay yourself upon the wedding bed, it is a foundation you are laying. A foundation laid upon loose rocks and pebbles, upon the sludge of *bowel secretions,* will crumble before it even sets."

Daidi's bells. She *does* know about Adalla. Someone must have seen us. Or maybe the amas' gossip has traveled further than I thought. But it's Matris I should be upset with. It's because of her that Adalla is an issue. And beyond her, it's this whole stupid system telling people whom they can love.

"Are you listening, Seske? Are you hearing my words?"

"Yes, Matris. Sex is a tool of manipulation," I spit back at her. "Marriage, a commodity. Checks and sums upon an accountancy ledger. And if I follow your lead, I'll be able to fuck this family back into solvency."

Her hand claps against my cheek, but I don't flinch. I keep my nerves steady. Blink away the tears dancing in the corners of my eyes.

"Young woman, you will listen, and you will not see that filthy girl again. Your thumbs aren't exempt from hanging." She gathers herself together, prim and proper, as if her hot handprint isn't flaring up on my face. "Now, as I was saying. I have given much thought to the suitors we will present to you at your coming out party. I think that you will be very pleased with the selections. Very fine matrilines. There are still so many details to work out, though. Have you given any thought to the colors you would like to present to? I was thinking cream and lime green . . . something uncouth to cause a little stir. Your mothers, fathers, and I all know how you like to cause a stir."

I clench my teeth and nod along. "Cream and lime green, Matris. That sounds lovely."

It's all I can do to not fall to bits right now. She's talking about this as if everything is normal. As if my heart isn't in shreds. As if those beastworkers aren't under her orders to kill the baby beast. As if hundreds hadn't died in that last quake, just hours ago—beastworker lives that will barely be mourned. As if our matriline isn't on the verge of being extinguished. As if our world—not just mine—isn't crumbling all around us.

This way of life, something has to give, or it's all going to break. Mother's too caught up to see it, prattling on about the dresses I'll wear, and the suitors she's chosen, and the hoisting chair, apparently carved from solid pillars of bone, that will be the tallest ever built. She will spare no expense, she says. This celebration will be talked about for generations to come, she says. She keeps talking, talking, ignoring the obvious all around her. That we might not *have* generations. If I yell at her, yell loud enough and long enough for her to see what she's doing to this beast, what she's doing to our people, maybe she will finally understand.

If I were anywhere near fit to be heir of our people, I would speak those words to her now, before it is too late, but me . . . the girl who should have never been born, I simply force a grin onto my face.

"Hoist me high, Matris. High enough for all matrilines to see."

ADALLA

Of Slow Beats and Fast Women

There's buildup in ventricle nine," my ama shouts. "I need a pair of workers down there immediately."

I raise my hand, but she looks past me, calls on Jameenah and Uridan, who, yes, have got years more experience than I do, but Jameenah is too slow and Uridan is too cautious. Thank every heart-father of memory's past that Ama's and my shifts overlap only once every three days, or I'd have been driven out of my mind these past six weeks. I've proven myself again and again, and yet to Ama, I'm as green as swamp moss.

Finally, her eyes meet mine. I stare until she looks away.

"That should be my assignment," I say to her once everyone is dismissed.

"When's the last time you've had a day off?" she asks me.

"When's the last time anyone's had a day off?" I sass back at her. I can't even remember the last time I hadn't worked a double shift. There're so many ways I can contribute, so many things I'm learning, but there's an unspoken network as well. Stuff I've just had to pick up along the way because no one is willing to say out loud how bad this heart is straining. They act like it's all normal, like this is the way it's always been. Like the arrhythmia hasn't cost the lives of a dozen women. Like any one of us could be next.

We keep the beat. Most always, it's on schedule. Sometimes, it's a few seconds late. Once in a while, it'll skip, and we'll stand around for another three minutes forty-seven and a half seconds, doing nothing, wasting time, waiting for beastie's beat to return. But every few days it'll beat prematurely, catching everyone off guard, washing away anyone who isn't lucky enough to secure themselves properly. This . . . we just have to put out of our minds, despite the numerous bodies we've dredged from receding pools of ichor.

My ama sighs. "I know you could do it. Better than half the women here. Probably more than that, but, child, your head is swelling. And this heart is swelling. And I don't have time to tend to both of you, you get me? Ventricle nine is easy compared to what's coming down the line. Keep your focus. Work each job like the beast is depending on you. Because she is."

"She?" I ask, eyes wide. Never in all my dizzy dreams had I thought that our beast was something other than a thing, an animate object, a sustainer of life. The idea intrigues me. Scares me some, too.

"It," Ama corrects herself. "It's our whole world, betcha girl. Your time will come soon enough."

I swallow my nerves, wondering how many other secrets she's been hiding from me.

And then she unsheathes her knife, and when the beat hits, she's off, leaving me sulking. I look at my ventricle, the one I've been picking at this entire shift. The plaque buildup is massive, more than a day's work, but it's not critical. It's right near the valve, just twenty steps in. I take my knife, pry at it. My bucket girl follows after me, a young thing, probably half my age, a pail hanging over each of her shoulders. She sets one down, waits for me to fill it, then goes to dump that one while I fill the other. She's got good lungs, and she's fast. Not many can keep up with my volume, but she can. I've asked her name, but none of 'em talk.

But I can talk. "This is a bunch of third-ass shits, is what it is, betcha," I tell her as I slice big chunks of calcified protrusions from the wall. "Third-ass shits! I should be in ventricle nine. Ama knows it too. If I'm to prepare for harder times, I need to be practicing, not playing it safe here." The hunk comes free and I throw it into the nearly full bucket. Normally, my bucket waif would run off about now, but she moves with me, trusts me with her life. She sees my need right now goes beyond an emptied bucket. Need to empty my heart, too.

"What are you going to do about it?" she says, not saying. Really, it's just me imagining her words and giving her a voice an octave higher than I speak. Between beats, working in the heart is mostly uneventful, and having someone to talk to helps pass the time, even if the conversations are faked.

"Well, I'll tell you," I say. "I'm going to prove Ama has nothing to worry about. That I'm more capable than she even imagines me to be. I can't learn anything down here, doing the job of a first season worker!"

"You are a first season worker," she says, not saying, her brow bent. "And I think your ama means for you to learn a little patience. She's been doing this longer than you've been alive. Don't you think she knows anything?"

"Whose side are you on, anyway?" I say back to my bucket waif.

"The beast's side. The side of all the generations sitting upon the labor of those strong shoulders." She smiles, looks at my arms. They have become quite muscular.

"You say the nicest things." I grin back at her. "I'm glad you're here to keep me company."

The beat is building in my body. I toss the last chunk in the empty bucket and pick it up by its handle. The waif protests, sullying myself as I am, but I don't care, so then she doesn't care, and we make our way back out the exit. Usually, I'd take a breather and wait for her to come back with emptied buckets so we could start again, but this time, I accompany her to the dump spot to get my mind off things.

She runs, and I run after her, catching stares. I know I'm not supposed to be here, but this forced separation between heartworkers and bucket waifs is just weird. Besides, the more I know about the process, the better worker I become. Maybe I can find ways for the other waifs I work with to shave a few seconds off their runs, so I'm not sitting around, waiting. Nothing to do with my own curiosity, sure is sure.

Finally, we come to the dump, an enormous pile of scaly rock: yellows of marbled fat, greens of jagged undergrowth and infections, and deep purples of fissure pack rot. One end of the pile burns, ashes sifted and taken off in another set of buckets. Nothing goes to waste.

I empty my bucket and turn, almost running right into a familiar face. My own, nearly. The waif girl averts her eyes, dumps her buckets. I'm staring. Staring so hard, I give her a moment, and she turns and runs back off, and before I know what my feet are doing, I'm following her.

My little bucket waif is after me, pulling at my dress, trying to steer me back into the right direction, but I can't. I take the artery that leads to ventricle nine. She must be working with Jameenah and Uridan on that big mass. My mass is nearly finished anyway. It can spare a beat or two.

"Go wait for me by the entrance," I tell my waif. "I'll be back in a few minutes. Just going to make sure everything up here is okay. No reason not to, right?"

Her brow bends at me so hard, but nothing comes out of her mouth. She gestures at me, the silent language of her people. I've picked up a little the last few weeks. She's warning me not to do it, not to go.

"Please. If you have something to say, say it. If you think this is a bad idea, let me know."

She's pissed off now, her gestures becoming hard and sharp, like a cuss.

But the other waif, the one who could nearly be me, has almost disappeared down the corridor.

"Ah, I'll carry your bucket for a week if you don't tell," I beg. "I just need to know who she is."

Eyes squint, but her hands stay at her sides. I smile at her, and then I'm off, chasing after the soft padding of footsteps. I move through the entryway, check my gut for the time, then duck inside the valve. I've got just enough time to scope things out, to see just how deep this ventricle goes. I keep my eyes open for tethers, hook in my one hand, waiting for signs of an early beat. I walk, knife blade to my belly, in case I get swept away. I remember that first lesson they'd taught us, knife always at the ready.

I'm so nervous, I forget to breathe. It's like my ama has given me a puzzle, expecting me to solve the thing even though she and everyone else are sitting on half the pieces. I need to know who this girl is who has so much of my father's face. I've missed that face.

Jameenah and Uridan are close, and oh, they're swearing like a couple of boneworkers. They're having a hard time of it for sure, because for someone to so brazenly curse the head-mothers, you've got to be at your wits' end, sure is sure is sure. I slow down, crouch behind the trunk of a tendon, so they can't see me. The both of them are fussing with a stubborn patch of crystallized fat. They're hacking at it, right at what's usually the weakest point of the structure, but they've missed how the fissures in this specimen are all lined up on the diagonal. If they struck at it six inches lower, the whole thing would shear off, no problems. But my thought is lost as I see the waif—my sister, I am sure—lay her bucket down at their side.

She sways as Jameenah and Uridan chip, in a rhythm, focus intent. Fingers flex, just like mine. Does she also see how dizzy-headed they're being? Of course, she would never correct their mistake. Couldn't speak if she wanted to. She has a patience I will never know, because if I were her, I would have snatched those knives away from them and shown them what and all, betcha.

Then suddenly she's up, charging toward them, and I'm thinking, *Yes! Yes!* She's grown tired of this sad display, and she's going to chop that entire swath of crystal off in one hit, and then I'll know she's mine for sure. But that's not what happens. Not at all. She's grabbing their clothing, pulling them away. And then I feel it too, a premature rise in tension of the heart muscle beneath my feet. Like it's about to—

Beat.

I scream out, but ichor fills my mouth, fills my lungs. I brace myself against the deluge, but it slips under me, unseating me from my perch, pulling me away. I swing my tether, hoping for it to find a grip. It digs into the flesh above, but the anchor hasn't gone deep enough, not with this turbulence. I press my blade to my stomach. Soon as that anchor gives way, I have to do what's best for all. I'll plunge it hard and deep, so deep my amas will have no sorrow, only pride for how I'd given myself for the sake of the ship, and for the knife that has been passed down for generations.

Oh blessed mothers, my anchor is slipping. I close my eyes. Feel the poke at my skin. The tear of flesh. And then a hand is around my wrist, pulling and twisting and wrapping me up, tossing me like a babe in my father's arms. Those familiar arms.

As the ichor starts to recede, as the ichor drips from my bleary eyes, I see the waif who may be my sister has anchored in on her own, muscled arms clamped all around my body. She releases as the pools lap to our ankles. Unclips. Smiles at me.

"I just saved your life. You owe me one," she says, not saying, in a voice that I imagine to be raspy and low, but for the first time, I wish bucket waifs really did talk. She seems like she has so much to say.

"Indeed," I say. "Thanks."

She looks back at Jameenah and Uridan . . . Jameenah screaming like Ol' Baxi Batzi's got ahold of her and Uridan still trying to catch her breath. Their anchors held, but the women got all tangled up in the beat and are now just a collection of limbs splayed all over the place. My waif sister raises a brow.

"I'd better attend to these two, and you'd better get out of here before you get in any more trouble," she says, not saying. The deepness of her voice scratches at my throat, but I've already committed her to this persona . . . the fearless waif who's as much of a badass at play as she is at work. "Meet me at the doldrums? After shift? You can buy me a lungful."

Her brows go high with that one, like she's amused by my suggestion. Have I pushed this putting-words-in-her-mouth thing a little too far? Maybe. Probably. But nearly drowning and nearly dying has put me in a ripe mood, betcha, and I accept her offer as if she'd actually given it.

"I'll buy you two," I say, then scurry out of there, fast as I can, hoping to get back to safety before anyone misses me.

CONFESSION: I'VE NEVER BEEN TO THE DOLDRUMS BEFORE. They're huge, cavernous, stretching a mile up, probably. Strips of spongy gray materials strung from bottom to top. If you squint, you can just make out the acrobatic workers, way up high near the gills, collecting the mad vapors for our consumption.

A lot of my coworkers come here after shift, but no one's ever invited me. I try to fit in, laugh at their jokes, but those rumors about Seske proposing to me have lingered like a mysterious stench, and maybe they're afraid of some of that embarrassment rubbing off on them. Or maybe they're all jealous of my talent. Or they think I don't deserve to be here. Or maybe they just don't want to waste their time getting to know me because they think I'll wash out of the heart sooner than later . . . either literally or figuratively.

That's not to say I haven't had mad vapors before. Sonovan pretends not to notice that I sip some from the envelopes he leaves lying around. Usually only a swallow here and there, enough to make my arm hairs prickle, enough to relax my brain and give pretty purple ripples to objects moving too quickly in front of me.

There aren't many waifs here, now. Three in all, and they're all servers, delivering hoses and overfilled bladders to customers, running this way and that. Suddenly I feel awkward for making my waif sister fake-invite me here. Will she feel comfortable? Will she even show?

Her hand is on my wrist again. I spin around, see her. Smile. "You made it!" I say. "I hope I wasn't too forward."

"Well, I'm here, aren't I?" she says, not saying. She looks around too, notices what I've noticed.

"We can go somewhere else, if you like," I say, but she's already heading for a table, claiming the space like she belongs here. I like her already.

We take seats across from each other. Our server comes by, drops a vapor palette in front of me, stalls a moment as she takes my waif sister in. She looks back at me, mouth gaping wide enough for a murmur to fly straight in.

"Um, she's a grisette," she mumbles. "We don't serve them here."

"She's not a grisette," I say. "She's a person. A person with a name . . ." I blink a few times, realizing I haven't even bothered to ask her what I should call her. But I have to save face in front of the server. I have to be convincing. "Parton. Parton Kendi," I say, proud and erect, giving her the demasculinized version of my father's name. Our father's name.

The server's eyes widen like I've smacked her across the face.

"We'll be having that other palette now," I say, sliding my knife onto the table in a completely nonthreatening way. Completely, betcha.

Her trembling hand puts a palette down in front of Parton, then she's off, probably to tattle to her boss. Who knows how long we have left to enjoy ourselves, but I smile at my sister anyway. If this is all the time we've got to connect, we'll make it work.

"So I guess you've noticed we look a bit alike," she says, not saying. But her brows don't pitch, so I'm fairly certain we're both on the same wave here.

"Yeah, I noticed," I say in my own voice. "But I get the distinct feeling that I'm not supposed to have noticed."

I take the length of bone pipe and pierce the lightest-colored membrane on the palette, sucking up the entire vapor sample, trying so hard to look like I know what I'm doing. I let the gas twirl in my mouth, cheeks puffed like I've seen Sonovan do a million times, then I blow out a pathetic wheeze, pale vapors immediately dissipating into the air. The flavor is sharp, cloying, so much fresher than the stuff I've scavenged. I resist the urge to scrape the residue off my tongue. I blink a few times, and my muscles start to relax. My eyes trace over every single one of her facial features, then I say to her, "It's so odd, looking at you. Sorry." I giggle into my fist. "I didn't mean for my words to come out like that. I wish you could tell me more about you."

I'm a lightweight, already halfway to gaffed on a single vapor sample. Still, I poke my bone pipe at the next one, a deeper-colored gas, swirling and shimmering beneath the confines of its clear membrane. I take a hard suck. This one's spicier. Waaay more potent. From my fading periphery, I see Parton's hands moving. I lean back. Watch. Try to put together her language of gestures. Purple ripples follow her hand movements. Mesmerizing. I don't know what she's saying, but I never want her to stop talking.

"Here's the thing," I say, leaning toward her, nearly falling off my seat. "I could really use a friend right now." I say *friend*, but *sister* is the word that wants so badly to tumble out of my mouth, but I'm nowhere near gaffed enough to say it in public. I've been pulling double shifts in an effort to work Seske out of my mind. Focusing on the heart that really matters. But as much as I try, I just can't put her behind me. "I've got no one else to talk to. And oh, I feel like I've got to talk, before my feelings eat me up alive. Get me?"

She nods, and the purple ripples now have some shimmering silver friends.

"Parton, is it okay if I call you Parton?" I look over and see the manager coming, our timid server trailing several steps behind. This will not end well. I take the bone pipe, pierce the darkest sample, a deep aqua blue closer to the pitch of ichor. My lungs burn so badly. My head is so spinny. Last thing I need is to stab someone, accident or not, so I stand up and holster my knife. "We don't want any problems here," I say to the manager. "We're leaving."

Parton is up and at my side, which is good, because the ground starts shifting beneath me. I think maybe I swallowed that last sample instead of blowing it out. I think that was a very, very bad idea. My gut twists and roils.

I walk as straight as I can, propped up on Parton's shoulder. We get twelve steps past the door when I spew all my dinner and most of my lunch up against a wall. Parton sits with me, her hand on my back, rubbing till I'm emptied.

I'm too tired to speak for her, but her eyes say thank you as I wipe the vomit from my cheek with my sleeve. She raises the palette and two bone pipes she'd swiped from the doldrums. Her eyebrows pitch. After a brief wave of nausea, my mouth waters after them.

"Yeah, okay, but where?" I ask. "We can't go back into the doldrums."

Parton looks around with apprehension, then nods her head, indicating that I should follow.

DEEP PAST THE TRACTS OF INTESTINAL FARMLAND, THERE'S A pile of gall husks awaiting breakdown. I follow Parton, while trying to watch where I step. Pools of acid remain in some areas, and sometimes they're deceptively deep. Sonovan says they can eat right down to the bone in a matter of seconds. He's been known to exaggerate, but I'm not willing to risk it either way.

Finally, Parton stops at a husk, round and brown, and as tall as the both of us put together. There's a hole on the underside, where the larva, a plump green thing with about a million legs, had bored out. Larval steaks will soon grace the tables of the Contour class. And we beastworkers will feast on the husks, ground down into shreds and salted and spiced to make them almost palatable. It's the same stuff they make paper out of, minus the spices. But this husk is empty, and I follow Parton up inside. There are a few pillows and a ley light in here, and it smells sweet and swampy, not the same funk that mars the air outside. There's just enough room for the both of us to stretch out. I lean back against the curved wall of the gall, rough bite marks from the larva's meals pressing against my skin.

Parton settles also and pokes the black membrane of the vapor palette, sucks, then blows a ring of smoke that dissipates right before it hits my face.

"Come here a lot?" I ask.

"You know, it's a home away from home," she says, not saying. "Do you like it?"

"It's cozy."

She offers a suck from the black membrane. I steady myself, then take the smallest of sips. And, girl, it hits my head like a brick. Instantly, I'm woozy. My body feels like one of those acid puddles.

"Maybe you should pace yourself some," I say as she takes another full suck. She lets the vapors loose, tongue undulating as the cloud turns into fancy shapes in the air.

"I'm a pro," she says, not saying. "So what did you want to talk about anyway?"

I just need to hear myself think things through. To have someone to nod along, to dump all my secrets on. Someone who I'm sure won't tell anyone else. But before I can say a single thing, Parton throws me a saucy grin, then lifts the hem of her scratchy gray shift, higher, higher—revealing her lean and muscular thighs. I press my hand to hers before it can go farther. She looks at me, brow raised.

"No!" I say, then bite my lip, realizing how she must spend her time here, realizing how a waif like her can afford such an expensive habit. "I want your time, but not like that."

"You just want to talk," she says, not saying. Suddenly, with a transaction looming between us, I feel even more awkward about putting words in her mouth.

"Is . . . that okay?" I wait for her response this time. Like, I actually watch her, paying attention to her, reading the words her body has to offer me. "I'll still pay, of course. In vapors?"

Her brows pinch; her lips purse out in that way my father's would when he didn't believe the lies I told about how his smoking pipe ended up broken, or how one of the pinch pies he'd baked must have been taken as favors by demanding spirits and certainly not eaten by a hungry girl, betcha. *Of course you're going to pay me* is what she's thinking, but I don't dare say it. She pats me closer. She will listen. I relax. Her arm slips underneath mine, and she pulls me in tight, and it's like we're best friends.

I tell her about my old job in the ichor vats, distilling copper from the beast's blood, and that it'd always been my dream to work the heart. I tell her about my old life, back on the previous beast, and how hard it was to leave behind during exodus. We're supposed to pretend those shallow roots that we dared to lay down didn't matter, but they do. We'd watched the world we'd fought so hard to keep alive for so long slowly wither and die all around us. You can't just ignore an open wound like that and expect for it to go away. But talking to Parton soothes the pain some.

I even find the courage to tell her about Seske and the almost-moment we'd had, in the most inopportune place, at the most inopportune time. Those raw emotions of my past were hard to relive, but even more tender are my hopes for the future even though the fissure between Seske and me continues to grow. Parton smiles our father's smile, and my words keep flowing. It feels so good to finally have someone I can confide in.

THE NEXT DAY, AFTER SHIFT, WE MEET IN OUR GALL CAVE. I bring a mirror, in case Parton hasn't ever really looked at herself. Our faces press against each other, and we both see it now, the similarities painfully obvious. I start to tell her about our father, but it's tedious. I love that she really wants to understand, but she stops me each time a word snags her. I have to explain *father*. I have to explain *mother*.

"Were you raised by beetles?" I ask her, mostly a joke, but then it occurs to me: I've been dropping all my baggage on her, without even trying to get to know something about her life. "I mean, seriously. How were you raised? No mother, no father?"

She pantomimes the word *baby*, which I'd taught her yesterday, then points to me. Then she points to herself and shakes her head.

"You were never a baby? Never had a childhood?" I think she's being melodramatic. Maybe her childhood was rough, but there had to be something there. "Come on, it's not like you were hatched out fully grown!"

She nods, then pinches her ear. Our little signal that I've

understood what she's trying to say. She then pulls a pillow into her lap, draws a finger in a circle, leaving a trail of up-turned fibers behind her. She points at herself and draws a dot.

"That's you," I say. "That's Parton?"

Pinched ear. Then she draws a bunch of other dots. Maybe eighty or so.

"Those are others like you? A bunch of you born at the same time? Like a brood?" She continues for some time, and ear pinch by ear pinch, I listen. As we build our vocabulary, the easier it is to get deeper and deeper. She teaches me a dozen hand gestures and I teach her a dozen words. The wall between our lives starts to crumble. Finally, I am able to explain who I think she is to me.

Brood sister, she signs at me.

I draw a deep breath, and when I let it out, a loneliness I never knew I had escapes with it. I love my family, and it has always felt complete. I have Sonovan and my head-mothers to worry after my learning. I have my heart-mothers to guide me toward my passions and my will-parents to ensure I make the soundest decisions. But now I know there was something missing all along, and she's sitting right in front of me.

I pinch my ear. *Yes, brood sister,* I sign back at her.

AMA ASKS FOR VOLUNTEERS. THERE'S AN INFESTATION OF heart murmurs in a cleave in the muscle surrounding ventricle nine, deep too. No room for two workers, and barely enough room to accommodate a bucket waif. They'll need the fast-est. The bravest. The deadliest. Most heart murmurs can be detached with patience and a little elbow grease, but ventricle nine supplies ichor all the way to the beast's brain, so there's no room for error. I raise my hand for the job, while in my head,

I rehearse the killing swipes of a knife. Single slit, eyes to tail; two inches deep for the grown ones, inch and a fourth for the youngins. Cut too deep and you nick the ventricle. Cut too shallow, and the murmur sends out a warning and the others dig in deeper, which makes everything ten times more complicated.

I raise my hand higher until Ama has no choice but to notice me. My record is spotless. I stare her in the eyes. She knows I need this to prove myself worthy of working the beast's heart.

"I'll go," I say, practically a challenge. If I don't get this, I'm not sure what I'll do with myself.

"You're sure?" Ama says to me.

I hold my knife out in front of me, hand as steady as steady gets. She nods. I breathe, and all at once, the tension I'd been clinging to slides right out of me. On the next beat, I'm sprinting, fast as my legs have ever taken me. My focus is tight, one hand on my anchor should the beat come again prematurely. I feel the fire behind my eyes, a tingle in my sinuses. I'm not about to cry. Don't have time for that either. A dozen bucket waifs trail behind me, but they don't need to be fast in, only fast on the way out.

I slow when I see the cleave, a jagged fissure in the smooth inner lining of the ventricle a few feet wider than my shoulders. One of the bucket waifs follows me in, and the rest wait outside. In the shallow light, I see a massive colony. Nearly a hundred heart murmurs. I don't waste time and start slashing, and they fall to the ground in gray-green piles, wings splayed, mouths twisted, eyes . . . I don't look them in the eyes. The waif works underfoot, silently stuffing her bucket full, then hauling it back out and sending the next waif in. Then the next. Then the next.

There's a massive one, as big as five murmurs put together

easily. I glance at my bucket waif, then at her bucket, already nearly full.

"You don't have to get them all on one try," she says to me, not saying, voice pitched high, like the child she nearly is. Her eyes widen. I haven't worked with her before, so she doesn't understand my awful little game.

"I know," I tell her. "But if I can, imagine how everyone will talk. I'll forever be 'Adalla, the heartworker who slayed eighty-eight murmurs in one go.'"

"I don't think anyone would ever call you that." Cynical, this one.

I slay the last five smaller murmurs, saving the mammoth one for last. The waif's bucket is full now, and it's way too late for any more waifs to be racing back. "Go," I tell her. "I'll carry this one."

I look at it, so big, I see it breathing, in and out. I don't have much time, but I take a second anyway to examine it. Four inches. That's how deep I should go. I raise my hand high, then slice down the whole length. One, two, three seconds . . . I'm worried I'll have to slice again, but finally its body goes slack and falls to the floor in a crumple, like an oversize blanket. Maybe I'll have Sonovan tan it so I can sleep under it, a constant reminder of being "Adalla, the heartworker who slayed eighty-eight murmurs in one go." I quickly bend down to roll it up, but from the corner of my eye, I see a little flutter. Eighty-*nine* murmurs. The tiniest, cutest murmur had been hiding under the wings of the big one. It's pale green, just like my little Bepok had been, but the markings on its back are different.

My heart twists, and I make the mistake of looking it in the eyes. I'm overcome with memories of the murmurs we kept on the last beast, mostly used to keep the warmth, but you grow attached to such things, and they become pets whether you want them to or not. Without thinking, I slip my knife under the ridge of its mouth and pry. It's so small, it comes off with a pop, no struggle at all. It's barely as big as my spread hand. I lay it upon my arm, and its suction grip returns. I pet it, just once, don't know why—muscle reflex, an ache for my old pet—but immediately I know it was a mistake. It's not tame. It's not mine. It startles and screeches, bites down harder into my arm with those tiny burrowing teeth.

I scream from the pain, and then at my feet, the giant murmur convulses. I hadn't cut deeply enough after all. In a half a second, it's got me wrapped up in its folds, climbing up my legs. I try to kick at it, try to run, but I'm tripped up and fall into a heap. In no time, its wings are suffocating me. Fangs sink into me, here, there. It rips my satchel from my hip, my anchor and all my tools out of reach, but I've still got my knife. My hand swipes blindly, blade cutting, blood flowing into my nostrils, my mouth. So much of it, I'm drowning here, under this murderous blanket. Yeah, so maybe I killed its entire family, then tried to take its child as my own, but if you start giving these things feelings, personalities, it makes it a lot harder to discard them. Sometimes these "things" look like moldy blankets. Sometimes they look a lot like you. My soul clenches up. The beat is coming, and soon we'll all be dead, so what use is it musing about such things anyway?

Only the beat doesn't come. The ichor doesn't flow. I count a few more seconds, praying it's not just coming late, but no . . . it's the arrhythmia. A skipped beat. I wait a moment for my own heart to stop pounding, realizing the luck I've drawn. I've got a whole three minutes and forty-seven and a half seconds left. I spend twelve seconds wrestling myself out from under the blanket. Four cursing all heart-fathers there ever, ever, *ever* were. Twelve retrieving my anchor. Eight rolling the blanket up into a nice roll. Four dusting myself off, trying to look a little less disheveled. And twenty-three sprinting back to the opening, where everyone is waiting for me, wide-eyed.

I throw the blanket down in front of me. "Eighty-eight killed in one go," I declare. They applaud. All of them except Ama. She takes one look at my anchor and the frayed end of the rope and at the murmur trembling upon my arm. It's scared. Alone, thanks to me. But I've tamed one before, and I can do it again.

Ama's eyes, though, they slit at me, sharper than the blade of my knife.

"Damned dizzy-headed girl! If the beat hadn't skipped, you'd be dead now. And for what? To prove yourself? Nothing, 'specially your ego, is worth risking our lives, Adalla. Strip!" she orders me like I'm an initiate on her first day.

"What?"

"It was a mistake not to complete your training, so we're going to complete it now. Strip, I said."

And there, in front of everyone, I drop my dress, letting it fall into a pile with the slayed blanket. I stand there, on display, in front of everyone. Ama draws her whip from her satchel. The first strike hits me square in the back. I don't flinch. The cuts burn, deeper and deeper, until everything feels inflamed. There's a long pause, so long, I think she's done, but she hasn't dismissed me. One more whip cracks into my forearm, right where the baby murmur is settled. Thing splits in two, sliced down right in between those bulging black eyes, and falls to the floor.

If Ama wanted to break my spirit, she's succeeded.

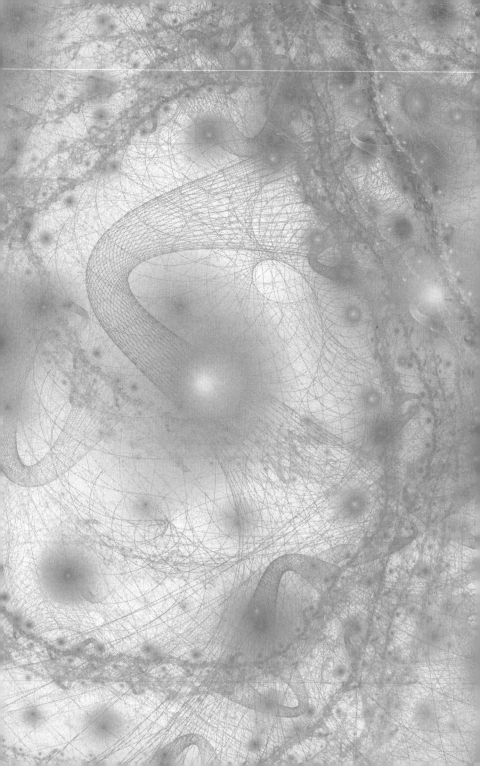

part II

. . . .
expansion

From the moment of conception, we are ever expanding—as cells, as individuals, as a people. It is our duty to look past the horizon, to ask what lies there and to wonder how we might strengthen our lines so that we may extend our reach.

—MATRIS MITTARK,
512 YEARS AFTER EXODUS

SESKE

Of Soiled Cloths and Pristine Dances

I can't keep an eight count for my life. My ama remains intent on guiding me through this final dance lesson, proudly swaying to the beat despite the number of times I've stepped upon her feet, her shins. One time, I even managed to kick her in the knee. Every time I start to get into any kind of rhythm, any time I think I'm about to enjoy this and just have a little fun perhaps . . . my mind starts wandering . . . about the baby beast mostly, hoping those lab techs haven't figured out a way to breach its membrane.

Here, my ama's hand is around my waist; the other holds my hand high up in the air as she spins and twirls me, preparing me for the pomp and circumstance of my big day, but really, I'm swimming, swirling, playing games with the baby beast, her tentacles picking and plucking at my skin—

"Seske Kaleigh!" my ama screams at me. I look down. She's

no longer holding me but now holding her shin. A rivulet of blood drips down, pooling upon the satin of her dance slippers.

There's a medic on hand. She comes over, applies salve and a bandage. This isn't my first dance rehearsal. She's got a cold pack handy too.

"I'm sorry, Ama. If you want to call the rest of the evening off, I'm okay with that." I press my hand upon her back.

"Bless the mothers, no," she says. "We have to have you in top form for tomorrow. Let's keep going." Ama tries to stand, but she winces and bites back a pained curse. "Sisterkin!" she calls, her voice reverberating through the dance hall. Sisterkin comes shuffling from out of whatever hole she'd been pouting in, probably lamenting that these should be *her* dance lessons for *her* coming out party. Not that she'd need lessons.

My insides cringe up.

"Dance the molalari baret with Seske," my ama demands.

"Yes, Amakin," Sisterkin says. "Original, palatial, or Courdarin version?"

Ama laughs hard. Too hard. She meets my eyes and they melt into something more compassionate. "The Courdarin," she says. The remedial version. She doesn't say it out loud, but I can feel it. All the flourishes that make the dance beautiful have been trimmed away. The moves are as basic as they'll get, but I'm still tripping over myself.

"Don't worry, Seske. We'll have you in prime shape before your coming out party." Sisterkin smiles at me, face and chest close in, but feet angled awkwardly and obviously away from me. "Feel the beat with me. Ready?"

She signals to the musicians, and they climb back up onto the gangliar pipes. Each pipe takes three people to play, and there are twelve in total, though only four are in use for these practices. They squeeze air sacs, clap copper cymbals over the release holes, until the soulful sweet tunes fill the cavernous hall.

"*One*-two-three-four, step-two, and *slide* . . ." Sisterkin demonstrates for me, and it's like she's floating atop a cloud of mad vapors. Her whole body sinks into the song, down to each and every finger moving with the grace of a dancer. "All you have to do is feel the rhythm. Your potential suitors will do the rest."

"I can't believe I have to dance with *all* of them," I grumble, feeling overwhelmed and lost within the cavernous walls of the dance hall. Florists are busy covering them in the most resplendent blooms harvested from the woodward canopies: lots of ferns, river lilies, and my favorite, the creeping nova with its silver tendrils and succulent purple petals. But it's hard to see their beauty when such frustration tears at my soul.

"You'll have the *pleasure* of dancing with them all," Ama corrects as Sisterkin pulls me back into her graceful arms, then twirls me senseless. "All from very fine families."

"And what if I don't like any of them?" I ask, *and three and four, and*—"Or what if I already like someone—"

Sisterkin slides right up onto the bridge of my foot. "Sorry," she says, giving me a stern brow. Matris must have blabbed to her about Adalla already. "Five men and seven women. Surely one of them will appeal to you, but if love doesn't strike you before the candle wanes, I'm sure Matris will understand."

From the pout on Sisterkin's lip, however, I can tell it would certainly not be okay with Matris. But there's something else on her face. Regret. She's said something she shouldn't have. *Five men and seven women.* She knows their identities.

"You have to tell me who they are!" I whisper urgently.

"I sat through the interviews. Just the preliminary ones,

but the front-runners were obvious. So much better than the others, Seske. The men all prim, painted, and obedient. The women all gorgeous, stately, and primed for guiding you into your eventual reign." Her voice has soured, but her smile stays tight and almost genuine. "You couldn't find a better set of suitors if you tried."

"Then you marry them!" I shout at Sisterkin. "That's what you want, isn't it? My family? My suitors? My throne?"

"This is about that beastworker girl, isn't it?" Ama says, hobbling toward me, nodding down at me like I'm a child. Good mothers, do they all know? "Sisterkin, could you go show the musicians the way to the refreshment stable? And the florists too. I'm sure they've all worked up a thirst."

"But, Amakin—"

"Please. It's going to be a rather long evening, and everyone needs to be in top form."

"Yes, Amakin," Sisterkin says, then with a sigh, she reluctantly slinks out of the great hall with the musicians and florists in tow.

When they're all gone and Ama and I are alone, she wraps her arms around me, and I suddenly realize I'm shaking. "Dear Seske, women like you, women like your mother, they don't marry for love. They learn to love, yes, deeper and harder than anyone, but sometimes there are people who get left behind."

I meet Ama's eyes and I see the hurt brimming there. "You?" I say, my voice trembling as well. It hits me hard, something both shocking and new and old and familiar at the same time. I'd seen the way Matris and my ama traded glances and held a special fondness that Matris never shared with her head-wife and -husband. Matris's hand was nearly a constant on Ama's biceps whenever they were in proximity. Cheek presses lingered during hellos and goodbyes. No intimate bounds were crossed. Matris would never risk that, especially with her record. But Ama and Matris, they butted right up against them.

Ama nods. "I was a match. A good match. But there was another who was better."

"My other head-mother?" I say, obviously.

Ama shakes her head slowly. "Not her."

Then who? The head–family unit consisted of two women and a man. That means the only other option is my head-father, which doesn't even make—

And then I'm hit, harder this time. I swallow, my eyes following her body up and down, looking for traces of the delicate procedure that made her ripe to receive her own matriline. Who was she before? What made her decide to go through with such a major transformation? When did this all happen? I have so many questions for her . . .

But I already know the *why*.

"You were cut and drawn for her?" I ask. "To be family. To be close." But never *too* close.

My ama nods. "She wanted to keep me near. And I wanted to be kept near. The position of will-father was already taken, so I did what I had to do, and I have never regretted it. I know your heart is young, but I also remember how hard it can ache. Put your suitors in order. Marry to strengthen your matriline. The rest, if it is meant to be, will come."

Ama hugs me again, and I rest my head against her shoulder, trying to pretend I'm not crying softly into it.

Sisterkin comes running back into the hall. I stand up straight, and Ama smudges the tears from my eyes. Sisterkin stands there alert, like a crib worm eager for feeding. I smile back at her, a wide, crooked smile. She's missed something.

She knows I know something she doesn't, and it bothers her. It bothers her a lot.

I TAKE A SMALL OFFERING TO THE SPIRIT WALL, CALLING UPON the guidance of my ancestors. I'm trying to be an obedient daughter, trying to learn how to be the thoughtful leader my people deserve, but so many things weigh on my mind, and perhaps they can help. The wall stretches out in an arc, twenty feet high, eighty feet long, a monument to our dead. Besides our Texts, it is our clan's most precious possession, moved from beast to beast with painstaking care. Faces stare out at me, the bodies of our most recent dead interred upon the oozing surface. Some of those faces are so fresh, I can still make out their eyelashes beneath the tacky gray coating, like statues that might reach out and grab you if you linger too long. Others are partially absorbed, just hints of foreheads and cheekbones and noses, suggestions of arms and legs. I can't even imagine how many layers of our ancestors are tucked inside, out of sight, but never forgotten.

I press seven copper beads into the wall's surface in honor of each of my mothers' lines, taking care that my fingers don't touch the coating. There are washing stations on the passage out, of course, but even just the thought of having that flesh-devouring slime upon me for a second sends a rigid chill through me. I shake it off, then step away and kneel next to the tribute candles. The scent wafts up and relaxes me, easing my mind into a heightened state.

"I know I haven't been coming as often as I should lately," I say to the spirits. "But I'm hoping you'll lend your guidance now. I spent our last expansion as a child, seeing the world through a child's eyes. Tomorrow I will be a woman, with the capacity and the responsibility to guide this expansion to-ward its full potential. Not only do I want our people to grow through creative, economic, and scientific endeavors, I also want them to grow their compassion and wonder. And maybe they will start to understand that looking at the world through a child's eyes is not a deficiency, but just another perspective."

A child's eyes.

My thoughts skip back to the baby beast. As much as I try to put her out of my mind, I can't help but wonder if there'd been something else there. If there is more to the beast than just a convenient package of flesh for us to consume.

I catch a movement on the wall from the corner of my eye. Fingers wiggling, maybe, but when I look toward the of-fending ancestor, she's completely still. I stare her in the eyes, wondering if she'll blink. But nothing comes. Paranoia closes in all around me, signaling that maybe it's time I get some fresh air.

I end my prayers by reading my lines and those of my mothers, each of them named after a constellation in our new sky. Then I blow out the candles and duck through the exit that leads to the washing room. Two accountancy guards sit there, watching to ensure none of the wall material leaves the room. It spreads fast and is a bear to clean up. I choose a washing station, and the wash hoglet wiggles from its perch above the basin. The creature recognizes me. I always bring them a small offering as well. I glance back at the accountancy guards, then put my hand in the pocket of my raiment and fetch a piece of worm jerky, and I stealthily plunge it into the hoglet's puck-ered snout. The hoglet sucks away the treat and, along with it, any traces of the wall material.

"Who's a good girl?" I ask her. She bucks excitedly against her tether.

"Don't interact with the wash hoglets," one of the guards says. "You'll rile them up."

Sometimes they break free from their tethers, and that's fun for everyone, as the guards have to leave their comfortable seats to capture the hoglets before they get at the wall and do damage. After the hoglet cleanses my left hand, I pat her on the head anyway, right before I rinse off in the basin. The guards manage to holster their annoyance as they inspect me on my way out.

And before I realize where my feet are taking me, I'm halfway to the womb. Am I really doing this? Am I going back to see the baby beast?

But then I'm there, waiting for the room to clear out, before stepping next to the cloudy membrane and pressing my hand against it. I get a little choked up, looking at the wound the technicians had inflicted. It's much longer than last time, wider. I look back at my hand, and beyond it, and I'm relieved to see the baby beast is staring at me, the membrane so clear, it's as if there's nothing but air between us.

"I'm sorry," I say to her, the words bearing so much weight inside me. Sorry I kicked her. Sorry my people are torturing her. Sorry we've killed so many of her kind.

After a long while, the baby beast moves a tendril next to my hand. I smile. She does something with her mouth that makes me think I've made a new friend.

Then the womb membrane parts for me and I quickly slip inside with the baby beast. I don't flinch this time when her tendrils explore me. It tickles more than hurts, and she enjoys the sound of my laughter through the womb water. I think it's the same water that fills our stasis pods during exodus, but it's so much fresher, so much more alive.

But as I look around and get my bearings, I see that the wound is getting deeper as well, jutting several feet into the womb, ridged and gnarly, coming to a cleaved point. If they continue, it will one day encroach so far into the womb, it will pin the baby beast to the other side. The day after that, it will pierce her flesh.

I'm saddened by this, but she nudges me, like she's trying to cheer me up. The lights across her body begin to pulse to a beat, and after a few turns, she does something amazing. She lifts these fronds she keeps pressed against her body, raises them to their full height, and flashes them. Suddenly, the entire realm of her womb is full of multicolored lights. The lights ripple and undulate. We spin.

Thin, inquisitive tentacles lick at the corners of my eyes. A couple plunge inside, trying to dig around my eye sockets and trying to get up my nostrils as well, and I'm too vulnerable to resist. She wraps me up completely. The thin tentacles slide deeper and deeper inside me, but there's no pain, only an odd sort of pressure behind my ears. Then I feel my fingers wiggling against my will. My toes. Knees bend slightly, elbows. The cocoon falls from me, and suddenly, I'm dancing. Not the remedial Courdarin version I had just learned, but the full palatial molalari baret, with every single one of the finger flourishes.

Music plays, a full orchestra, but I can't tell if it's coming from inside the womb or inside my head. It doesn't matter. I dance. Like a plaything. Like a puppet on strings.

I dance. For hours, it seems, until my muscles have memorized every movement, every turn and swirl. When the baby beast has explored every inch of my being, every memory, she curls me back up into her tentacles. Inch by inch, the thin, inquisitive ones pull out from my eye sockets, my nostrils.

And suddenly, it's all over, like it had all happened too fast. I'm not sure how to process it. It wasn't really pleasurable, but not really painful either. There's just a door inside me, one that's been closed my whole life, which has now swung wide open. What's on either side of that door is still the same, but there's something fundamentally changed. And Daidi's bells, I'm crying like a babe.

Then the scar flashes white, pulses. Grows. Three inches. Four.

Is it morning already? I'd come late, when no one lurked about. But now, now I'll have to stay here until the next shift change. I feel each pulse at the roots of my teeth. I keep them clenched, and in turn, the baby beast keeps me clenched close to her. Now I'm her rag doll.

I don't mind. I drift off to sleep, and in my dreams comes velvety black space filled with the flickers of beast light. The big beast next to me flickers. It is our beast, I can tell that, though I'm not sure how. She tells me a bedtime story with those lights, a story that has been passed down through her kind since near the birth of everything. It is not Vvanescript she flashes at me but a language much more ancient.

It is the story of a hero, a rescuer. A story of sacrifice and valor.

The baby beast wakes me before I know how it ends. It's quiet outside now. No more sizzling in my teeth, no pulsing at the scar. It's grown by nearly half, though. I exit through the thinned membrane and crouch quietly as my body transitions back to breathing air. I've gotten better at this part at least, just letting it dribble from my nose and open mouth instead of suppressing a coughing fit.

I need to hurry, to get back home so I can prepare for my big day, but first, I have other business to attend to. I look over at the shock gun sitting there unattended. Four screws are all that separate me from its inner workings.

MATRIS TAKES MY HAND LIGHTLY IN HERS, IGNORES THE OIL stains that refused to budge from beneath my fingertips, ignores the tentacle marks that my patinas hadn't been able to cover up, ignores the fact that I was nearly thirty minutes late to my own coming out party. She should be furious right now, and I should be melting under her ominous brow, but instead her face is one of pure relief, of pride, and of impossible calm.

She's had a sip of campadin wine, for sure. Maybe a couple sips, the way her eyes are shining.

"Distinguished lads and gentlewomen, please allow me to present Seske Ashad Nedeema Orshidi Midikoen Ugodon Niosoke Kaleigh, a true daughter of mothers," she says, taking the time to slowly enunciate each of my mothers' matrilines, not caring a lick how far we are behind schedule. "From Ekondah Shedita Mendaleigh Amida Gazra Jomari Saseem Paletoba, a true daughter of mothers . . ." Matris then ambles down the lines of my will-mothers, my heart-mothers, and, finally, my head-mothers, extending her own matriline back twelve different ways to Matris Abinaya, the first of her kind. The whole procession takes nearly twenty minutes, and not once does she falter or consult the Texts. The audience stands rapt, the occasional ululation when someone's matriline is mentioned.

Me, my eyes and mind wander, first to the hoisting chair. Matris was right. I'd never seen one higher. Its three legs were meticulously carved from the whitest, softest bone and bear embarrassing pictures of me, chronicling my infancy on one leg, my childhood on another, and the woman I've become on the third. My amas will stand at the base, each holding a leg, and together will hoist me high. It's all an illusion, though. The chair is latched firm, with legs that will retract upward half a foot, giving the semblance that they've lifted me and some seven hundred pounds of beast bone. It's ceremony. It's tradition. But I can't help but get a sour taste in my mouth, remembering how it felt to have Adalla's amas tossing me up and about. That was personal. I'd felt the love. Here, I just feel the expense. The pretension. The eyes all upon me, drilling into me.

Then I notice that Matris has finally stopped talking. I swallow, trying to remember what I am supposed to say. I bow deeply, since I know I'm supposed to do that. I count to twenty, then I stand, and all my suitors have filed in front of me, and for the first time, their identities are revealed. It is as Sisterkin had said, seven women and five men. In perfect unison, they bow back at me.

"In the pursuit of family," I say, trying not to hyperventilate. "It is my honor to strengthen my lines, to honor our past while building our future."

Matris throws my bloodied cloths in front of them, proof of my womanhood. The entire hall erupts in applause. Then quiet descends as the soothsayer hobbles up to the cloths. She carefully spreads them out in sequence . . . first day, second day, and third day, which was just barely any spotting. She considers the patterns.

"Strength!" she declares at the first rag. "The ancestors speak of strength of *will*, of resolve. A logic that will guide us through many tough decisions." I look over at my will-parents, and they are gushing of course. When the time comes, I will be a will-mother. The entire hall fills with the piercing whistles from will-mothers everywhere. The last will-mother Matris was seven lines ago. My Matris, she does not look pleased with this news, but her smile stays firm. Too firm. Finally, when the murmurs die down, the soothsayer looks at the second rag.

"Agility!" she shouts. "The ancestors claim hers a nimble, agile mind that never rests. Such a leader shall never be cornered and will forever be thinking forward." The head-mothers hum loudly in unison.

Finally, the soothsayer leans in over my third cloth, bearing just a few light pink spots. She frowns, flips the rag over and back as if there must be more hidden somewhere. She chews her lip, probably trying to figure out how to best spin the results. The silence runs thick.

"Idiosyncrasy," she says, not quite sullenly. "A heart that beats to its own rhythm." The heart-mothers orchestrate an open-palmed clap that echoes in my ears. We all pretend we hadn't noticed that the soothsayer hadn't mentioned how well my heart would serve the people. And before anyone can give it much thought, I'm climbing the rungs of my chair, dress flowing down behind me, so long, the tip of the tail still touches the floor when I'm fully seated.

My amas pretend to hoist me, and the feast starts, and everyone's so intent on cramming their bellies full of fermented eggs and tiny, flaky bites of layered pastries that, for a moment, they forget all about me up here, and I can't say I'm bothered by that. Then my fathers sing an aria, from the Legends of Orinsi, of the trials of Matris Machelle, whose tact and grace moved us through the dark times and who had the idea to move into the beasts, instead of just plundering their resources.

Their song is lovely, even though the notes they hit strain in some places. But that's just like how my heart strains, knowing the truth about these beasts. All my life, I'd never given it a thought, never considered that these beasts were sentient. That they could communicate. I want so badly to stand up and yell at everyone, to tell them the toll our lives are taking on these creatures. I want Matris to command us all back into our ship and as far away from the herd as our engines will take us.

It would be a death sentence, though. Where would we be without enough resources to feed our people? There isn't enough room in our ship for any type of life, for sure, but even if we all returned to stasis, our bodies would still need nutrients, our engines would still need fuel. Even our hops from beast to beast take a toll. I bite my tongue, smile, try to be the daughter Matris wants me to be. I'll have decades yet to learn, to observe, to find new solutions to centuries-old problems. Then, when it comes time for my reign, things will be different. Better.

I sigh. My stomach grumbles. I'm not supposed to partake in the feast, symbolizing that I'll put the needs of the ship above the needs of self. I'd tried to eat beforehand, but my attendants were so busy stuffing me into all these layers of dresses, sharpening the edges on my naxshi, and scolding me for my tardiness and unkemptness, that I hadn't been able to get a word in, much less food in my mouth.

Finally, the flame bearer comes before me, a young girl probably half my age. She calls me down in song, voice high like a gnat buzzing in my ears. I pitch my dress, kick off my shoes, and stand tall upon the seat of the chair.

In file dozens of beastworkers, forming a single line between the flame bearer and the base of my chair. As they crouch down into fetal positions, foreheads pressed against the floor, I can't help but search their faces for that familiar one I don't dare wish to see. Matris wouldn't make the mistake of inviting Adalla here, for sure—but still, hope springs. The next row files in, wedging their bodies on top and in between. After a few minutes, after all the rows of beastworkers have been piled on top of one another, in a wedge that leads from the floor right up to the tips of my toes, I step upon the first back, find my balance. Down I go, feeling the spines under the soles of my feet. Feeling the people who serve as the backbone of our ship, through their labor, their dedication, and the many who give their lives in the process. On occasions like these, the Contour class allows itself to remember simple truths.

As I step down from the last back, I take the match from the flame bearer and light the ceremonial candle, a pillar of laced wax. When it burns out, the last of my childhood will be marked by its extinguished flame. I will be a woman, true and whole and judged in our way. The thought of that should frighten me more than it does. I stand, watching the flickering light, caught up in the moment, wishing for time to slow down or speed up, or do anything besides this monotonous flow of seconds in which I will have to set my life on a path with a person I know nothing about.

There's a tap on my shoulder—my ama. I turn and smile at her.

"It's time, Seske," she whispers to me. "Just remember your steps, and you'll do fine."

I nod, then look at the first suitor, her arms outstretched to me. All I have to do is follow her lead, dance for a few minutes. Maybe laugh and joke some about how awkward this all is. Her smile is kind, and her facial tattoos glint brightly—blue and gold patterns pop against the deep brown of her skin. Her hair in a wonderfully intricate braid that rests down upon her shoulder. Her arms are well muscled, her hands the same as they press to mine, but not rough, like she's done labor. There's something about the way she holds herself. Like a dancer. Then I realize: she *is* a dancer. I recognize her from one of the recitals that Matris sometimes drags me to.

I stiffen. My nerves are now ten times worse than what they were before. My first dance with a professional? I can't imagine how badly I'll embarrass myself. The orchestra begins, the sound of sullen pipe organs filling the hall. My suitor nods at me, getting me ready and on beat. She guides me to my left, but my feet refuse to budge.

The organ music becomes more intense. I glance over at the musicians, scaling the organic pipes, pumping the air sacs, and covering the openings so that the wheezing notes spew out in a pleasing chorus. They're more acrobats than musicians. My glance has turned into a stare . . . I'm stalling, I realize, as my suitor taps me on the elbow.

"One-two-three-four, and *step* . . ." she whispers at me, reminding me as the count rounds again. Another attempt at moving me fails. Now people are staring hard, half-eaten pastries hanging from their mouths. I hear their whispers even above the grind of music. "Just follow my lead," she says to me, nothing but patience and kindness in her voice. "I'll take care of you, I promise."

I know she's just talking about the dance floor, but my mind gets all twisted up, and suddenly, I see her taking care of me in our home, snuggling under a blanket, baby bouncing on Daddy's lap, big ol' crib worm sucking at the baby's thigh as she makes cooing sounds at us. It's all so . . . so perfect. So easy. So wrong.

"I'm sorry, please excuse me," I say, then peel my hands from hers and run as fast as my feet can take me, ducking out of the view of all these strangers. I come to the doors: two guards stand there and refuse to budge. Can't get away that easily. I duck through the crowd, head to a dark corner behind one of the buffet tables. I lurk, my hand reaching up top, pulling a fermented egg from the table, peeling back its fuzzy pink shell, and then stuffing it into my mouth.

I want to cry, but I don't dare smudge my patina. I'm going to have to go back out there eventually.

"Napkin?" says a voice. A familiar voice. I look up and see that male accountancy guard next to me. He nods at the front of my dress. There's a big goopy stain dribbling down it. "Patriline Wheytt Housley, at your service."

"What are *you* doing here?" I ask. It comes out harsher than I'd intended, but I've just embarrassed myself in front of six hundred people, so I hope he'll forgive me. I take the napkin, wet it with a whole mouthful of spit, then go after the stain before it sets.

"I received an invitation from Matris Paletoba."

"To be a guest, or to spy on me?" I say, giving him a once-over, checking for the bulge of his ledger in his pocket.

"I kind of get the feeling I'm here to show off how progressive she is."

"Ah, another of her distractions. But somehow, I doubt you shaking hands with all the guests is going to overshadow me running off like that." I relax some. It's nice talking to someone who's not trying to plan the next fifty years of my life.

"I doubt anyone even noticed," he says, another one of his bold, yet useless lies. "And you're not the only one having an awful time. Everyone keeps asking me to fetch them tea or napkins."

"You fetched a napkin for me," I say.

"You're different. I'd fetch tea and napkins for you any time. Can I help you up?" He extends a gloved hand. I take it.

"Escort me back to the line?" I ask. I'm not sure I trust myself to get back there under my legs alone.

"Absolutely," he says. And then we're walking, slowly, as if the floor were going to crumble beneath us. Still, I try to keep regal airs about me.

"I don't know if I can do this . . ." I mumble. "I don't want to have to choose."

"Don't think of them as suitors. This is just an opportunity to dance with a couple someones. That's all. Maybe one will suit your fancy. Who knows? Either way, you don't have to marry anyone."

"You don't know Matris very well. I'll be as good as engaged at the end of this night."

He says nothing, and I'm oddly grateful for that.

Finally, we're back before the dreaded line of possibilities for my future. Wheytt's hand is still in mine, and despite his fingers trying to pull from my grip, I don't let go. Suddenly, I want nothing more than to dance with him. Not because of his kindness, but because if I'm dancing with *him*, I can't be dancing with *them*.

I turn to him and take his other hand in mine. His eyebrows pitch over his goggles, and even though I can't see his eyes, I can feel them locked on me in horror. "Matriling Kaleigh!"

"I told you, you can call me Seske."

"Seske, everyone is staring."

"Let them. I can't dance with any of those suitors. I don't even know anything about them!"

"I can help with that," he says, a whisper in my ear, a smirk in his voice. "Accountancy Guard trade secrets. What do you want to know?"

"Everything that will fit in the time it takes to dance the molalari baret," I tell him. "Just follow my lead." I nod the count out, but the music hasn't started. Probably won't start. This is not whom I should be dancing with, after all. I do a practice count in my head and then make the first step; Wheytt follows along, adequately, and together, we fall in sync to an imaginary beat, and he whispers to me what he's observed about each of my suitors. Once we're a few counts in, the music finally starts up in an attempt to defuse an already awful amount of tension in the room. I just hang on to Wheytt's words, hoping they'll help me make a choice I don't want to make.

And once he's done, I steel my gut and add a flourish on the next count. The crowd aahs, stoking a fire within me. I add more flourishes, each turn now, as everyone watches in stunned silence as muscle memory from my dance with the baby beast takes hold. Even my dancer suitor stares back at me, her jaw hanging wide.

"Thank you," I whisper to Wheytt, my cheek to his cheek, as I prepare for our final flourish. On the slide, I step off into a pirouette, steal the collective breath of the entire hall, then swirl until I'm face-to-face with a suitor. Wheytt had described him as well-read: he could see the book ink on his fingertips. He smells tar mint on his breath, covering up the cigars that he smokes, which means he's not above breaking a few rules. And Wheytt noticed the trembling hands, even though they were clenched behind his back, which means he's just as scared as I am.

Plus, choosing a male suitor would fluster Matris, which would be a happy bonus.

I bow, and he curtsies: eyes seem bright and honest enough, smile seems genuine. "Sir, may I have this dance?"

"Most certainly," he says, so much patina on his face that it crinkles around his eyes when he smiles. "I'd be honored."

His name is Doka. We dance, we laugh; he tells the best jokes. Three of his mothers are Senators. Not many matrilines wield such influence, which is likely why he'd ended up on the list of suitors. Three Senators tied to our line would earn

Matris favors, for sure, and maybe they'd be less likely to unseat her from the throne, should her faulty decisions continue to haunt her. Doka has taken after his mothers, it seems, and runs circles around me in the game of politics. Never once does he shame me, nor is he ashamed for his odd interest in a realm strictly off-limits to husbands. I kind of almost admire him for that. Over the course of the evening, I dance with a couple other potential suitors but keep coming back to Doka. And even when our feet tire, we find a quiet corner, and he slips me a buttered biscuit, and it is then I know he is for me. Or at least, he could be.

I glance at the candle: only inches left. I should do it now, declare him my suitor and confirm our engagement, and get it all over with in one fell swoop. I clear my throat, ready to speak the words that have terrified me right up until now, but then I see an almost familiar face staring at me—

"Adalla," I scream out. She stands there in a ball gown that would befit a matriarch's wife. Her braids are so fine that her scalp shows, a weave of patterns denoting her lineage. Not an ichor smudge to be seen on her face. She smiles, but her eyes are so, so hesitant. Then I notice Sisterkin next to her, so proud of herself.

"I thought it only fair that *all* your friends be in attendance on your special night," Sisterkin says to me.

"*Oooh!*" I squeal, then hug my sister tight. Oh, I know she's up to something, but my arms need to be filled right now, and imagining my body pressed up against Adalla's is giving me way too many feelings, so I settle for the next to last best thing. "Thank you," I say to my sister, then introduce Adalla to Doka. His eyes have already read her beastworker braids, and yet his curtsy is as deep as it was for me.

"Pleased to meet you. Any friend of Seske's is a friend of mine." He bats his gilded lashes.

"I'm so glad you're here, Adalla! I had hoped Sonovan would have sent you to deliver the tome that night after the quake."

"I was busy. We're always busy." Her voice is curt. Her eyes cut at Doka.

"Oh," I say. "Well. Busy is good." There's a long, awkward stretch.

"Seske, why don't I get some refreshments for our friend?" Doka says, sensing our need for a little space. Then he leans over, whispers in my ear. "I'll sneak a couple buttered biscuits for you as well?" His lips touch my ear as he speaks. My eyes alight at his boldness, but I nod, and he's off, and Adalla and I are alone, give or take about six hundred onlookers.

"I should have come to visit you," I say. "I just wasn't sure my heart could handle it."

"We've all got our priorities," she says, throwing a glance toward Doka at the buffet table. "He's cute at least," she offers. "I was kind of hoping you'd end up with a suitor who's perpetually got a sprig of kettleworm wedged between their front teeth and a booger dangling from their nose."

I glance back at the candle burning through the minutes left before I enter womanhood, and only a sliver remains. Just enough time for one last reckless moment. My lips part. I move them closer to hers. "That day in the fissure, there was something between us, right?"

"Maybe. But maybe that quake happened for a reason. Maybe there shouldn't be anything between us."

"Then why do you want to be here now?"

"I don't. Your sister practically dragged me."

"Oh," I say. If Sisterkin initiated this, it could only be a setup. A giant temptation. She thinks I'll choose Adalla as my suitor, bring shame upon our name—any reason to have me tossed from the line so she could step in. Oh, I know she's not even in the running, but any future Matris would listen to her, and she'd be the force behind it all. Well, I'm not falling for it.

"I talked to my ama," I say. "Turns out there's another way we could be together without risking a scandal."

Adalla looks up at me, suddenly hopeful. My heart stills. There is something there, something I thought I'd been imagining.

"I'll marry well, strengthen the family lines. Then, two or three years from now, when I start to extend my family unit, I'll bring you in as one of the heart-mothers."

"Cheating between family units is the biggest offense!"

"We wouldn't be cheating. Just close. Very close." I touch her shoulder, running my hand down to her elbow. It lingers.

Her eyes inflame. "I don't want to be your pet, Seske," she grates at me. "I don't even know if I want to be your wife. I just want a chance to see where this will take us, to see if I even want this!"

"Seske!" Matris says, interrupting this moment. Sisterkin stands next to her, a vicious little smile on her face. "Please, we need to get back to the ceremony. Now thank your friend for her well-wishes and let's go."

"No," I say.

"No, what?" Matris demands.

"I won't say goodbye. She deserves my attention more than any of those strangers over there."

"You may visit with her another time then, but not today!" She grabs my elbow, but I pull free.

Adalla stares at me, panic in her eyes. She wants to know

if there's any spark between us. I can give her that, at least. And if there is, well, we'll figure something out. A quick glance back at the candle, and it's just a thin layer of wax now, wick barely standing upright. I've got about one minute left before I'm fully a woman, before the rules of womanhood will fall on me. If this is just a childish folly, I will know it from this kiss.

I press my lips to Adalla's, soft and slickened with balms. The flavor of her mouth ignites my heart; her warmth fills me. I am lost and found and lost again. I move my arms to embrace her, and her hands pull me in so hard, it's like she's trying to make us one.

Finally, too soon, we part. I have to force the next breath into me, because she's all but taken it away. Our eyes lock. Our fingers lock. Our hearts lock.

Matris is wailing. I look over, and the flame is out. Our kiss—how long had it lasted? The families of the suitors are all up in arms; my fathers try to calm them, to reassure them, but then punches are thrown. There's mayhem. It isn't fair. Nothing is fair. My people's future is dependent upon me being miserable, forced into a life I don't want and never asked for.

"Seske," Adalla says, as if she can read my mind. "We can't have this."

"But—" I say, but her finger presses to my lips, then she points to the wisp of candle smoke still lingering in the air.

I run, fast as I can, grab a match from the flame bearer, and then yell above the shouting. "The light isn't out yet. I can still choose!" I strike the match and hold it high in the smoky wisp dissipating before my eyes. At first, there's nothing, but finally, a small bead of fire sits midair. It travels down, down, slowly.

"Doka. Doka Taylan," I say. "I choose Doka!"

"*Tay-li-an*," his head-mother corrects, enunciating each syllable like she wishes they were claps against my cheek. This should be a proud moment for her, for Doka. For my family, for our people. But I've completely ruined it for everyone. I cringe at the thought of how this event will be replayed in the Texts.

Doka takes my side, smiling like the last five minutes hadn't happened. "I am honored, Seske!" he says. "Let us all dance and rejoice in this arrangement. I cannot wait any longer. Let us dance. Let us all dance!" His voice is so commanding, so regal, that the guests cannot help but obey. And then we are dancing, me keeping a strict and steady count in my mind to keep from falling into a puddle of tears. On our first turn, I catch a glimpse of Adalla standing in the exact spot I'd left her, arms down at her sides, looking utterly deflated.

On the next turn, she is gone.

ADALLA
Of Silent Girls and Loud Mothers

I take each step carefully, quickly. Keep a smile on my face. Eyes focused forward. Eyelids up. I'm passing for sober, I think. "Hello, Uridan," I greet my partner for the shift. Ama won't let me work on my own anymore, but the heart needs me. Even gaffed to my eyeballs, I'm better with a knife than most of these women ever will be.

"Hello, Adalla," she says, not bothering to look up at me.

The ground is swaying beneath my feet, but no one else is, so it's all in my mind. I bite back the giggles. Straighten my smile into something more serious. My ready-for-work face.

"Crude fat ventricle six today. Shhh-should be an uneventful shift." My tongue is too swollen in my mouth, and I'm starting to slur. Probably should keep my talking to a minimum. "Have you heard the one about the beastworker, the matriarch, aaa-and the heart-father?" I lean toward her, nearly stumbling.

It's then she looks up from polishing her knife, so shiny, I can see the glassiness of my bloodshot eyes. "Adalla," she whispers. "Are you on mad vapors?"

"Me?" I ask. "Of course not! What kind of person would report to her shift high?" I almost raise my hand. Maybe I'm worse off than I thought. "Just tired, is all. This is my thirteenth shift in five days."

"Maybe you should sleep this one off, then. You look like third-ass shits."

"No, no. You look as bad as me." I pinch her cheek, peer into her drowsy eyes. "And look." I unsheathe my own knife, lay my hand flat against a fat slab, then run the knife's point into the spaces between my splayed fingers a half dozen times in fifteen seconds. I show my hand to Uridan, front and back. All the fingers are still accounted for, nothing's bleeding.

She nods, and I breathe easy. I fill twenty buckets to Uridan's thirteen. I might be gaffed, but I'm focused, right here, right now. I've made it three months without pining over Seske, without fretting over what additional cruelties my ama will bestow upon me, without dwelling on the life I wish I had. Right here, there's just me and my knife and this big slab of fat. It's not perfect, and this isn't the first time I've shown up to shift like this, but it works.

It's the only way it works.

THE PATH TO OUR SECRET HIDEOUT IS FAMILIAR NOW, ENOUGH so that I could lead the way if I wanted. Parton walks ahead of me, though, a skip in her step. All throughout our shift, she's had a sly smirk upon her face, and I've been beside myself wondering what it could be about.

Just twenty more steps until we reach our gall, and after the hundreds of held glances we'd risked today, the dozens of brushed shoulders as we passed each other too closely in vein 5P3, and that one bold time we'd locked pinkies together, just for a few moments after an arrhythmic beat and everyone was too harried to notice—the reason for all of that frivolity will finally be revealed.

I veer toward our gall and tuck up into the bore hole, the only blemish in the spherical cocoon. It's a tight fit, but we wriggle inside, then the room widens out as we make it to the gall's core.

"So are you going to tell me or what?" I say around the bone pipe dangling from my lips.

But Parton is already two puffs deep into the purple-black gas held back by a thin membrane on her special-order palette. She holds her breath for a while, or forever, and then finally blows a ring of smoke that dissipates right before it hits my face. I breathe it in, then take my own puff from her pipe, so deep it fills my lungs and even manages to sneak into those hollowed-out spaces of my soul. I hold it just as long as Parton had, maybe longer, then blow back at her, five small rings, each chasing after the next. I watch her hands closely, waiting for her to sign some sort of compliment, but they stay still in her lap. No, not completely still. They're trembling.

"I know a way to solve your problem with Seske," she says. *Really* says, with her own actual voice. It's deeper than I'd imagined, still scratchy, though.

My eyes go wide. "You can talk?"

"I can. With you."

"Why didn't you before?"

"We're . . . not supposed to."

Something in the back of my mind prods me to ask her more, but my head is still spinning from the mad vapors. I take another puff, shuddering at all the secrets I'd spilled to Parton in the early days of our friendship, back when it was more transactional. I'd plied her with vapors, and she'd lent me her time. Same arrangement she'd had with Uridan and a couple of the other too-lonely women on our shift.

"My problem with Seske?" I ask as soon as my mind loosens back up.

"You can be together. You still want to be with her, yes?"

I sigh. It was so much easier when Seske had been tucked away in stasis. Those months hadn't been easy, but my mind was still able to focus. I'd lived a normal life. Now it's like I'm neck-deep in silt sand, treading, treading, just to be cranky and miserable.

"Okay," I say. "What's your idea?"

"The Hundredth Night Masquerade. All the other grisettes have gotten their invitations. A party to celebrate and recognize our hard work. They say there will be dancing, music, and a 'feast to end all feasts.' Please come. You can both be my guests. Wear masks. Dance together. Maybe more?"

Hands like mine, they are used to the force and exertion needed to rip tumor from flesh. Feet like mine can nearly outpace a tidal wave of ichor, betcha, but I know nothing of stepping to the rhythm of my own heart. Of dancing.

With Seske.

For a moment, I imagine us together, swaying to music, my hand around her waist, our faces hidden behind masks. Our identities unknown. There would be no one to care about who was royalty and who was a beastworker. We'd be equals for once.

"So?" Parton asks. I'm so deep in thought that her voice startles me again, like I'm hearing her speak for the first time. There's so much for me to process right now, I can't even figure out where to start.

"I don't know," I finally say. "I don't know how to dance."

"You dance every day. With the beast. But I will show you how to dance with a woman." She goes to stand, then topples over. I catch her in my arms, and we both break out in giggles. "Tomorrow," she says. "I will teach you to dance tomorrow."

I THINK I MIGHT HAVE LIED. FINDING MY WAY TO OUR GALL cave is trickier than I thought. Parton wasn't at her shift today, but my heart is racing, hoping that she'll show up here. My feet press through the soft flesh of the farmland tracts, budding galls knocking against my shins. Here, stuck in the quiet with only my thoughts, I hear the hundreds, thousands of larvae scritch-scratching inside their fast-growing encasements. They'll be harvested within the next few weeks—before they start their metamorphosis into big, unwieldy beetles—and more larval steaks will grace the plates of the Contour class citizens.

Finally, I spot the pile of husks and notice the dim glow of our ley light seeping from the bore hole. My heart jumps. My feet are light. I'm ready for my first dance lesson. The Hundredth Night Masquerade is still a few days away. I'll have time to perfect my moves by then, sure is sure.

I pop up into the hole, crawl my way to the core, then feel my smile go frigid. It is not Parton who sits among our pillows. It is my ama. I nearly fall back through the hole, but her stare holds me.

"Uridan says you've been showing up to your shift gaffed. I knew you were off, girl, but I never thought you'd defy me such. You've burned me, girlie. Burned me badly."

I resist the urge to apologize. Parton and I have done nothing wrong. Still, Ama won't see it that way. I steady my nerves, ready to dodge her pinch or slap or worse. "You warned me off her, Ama, but you never told me why. I think it's you who's burned me. I look into Parton's eyes and all I see is my pai."

"Parton?" she asks with a brow raised.

"I gave her Father's name. She had no other name to claim."

"She's a grisette. She doesn't have a name. Doesn't *need* a name."

"Am I wrong, Ama? Tell me the truth. She's my sister." Never in my life would I have thought my mouth capable of saying such a slur in front of my ama. But I've said it, *sister,* still bitter and slick on my tongue.

Ama still doesn't flinch. "There is a hierarchy among beastworkers, Adalla girl. Your head is too full of Contour class dreams for you to notice, but we're at the top of that pile. Our work is prestigious. Our matriline is solid. You go around consorting with the likes of a bucket waif, and you'll bring down shame upon your head, and the rest of our family too."

"Shame? Just for making a friend? For showing kindness to someone at the bottom of the pile?"

"She could only wish to be at the bottom of the pile. Adalla girl, grisettes are tools, not people. A mechanism to move buckets for you. It oughtn't be important where the bucket ends and they begin. They are one and the same."

"Things to be used? Abused? I won't believe it, Ama. And I know you don't either. You pretend your heart to be so cold. Prove to me it's not!"

Ama stands, and it's like she's suddenly filling up the entire room. "Girl, she is the *reason* my heart is so cold!"

My eyes go wide. She recoils, like she hadn't meant to speak such a thing, but there's a crack now. And I see it, all those parts of Parton that don't line up with Pai, they line up with my ama . . . And I know. I know for sure Parton is Ama's daughter too. My sister, truly. "She's ours, isn't she, Ama? She's smart. She knows so much about the heart. She's got more intuition than me, even. She's as stubborn as you. But you and Pai . . ." Ama and Pai had to be her parents. But such a romantic entanglement was forbidden. A head-father frolicking with a heart-mother? The thought brings bile up into my throat, but I have to know. "How, Ama?"

She sits, folds into herself. Suddenly, she looks as formidable as scraps of parchment. Her fingers find the frayed edges of her dress, and she lifts it up until her belly is bared. There, a tiny faded scar to the right of her navel. "Because of this scar, child, you have never known hunger. You've never had to live a life of scavenging. Never worried about having to work any of those lesser organs that slowly fill your body with poisons and tumors." There's a long sigh, and Ama pats the spot next to her. She is hurting. Worse than I am. I go to sit by her side to help her through this best I can.

"I'm sorry, Ama. I opened up this wound."

"No. You need to know. You'll soon be old enough to make this decision yourself, should we survive long enough on this wretched beast. The first day of exodus, after the Contour class is packed back into stasis, the accountancy guards compare ledgers, and a list with the names of the most efficient, most talented beastworkers is made. Those women are asked if they will donate eggs. They pay nicely for the eggs, and the procedure doesn't hurt much. Just a few drugs and a little pinch here." Ama pokes at her stomach and smiles a sad sort of smile. "Men are asked to donate too. Your pai did. That was way back, before our family was even a thought. We weren't supposed to know, but we were paired together. Eight embryos. Frozen nearly twenty years ago now. You see how many workers we need to get us through excavation and expansion as quickly as possible. When it's time, as soon as the harpoons take aim at our next beast, they start growing the embryos quickly; and by the start of excavation, they're big enough to help. By expansion, they're full-grown and able to assist with building and heavy lifting. Without them, none of this would be possible."

So Parton's story about her origins had been true. That doesn't make it any easier to swallow.

"This isn't right, Ama! Those waifs should have families, not be raised like animals."

"It is what it is, betcha girl, and you will not see her again. I've sent her to work the doldrums. Be thankful it is not you I've sent there instead."

"Why did you keep her so close to us to begin with? You wanted her near, didn't you? You wanted to see the child you'd sold into labor, and yet here you are telling me I've done something wrong! I'd hate myself if I'd done what you have!"

Finally, the slap comes, clean across my cheek. I press my hand there, feeling the warmth bud beneath my skin. Tears rim my eyes. Not because of the sting against my cheek, but because maybe the system has already broken me. It's taken Seske from me, my father, my sister, and now my ama is lost to me, too, her eyes now colder and more distant than they've ever been.

"Take tomorrow off," Ama tells me. "Rest. You'll need your strength for bonework."

At first I don't understand . . . and then it hits me, what she just said. *Bonework.*

I am no longer part of the heart.

I stand there trembling, not knowing what scares me most—being cast down to labor alongside the ruffians and riffraff who work the beast's bones, or spending another moment here, staring at the contempt on my mother's face.

SESKE

Of Unseen Men and Overheard Plans

So Doka is actually kind of amazing, totally unlike other men. He's smart, quick-witted, and adventuresome. His interest in politics is intense, which is great for me, because it gives us an excuse to be together when we discuss things. Not that he's tutoring me. That would be ridiculous, but I like the masculine slant he brings to the issues.

The Texts are spread out in front of us. He's been through replicas, of course, but he's never seen the real thing. He examines the book, tracing the contours of the spine, smelling the pages, eyeing the barely visible ink blotch on the back.

"Of course, we can't eat or drink around it"—*or have bloody noses,* I add for my personal benefit—"but Matris says we can use it all we need."

"So much history these pages have seen," Doka says. He lays the tome flat on the table between us. He flips open a page and reads.

"Ahem," his honor attendant says at us. She's a matronly woman, with a strong, stern face, here to make sure Doka's honor stays intact. I notice Doka and I have drifted closer while looking over the Texts, well within the three feet we're supposed to keep apart.

"How are we to study, Kiravi, if we cannot even read from the same page?" he asks her. "I promise, my honor will hold. We are merely studying. Can't Seske scoot a little closer?"

"Closer, but no touching," Kiravi agrees with little more than a grunt.

I draw my chair closer and smile at Doka for his forwardness. "You're so well-spoken," I whisper to him.

He gives me a strained half smile. "Thanks?"

"You're wel—" My brow bends. "Wait. Was that a question?"

He shakes his head, flipping three-fourths of the way through the tome, his finger running mindfully down the page. "No, it's nothing. Here, let's look at how the Senate gets chosen again . . ."

"No, tell me. What did I do?" I ask, so struck by his sudden change of tone. "Did I scoot too close?" I whisper.

"You said I was 'well-spoken.'"

"Well, you are! How did that offend you?"

"It's not what you said. It's the part of the sentence you finished in your head that's the problem. 'You're so well-spoken . . . for a man.'"

"But that's not . . ." I clear my throat. "Well, I didn't . . ." I fumble over my words, again and again. I want so badly to defend myself, but maybe that was what I was thinking. Just a little bit. "I'm sorry. I'll do better."

"Thank you," he says, not a question this time.

So we study. He leads me down the Lines, but not like my pai takes me. He tells me the stories, shows me the artifacts they'd left for us. Doka also teaches me a song to help me remember the order, and my favorite part is the staccato parade of names from right before the Great Mending, when the average length of the reigns could be measured in weeks. Coups were aplenty back then, and it takes me a few tries, but finally I'm able to get all those cursed names out in one breath.

Somehow, Doka makes this dusty old book seem relevant. On the tenth matriarch, he reaches out his hand. I reach with mine. Our pinkies lock. The Texts are just bulky enough to keep this transgression out of Kiravi's line of sight. If his honor attendant caught us, we could both be strung up by our thumbs for such an act. Doka smuggles me a tight-lipped smile as he continues to read.

We spend two heavily scrutinized hours together each day for his lessons that are not lessons. Weeks go by, and while I enjoy our time together, it always feels like he's putting on a performance.

Then one day, Doka puts the Seven Tenets of the Ancestors to song. Usually, his songs are upbeat, with a tempo that makes them easy to remember, but this one's a sweet lullaby. His voice is so melodic and lilting, I catch myself drifting, imagining what he really looks like under all that patina and glitter. He's only halfway through the tenets when Kiravi starts to drift as well, lulled to sleep by Doka's gentle voice. With his protectorate's eyes half closed, he becomes bolder and presses his finger against my open palm, and suddenly, I'm wide-awake. He traces a Vvanescript letter into it, an *I*, but I clench my fist, painful memories of doing the same with Adalla too much for me to bear.

I like Doka, I do. Being with him is a thrill. A novelty. He's friendly and interesting, and he makes the best jokes, and I know he'll be a wonderful and obedient husband, but I do not yearn after him like I should. I know I must try harder. It will make our eventual marriage go smoother.

"Have you spoken to your mothers about us?" I say softly to him instead.

"Of course." He grins. "My fathers, too, and all of my grandparents. They're all very excited about how our courtship is progressing. Aren't you excited?"

"Of course. My parents are excited as well. They all agree it is a very good match."

"*Extremely* good," he says with a laugh. "Strengthening the ol' family lines . . ."

"You sound like you got the same talk from your headmother that I did."

"That's the one." He laughs. "You know, we've spent all this time together, but I feel like I should know more about you by now. But it's tough with you-know-who always looming over us."

"I was thinking the same thing. But maybe we could get to know each other a little better now . . ." I say, and for some reason, I'm ready to bare it all to this near stranger. "Tell me a secret. Something you've never told anyone before."

He looks at me, blanking, mouth gasping for words.

"Fine. I'll go first. I slept with a crib worm until I was twelve years old."

He raises a brow, takes a long moment to think it over. "Okay, I'll play. Once I got a cowrie shell stuck up my nose. So far up there, I almost needed surgery to remove it."

"Good start. But if we're just going to talk about stupid stuff we did when we were little kids, we'll be here all night—"

"I was sixteen."

I smile at that. "Fair enough, then. I've done beastwork. Dressed up in a leather tunic and went to work on the doldrums of our old beast. Every day for a week, and no one batted a lash."

"Eesh, well, that's something . . ." he says with a scowl. "So, we're really doing this? Right now? Spilling all of our secrets to each other?"

I cross my arms, my stare firm. "When we're married, we shouldn't have any secrets. Might as well get them all out now."

"Married? Is this a proposal? Are we making this official?"

"Doka Taylian, you will *know it* when I propose to you, I promise. This is a hypothetical."

"Okay," he says. "Here's a big one for you: I once took my will-mother's place in the Senate when she was sick. She sent me on an errand to tell them she was too ill to attend. I decided the spirits were tempting me out of my station, but if I was going to fail them, I would fail them in the most spectacular way. I wore my mother's robes, borrowed her credentials, and faked her naxshi with some blue and gold patina. I watched the Senate proceedings closely, and for all the decorum the Senators project in the public eye, they certainly leave it as they enter the chamber doors. There was yelling, swearing. Pettiness. One Senator even decided to hold the floor for nearly an hour, not conceding until she received a formal apology from the Senator who had bad-mouthed one of her proposals. It was so amazing. I even cast three votes. No one noticed."

"Impressive," I say, noticing how proud Doka seems for defying the ancestors' will. "No wonder you know so much about the Senate."

"That, and I sneak down into my mothers' studies almost every night."

"So you're good at sneaking?" I ask, tossing a glance at the honor attendant, arms crossed over her chest, head cocked back, still snoring. "How long do you think she'll stay asleep?"

"She usually naps for a couple hours easy," Doka says, a grin spreading across his lips. "What do you have in mind, Seske Kaleigh?"

"A small excursion." I smudge my thumb through the patina on his cheek. It's so thick, it just kind of glides across his skin. "We're going to have to do something about this, though." I gesture at his entire ensemble. "I'll go fetch you some women's clothes. You go wash up. Let's see what you've got under all of that patina."

Doka balks. "Do you know how long it took to put this on?" he says, gesturing at his face. *"Hours!"*

"Well, we can't go sneaking about with you looking like that."

"So it seems." He leans forward; our noses nearly touch. That honor I'm supposed to be keeping away from, I can practically smell it radiating off him. A throb of tension. A palpable wanting on his breath.

I think this is the part when I'm supposed to say something risqué. To invite him to my room, just for a look around. To accidentally brush my hand across the smoothness of his abdomen. I look back over to Kiravi and see one of her eyes cocked open. She quickly shuts it, then begins snoring loudly.

Ah. Games, then. What better way to seal a marriage than under threat of stolen honor? He needn't worry about that. I take the rules of honor very seriously. The rules defining the proper behavior for a matriarch in training, not so much.

"Come on," I whisper, taking him by the hand, and as his clammy palm presses against mine, all manners of mischief fill my head. "There's something I want to show you."

I lead him down the hall, past my bedroom, to my bapa's dressing room. I pick the lock and open the door to reveal men's silks and wraps hanging upon hooks. A full display of patinas sits out upon an intricately carved bone vanity. It's yellowed and smoothed over, unlike the pristine white of the furniture that surrounds it.

"Seske," Doka says, his hands running along the vanity's surface. "How old is this?"

"I don't know. Old as me at least." I pull one of the silks down and wrap it around my shoulders. Then I dip my finger into a warm orange patina and rub it onto my face. "If you won't dress up as a woman, I'll dress up as a man. You'll help me, right? And then we can see what mischief we can get into."

"Seske, we can't be in here. Don't you realize how priceless this is? How many favors your father and your *grandfather* must have pulled to have this vanity put through exodus? Even this patina, it's way too old to be from this beast."

"Sounds to me like you're uncomfortable sneaking around . . ."

"No, I . . ." Doka fumbles for words. He tries to relax, but political calculations are spinning around in his head for sure. "I'll help. But be careful, not like that!" And he pulls my hand away from the patinas and goes for a big, fluffy brush. "Sit still," he says, and bites his lip, looking at my face like it's an empty canvas, then begins covering up my naxshi with a thick layer of patina.

BEING A MAN, IT'S LIKE MAGIC. A SHIELD OF INVISIBILITY. NO one talks to you. No one looks at you. We're in the central market, caught among the bustle of women scurrying from one bone-white storefront to the next, buying clothes, food, medicine, and gifts to appease the ancestors. For the most part, we go unnoticed, but I catch them risking glances at us now and again. Some of them even dare to ogle our foreheads—a man's most sacred place of honor. It is there that his wife's matriline will be set in ink on the wedding night, a fine brush tracing the celestial claims of her ancestors upon him.

I blink. My eyelids are so heavy, holding up to a dozen tiny gemstones each. My whole body feels like I've been dunked in slime, but my, how I glisten. I've never felt so bold, so beautiful. Doka made me practice my walk while mimicking his gestures. He spoke of calling upon the honor of my patriline, and now I am enjoying the fruits of my toil, no longer Seske Kaleigh, but Sesken Pmalamar, son of fathers. My temples bear the stark black markings of my pai's line, my forehead blank for when I am taken into matrimony.

"Here," I say, looking up at the Muirabuko Emporium, tugging Doka toward the front door. "I love this place. Or what this place had been on our last beast." I glance through the window and see nothing has changed. The purple paint on the ceiling detailing the family's celestial lines in glittering gold, the copper bead wall separating the cheap trinkets from the more expensive novelties in back, and there's even the old puppet theater, with a show going on right now in fact! I'd watched the gel puppets perform when I was a kid, mesmerized with how those moldable waxy figures moved and shook on their own. Completely lifelike. Seeing these familiar things is more of a comfort than I realized . . . a little stability in the volatile state of our clan's existence.

"Come on," I say, tugging at Doka's elbow. "Let's go see what's playing."

"We can't just walk in there!" Doka whispers at me. "We use the men's entrance."

Right. He leads me around the side. Not so grand here, not so spectacular. The section is about a fourth of the size of the main part, selling mostly scarves, patinas, and hobby kits for

carving the custom bone beads young lads like to adorn themselves with.

"I don't see any gel puppets," I tell Doka. "I'm pretty sure
they have them all up front."

"We'll ask a clerk to fetch them, then," he says.

"I'll go. I know exactly where they are."

"Sesken," he says, using my fake name. "Remember your
station."

"What? My fathers and I come here all the time. We never
have a problem."

"*Seske* wouldn't. Sesken would. If Kiravi were here to su-
pervise us, we'd be fine."

I nod, taking his point. "But if Kiravi were here, we'd be in
trouble."

Two women enter the back with us. Doka and I look down,
pretending to shop. It's the Muirabuko head-mother—matron
of the family—and in at least a dozen layers of silks, she definitely looks the part. Their son had married right before our
last exodus. They were progressive and let him work a few
days a week at the counter.

"Matron Muirabuko," says the other woman, and it takes
me only a moment to place the voice. I glance over in shock.
It's Sisterkin. "Your son's marriage has strengthened your
business's supply chain, and now a political move could help
strengthen your solvency. Imagine your taxes being lifted."

The matron nods along, but I can tell by the cinch of her
lips that her heart will not be swayed. "We are progressive, Sisterkin, but the moves we make are seen by all . . ." Then her
voice trails off among the laughter coming from the front of
the store.

Doka nudges me closer to them. We keep our heads down,
speak in whispers. They're discussing this delicate information

not five feet away, and they've yet to pay us any notice. We truly are invisible.

"... would just be too much!" Matron Muirabuko is saying. "Giving names to someone who is nameless. It's just not done by someone in our position. But just because we won't doesn't mean no one will. Perhaps ask the Atirans or the Roushans?"

"I've asked them already," Sisterkin says with a hint of bitterness. "And the Bulwards and the Ranyanks, and the Cruszans and the Pleletans. I wouldn't dare bother you, Matron Muirabuko, if you weren't my last hope. I can see to it that your shop is always profitable. That *any* shop you open will be profitable and favored by Matris."

This gets the matron's attention. She stops shuffling baubles and stands straight up. "Are you saying that you could get Matris to grant me another shop site?"

An involuntary noise escapes my mouth. Sisterkin looks at me, locks eyes with me for a brief moment, but there is no recognition there. She looks away just as quickly. "Maybe there's a more private place we can speak?" she asks the matron.

Matron Muirabuko agrees, and then they're gone, completely out of earshot.

"Sisterkin is trying to get a line name!" Doka says. "This is bad, Seske."

"She's been trying to steal my line name since we were kids. Nobody wants to shame their ancestors by giving her theirs."

"Most won't. But all she needs is one. And she's promising people store space. That doesn't come around often. This iteration of our city is less than a year old, and at the same time, nothing about it has changed for centuries. My great-great-great-great-grandfathers probably once stood upon this very spot, in this very store that's been replicated and replicated again and again. If Matron Muirabuko doesn't take that offer, then someone else will."

"That's just like Sisterkin, going through all that trouble, and for what? Just to have a line name to rub in my face? She doesn't even have a given name!"

Doka stares at me, like he's giving me a chance to go back and correct something that I've said wrong, but it's not coming to me fast enough.

I try harder, remembering the time Sisterkin had made up a name for herself. Khasina, she'd said, because it sounded pretty and regal. She'd asked me to call her that, but I'd said no. *What's the problem?* she'd asked. *It's just a made-up name tied to no family line.*

And I'd given in to Sisterkin's persuasions. And the first and only time I'd said it—Khasina—oh, how Sisterkin glowed. That was the first time I realized how powerful names were, and soon after that, I realized the magnitude of my mistake.

She had played with the name for nearly a week, though I mostly ignored her. But then I'd heard her playing tea with all her dolls. Only now in hindsight do I see how finely her dolls had been dressed, thirty-seven dolls. Thirty-seven women in the Senate. But then, I hadn't noticed it . . . only her singing "Khasina! Khasina! Khasina!" over and over again, and one time she said "Khasina Kaleigh!" She'd stopped her singing and dancing and turned to look right at me. Had it slipped out? Or was she challenging me then? I hadn't stuck around to find out. I'd run straight to my pai and told. I didn't see Sisterkin again until a week later. For months, she'd barely looked at me. Nearly a year passed before she'd spoken to me again. Whatever power there was in giving a name, there was something darker and much more powerful in taking it away.

"She'd need a line name to challenge for the throne," I say to Doka, my voice a rasp with the onset of too many emotions for me to process at once. "And if she's found the power to bribe someone with a storefront, she must be serious about it." Maybe she'd played at having a name when we were kids, but this isn't a game anymore.

"Maybe she's found a loophole."

I nod. "She's always holed up, studying the Texts. Well, we can't let her do this. We have to figure out what she's up to."

"Seske, we've been gone close to an hour already. We need to get back before Kiravi wakes up."

"Don't pretend, Doka. She was awake when we left. I get the keen feeling she wants you up to no good."

"Maybe a little frolic in your bedroom! Not espionage against Matris's daughter."

"I'm Matris's daughter . . . Sisterkin is just Sisterkin. You want to marry me, you'll have to get that straight, first of all. And second, you'll have to get used to taking risks, because honestly, marrying me is a risk the way Matris's reign is going. If Sisterkin is planning something, it's in both of our interests to know about it."

Just then, Sisterkin exits the private office of the matron. I steal a glance at Doka, and reluctantly he nods. Yes. We are invisible, and I intend to use this power for my own good.

We trail behind her several paces, following her from the posh streets of the central market down alleyways to a less pretentious area, and watch as she enters a jewelry store. Doka and I make our way around the back and pretend to browse necklaces, when the women enter. It's quieter here and we get the whole conversation this time. Here Sisterkin speaks ill of me, saying she's worried about the decisions I'm making and is unsure she wants to stay aligned with me. It cuts, I won't lie. I may never have accepted Sisterkin as family, but I've always tolerated her presence. Sometimes, I've even enjoyed it. She's ready to be done with me, however. Completely. She whines about how it was unfair, how I shouldn't even be alive, much less in line for the throne. She doesn't come outright and say that she wants it, but she alludes to it a lot. She claims Matris will support her decision fully, then makes promises of shop space and favors in return for the shop owner folding Sisterkin into her matriline.

I'm feeling so sick, I can't stay a moment longer. Doka helps me out, leads me back toward my home. If Matris approves of this, it certainly can't be good. Had I pushed Matris too far, embarrassed her so wholly at the coming out party that she'd rather deal with the drama of announcing Sisterkin as her successor?

We climb back through the scaffolding leading up to my bedroom window, then we're alone up in my room. I wipe my patina away, wishing Doka would do the same so I could see the man who might have just exposed the coup of the century. I hand him a wet cloth. He looks down at it, then wipes. He needs three more cloths before I can see him. *Really* see him. "You're beautiful," I say, and he flushes.

"I'm sorry you found out about your family like that," Doka says. "I feel weird for being mixed up in it."

I shake my head. "No, thank you for wanting to get tangled up in this. I need an ally. I need a friend." When I'd chosen him as my suitor, I'd imagined I'd do everything I could to sabotage the relationship and leave it dead in the water. Just another mess for Matris to mop up. But the more time I spend with him, the more I see him as something else. It takes a moment for the words to make it to my lips, but finally, I say them. "A husband."

He looks up at me through those thick, natural lashes, more beautiful than they'd been when they bore so many jewels. I touch his forehead—a spot so sacred, I might as well have taken his honor right here in the middle of the floor. He shivers at my touch.

"I think we are a *very* good match," I say.

The door bursts open; Kiravi stands there, taking up the entire doorway, and sees my finger upon Doka's forehead and nearly faints. "Your honor, my Doka," she says, crying into her sleeve, an act she has obviously been building up to for some time. "It was my only duty to protect it, and here, I have failed. We must tell your mothers immediately so that I may take my lashes."

"No," I tell her, grabbing her by the arm. Am I going to do this? Fast-track our marriage. I mean, I like Doka. He's quick-witted, up for an adventure, and unapologetic for his quirks. He's everything I want in a friend. But I'd be getting much more than a friend. I'd be getting a lover, too, and that part scares me quite a bit. I won't be able to avoid it forever, and at least Doka and I get along. Chemistry will come—he *is* quite pleasing to look at. And I can't even imagine the fit Matris would have if she found out I'd taken Doka's honor. She'd disown me for sure. "No, there's no need. Honor has not been taken. I was just . . . proposing."

Kiravi throws her hands up, then pulls both Doka and me into an enormous embrace. She presses her hands upon his cheeks, looking perturbed by the naked state of his face. "Oh, no no no. We can't have you looking like this in front of your future wife! We have to get your patinas!"

Then she tugs him away, big goofy grin on his face. I wave at him. And then they're gone. I suppose I'll have to tell my parents.

And then I'll have to figure out what to do about Sisterkin.

ADALLA

Of Sharp Knives and Blunt Messages

I've got about a dozen slivers of bone cutting up my hands, but I push past the pain, just like I've pushed past the pain of being cast into boneworks by my own ama. The hunger pangs, though, they're more difficult to ignore. I'd skipped breakfast, the morning gruel unappetizing, but I was sure lunch would be better. It wasn't. Same dank, cold paste . . . looks more like spackle than food. I'd choked down a spoonful then, not nearly enough to sustain me through a single shift of bone-work. Down here, the rhythm is on the scale of seconds, slice and saw, slice and saw. Chop and chip, chop and chip. Mind-less work. Soulless work.

And now here, after shift, I'm staring down at my dinner. More spackle. Thicker, this time, and lukewarm. Small bits of rubbery stuff—cartilage, maybe, or specks of liver giving the bonemeal more sustenance? I pick one up, examine it. Hold it to the tip of my tongue. Balk at the taste. So bitter.

The women from the next table over laugh. It's then that I notice I have an audience. Boneworkers, all of them, though that's the only kind that frequent a dive like this. I try not to stare at the scars across their chests, deliberate ones made into all sorts of shapes from tiny, thin scratches. The sides of their heads are shaved, leaving a line of hair, tangled and twisted with bone slivers. They're broad and muscular from decades working beast after beast.

"It's worms," one woman says, the broadest, biggest one with the most scars. "Bone worms. They leave them in the mash to provide a little protein. Where you from, worm-licker?"

The others laugh.

"Don't want any trouble," I say, staring into my mash. I force a bite, hoping it'll stay long enough in my stomach to get some nutrients. It makes gall hash seem like the gourmet stuff they served at Seske's coming out party.

"Telling me where you're from won't cause you any trouble. Not telling me might." She stands, comes over, and sits across from me. I can smell her—pungent, spicy. Like her body hasn't known a sliver of soap in all her life and has made up for it by collecting an assortment of potent odors as a cover-up. "No scars. Wearing a shirt. Limp hair. You an organ girl?"

The way she says it lets me know that admitting I'm from an organ, any organ, would be a bad idea. Telling her I was from the heart . . . they'd have me strung up and beaten so fast. I shake my head. "Ligaments," I say, rounding out my vowels like they do, practically chewing the words. "Cut the wrong one, and they sent me down here."

"Ugh." The woman nods. "I've got five chits on you that says you can finish your gruel. Don't want to prove me wrong, do you?" She lays the cowric fragments on the table, and her friends come over and crowd around me after laying down their own bets.

"Probably not the wisest bet," I say.

"Little thing like you needs to eat up. Here." She raises a hand. The server comes over, slams a cup of malt cider in front of me. "That'll make it go down easier. Now eat up."

From the tone of her voice, it isn't a suggestion. I pour a bit of the hot cider into the meal, stir, then take a spoonful. It's marginally better—warm, and the spices make the bone mash go down easier. I swallow, manage to keep it down. Then go for another. I'm five spoonfuls in when it all comes back up, covering the table and a couple of the women. They just laugh and wipe the offending bits off with the backs of their hands.

"Acquired taste," the brutish woman says. "Kaieda, get this girl cleaned up!" She scoops my bowl away and returns it to the server.

"Wait!" I say. "I think I blew some chunks in that."

The server shrugs, then scrapes the whole thing back into the serving pot.

"No waste," the woman says to me. "We're so scrappy around here, even the lash counters have stopped hounding us. Besides, it hardly even touched your stomach before coming back up. Just as good as new." She laughs, then goes to help me out of my soiled shirt, but I balk.

"No, I'm okay. I'll clean up at home," I say.

"Nonsense," she says, tugging my shirt again. I hear the stitches popping. I stand up abruptly, my eyes focused. I won't be bullied, not even by someone twice my size. My hand goes to my knife. Their eyes go to my hand.

"Like I said, I don't want any trouble."

"Aw, you're no fun," the woman says. Then she turns her

attention to three waifs, hunched in the corner, on the floor, fingers all dipping into the same bowl of bonemeal. "Eh, look at them. Scarfing that down like it's their last meal. Like they won't be feasting tomorrow night!"

"All that bare, soft skin," another woman says. "An empty canvas." She takes out her knife, flicks it open. I flinch. I leave now, and those waifs are going to get worse than they'd ever deal me. I'd seen the way they treated the waifs today. Not simply ignored, like up in the heart, but kicked around, cussed, abused. And there are so many more of them here too. Almost as many as there are boneworkers.

"Wait," I say, pulling one of the two chits in my pocket out. "Let me buy you all a round of ciders. It's the least I can do for losing you a bet. And for blowing my dinner on you all."

The brutish woman turns back at me with a smile. "Now them's the kind of words I like to hear, worm-licker."

"The name's Adalla," I say, offering her my hand.

She takes it in both of her hands, shakes it, but doesn't let go right away. "I'm Laisze, you met Kaieda. That's Malika, Sandris, and Josoki."

I'm nervous, having them crowding me like this, 'specially when I'm pretty sure they're all armed, but as I look around the bar, I see that it is merely the boneworkers' way. I'd seen it as I worked today too. How all the women stood so close, touched so much. Just simple conversations, but there'd be a dozen touches between them, single presses of the hands to forearms, to shoulders, to the chest, to the cheeks.

It's odd. The people back home are all very friendly, but there's always an unspoken barrier between us. We spend so much of our time pretending that our neighbors don't exist, even though we can see them clearly, for lack of any real kind of privacy. Only one of my friends has ever dared to cross it, and if thoughts of her are going to be swimming around in my mind, I'm going to have to do my best to drown them. I put my hand upon Laisze's forearm, trying the custom out. Maybe it'll help me blend in and sell my story about being from ligaments.

When the warm mead ciders come out, I slurp mine down faster than I should, 'specially on an empty belly. The buzz hits me quickly, the stickiness both sweet and tart on my lips. I'm pulled into their rough huddle, laughing, joking, trying to seem like I'm relaxing, while studying their body cues and posture so I can learn to speak and act and think like they do. Then suddenly, Sandris is buying another round, and my cheeks are warm, along with every other part of me, and I'm wondering if this is where I'd belonged all along. Here, I'm not Ama's child. No bloodlines to live up to or worry over shaming.

Being handsy must be easier when I'm drunk, because now my hand is on Laisze's shoulder, admiring the scars of a clockface. "It's beautiful," I say. "What is it?"

"My great-grandmother's pocket watch," Laisze says, voice caught between pride and remorse. "Smuggled seven generations, but that ended with me, two beasts ago. Got randomly selected for a cavity search, and it got left behind, or more likely became some lash counter's souvenir. But I've got it with me here, still." She rubs her shoulder. "They can never take that away. Can't take any of these away." Her hand swipes over the scars along her chest and breasts, down to her stomach. Each of them a memento from the lives she's had to give up, time after time. My eyes stop on the scars depicting a crib worm, tail swirling around her navel. Childhood pet to be certain, and it all just sort of hits me . . . the life I'd left behind on our old beast. I was so young during my first exodus, and I can't even remember the transition, only the part where I'd lost my pai. I was too young to help with excavation, and all through the long course of our expansion, my wounds slowly healed. By the time the signs of extinction started to arrive, I was so caught up in the prospect of working for the heart that I didn't have time to process the parts of my life that we'd abandon on the beast. Our possessions. Our pets. Our home.

"We had a murmur named Bepok," I say. "In that old life. She was thin as tissue paper, but she still kept me warm on cold nights. The way she purred tickled me so much. Left little heart-shaped hickeys all over my legs. I miss her."

Laisze claps her hand down on my back. "To Bepok," she slurs. "Best damned murmur anyone ever had." Glasses are raised and clinked. Another round guzzled down. Finally, when we leave the dive, we're all arm in arm in arm, for physical support more than emotional, but just barely. I'd intended to return home after my shift, but when my turnoff comes, my feet keep walking by it.

"You got room for me to stay the night?" I ask.

"Oh, yes, honey, there's room for you."

Laisze nudges me in the ribs, and I look up at the enormous wall standing before us. My vision blurs for a moment, and then I notice hundreds of oval-shaped gouges cut into it like a giant gray sponge. A few of the holes are lit by ley lights, where I can see a person in each small room, just larger than a bed. The rest are dark, with just hints of the silhouettes of people milling about.

"Block ninety-nine, best block there is." Laisze points up high. "There are a few empty lofts up there. New meat like you, I can guarantee someone will come milling around, hoping to get at your humble bits. Just pretend you're asleep, and they'll take the hint."

I swallow. My humble bits? Maybe I should have gone home. Maybe it's not too late to change my mind. I start to take a drunken step in that direction, but Laisze snags me by the shirt and steers me up the first couple footholds. "I still don't understand why you insist on wearing this thing, when it'll just get ripped or stained, or get you caught up in a bind."

Then her hand is on my ass, pushing me higher and higher. I shouldn't be climbing. I can barely walk. I dive into the first loft I come to. It's smaller than most, just enough room for me to lie down and sit up without banging my head. Probably why it's vacant, but I can't risk falling by going higher for more space. I snuggle in, and sleep settles over me. But soon enough, I'm woken by someone pushing up next to me. I'm so shocked, I make the mistake of opening my eyes. I'm staring right at her, a young, thin boneworker with bright eyes and voluminous lips. Her hair is more bone than hair.

I clench my eyes before I can see more and start to snore. Loudly. Obnoxiously. Laisze was right, though. She slithers out of my bed so quickly, so lightly, I barely feel her leave. I clutch my covers tight to my body, only a little shaken. My second visitor, things go more naturally . . . realistic snoring, and I don't open my eyes, even though she smells really nice, her entire body like one tensed muscle next to mine. I think I'm getting the hang of things, maybe even enough to trust myself to get some real sleep, but then the bone around me creaks, and someone's pelvis settles itself right on top of mine. I snore loudly, but she doesn't move. I snore even louder, high-pitched inhale, blubbering exhale. Tossing and turning restlessly from the waist up.

Then she's pulling my shirt up and over my head, and I've got no choice but to confront her. It's Laisze. She's drunk. Drunker than I'd left her. And she's got a knife.

"Get off me!" I scream.

"Relax, I'm not here for jollies. I'm here to cut you." Her

thumb presses my left nipple down, and she wipes pink gel across my breast and underneath. "Here, right above the heart."

I struggle to free myself, but my arms are caught in the fabric of my shirt. Laisze gives me a sloppy I-told-you-so grin.

"You're drunk. You don't know what you're doing."

"I do my best work when I'm drunk," she says. I try to buck her off, but she's too heavy and she squeezes me tight between those rock-hard thighs.

"Shh . . ." she says. The look she gives me is crazed, yet earnest, and it settles the thoughts still rearing inside me. "You asked for this. Bepok. She'll be right here with you, forever and always now. You'll never leave her behind again. Okay?"

I nod, and with that, the tip of her knife bites into my flesh. She blots the blood away with a questionably clean rag, and memories rush forth of the first signs of extinction on our last beast—of walls weeping blood and of a multitude of tumors budding, growing rapidly, and finally hemorrhaging. The lash counters were so busy yelling at us to prepare for exodus, that I never had time to fully process the trauma of seeing the world I'd grown up in completely and utterly ruined. The illusions of home and permanence had crumbled so easily.

And now, my eyes are tearing up, and not just from the physical pain of Laisze's knife. This scar will be the first thing I truly own.

Laisze leans in close, her hot, spiced breath spilling over my skin. A few more minutes of cutting pass, then she's massaging oil into my skin. She releases her grip and slides off me. It stings like the nettles, but when I look down, I see her there—Bepok: a red outline of cut flesh upon my brown skin, her wings spread, tail coiling around and around my nipple.

I turn to thank Laisze, but she's passed out next to me, like a hunk of stone. The bed's not quite wide enough for the both of us, so I lie on my side and press close to her, feeling the roughness of her scarred skin against the smoothness of mine.

TURNS OUT BEING HUNGOVER IS GOOD FOR BONEWORK. MY heart is beating in my head, the exact right rhythm for my knife to be digging into this storefront sign. The Vvanescript lettering comes back to me, letter by letter, and I remember how Seske had traced each of them for me hundreds and thousands of times. ABACCA'S JEWELERS, DEWSIDE, the sign reads, replacing another sign that had already been hung. The whole inside is getting a new treatment, in fact. A rush job, with three dozen boneworkers converting aisles and lighting to the Accountancy Guard's specifications.

"Looking good, worm-licker," Laisze calls up to me. I toss a bone fleck back at her, and it hits her square between the eyes. She laughs, then says, "Almost done? We need to disappear before the posh arrive." She nods off in the distance, where two Contour class men stand, staring at us, gilded up in patinas. Just plain staring, like we're in the way. Like they can't wait ten more minutes for us to clean up and move on. I puff my chest and stare back, my new scar proudly on display. The air cool on the shaved sides of my head. I was half asleep when I'd agreed to the cut this morning. Laisze's idea, of course.

Kaieda did the actual cutting this time, tugging the razor up against my skin. When the first swatch of hair fell to the floor, I'd nearly fainted. All my life, these same braids have been a badge of honor worn upon my scalp, of both the lines of blood and the lines my ancestors had drawn between stars in the sky. But as much as it was a shock to my system, it didn't feel wrong.

And when Kaieda had styled what was left of my hair,

tugging it and teasing it and adorning it with slivers of bone . . . that felt right.

It's a lot of change, all at once, but now I look like I belong. I *do* belong.

I turn my attention back to the sign, take a dozen more whacks until it reads just right, then I join Laisze back on the ground. "Going to that dive again tonight?" I ask, because I'm thinking of asking her for another scar, but I need a few ciders' worth of courage first.

"Not tonight. It's the hundredth night of expansion. You know what that means."

I shake my head, but then my last time with Parton races back to me. "The masquerade party? I thought that was just for waifs."

"We crash it every beast cycle. It's a feast, Adalla. Bigger than you can imagine. Music. Dancing. You'll come with us? Malika has an extra mask you can use . . . a fox."

I nod. A fox, a creature of the time before—similar to a dog, if I remember right. Or maybe a cat? They're all so foreign. What matters is that this will be another night out. I could get used to this. And come morning, if I'm still in a fog, I can stagger in to work, and the worst that will happen is that I spell a word wrong on a sign. No veins getting nicked, no millions of lives depending on the steadiness of my hand.

I think of Parton, missing her, hoping she's doing fine where my ama sent her. But she will be at the party, and maybe if I pray to the spirits, I'll be lucky enough to run into her.

The men are still staring as we start to clean up.

It's weird—one of them seems familiar, but I'm sure I'd remember a face like that.

Laisze's hand comes down on my shoulder. "Something wrong?" she asks.

"That man over there. He reminds me of someone. Someone from another life."

"Maybe they share an ancestor some ways back. His great-grandfather took up with some beastworker on the sly. Unless you're accustomed to hanging out with the Contour class?"

I shake my head, hearing the venom in the word *Contour*.

"So, was this someone a neighbor? A friend? Or something more?" Laisze asks, and I laugh at the hint of jealousy in her voice.

"A *friend*," I say to Laisze, feeling the heat rise in my cheeks. I stare at my feet, and by the time I've gathered my thoughts and dare to look back up, the men are gone. "Isn't it odd that some of the things that we left behind in that other life are still here haunting us in this one?"

"If I had a scar on my skin for every scar in here"—she thumps her chest, right above her heart—"I wouldn't have a scrap of me that hadn't been touched by a knife."

MY COSTUME'S "FUR" IS SHEDDING BITS OF RED MOSS ALL OVER the place. My mask is stuffy inside, smells faintly of mildew, and the entirety of my vision is reduced to two jagged holes, but even through all these issues, I've never been so excited to wear anything in my entire life. The Hundredth Night Masquerade is more than I'd imagined, thousands of waifs dancing and swirling under twinkling ley lights made to resemble the pattern of stars that had shone over Mother Earth. There's even a giant disk hanging above called Luna, or so Laisze tells me, the moon where their spirit mothers lived.

I shove a pastry into my mouth, so delicate that its flaky layers melt right on my tongue. And there are gall steaks, cut into little cubes, marinated in a deep red sauce that tastes both sour and sweet. And cheese cubes with the thorns pre-shucked! I pop three in my mouth and chew, savoring how smooth and creamy they are, nothing like the gritty ones So-novan sometimes brought home from the market when they were in season.

Laisze's dressed as a cow, a beast that produces milk. Ma-lika is a snake. Kaieda is a tree with leaves made from copper foil. She makes a beautiful noise when she rustles. Sandris is some sort of eight-legged sea creature that everyone agrees must be mythological in nature.

Laisze moos at me. I raise a brow. "It's what the cows said," she explains.

"Ah," I say with a nod. "And what does a fox—"

"Help! My legs are all tangled!" Sandris says. "How can anyone think this thing actually existed?"

Malika doesn't have arms, and Kaieda is all tree limbs, so it's up to Laisze and me to do the untangling. Grumpy and frustrated, Sandris starts complaining about a waif who'd accidentally dumped a pan of bone dust into the hole she'd bored this afternoon, but Laisze cuts her off with a hard stare.

"Talk bad about them any other time. Not tonight," Laisze says.

I catch something odd in Laisze's eyes. That don't-play-by-the-rules look she's always sporting has suddenly vanished. She notices me noticing, and then with that diligence she'd shown me last night as her knife pierced my skin, she's untangling costume legs from one another, then boots Sandris in the ass when she's done. Sandris goes off and grabs the first waif she sees, dressed in a sad excuse for a bird costume. San-dris tries dancing with her, but the waif breaks free. Spurned, but not dejected, she moves on to the next dance partner.

I stretch my neck, looking for signs of Parton, but it's so

crowded, it's impossible to make out much of anything. So many faces obscured by the masks of Earth animals that seem more like fables than part of our history. If I do see her, I'll apologize a thousand times for getting her sent to the doldrums. For some reason, Laisze makes sure all us boneworkers stick close, though, never venturing out of one another's sight. Still, I look. Hopeful.

Laisze extends her hands toward me. "I like this song," she says.

"I'm not much of a dancer," I say, tucking my hands into my armpits.

"That's obviously because you've never danced with someone who knows what they're doing." She smiles, so full of herself.

I laugh. Mothers' mercy, it feels so good to laugh again. "Is that so?" I timidly place my fingertips in her palm. She grabs my hand and yanks, and somehow the world goes spinning, and the next moment, I'm pressed up against her, one of her hands at my back.

"So, what's the deal with you, worm-licker?" Laisze says, as we fall into the beat of the song, a staccato flutter compared with the beat of the beast's heart. "I've worked ligaments, and you're not like any ligaments girl I ever met. Pet heart murmur. Talks funny. Writes Vvanescript. And I've seen the way you tense up every four minutes."

"Three minutes forty-seven and a half seconds," I correct her. The words slip right out of my mouth, and as they echo around in the confines of my mask, I wish so badly I could take them back. But they're out now, and Laisze isn't the type to back down when there's gossip to know. So I lay it out there in front of her. "I worked the heart."

Her eyes go wide, and her hand goes over the mouth hole

on my mask. "Shh, girl, you don't want the others to hear you say that. Well, that's some third-ass shits. I'd guessed gills or liver. Heart? Really?"

"Really."

"Shits . . ." she says, dragging the word out for three seconds. "And this is your first time working bone? That's gotta be a change."

"Yeah, but I've felt more comfortable there than I ever did back home." It feels wrong calling it home anymore, not when I've got our block to go back to tonight. I get weird cramps when I think about last night, pressed up to Laisze, listening to her snore. A loud, ridiculous snore. A real one. I catch myself feeling guilty for these thoughts, like I'm betraying Seske, but Seske's made her choice for her future, and it doesn't involve me. It's time I make my own choices.

"So, if I get you drunk enough tonight," I whisper to Laisze, "is there any chance you'll give me one of those?" I point to the BLOCK 99 scar on her right breast. Maybe I'm pointing at the scar.

"Not too drunk tonight, dear. We'll eat, be merry, and give the waifs a good send-off. Pretty soon we'll need to get out of here before we get swept up in the mix."

"Send-off? Where are they going?"

"Oh, Daidi's bells. You don't know?" She takes my fox mask off and looks me in the eyes. "Expansion is in full swing, Adalla. All those people who have worked to get the beast up and running, what work do you think there is for them to do now?"

"I don't know! There's bound to be maintenance." Truth is, I've never thought much about it. Truth is, too, I don't even remember ever seeing a waif on our last beast.

"We do the maintenance, and there's more than enough of

us for that. The rest of us will get assigned to janitorial or agriculture. The waifs, there's just too many of them to do anyone any good."

"So . . ." My mind swirls. What can she mean? Then: "They *kill* them? Waste their lives, just like that?"

"No waste, Adalla. There's never any waste."

I try to swallow the lump in my throat. It can't be true. But I think about it. Most of the hard work in the heart has been done. No more excavations and reroutings. All the murmurs have been removed, and even if colonies crop up from time to time, everything could be taken care of by our teams of heartworkers. No buckets to haul.

This is why Ama didn't want me to be close to Parton. Not because she was embarrassed of her, but because she knew she was going to die. My head starts twisting this way and that. I have to find Parton. I take a few steps, but Laisze's hand comes down upon my wrist.

"Stay close," she says, but I shake her off. And then I'm lost in the sea of masked faces. I pull them off, one by one, seeing stranger after stranger. I'm heaving and sobbing, and nothing is coming out but garbled screams lost in the music and laughter.

SESKE
Of Given Names and Stolen Lives

Doka and I stand there, jaws dropped, watching the beast-workers put the final touches on the Abaccas' new jewelry store in one of the most prized spots in the central market. The flawless facade gleams, setting it apart from its neighbors, which have been meticulously re-created each beast cycle and bear all the stray marks they've accumulated over the past few centuries. It is too early for fanfare—that will come later—but this is the first time in over two hundred years that a new store has opened its doors. Now, with this unprecedented change of ownership, those gouges in the floor, streaks on the ceiling, and dents in the shelving are being smoothed and polished over. I've never seen bone shine so brightly.

"I can't believe she actually pulled this off," Doka says.

"I can. Sisterkin is relentless," I say. "People would kill for this type of real estate."

Doka nods. "Maybe someone already did."

I won't rule out any means with my sister. What could she have possibly offered to get them to give up their claim to a storefront, not only for themselves but for all their generations to come? A wave of nausea overwhelms me.

"Tonight, we'll do more digging," Doka promises. The back of his hand grazes mine in a small gesture of reassurance.

I can tell he wants to hold it, but we're risking enough being up this early, two patinaed men milling leisurely about without supervision. That boneworker over there carving the Abacca name into the sign, chest bared like she owns the place, is giving us hard looks. She must be new . . . only one scar. I need to be planning tonight's sleuthing with Doka, but I can't take my eyes off her.

"She looks so familiar," I say.

"Who?" Doka asks, distracted. He's probably already trying to figure out how we can get access to the Senate's accountancy ledgers, to see if they have recorded any newfound wealth or money being passed into the hands of the previous owner.

"That boneworker, the one up on the scaffolding. But . . . it can't be." That last part comes out as a whisper. The girl could be Adalla's twin, but she doesn't work bone, let alone wouldn't be so bold as to have her breasts on display like that. And that hair!

"Beastworkers all look alike," Doka mumbles. "It's nothing. Now, I'm thinking we should sneak into the Senate house tonight, check the roster for new names . . ."

Usually, I'm the one with the foot in my mouth, but now his words bite at me, so easily dismissing one of my lost relationships. I've told him about Adalla. I've told him almost every secret I have. He knows how I feel about beastworkers. I glare at him, hard. He's two minutes into his plan before he looks up at me, notices.

"What's wrong?" he asks.

"What did you mean by that? 'Beastworkers all look alike.'"

"Huh? Nothing! I didn't mean it like that. It's just that they've got their world, we've got ours."

I wince. His patina starts to go uneven, rivulets of sweat trying to break through the golden barrier. I thought he was different. And yet in a moment of distraction, he talks just like every other Contour class snob, showing his true—albeit patina-covered—colors. He hasn't repulsed me this much since we first met.

"I need to get back home before my parents notice I'm gone," I say flatly. "And I can't sleuth with you tonight. My bapa is already starting to get suspicious. I'll send word when he starts letting his guard down again." I turn and leave. Doka runs after me.

"Wait! Men out all alone . . . we'd draw too much attention."

I curse my stupid disguise. I can't even storm off like I want to. I wait for Doka to catch up and then move as briskly as possible. The walk is awkward and excruciating, him trying to play nice, him listing all the names of the beastworkers who tend his estate, the parties his family has thrown for them, the tips he gives them. He won't stop. He thinks he's helping, but the more he says, the more I see how he views them. Yes, he's kind—kinder than most. He thinks beastworkers should have decent working conditions, and he murmurs of small-talk social justice, but he'll never see them as equals. He'll never see them as people.

Finally, finally, we part ways, and I'm climbing back up through my window. I take my time, careful not to disturb the rest of the household's sleep. I ball my clothes up and stuff them into a drawer, wipe down with soap and a wet towel, just to get all traces of the patina off me, and then I slip into my night clothes.

As a precaution, there's the dummy made from puppet gel, mimicking my breath under the covers. A few braided sprigs of dried moss sticking from the top of the blanket will pass for hair in the night if anyone happens to check in on me. The dummy doesn't look like much in the light, but she's lifelike enough to fool bleary-eyed parents. Her body wiggles and jiggles as I disassemble her into parts, creepy eyes just staring at me. Maybe I'd done too good of a job on her face. I hide the parts behind my pile of ancestor dolls that maybe I should be too old to play with, but they're collectibles, or so I tell myself. Then I put the moss back into a vase. I'm about to hop into bed, when a soft knock comes at my door. I freeze, then pretend I'm snoring.

A harder knock. "Seske . . ."

It's Sisterkin. My heart jumps into my throat.

As I pad over to the door, I'm wondering if I should spill the news that I know about her plan, or if I should hold on to it so I can put it to best use. If I expose her now, she might be able to change course and come up with something even more sinister. No, I'll wait until I know exactly how deep her treachery goes.

"Seske, Matris needs you. Now," she says through the door.

"What is it? More wedding planning? Can't it wait until a decent hour?"

"No, it's something else completely. Please, there isn't much time," she whispers through the crack of the door. "Matris is sick."

❖

EVEN IN HER WEAKENED STATE, MATRIS IS STATELY, LAYERS OF all her gowns flowing over the sides of her bed. She looks miserable, bothered, and irritated—in other words, her normal self, except that she's lying down instead of towering over me.

I can't help but notice the bloodied kerchief she's clutching.

"Matris," I say. "How long have you been ill?"

Our visits have been short and infrequent lately, now that I think about it. I'd been avoiding her since the coming out party, hoping to stretch out my courtship with Doka as long as possible, and after our engagement, I'd been avoiding her because I wasn't ready to deal with all the wedding planning. But now I'm wondering if it was Matris who'd been avoiding me.

"It's nothing, child. Just a bit of fever. It'll soon pass."

"Favor from the ancestors," Sisterkin says somberly.

"Favor," I say in response, trying to ignore the fire Sisterkin has put in my heart. I don't dare look at her again. They haven't been colored in yet, but she's got black outlines for naxshi on her forehead and cheeks, clunky bold patterns of a celestial line that doesn't run very deep, nothing like the intricate patterns that Matris and I wear. But the Abaccas' shallow line is infinitely more powerful than no line at all. This power has me rehashing Sisterkin's betrayal, instead of worrying over my dear, sick mother, so I force my attention back. "Do you need my help, Matris? What can I do? More pillows?"

"Bid the ancestors for me, for long life and health," she says, slipping her offering into my hand. Seven cowrie shells, but they're pale and brittle and oddly shaped, nothing like the black and blue spotted ones we harvest from the rivers. It takes a moment for me to realize why.

"These are from . . . *Earth*?"

Matris nods, then coughs into her kerchief.

I've never held anything from Earth before. I get dizzy,

ESCAPING EXODUS / 165

worrying about breathing on them too hard. My mind can't even fathom how valuable these are. Then the fire in my blood goes cold. An offering of this magnitude means Matris must be sicker than she's letting on.

"You'll also tend to my duties tonight. A short speech at the Hundredth Night Masquerade. It's trivial and won't take long."

"Yes, Matris. I will do what I can to lessen your burdens so that you can heal rapidly. I will serve in your stead." Inside, though, I know I'm nowhere near ready for this. What do I do? What do I say? And if someone asks where Matris is, what then?

"A fine daughter I have in you. Sisterkin will . . ." Matris blinks. "I've misspoken. *Khasina* will accompany you and guide you through it. You can depend on her if you have any questions."

So my sister has secured a given name in addition to her new line. How she beams at finally having one. Doka had assured me that the Abaccas' favors with the ancestors were few, they had no connections to the Senate, and the only one in their line of any significance is a chief auditor. A line like that wouldn't have the pull to challenge for the throne, but somehow, Doka's assurances had failed to put me at ease. Because *she* seems to think it's enough.

"We'll head to the spirit wall for prayer. We'll pray hard for you, Matris." She lays her hand upon my mother's, but I can tell the kinship between them was never built upon names. Theirs goes deeper than I can ever understand.

"You will make your mothers proud," Matris says with a nod, then a cough. The red stain spreads, and there's not much untouched kerchief left.

We take our exit then, urgency nipping at our heels. We greet the guards at the entrance to the spirit chamber, then stop to cleanse our hands in the vestibule. The hoglet looks at me, begging for food. "Sorry, girl," I whisper to her, and give her a soft tap on the head. "Not today."

Finally, we stand before the wall where our ancestors have been entombed for centuries. The mothers of the past all stare back at us, bodies held tight in the formation. Their flesh, their bone, that's all been eaten away, but their faces are clear as day, set in the calcified remains. The detail is remarkable on the mothers from the past century, after advances in the embalming process were made. This one's even got age lines in the corners of her eyes. She's smiling. So lifelike, it's as if she's about to tell a joke, except for the ghastly white of her entire body, a dead giveaway.

Sisterkin lights the candles. *Khasina,* I remind myself. I won't be so petty as to ignore her newly given name, though I wouldn't in the least mind ignoring her altogether. We're now supposed to pretend that this is how it's always been, that she was born a daughter of mothers of the Abacca line and not a stain upon our family.

The candles' spicy scent relaxes me, making it easier to commune with the mothers. Khasina starts chanting, and I follow along. I get into a rhythm, my eyes flutter, and the mothers sway in front of me. It's hard to keep focus. I look over at Khasina, a few paces away, caught in a meditative state. I've never been able to focus this deeply before.

"Seske," the mothers whisper to me.

"What? What is it, Mothers?"

I watch their mouths. Their lips are not moving, but still they speak. "Seske, come closer."

"Will you cure Matris? She calls upon your grace. She is too ill to be here at the wall, but Khasina and I, we pray in her stead." I place the cowries into the wall, carefully, so the sticky substance doesn't get on my fingertips.

Something catches my attention out of the corner of my eye. My head swivels, heavy, disjointed. I look, but Khasina is no longer there. I lose my balance, and then I'm falling. Falling toward the wall. My cheek hits with a dull smack. I sink into it, held tight by the spirit wall's sticky grip. I try to pry myself off, but I only end up lodged farther in.

"Khasina! Khasina! Please help," I call, but there's no answer. The digestive mites work their way toward me, ready to inject me with their embalming juices. I struggle, and they skitter away—I'm livelier than the flesh they're used to dealing with. "Guards!" I yell at the top of my lungs. They should be able to hear me. I call again and again until my voice is raw and hoarse. The more I struggle, the deeper I get. Hours pass, the candles extinguish, and soon, my senses return. Their hallucinatory properties are well-known, but that batch must have been made doubly potent. The mites have grown used to my yelling and moving already, and I can feel them at my feet, my fingertips; tiny pinpricks injecting their venoms. I need to find a way to free myself. I can't believe Khasina would just leave me like this . . . well, actually, I can.

A daughter of the Abacca line might have no claim to the throne, but with me out of the way, that would leave my parents free to adopt. Rule of Tens . . . nine parents, and one child to share between them. They couldn't adopt a nameless Sisterkin. That would be out of line.

Khasina, though . . .

She'd knocked at the doors of every matriline that had yet to conceive a child or had lost one through death or marriage, until she'd found one desperate enough to soil its name for favors. I feel foolish for underestimating the depths of my sister's tenacity. The thought of losing my line is more upsetting than losing my life, because if I go, I will be erased. It will be as if I never existed. Not even a failure—a never-was.

I quiet my mind and think. The guards are gone. Bribed, likely. No one else has come to pray. They must have closed the chambers off. That means there's no one coming to my rescue, and I'll have to do this all on my—

Wait. I have just enough wiggle room to reach the pocket in my raiment. I hold a tiny piece of jerky meat between my fingertips. "Who's a good girl?" I yell into the room. My voice echoes, but I listen. I can hear the hoglets rustling against their tethers. "I've got a treat for you!" More rustling and straining, and with no guards there to wrangle them back, maybe I'll have a chance to get free if I can rile the hoglets up enough.

"Treats! Come and get it!" And then I whistle, and they squeal like someone's torturing them. Then I hear one splash into the basin and then thump on the floor. One is coming. Then another. Bodies flip-flopping toward me, stumpy little clawed fins propelling them sluggishly across the floor, eyes wide on my little morsel. It's perhaps the slowest rescue there ever was, but they're coming, and finally three of them are climbing up the wall. They fight over the morsel, and when that's done, they take to their second favorite treat: licking the spirit wall. Their saliva neutralizes the tacky grit surrounding me, and I wiggle and twist, until finally, with one last turn, I peel away from the wall, and my feet settle back on the floor. My toes and fingertips burn, but the damage isn't too extensive, which is bad news for Khasina.

I wrestle the hoglets back into their tethers so the wall isn't completely destroyed, and go to create some destruction of my own.

THE HUNDREDTH NIGHT MASQUERADE SHOULD BE WELL UN-der way by now. Everyone will be wearing a mask, which I'll use to my advantage. I steal some pond fronds for feathers. A broken shell for a beak. I'm a sad, sad-looking bird, but no one will recognize me.

I make my way to the party and get sucked into the crowd. I keep an eye on the stage, pushing closer and closer to it, so that when Khasina appears, I'll be close enough to confront her, here, in front of everyone.

A waif grabs me, dressed in tentacles of some mythological sea beast. She tries to get me to dance, but I keep my focus on where it should be. And then I see someone, standing there—a reddish-brown creature, pointy snout and ears, bushy tail. I get closer, peer through the mask. Her eyes, yes, they are Adalla's. I can almost feel the ancestors smiling down upon me, to grant me a chance at fate such as this!

I'm struck still, and all the world fades away. It's as if my mother isn't terribly, terribly sick. It's as if my sister hadn't probably most likely left me for dead. As if we aren't a bunch of parasites, murdering beast after beast.

It's just a lovely night, a simple, pleasurable moment that can be measured by the beat of a song.

"I made a mistake," I say to her. "I should have chosen you. Given the throne away. I've done nothing to deserve it anyway. I've done nothing to deserve you."

"Seske?" comes a muffled voice from beneath the mask. Yet it is not Adalla's voice, but something harsh and scratchy.

She takes off her mask. I nearly faint. It is not Adalla, but this girl . . . she looks so much like her, they could be sisters. The very same sister Adalla and I had gone exploring the second ass for. "You must be Seske, the one I've heard so much about."

"You've talked to Adalla?" I ask. "Have you seen her lately? Is she—"

There's a scream not far from us, a waif gone mad—no, looks like a boneworker, judging by her hair. She's ripping masks off everyone's face. I tug Adalla's sister away toward safety. Accountancy guards show up a moment later to resolve the situation, and after a brief altercation, the woman is dragged off, kicking and screaming. For a moment, I think—

No, it can't be her. Just my mind playing cruel tricks on me.

"I haven't seen her in a while," Adalla's sister says once things are calm again, "but I suggested that she invite you here, and since you're here, I'm sure she's around here somewhere."

"She didn't invite me," I tell her. "I've come to give a speech. Up there." I point to the raised podium on the stage twenty feet above us. Khasina has just now arrived, dressed in splendid gowns, not the humble ones she'd worn to the spirit wall. Her naxshi are completed and now gleam. The orange and silver paint are in the same pattern as the naxshi of the woman in an auditor's uniform standing by her side. Must be Chief Auditor Abacca.

I walk three steps toward them, but then servers are shoving glasses of ale into everyone's hands. One falls into mine. I look back at the girl who could be Adalla's sister. My mind wants to tell me something . . . it's so close, I can hear the whispers, but I can't make out the words. Something here is not right.

The music cuts out. "Dearest workers," Khasina says from her perch upon the stage. "It is with great honor that I stand before you today to celebrate your hard work with a congratulatory toast. I am here carrying out the will of our Matris. She wishes to be here more than anything to celebrate your dedication. In just under eight months, you've helped to turn this hunk of space beast into a living, thriving city . . . a feat that could not have been done without you. So, it is with great honor that I, Khasina Kaleigh, true daughter of mothers, salute your service." She raises her glass. "Let us drink to you!"

My drink slips from my hand and spills at my feet. Kaleigh! That's my line!

Kaleigh, Abacca, Khasina, Sisterkin . . . suddenly the girl with no name has too many. She sees me. I run up to the stage. Adalla's sister gives me a boost, and I climb. Soon I'm standing eye to eye with my sister. "Khasina, true daughter of mothers of the Kaleigh line? How can that be when I stand here before you? Surely you have misspoken."

"I . . . you must have misheard me. I said 'Khasina Abacca.' Didn't I?" She turns to the auditor chief, who nods like any good lackey would. But Khasina's naxshi go pale.

"You look like you've seen a ghost," I shout at her. "Well, me, I've seen several, and you know how our ancestors feel about those who step out of line. The Senate will hear about this violation. There's no weaseling your way out of it this time. I've got thousands of witnesses." I gesture at the crowd.

The girl with too many names laughs at me, then pulls me in close. "All of your witnesses will be dead within the hour."

"What?"

"They're grisettes, Seske."

"What's a grisette?"

"Really—and *you* think you're worthy to guide our people?" Khasina shakes her head in contempt. "They're temporary beastworkers. Matris really has protected you, hasn't she? She knows you can't handle the truths about how our society functions, that this mind of yours is too shallow for such big ideas. But you go ahead and tell her. She wants this adoption to happen as much as I want it to. As much as our people *need* it to."

The cries start coming then. Below, by the dozen, people are falling to the floor. "What was in that ale?" I demand.

"Cell destabilizing agents. Don't worry. It will be painless. They'll turn into pools of dense fertilizer for the plants. This year's harvest will be beyond exception."

"This is barbaric!" I say. I have to do something, but the workers are falling so fast. So quietly. I pray to the spirits of the mothers to intervene, to give me strength. Neither of those things happens, and I'm groveling at my sister's feet, begging her to undo it.

"It cannot be undone," she says with disdain. "And even if it could be, we have no room, no resources for them. No work for them to do. It's unsustainable."

"It's murder. I'm telling Matris!" I say, feeling like a helpless child.

"She's the one who sent us here, Seske. She would have been here herself if she could. I know this is a lot, but this doesn't even scratch the surface of the fortitude it takes to keep our beast up and running, to keep our people safe. This is the way it is. This is the way it's always been."

Then she walks off, even as the hundreds and hundreds of waifs behind her dissolve into nothingness. Just as Sisterkin had expected me to hours earlier.

And with the same amount of remorse.

part III

extinction

When our first foremothers saw the signs of extinction, they did not bemoan the end of their world. Worlds end, again and again. Extinction is a time for celebration, for what is lost makes room for what is to be found.

—Matris Tayg,
670 years after exodus

ADALLA
Of Strange Fruit and Familiar Signs

This is the way it's always been," Laisze says, rubbing a cool cloth over my swollen eye. The cut still stings, but her touch takes most of the tenderness away. "What you did was foolish. You put us all at risk."

"I know, I just thought . . ."

"Don't think. The truth is hard. Life is hard, but we've got what we've got. If you want to help, keep your mind on bone-worker issues. We've got plenty of our own."

The lash counter in our section of the field scowls at us. We've been talking too long, which means the fruits aren't being harvested, which means I'm setting myself up for yet another beating. I can't believe Laisze and the others just accept it. All those lives, lost for what? So the Contour class can move into their homes sooner and without dealing with any inconvenience?

I guess I'd been sheltered from it all as a child, but life comes at you fast once you're grown. One minute, you're a prodigy in the most prestigious organ on the beast, and the next, you're knee-high in a boggy fruit patch, swatting away flies and picking ticks off your calves. But I'd take those little annoyances any day over that other thing that's pestering me. *Haunting* me would be a better word. I glance over my shoulder. She's not there now, but I've seen Parton's ghost, standing not twenty feet away from me. The guilt overwhelms me. I chase it away in the evenings, guzzling my meager wages down with watered-down mead. It helps ease the guilt. Some. But never for long.

I twist the next fruit head, shuck the outer shell, then toss it into my bag with the others. On to the next. My hands are stained deep purple with the fruit's thick juices, which makes it impossible not to think of the lives of those sacrificed and turned into produce. I can't help but think of how many of Ama's eight embryos had suffered the same fate. How many of my sisters had died at Matris's hand? How many of them are left, not yet born? No wonder this ship is haunted.

I slash the next fruit, but I notice it has a weird growth. It breaks open in my hands, and among the shiny black seeds sit four white ones . . . underdeveloped, I think at first, but they're squarish. I look closer and realize that they're teeth. Human teeth.

I scream, drop the fruit. Laisze comes running, and she looks down, sees it too. And it's not like the other times I've nearly fainted on the field, not like the first time I saw Parton's ghost. Laisze had tried to calm me down, telling me there was no such thing and I had nothing to be afraid of.

Tell that to me now.

"It's a sign from Parton. I can't just sit by and let her—"

"She's already gone, 'Dalla. Already gone. It's just teeth. It happens sometimes. Not everything gets rendered down properly. Usually toward the end of expansion, when extinction is about to start up, but it's much too early for that."

I try not to think about it, the cycle that keeps our people alive. One day, you're eating crops; the next, your body is nourishing them. And there had been so, so many bodies at the masquerade. And then I'm crying like a baby, and Laisze clutches me closer, and my tears are running all down her chest, and I feel weak. Useless.

The lash counter comes over, pokes her baton between Laisze and me and wedges us apart. Then she takes a look at the fruit and gives a terse laugh at the teeth tucked inside. She smashes it with the baton, then pokes me in the ribs. The slick juices run down over my hip, and I think . . . I think I feel one of the teeth sliding down too, but I don't look because I couldn't take it. That could be Parton's tooth. Parton's tooth that's so funny to the nasty lash counter, who thinks lives are tallies. My fists ball, and Laisze notices, grabbing my hands and forcing hers into mine to keep them occupied.

"Come on, 'Dalla. We've got a lot of crop to harvest," she says, before I can make this situation worse.

I need to do something to avenge Parton's death, to make things right. But breaking one lash counter's jaw wouldn't solve anything—can't do much if I'm hanging by my thumbs. I need a bigger plan.

That night, after I think we've both had enough time to sober up some, I make the climb down from my bunk to Laisze's. She's fast asleep, snoring. Real snores. I slip under her thin blanket, drawing comfort in her warmth. Her bed is large, one of the largest, and only three stories up from the ground. Which is good when you've binged on mead all evening. Not so good when you want to keep secrets secret. The lash counters watch. They listen. But I can't make myself care.

I jiggle Laisze's side until she wakes. Glassy red eyes pry open, first one, then the other.

"'Dalla in my bed? I must still be dreaming," she says with a sloppy smile. She reaches for me, pulls me closer, but I am not here for that.

"Laisze, I can't. I can't just forget. Parton was my friend. She was my sister." I say this word too loud, and I feel the tension cleave through the air. Loud enough to raise lash counters' hackles for sure.

"Shh . . ." Laisze tries to calm me, but I won't be calmed.

I inch closer, until my lips are all but upon Laisze's ear. "All throughout our history, we sing of two kinds of women . . . those born into power and those who disrupt power. I intend on being the latter."

I feel her body tense. She throws the covers over our heads and says, "Moan."

"What?" I ask. I'm still a little dizzy, still a little drunk.

"Moan. To help cover my words."

I nod, finally getting it. I take a moment to gather myself, then let out a smooth, throaty purr.

"You're just one person," Laisze whispers beneath the sound. "One boneworker picking fruit. What power do you have?"

"We're two, if you'll join me," I say, and she moans now, to give any eavesdroppers a sense that we're simply finding pleasures in each other's bodies and not plotting to bring this system to its knees. "Together we double our chances. Hands like ours have touched every single inch of this beast. We built this infrastructure. We know its strengths and its weak points."

"Daidi's bells, those guards must have beaten the sense out of you, 'Dalla. It sounds an awful lot like you're planning a revolution," she says, and I moan, a roar of satisfaction. These are words that must not be heard. "Like *we're* planning one," she says with a smile.

"Settle down, you two," comes the voice of the bone-worker in the bunk above.

And so begin our plans, now pressed up together in my little hovel of a bed, covers drawn, whispers passing between us like those of doting lovers. Still, even though we've moved up here, whispering is not enough when so many ears are about.

I think of Parton and her language of signs. And when I teach them to Laisze, I am still consumed by anger, but it's not the sort of anger that is resentful for the past, but the kind that fuels hope for our future. We are pressed together so close that our signs become more like caresses.

Difficult concepts that cannot be summed up in a touch of a thumb to the inner arm or a brush of knuckles against a collarbone are scarred upon my skin: diagrams of buildings, tactics, weak spots, hidden among illustrations of my past.

And then next thing I know, Laisze's telling me the location of a secret meeting spot, her mouth hot upon mine, her tongue twisting, twirling in my mouth—each turn and counterturn a set of directions on where we are to meet. A neat shortcut, one I didn't know about. She pulls back, licking her moist lips. "Good?" *Do I understand,* she means.

I nod, picturing the exact spot in my head. "Yes," I whisper, and then I trace more of our signs upon her skin.

But just in case, once again . . . and take me the long way around this time.

Somehow, I manage to grin without salivating all over myself.

Her eyes alight, and she takes me on a journey, through dark corridors, around corners, under passageways—so deeply, so thoroughly, that I feel I'll never get lost upon this beast again.

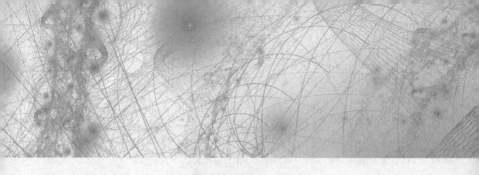

SESKE
Of Questionable Crimes and Undisputed Punishment

Matris denies everything . . . well, not *everything*. The mass murder, she'd sanctioned. Only she won't admit it's murder. She claimed the grisettes are not even real people. Artificially birthed and grown in vats. "They've barely got brains" were her exact words, but hadn't I stood there and talked to the girl who had to be Adalla's sister? Same bright stars in her eyes, despite everything she'd been through?

I've never hated anyone so hard as I hate my mother right now. She won't budge on the matter, and she refuses to allow me to speak otherwise. But on the issue of Khasina's attempted coup, Matris insists it was all an unfortunate misunderstanding. Khasina would never do such a thing, and for me to think otherwise is an insult to the throne. My sister had felt sick at the spirit wall, that's all, overcome by the potency of the fragrant candles. The guards had escorted her home, just to be safe.

Convenient.

I poked holes in their lies, but they kept digging deeper ones beneath me—that I'd misheard Khasina or that she'd simply misspoken. That clearly, I'd been too distraught from my misfortunate event to process my thoughts correctly. So I left my mother and sister before I found it impossible to climb my way back out of their pit of deception. My allies are few, and those with the power to help me are even fewer, and those I'm on good terms with . . .

Well, I go to Doka's house anyway. I know we don't always see eye to eye, but he has a good heart, and he'll help me figure this out before my sister tries to kill me again.

"Seske!" Doka's will-mother and -father greet me at the door, pulling me in for a tight embrace. The commotion draws out Doka's other parents, and before I know it, I'm surrounded, greeting each and answering questions about what I've been up to lately.

"Oh, you know, just wedding planning mostly," I say, a huge smile plastered across my face. The muscles in my cheeks feel like they're going to snap from the tension, but I can't go raving about coups in their company. Not yet, at least. With three Senators in this room, it's best I play to their good sides, build trust, and then when it's time to strike, I'll have them in my corner.

"Doka's in his room hosting his little patina party," his will-mother says, the youngest of Doka's mothers, and definitely the most talkative at the dinners I've attended.

"Fussi!" his will-father says, pinching his wife in the side. "You know full well it's a proper social club."

"Aiee, again . . ." She turns and whispers to me. "You give

them a little leash, and this is what you get. Mind our sweet Doka, yes? Keep him in place? He's got his father's fancies, I'm afraid!" She nudges me, and her husband just shakes his head.

"I'll go get him," he says.

"And fetch his honor attendant too!" Fussi hollers after him.

"Your feet work just as well as mine do," he mumbles.

"What, dear?" Fussi asks, even though it's clear from her exasperated smirk that she's heard him.

"Nothing, dear! I'll call her right down!"

While he's gone, the other parents fawn over the gift I'd presented them when I'd officially proposed, a detailed replica of the relief of the twelve mothers who were the first of their line. Both Doka's and my ancestors were among them. *Isn't it amazing?* his parents say, their voices all a blur in my head, sounding distant like they're miles away. *There are three slivers of real actual wood from the original mixed in with the beast bone. Pine, I think it was called. Is it pine? We'll have to ask your mothers.* I just nod and smile. Like I can still see beauty in the things created by the same people who pressed this unjust system upon us.

Finally, Doka's here, and his eyes light up when he sees me, and I want to go to him, to tell him everything, but we maintain a respectable distance, not willing to defy Doka's parents like we do with his honor attendant.

"Seske, it's good to see you." He looks around at his parents, then back at me. "Did we have a study session I forgot about?"

"Doka's always got his nose in a book, doesn't he?" Fussi says. I can feel her grin on the back of my neck, along with those of Doka's other parents. I can feel their stares too. It's all eyes and teeth in here.

"Nothing planned. I was just hoping to schedule one soon. So . . . um, you remember what we were talking about the other day? About names?"

"Baby names?" a mother, not Fussi, says.

"Hush, dear!" says Doka's head-father. "They're not even ready to think about extending their line!"

"No, no. Not baby names," I say, assuring them with a quick shake of my head.

Doka steps around me and addresses his parents. "You know I love each and every one of you, but please . . . can't we have a semblance of privacy?"

"Two minutes," Doka's head-mother says, one of the Senators. "And your hands stay in your pockets at all times."

I breathe a sigh of relief, shove my hands deep into the pockets buried under the layers of my silk skirts, and follow Doka a few steps down the hall.

"What's wrong?" he whispers to me. "Is it Khasina?"

I nod. "We were right. She tried to kill me. And I'm sure she's going to try again."

"Okay, this is serious," he says, hands also in his pockets. He thinks for a long moment. "What if we move up the wedding? We could get our house in order and our lines strengthened. Khasina might be desperate, but no way would she risk riling a family with Senators three-deep."

"I don't know, Doka . . ." My brain is already wrecked. I can't handle anything else right now.

"Seske, it's going to be okay. We'll figure out how to protect you." He bites his lip, then leans forward so that our foreheads nearly touch. "Remember I told you about that time I snuck into the Senate? That wasn't my biggest secret . . ."

"It's that you smoke cigars?" I say. "It's fine. I think it's charming."

"No, what? I . . ." He shakes his head, probably wondering how I knew that. "I mean, yes, I do. But what I mean to say is I've got some friends visiting. Male friends. We meet once a week to discuss all kinds of things, but we often talk about how we can get men into positions of power."

"Wow. Okay." It takes me a moment to process this, but the way he's looking at me spurs me toward a more articulate response. "Yeah, I think that's great. Well, when I'm Matris, we can definitely make that a part of my platform."

"That's decades from now, Seske. We're seeking action *now*."

"To promote men's issues?" I say, wanting to understand.

"To promote the betterment of us all. To help set up rules that protect *everyone,* men and women, and those who don't fit neatly into these narrow roles we've defined. To protect the Contour class, beastworkers . . . the Accountancy Guard . . ." His voice trails off.

But I'm rapt. He's really thought about these things. I haven't the nerve to entertain hope right now, but maybe one day, with him behind me, I could find it and do some good with it.

"And there's one more secret . . ." Doka grimaces. He whistles, and a door down the hallway opens.

He's not dressed in his uniform, so it takes me a moment to realize who it is, but when I do, I feel like I've taken a kick to the chest.

Wheytt. Now it all makes sense. "You planted him at the coming out ceremony to talk you up so I'd choose you as my suitor," I rasp. Meanest rasp there ever was.

"No!" Doka whispers with fierce urgency. "He didn't join the group until after that. I approached him, and he said no the first few times, but I persisted. So if you're going to be mad at anyone, it should be me."

"Oh, I've got enough anger inside to spread between the

both of you," I say, trying to figure out what this emotion is that I'm feeling. Jealousy? Resentment? Distrust? "Why didn't you tell me?"

"We knew it wouldn't look good if you found out," Doka says. "But I could tell Wheytt needed the camaraderie. Being the only male in the Accountancy Guard was taking its toll. The stories he's told us haven't been pretty. A lot of harassment and crude jokes. We gave him the support he needed, and now he's being considered for a promotion."

"I've had enough lies thrown at me today. I don't need any more," I say.

"He's telling the truth," Wheytt says. He's bad at lying, and none of his usual tells are showing right now. "About everything. I've navigated the system, and now I want to help others. We've even got a guy we want to try to put in the Senate next session."

"Okay. But how are you going to do that without a matriline?" I ask. "It's written into the Senate's mandates. *You* taught me that," I say, my words striking at Doka.

"He has one. We've found a loophole."

"How?"

"He was born with a matriline."

"Born a girl . . ." *Halli the Mangler* is the first thing that comes to mind, born a girl, but her parents hadn't braided her hair before her first tooth came in, and the old spirit turned their daughter into a son. But then I think of my ama and how she'd changed herself to become a part of our family. A man wanting to become a woman, and all the privileges that came with that honor . . . that made sense. *This* definitely doesn't. "You mean she was cut and drawn? But in reverse?"

"*He* was. And yes. Something like that."

"But why would anybody want to—" I clap my hand over

my mouth, realizing what's about to come out. Worse than calling Doka "well-spoken" for sure.

"I think our two minutes are just about up," Doka says. "Supper's nearly ready anyway."

"Wait!" I say. He's trusted me enough to share this big secret of his with me, and I've managed to insult him in return. "Please wait. Give me another chance. I've got something to tell you too. Something that could help us gain some leverage over Matris and my sister."

I open my mouth to tell them all about the baby beast, but I can't figure out where to start, and even if I could, it wouldn't do her justice. "You have to see for yourselves . . . meet me at the second ass tonight."

I PACE BACK AND FORTH THROUGH ANKLE-DEEP SLUDGE, CAN-dle lit for peace of mind. Too bad it's not working. If this place wasn't haunted before, it definitely is now. The village where the grisettes had once lived now lies empty. Doka and Wheytt are running late. Curiosity gets the best of me, and I venture deeper into the village with all the respect I show when visiting the spirit wall. I need to feel this emptiness. This wrongness. It needs to latch on to my soul, so I can convince the Senate that we need to reevaluate our culture and traditions. I need them to see that our ancestors so long ago had destroyed one world, and here in space, we've only gotten better and better at that destruction.

I see a broken piece of pottery lying in the sludge. I scoop it up, run my fingers along the smooth inside, then the carved outside. I imagine the meals it had held. The water it had hauled. Maybe even the flowers it had displayed. Was there even beauty like that down here? A million other questions run through my mind, but I will find no answers. Whoever had used it is now long gone.

In the quiet, the unclenching of the sphincter is incredibly loud. I run over and help Wheytt through. He lands ungracefully in the sludge. Gets up, dusts himself off like it's no big deal. I look out into the dark of the first ass, but there's no one else.

"Doka got caught by his honor attendant," Wheytt says, looking down at the carpet of critters crawling up his boots. "I'm really sorry, Seske, about not telling you."

"It's fine. We're just friends. *Barely* friends. You don't owe me an explanation."

Wheytt's brow crumples. "What did you have to show us?"

I ignore the hurt on Wheytt's face, and the inkling of remorse in the pit of my stomach, and lead him through the tuck in the wall, all the way to the womb. It's quiet, but the stench overwhelms me immediately. The scar is no longer solid. It looks infected, white pus oozing. It's so deep, so awful, I almost turn away, but then the womb wall goes transparent and I see the baby beast inside. There isn't much room for her to swim around. She just floats listlessly, staring at me.

"Whoa . . ." Wheytt says, jaw dropped. "Is this what I think it is?"

"She's what you think she is, yes." I press my hand against the womb, and the baby beast does the same with one of her tentacles. She seems to perk up. "We need to visit with her," I tell Wheytt. "Maybe your heightened senses can catch something I've missed."

"Visit?" he asks, but before I get to explain, the membrane thins, and I'm passing through it, suddenly surrounded by liquid. I reach my hand back toward Wheytt, and he timidly takes it.

The baby beast looms in front of us, its many tentacles waving, glad to see me and very curious about this new friend I've brought. She's slow and gentle with him, offering tendrils one by one. Wheytt looks over and sees I'm already covered with them, sees them snaking inside me. I think this scares him more than reassures him that it's safe, but as soon as the first tendril makes its way up his nostril, I feel something different from what I've felt with the baby beast alone.

I feel what Wheytt feels. I see his thoughts, taste the cool liquid in his mouth.

I'm behind his eyes, seeing what he's seeing, which is me looking at him. It's weird. It's exhilarating. Then I'm falling into his mind, like a trapdoor has opened beneath me. I tumble and tumble, deeper and deeper. I find the memory of us dancing together. His senses are so much more acute, and as I relive this shared memory, I find his experience was completely different from my own, even though we'd been only inches apart. His eyes are fiercely focused on my suitors, picking up little clues about each of them, all to make them less of strangers to me. But then I catch whispers of the very thoughts in his head, about how he wished this dance with me would never end.

Patriline Wheytt Housley having those kinds of thoughts about me?

One-two-three-four . . . The dance count becomes louder in my ears as he tries to distract me from his thoughts, or maybe he's trying to distract himself. I feel him flushing as he tugs back against the memory.

But it's too late. We're connected now, and there are no more secrets that can exist between us. I tug at tendrils and his toes twitch and his brain releases endorphins. He goes slack all over. I replay that dance for him, feeling his arousal . . . or maybe feeding it. Tendrils tighten around his biceps, his mouth becomes slick with saliva, pooling into the cool waters that surround him. Each and every pore stands on edge.

And soon I feel him, crawling around in *my* brain. Prying at my thoughts. Wondering what I'm doing to him. His entire body frowns, then he's tugging my tendrils like reins, and I'm yanked back, completely frozen. I feel something slip inside me, like I am an ephemeral hand puppet, and then limbs that don't exist begin to dance. I'm falling into a rhythm, and now we're dancing again. Wheytt throws back his head and laughs. I press back, trying to regain control, but he is so much better at this than I am. Or so he thinks.

I rewind through time and play the instant before he'd saved me from getting crushed by scaffolding, so long ago. Instantly, he's more receptive. I weave the memories together, our kiss, our dance, and bitterness drops away.

Then our world drops away.

It's just him and me, surrounded by nebulas, the cold of space pressed to our skin. Together we stroll between stars on a timescale that feels like minutes, but the drastic shifts in the sky surrounding us suggest otherwise. Below us, a star system with two suns, one grand and one smaller; we dive toward them, feeling the tug of their gravity. And then I see it— a planet! A big, beautiful ball of blues and greens.

The planet draws closer, and the details of mountain ridges and lakes become clearer, offering a picturesque background to our intimacy.

We are careful, taking only what the other offers, knowing that a connection like this is deeper than either of us can fully comprehend. He reads poetry to my spleen. I tell fairy tales to his bile ducts. The inside of his navel is a vast, unexplored desert. He lounges upon the cushion of my lips. His desires rise, and I pretend not to notice, diving right into the pool of tears caught in the corner of his eye. I don't make a single splash. And while I swim laps, he hikes across the boundless expanse of my molars, and then I'm climbing up his chest hairs.

We're curious, playful. Adventuresome. The landscapes of our bodies like the foreign world we orbit. Is this how the beasts communicate with one another? A life without secrets? Becoming intimately familiar with everyone you touch? If I were still that naïve girl whose biggest problems were running from carnivorous plants in the woodward canopies, I'd dare to hope my people could one day experience such openness and honesty, but I am no longer that girl by a long shot.

Our connection severs.

My eyes open. I see the womb all around us, but it's gone completely clear. Completely vulnerable. Outside, I see four technicians holding their contraption right up to the scar. The tip blazes. Wheytt shudders, then screams bloody murder; my world goes white. I convulse. The baby beast convulses. She spits us out of the womb, but we've still got her tendrils up our noses, in our mouths. The baby beast tries to close the black protective web around her, but her tendrils are in the way of a perfect seal.

She retracts them, but not fast enough. Many are caught, cut clean off as the web slams tight this time. I cough them up, nearly spew out my weight in severed tendrils as they pile onto the floor.

The web flickers, then the womb goes transparent again. The baby beast is in distress. For months, she'd been able to resist the worst of the assault, but now the scar has pierced her skin. Our world shakes all around us, worst quake we've ever had. Wheytt realizes what's going on too, and he kicks the lead technician square in the gut. She stumbles backward, then charges at him, a sudden pause as she considers if she should hit a man, but in that moment, my fist comes down on her jaw, and she's knocked out cold. The others, with nowhere near her stature or bravery, back up. Whatever fire they see in my eyes is enough to subdue them.

I breathe in, breathe out. The entire floor is drenched in womb water, the scar is ruptured, and the only heartbeat I feel is my own. I find myself wishing it would stop too.

I pull the remaining cold dead tendrils out of my nostrils, my mouth, and pluck them from the corners of my eyes. I take one last look at the dead baby beast, too stunned to cry.

I think this is the worst thing that's ever happened to me, but then Wheytt points to a rivulet of blood dripping from the wall.

Walls weeping blood. My fathers had tried to shield me from it on our last beast, talking loudly and excitedly to distract me from looking around too much on our way to the stasis pods, but I do remember it clearly.

Extinction has already begun.

ADALLA
Of Secret Sisterhood and Public Apologies

I see another distended fruit, but I ignore it, carefully setting it in my bag so it doesn't split open. Parton's ghost, however, has become more curious, and she works beside me for part of my shift. Something in my mind is broken, that's all. I know better than to try to talk to her—Laisze's already too worried about me—but I acknowledge Parton with a nod of the head and a promise in my heart that her death will be avenged.

Parton smiles, then dissipates as Laisze and Kaieda walk right through her, Malika dragging behind them.

"Kaieda and Malika have agreed to come drinking with us tonight," Laisze says.

I startle, about to tell her that we've got *other* plans, but then I remember *drinking* is our code word for *meeting*. But still. We hadn't agreed upon letting others into our fold just yet.

In the fields, we can't stand close enough to touch or to whisper, so we're left to our voices. We all pick fruit within earshot of one another and certainly within earshot of the lash counters.

"Wonderful," I say, our affirmative that means the opposite. It's not wonderful at all, but with Kaieda and Malika standing so close, I have to use our coded language. "But I thought it'd be just you and me drinking tonight."

Laisze raises a brow. "You said it was okay to invite them. Last night, you were quite enthused."

Last night. I remember the enthusiasm, for sure. Her thumb had slid across the peak of my pelvis bone—our sign for *invite*—and hit me just right, I guess, because a chill ran through me and my humble bits seized up, and my mind wandered as her hands wandered, and I'd lost track of the whole conversation. It seems our ingenious communication scheme has a big flaw.

"Of course," I say, saving face. "I am excited to have them." And I am. Mostly. Glad this rabid idea of mine is taking root in others. But then I imagine Laisze giving them directions to our first meet-up, her tongue swirling in each of their mouths, and waves of jealousy and nausea hit me at the same time. My knees buckle and I stumble backward and land upon a cluster of fruit. Pulpy juice and spiked leaves press into my bare back. I blink a couple times, looking up. Both Laisze and Parton are staring down at me, worry on each of their faces. They both reach down to help me up, but luckily, I choose the hand that won't dematerialize on me.

I look around, and Kaieda and Malika have both moved on, picking fruit farther down their lanes. A lash counter is on her way, brow creased, dark goggles aimed right at me. She sees all the fruit I've ruined. She cusses me and types a note into her ledger. My payment will be short this afternoon. I bite my lip, apologize profusely, and try not to stare at Parton, looking right over her shoulder.

FIVE OF US MEET IN OUR SECRET MEETING SPOT. WELL, FOUR OF us who count ourselves among the living. We don't have long. Curfew is in an hour, and we need to stagger our traveling so we don't draw suspicion. All eyes are on Laisze, waiting for her to command us, but she smiles and pushes me front and center.

"This is your cause, 'Dalla," she whispers into my ear. "You need to own it."

I gulp. Who am I to lead anything? But I must try to channel something within me: Seske's freethinking. My bapa's tenderness. Sonovan's know-it-all-ness. Even my ama's stubbornness. I pull on all those parts of me, which will always be parts of me no matter how hard I try to forget about them.

"This system, the one we've held on to for so long, it's killing us," I say defiantly, readying myself to present my case. "All the bad choices we've made, all the apathy we've cultivated, is coming back to haunt us." I crack open a distended fruit, showing the others the contents. Two finger bones, fused into a curl. "These are the artifacts of our sins. These are the artifacts that we can see. Who knows what else is there, damaging our hearts, our minds." I sneak a glance at Parton. She nods back at me, listening as intently as the others.

"It's true," Kaieda says. "I heard the river has gone rancid. Nearly all the bathers on block sixty got sick."

"Word from the doldrums is that the air's gone bad on block thirty-three and it had to be evacuated," says Malika.

"We've been upon this beast not even a year, but already

the signs of extinction are upon us," I say, thinking about how bad of shape the heart had been in when I'd left. Thinking of the quakes we've had. We were all so busy, working our way through expansion, that no one stopped to compare notes.

"We need to demand answers!" Malika says. "We need to go straight to the top!"

"Matris! We need to hear it from her mouth . . . an account of all that's wrong and what we can do to fix it," Laisze says, clasping my hand in hers. "Dalla, here, will take us there."

"Wait, what?" I say. I thought we'd just complain to the lash counters, get them on our side, maybe have them look into things.

"You've got connections us boneworkers don't have. It's time to use them." At first I think she knows about Seske, but then Laisze pounds her chest, right over her heart. Our little secret, but maybe it's time it comes out.

"Aye," I say. "Maybe they won't listen to boneworkers, but maybe they'll listen to heartworkers."

"Who on Daidi's hairy bells do we know with that kind of clout?" asks Malika.

I clear my throat. "Me," I say. "At least I used to have it."

There's a collective gasp. "You?" They look me over, faces caught in between being disgusted and impressed.

"Yes. And Laisze is right. I can get us through if we don't look like this. If we wear shirts, fix our hair. Look presentable." The tension in the room doubles. I've said the wrong thing.

Boneworkers are proud, if nothing else. I'd just degraded them, even though I hadn't meant it that way. Or maybe I had, and it's my old ways of thinking shining through. "Shits," I say. "I'm sorry. It's not *your* way that's the problem. It's *theirs*. They see your bare breasts, your bone-studded hair, and don't bother to look past it. We shouldn't have to bend our ways to be seen as equals. It is we who must make *them* bend and see that we are one united front."

They nod, and I know we have their support. But we're still missing something. We need a symbol. A name.

I am far from anything resembling an artist, but I scrape Parton's face into the bone column of our meeting place and, under it, write *Sisters of Lost Lines.* Provocative, with the word *Sisters* in there, the mere mention enough to cause questions to our way of life. And *Lost Lines* for all of those forgotten through history, whom I intend to give a voice.

BY THE TIME WE'VE DRAFTED OUR DEMANDS, THERE'S STANDING room only in our little hideout. We've recruited people from the gills and their branchial hearts, from both the front and back bladders, from gall harvesting and musculature. Our web of trust is fragile, but from the testimonies we've vetted over the past few days, people have been feeling this way for a long time. We all want this change and realize what we are risking to get it. If we are successful, we will have a chance at healing our entire civilization. But just like a badly set bone, things will need to be broken before they can begin to heal properly.

"Point one," I read from our list: "The Matriarchy will recognize its complicities in the willful destruction of life."

Everyone nods. They have all witnessed it, either directly or indirectly.

"Point two: All Lost Lives will be documented in the Texts and bestowed proper given names and matrilines to the best of the matriarch's knowledge.

"Point three: Any and all remains discovered will be taken to the spirit wall for proper burial."

We have a case full of pieces and parts already—bones, teeth, fingernails, hair—all carefully plucked from harvested fruits. Plus we've got two allies in processing now who catch what we don't.

"Point four: On the division of labor and the redistribution of wealth . . ."

Eyes perk up. The depressing, but necessary, parts out of the way, we get to the real reason so many people are here supporting the cause. Still, confronting the blatantly unfair class system had taken many discussions. We all agreed it needed to be done away with, but the suggestions on how to best carry that out were as varied as our members. Some wanted baby steps, thinking the Matriarchy would be more open to small changes. Others wanted to bring the whole system down to its knees, scrapping everything and starting from scratch. Me, I wanted the Matriarchy to feel like it was being brought to its knees with a series of manageable and strategically placed steps.

"All citizens, regardless of status, will be assigned to beast-work upon future excavations. Training and lots will be drawn prior to exodus. Citizens who have not as yet participated in said labor shall be taxed upon their assets and inheritances, eighteen thousand chits per beast cycle, accounting for the past seven beast cycles. Half the total received monies will be divided upon citizens who have labored, based on the number of beast cycles they've worked. Half the total received monies will be allotted to development of infrastructure in beastworker territory, to bring it up to the same standards as Contour class accommodations, and services for those unable to perform beastwork."

There are hushed cheers at this.

"We are asking for what we are owed and not a chit more.

This beast belongs to all of us, and we should all have a hand in its growth. No longer will fields be flooded with the blood of the downtrodden."

Laisze wheels a bone sculpture into the center of the room, elbowing her way forward. It is Parton's image, sure is sure is sure, carrying two tablets in her arms, our demands chiseled into each. "Sisters of Lost Lines, may I present our matron."

I've never been so proud of anything, not even my feats as a heartworker. Tonight, right before curfew, we'll deliver the statue to a public area and wait for the Matriarchy to make its move. An apology will come. If not, we've got friends all over who will start making things miserable until our words are taken seriously.

SESKE

Of Lively Puppetry and Deadly Lace

A great cross section of people stands in line, waiting for me to hear their concerns. Farmers with tainted crops. Store owners with flooded shops. Beastworkers with tallies of tumors and fissures and open wounds growing upon our beast.

"Send three more auditors to assess flood damages," I shout at my tactician. "Raise the dams a foot higher in block forty-two!" I shriek at an accountancy chief. "And place all beast surgeons on triage duty until further notice! Extinction is not happening. It can't happen." Papers fall from my desk. Books too. I pat down piles, looking for a pen to sign my latest proclamations.

Wheytt steps up next to me and, without a word, plucks a pen from my hair and lays it into my hand. I take a moment, my eyes meeting his, then I sigh, exasperated. "Please have all available accountancy guards perform resource audits for each block," I say to my tactician. "All quota breakers should be reprimanded and sent to—"

"And what about the demands we received?" Chief Abacca says, elbowing her way through my attendants and aides. She's been like a fly in my ear, but I haven't a swatter big enough to slap her away. Khasina all but shoved her mother onto my staff, and Matris agreed it was a sensible move.

Sensible for *whom* is the question.

"It's been days already," Chief Abacca continues, "and it's imperative that our decision be swift and just. The Sisters of Lost Lines! How despicable!"

"Yes, yes . . ." I say, turning my attention toward the chief, but then my seamstress barges in, demands another gown fitting. With the wedding moved up, everything is happening so fast. There's no time for me to breathe.

I excuse myself from the agitated crowd and step back into the privacy of the throne room. I step behind a partition, but even as I'm being twisted and pinned, I continue to brainstorm ways to avert the impending crisis as layer upon layer of silks are hefted upon me. Water rations. Food rations. Curfews. Favors to the ancestors, it won't have to come to that, but it might.

"I'm going to have to take this in. Again," the seamstress says, annoyed. Then to Wheytt she says, "Please make sure she eats. She's already lost too much weight."

"The sculptor is here," my tactician announces.

Frustration crawls up my throat and lashes out before I can stop it. "I've seen the sculpture already! You showed it to me this morning!"

"Matriling Kaleigh, that filthy thing was created by beast-workers!" my tactician says. "The Sisters of Lost Lines, are you not even trying? How could you even think it was your wedding sculpture?"

"How am I possibly supposed to keep up with all of this?" I scream.

"We can call in Khasina if you're in need of assistance," Chief Abacca offers. She'd like that, wouldn't she?

"No!" I say, feeling my heart strain, muscles tense. Sweat runs down my brow. It's too much. Many of Matris's duties have gone untended during her illness, and people are starting to get suspicious. So she'd pawned a lot of it onto me, under the guise of a proving ground for my fitness as future matriarch. Or perhaps she's trying to prove the opposite, trying to prove how awful I'll be so Sisterkin can swoop in again and take what's rightfully mine. I'm trying to keep it all together, but if I keep going at this rate, my health will suffer.

"Out! Everyone out!" Wheytt says with the same fierceness he had the last time I'd had a panic attack. My audience stops and stares at him.

"You heard him," I cry. "Leave, please. I need a moment." They file out of the throne room, leaving me standing there in my wedding gown. My right sleeve keeps sliding down.

"Sorry. You just look like you'd had enough," Wheytt tells me. I've kept him by my side since the incident with the baby beast. We don't talk about it. I don't even have words to describe what had happened, so I couldn't if I wanted to. But having him close feels right.

"Thank you," I say, slowly gathering papers from the floor and placing them into neat stacks.

"Would you like me to leave too? I'll be right outside if you need me."

"No. Stay. Help me with this. Where do I even start? I can do this. I know I can, but I can't have people yelling at me from all directions."

"Here. This pile. Start at the top and sort everything into

three stacks: urgent, important, urgent *and* important. The rest you can probably just ignore and wait for Matris to tend to once she's back on her feet."

"You're too logical sometimes, Patriline Housley," I say.

"I'll take that as a compliment, Matriling Kaleigh," he teases back. "Your dress is stunning, by the way. But the seamstress is right. You need to eat more."

"I love how everyone loves to tell me what I should be doing. 'Seske, you're too thin.' 'Seske, I can see your ribs.'"

"I didn't mean it like that. You just need fuel for your body, is all I'm saying. You're running on fumes."

"Fine, you want me to eat. I'll eat." I take a big bowl of steak cutlets drenched in red sauce, then lower it. "Let me guess. Now you're going to tell me I shouldn't be eating in my wedding dress. That I'm going to stain it and the wedding will have to be postponed, and then I'll have to deal with Doka's disappointment and my mothers' . . . Uh, sorry, I forgot. He's your friend."

"Yes, but you're my friend too. At least I think of you that way. If you don't want to get married to him, don't."

"Are you kidding? Do you know how much money Matris has already spent on this wedding? How much of our future she has tied up in it? There's no getting out of it. I'll just put up with Doka for the rest of my life. He's not *awful*." I look over the top sheet on my pile. "Flood in block seventeen. Sounds urgent. I'll have the auditors get on that right away." I set the sheet onto the urgent pile. "Two farmers reporting crops wilting in their fields. Seems important, but it can wait a few days." I file that in the important pile. "I think this is working! Next, several demands have been made against the Matriarchy, a new group called the Sisters of Lost Lines. This must be what Chief Abacca was screaming about. Said I need to 'take action.'"

"What kind of action?"

"I don't know. What's the going punishment for putting up awful statues in the middle of the market square? We hire artists to construct the very same thing. Maybe they just saved us some chit." I smile. "Doesn't seem too important or urgent, is all I'm saying. I'll leave it to Matris."

"You're sure? What are their demands?"

I flip the page over, then back. "Doesn't say. See, if it was important, they would have been more specific." I let the paper fall in a newly created fourth stack. Unimportant. Not urgent. It grows faster than all the others. I can tell Wheytt wants to say something to me about it, but my panic has subsided and I'm actually getting stuff done. After a long while, I've got three manageable, actionable piles in front of me. "See, I knew I could do it. All I needed was a little help. And now that I've done some grueling, agonizing work in my gown, I'll be used to it when the wedding rolls around."

I huff and walk out to the balcony overlooking the sprawl of our city. I never get tired of this view—the bone brick facades of thousands of homes and storefronts stretching down and around and above in a grand circle, strands of ley lights running through the center of the beast's belly, carefully placed to mimic the constellations named by our ancestors. No matter where you stand, you can look up and see them—from the classiest Contour neighborhoods to the tallest beastworker tenement blocks.

"If we have minds sharp enough to build all of this, we should be able to figure out a way of life where we're not being so destructive, so wasteful," I say. "Maybe Matris's illness happened for a reason. Maybe it happened so I can convince people that this is not the way, that we need to return to our original plan of finding a habitable planet!"

"Seske!" Wheytt says. "Your words are getting awfully close to being mutinous."

"What about the planet the beast showed us? It's perfect!"

"It was a dream. A hallucination."

"Maybe. But what if it wasn't? What if it was a map? What if this planet is our future?

"Our way is unsustainable. We've got a hundred years left of this way of life, if we're lucky. And now we've been given a way to escape it. All I have to do is convince the fifty thousand people on this ship to give up everything they know and follow me there."

Wheytt nods, but he still doesn't look sure about it. He stares at me. I stare back, projecting as much confidence as I can muster.

"Fifty thousand minus one," Wheytt finally says. "I'll go with you. I don't have a doubt in my mind that you want the best for your people and won't stop until we've achieved that."

There's a knock at the door.

"Should we let them back in?" I ask.

A bigger knock comes, a knock that rumbles the entire city and sends us both to our knees. Wheytt helps me up, and together we look over the balcony to see smoke coming from the central market, a pile of bone rubble where there used to be several storefronts. I look at Wheytt.

"Another beastquake?" I ask him.

He shakes his head. "I would have sensed it coming."

If not a beastquake, then what could have caused this type of destruction? Something so precise? Something so deliberate?

Seconds later, the door to the throne room swings off its hinges, and my tactician runs in. "Matriling Kaleigh!" she screams. "We need to get you to safety. There's been an attack by the Sisters of Lost Lines."

I grit my teeth, anger coursing through me and not fear. I push the tactician aside. "I won't hide from such blatant disrespect for the throne," I say and venture out into the devastation, covering my face with the silks of my dress so I won't inhale bone dust, stepping carefully around slivers of glass. Wheytt sticks next to me, eyes scanning the debris, kicking bits of rubble with his boots. Medics search the collapsed buildings for victims. Even if no lives have been lost, the goods belonging to several of the wealthiest, long-lined merchants lie in waste. The economic impact will be felt for months, if not years. "Wheytt, you have to figure out who did this. If there's material evidence, I know you'll be able to find it."

"Yes, Matriling Kaleigh," he says, but now other guards have gathered around, sifting through the piles of debris with their honed senses on high alert. They all outrank him, and I get the feeling they want him to stay out of their way.

"Wheytt should take the lead on this investigation," I command, trying to resolve the matter, but it appears I have irked the guards further. Soon, however, they are all working together, looking for evidence of what doesn't belong.

Wheytt turns over a brick of bone and stiffens.

"Did you find something?" I ask.

"No, nothing here," he says, and that look he gets when he's lying . . . it's back.

Tensions rise. The people want answers, but I have none to give them. Chief Abacca is breathing down my neck at every turn, and Wheytt has been avoiding me for two whole days. Finally, I corner him, and when I ask for a status update, his face is perfectly blank, as if he'd been stripped of all emotion.

"What is it, Wheytt?" I ask.

"I've found them. The Sisters of Lost Lines. I don't think you're going to like it."

He hands me the list. I look the names over, and when I come to Adalla's, somehow I manage not to flinch. I don't react at all, my face as still as stone. "You're sure?" I ask.

"One hundred percent. You know I'd do anything to spare—"

"Enough. I'll have them all brought before trial. You're dismissed."

There are twenty-three of them on the list. They're a diverse bunch, workers from all over the beast, which makes me shudder. They could end us so easily.

If we don't end ourselves first.

TOMORROW IS MY WEDDING DAY.

Today is the day I send my best friend to her death.

I stand with the list clenched in my hand, and I'm sweating so hard, I'm worried I'll wash the names away. Matris is beside herself. Such an act of dissent hasn't been experienced in seven reigns, and for Matris to experience it . . . well, it's making her sicker than she already is.

"We should make an example of them," I say. "Public lashing."

My mother shakes her head. "They're the ones who've made a mockery out of the Matriarchy. Those demands—" She falls into another one of her coughing fits. Part of me wants it to go on forever, because I know the words that are coming next. Finally, she takes a sip of her tea, then clears her throat. "If they find it so hard to live under the rules within this beast, let's see how they like the rules outside of it. Give me the list."

I clench it harder, now wishing my sweaty palms *would*

wash away the ink. "Please, Matris. Maybe not everyone on this list is truly guilty. Maybe some have been swayed by rhetoric."

"Give it to me!"

I step to her bedside, place the paper in her hand. She opens it, her glassy eyes reading over each name. She looks at me. "Adalla? Is this *your* Adalla?"

My heart cinches. All this time I've wanted Matris to think of Adalla as my Adalla . . . but it's come at the exact wrong time. All I can do is nod. Adalla couldn't possibly have found her way into such trouble. She'd been brainwashed, maybe. Or maybe she's being blackmailed.

"I warned you about her," she mutters.

"A public lashing—"

"Execution via expulsion from the beast. I will demand the sentence before the Senate myself if you don't think you have it in you."

I don't. I really don't. I stand there staring, looking pitiful, hoping Matris will change her mind. But now she's getting out of bed, and for the first time, I get a good look at what this sickness has stolen from her. Through her sleeping gown, her gauntness is overwhelming. Her aide scurries over and wedges a shoulder underneath Matris's armpit.

"I will demand it myself, then. And you will watch by my side."

I seize up as she hands the note off to her tactician.

"Quickly. Round these indigents up."

Watching my mother move, I see she doesn't have much energy to give, but she's so determined to save face. Her aide helps her into flashy, lightweight gowns, not the usual layers she dons, a carpet of weighty fabrics. Her groomers fasten down the edges of her styled wig, same braided knots we've always worn. I pretend not to notice, but sometime during her sickness, her hair began to go brittle and fall out, all but severing her from our matriline. If anyone beyond these walls ever realizes it . . .

A light layer of patina goes on, bringing a copper-brown sheen back to her pallid face. She straightens as we walk out into public, and through the pure force of will, she's no longer carrying herself like it is a burden. Her gait is slow but steady. An occasion such as this, no one would expect anything else from her, especially now when the Senators are biting at the chance to unseat Matris for any show of weakness.

The offenders are marched into the room under the watchful eyes of the full Senate and several hundred onlookers. I breathe a sigh of relief when Adalla is not with them. A few workers from pulmonary, some dressed for musclework, and the rest boneworkers, their bare breasts on display without regard for humility. Maybe Adalla got away. Maybe she's safe, hiding somewhere.

"Who speaks for you all?" Matris demands.

One of the boneworkers steps up in front of the others. The leader. Bone in her hair, scars all over. Her eyes flick to meet mine, however briefly, but my entire life passes before me in that glance. I nearly collapse.

"I do, Matris." It is Adalla. Adalla is the leader of this sect. And I had missed her. Dismissed her. "We stand behind our demands. Do you wish to admit your guilt and complicity in the lives that have been taken so mercilessly?"

Matris flushes. Never has anyone spoken to her like this. "Insolence!" she yells. "Who will speak in your favor?"

I almost yell out. Almost. I could plead for her innocence,

but that wouldn't do anything but show weakness in our line, a vulnerable split. The room is silent. No one will tarnish their name in such a way. But then all those nights studying with Doka come back to me, him fussing over the details of Senate proceedings. I realize that I can speak *against* the traitors, as it is my right. I can admonish them, support Matris's wishes. And if I can talk long enough, not all will be lost.

"I'd like to speak against them, Matris. May I take the floor?"

Matris smiles at me, like maybe I am a worthy daughter after all. "I concede to Seske Kaleigh, true daughter of mothers."

I step up in Matris's spot, then stare down at Adalla. "I am moved to terrible sadness to see these traitors before me. Some faces that I know, that I trusted, who have destroyed valuable property and have made a move to deconstruct the Matriarchy with dangerous ideas. We cannot allow such a disregard for our ways. No, our history is not spotless, and some of it is outright disturbing. Those ways need to be challenged. We need to change. But not like this. Violence is not the way. It is never the way."

Matris steps up to me, a slight falter in her step. She's getting weaker by the minute. She won't be able to last much longer, and I'm counting on it. "Thank you, Seske. You are—"

"I'm not done," I say to Matris. "I'm just starting, in fact. I've been thinking a lot on this, actually. All the things we should open for discussion. Seeds of ideas that we should implant into others' minds, so that we can contemplate the ways we can do better as a people . . ."

I continue, a full ten minutes, speaking of the atrocities we've committed in the name of the ancestors, of the beasts we've destroyed, of our goals . . . our original goals of finding a new planet to call home, where we could spread out and thrive and put this harsh reality behind us. Finally, Matris staggers, and her aide comes to prop her up. Matris fights her off, not wanting to lose respect in front of the Senators, but clearly knowing it's too late.

"Are you quite done now, Seske? I'm drifting off from boredom."

"I'd like to still hold the floor, if that's fine with you, Matris. If you're feeling tired, I can hand the sentence down once I'm finished."

There. I've said it. Directly challenged her. She can leave now, with her grace and dignity intact, or she can wait me out and risk fainting, falling, or breaking down into another coughing fit with bloodied kerchiefs.

"My sweet daughter, if you think you are capable of handing down the appropriate punishment, I will leave it to you. It is truly time that we test your fitness as future matriarch. Your decisions here will mark your line for generations to come." She glares at me, but it doesn't scare me like it used to. "I have more important things to tend to."

And with a flourish and a slower and more deliberate gait, she leaves us. I talk five more minutes, my mind racing over her words. I can't let them off easy, especially with the way the Senators are watching me. Plus, with a light sentence, there would be disorder to follow, probably more groups springing up. But I can't sentence them to death either. "And with that said, I must pass judgment. Five lashes each—"

The crowd rumbles; the Senators' eyes flash, seeing their chance to claim the throne incompetent so they can seat their own choice. But I have not yet finished.

"—from the Ancestor's lace. Bring the leader before me."

The audience gasps. The Ancestor's lace hasn't been used in many, many years. It was cruel. It was unusual. It made a statement. Then I notice the boneworker next to Adalla is holding her hand, their fingers entwined. They exchange a meaningful glance, falling into each other's eyes, a knowing I can feel from here.

Adalla steps forward, her fingertips touching with the other woman's until the last possible second. Then finally, she is mine. I will show her both my strength and my compassion in this moment.

She kneels before me, head so low, her forehead nearly kisses the ground. I will strengthen my line with the ones I slash across her back. The first strip of lace is placed into my hand. I dip it into a solution made from the acids harvested from the beast's belly, mist rising off its jet-black surface. I fish the strip out with tongs, then place it upon her back, right between her shoulder blades.

Adalla screams.

Screams so loud, I'm sure all her ancestors to the beginning of time have heard her. The acid burrows into her flesh: eats away the skin, then keeps going, searing deep tissue and muscle. She will always feel this pain. I make the mistake of looking up at that other woman. Decades older, decades meaner. Her eyes cut at me, promising revenge should she and I ever be caught alone in a room together. I cut my eyes right back at her, unflinching. If it weren't for me, they'd all be breathing the cold dark of space right now. I turn my attention back to Adalla, and when her body has stopped convulsing, I lay the next piece of lace.

"YOU KNOW WHAT THEY'RE CALLING YOU NOW?" DOKA SAYS during our first dance as woman and husband. "Kaleigh the Cruel." He smirks. It is an awful smirk, as if watching the girl who fuels my heart being maimed and falling into another's arms holds any sort of frivolity. Maybe I am cruel. Maybe the name is fitting.

Matris sits far up on her stilted throne, waving down at the festivities. She's so far up, probably no one but me has noticed she's a stand-in. My stunt yesterday had taken more out of her than I'd guessed. Either that, or she's so mad that she'd willingly miss the wedding of her only daughter.

"Anyway, I suppose I should give you my present," Doka says, gently pressing a finger against the side of his head to soothe the tug of the fresh braids that now give tribute to my family line. *Our* family line, I realize with a start. "Your concerns about Sisterkin—you don't need to worry about those anymore."

"What? You mustn't call her that. She has a name now."

"No," he says, smiling. "She doesn't. I've had her adoption into the Abacca line annulled. I brought my concerns to my mothers. They agreed that recognizing her would delegitimize the importance of names."

I glance over at Sisterkin, dancing fitfully with a wide smile on her face. "They haven't told her yet?" I ask.

"They'll leave that to you. That's part of the gift, I guess." His lips move toward mine. My mind seizes up. I can't. Can't kiss him. Not right now.

"I'm feeling a little queasy," I say, dropping my forehead against the bridge of his nose. "Later?"

"Of course, love. We have the entire night to ourselves, if you'll have my honor."

The silence between us, it's like all the distance between all the stars. I watch his smile drop. Was there something on my face? "What, you don't find me pleasing?" he asks.

"No, no. Of course I do! I . . . I told you, I'm just not feeling well. I couldn't sleep last night, couldn't eat."

"Nerves," he says. "I've got them too. But this is a great match, Seske. A strong match. We're good together. The love will come."

I nod. "It will come." If I nod hard enough, maybe that'll force it to come true. Finally, the song comes to an end. Our lines are drawn; our sculptures are presented. Drinks are served in celebration. It all flows so easily, so flawlessly. Flows by too, too fast. When the first guest departs, I start to panic. Soon, I'll be alone . . . with Doka. There will be expectations. There will be hurt feelings. He talks with his mothers—talks too much—and they'll know our marriage hasn't been consummated and the ties between our family lines have not been knotted.

My eyes catch Wheytt, in civilian clothes, apart from his goggles, over by the hors d'oeuvres. He looks about as uncomfortable as I feel. I go over to him and put small morsels on a plate, though my stomach bucks at the idea of food.

"So, are you here as a friend of the bride or the groom?" I ask him.

"Both," he says. "It was a lovely ceremony. Congratulations."

"Thank you."

"Sorry to hear about what happened with Adalla. I feel responsible."

"No. It needed to happen," I say. "You did the right thing. I know it wasn't easy for you."

"Likewise. Don't beat yourself up. What you did, you saved twenty-three lives. Really, you saved us all. There's no room for rebellion when resources are already so tight."

"Even if their cause had merit?"

He looks surprised. "You finally read the demands?"

I nod. I'd found the list buried under the not important/ not urgent pile, and now I'm seriously rethinking that whole sorting system. "All of it. All of their ideas made sense. I could have worked with them. We could have avoided this whole awful situation."

"You know, the Sisters of Lost Lines may be disbanded, but their ideas don't have to die." His voice is merely a breath.

The idea moves me, but I grunt. "Listening to you is what got me into trouble in the first place." I nod toward Doka and sigh. "Any chance I could hire you as my honor guard tonight?"

"Oh, Seske. He's probably as nervous as you are. It'll be over before you know it."

"You aren't helping," I tell him, then stare down at the jellied currants jiggling on my plate, almost as if they have a life of their own. They remind me of puppet gel, and all the times I'd used it as a prop in my bed to fool my parents when I'd snuck out at night. If I could fool my half-asleep father, then maybe a drunken Doka might fall for it as well. But I'll need some help. "If you had to choose," I ask Wheytt, "whose wedding guest would you be tonight? Mine or his?"

"Yours, Seske," he says. "Always yours."

"Good. I've got a job for you, then."

I SUCK IN A DEEP BREATH, MY HAND PRESSED AGAINST THE door to our new bedroom. Doka leans on me, drunk, but not drunk enough. He whispers sweet nothings into my ear, reeking of beer, eyes bloodshot.

"Welcome home, my dear!"

He stumbles forward, and the door swings open, revealing

our love nest to us for the first time. The bed sits at the center, a four-poster made from bone that extends from floor to ceiling, with the histories of our line carved meticulously into each post. On the nightstand sits a bottle of ink and a fine-tipped brush for me to mark my line upon his forehead once the deed is done.

He pats the bed, bids me over. I pretend not to notice and head for the dresser and pour us both a shot of liquor.

I take a taste. "Love, you should try this!" I look at the vintage, from seven beasts ago. Beyond priceless.

"You can't mix liquor and beer," he says, covers drawn back now.

"Please, for me? A toast to our honor." This gets his attention.

"That, I will toast to!"

I bid him over, watching closely. Three shots will probably do it. I sip mine slowly, keeping my wits about me. Waiting to give Wheytt the signal. Finally, Doka's eyes are glazed, and his pants have fallen down to his ankles, and his sweet nothings are even less sweet than before. He sways left, right, left again. I think maybe three shots were too many. I don't want him passing out before we do the deed.

"I'm just going to slip into something more comfortable," I say.

Doka nods, then embarks upon the monumental task of figuring out how to get his pants to slip over his shoes. It might take him a while. I go to the closet, where Wheytt is waiting for me. He's got the puppet gel, shaped like me. Highly accurate, but I guess after our experience with the beast, he knows my body more intimately than I do, down to the depth of each and every pore.

"She looks just like me," I whisper. I touch her arm and

the gel reacts, jerking up and around, like she's trying to embrace someone in a hug. Her body jiggles, wiggles. The brown patina he'd used is an exact match to my skin. Eyes. Nose. Everything is eerily perfect. "I think this will work." I help her into my bridal nightgown, a wisp of silk coming to just below her buttocks. I slip into an identical one, while Wheytt throws his attention toward the bedroom, peeking out the closet door.

"Oh, he's definitely ready," he says, and I can feel the grimace on his face.

"Let's do this." I nod at Wheytt. I exit the closet, put on my best prance. "Hey, love," I say, drawing the curtains, blowing out the candles. Darkness consumes us, and I make my way to the bed. Wheytt's tiptoeing right behind me. I touch Doka on his chest, his belly. "Are you ready?" I ask.

"Uh-huh!" he says.

Wheytt slips the puppet gel onto the bed. I sit, just out of view, next to the bed, poking the puppet to animate the gel and forcing a moan as Doka mounts her. I hear the squelch of splitting gel, a horrid wet rip, and then the poor puppet takes on a life of its own—jiggling, wiggling, limbs flailing wildly.

"Daidi's bells," I whisper to Wheytt. "I think he's got her in the belly button." My stomach curls.

Doka is quick and enthusiastic, and his ride is wild and short. Three minutes twenty seconds later, he's snoring, face pressed to the puppet's breast, drool dripping over her nipple. I let loose a breath and realize I'm shivering. Wheytt presses closer, drapes a robe over my shoulders.

"You okay?" he asks.

I nod. "That was only twice as awful as I thought it'd be. Not nearly as awful as it could have been, though." I light a couple candles, trying to keep my eyes from that horrid rip in the puppet's navel. "I think I'm going to puke."

Wheytt hurries toward me with a bucket, holds my hair, but all I've got is dry, painful heaves. He pats my back. "Can I get you some water?"

"How about some liquor?" I nod at the bottle on the dresser. He snags the shot glasses also. "Just bring the bottle," I say.

We settle on the floor, watching Doka snore. The bottle passes back and forth between us, and my mind starts to unknot. My head finds its way to Wheytt's shoulder. My hand finds its way to his chest.

"What are you doing, Seske?" he asks nervously.

"I don't know. I thought that I might try to kiss you," I blubber. "You were my first, you know. You're a good kisser."

"You're drunk."

"So are you. I still want to kiss you. For real this time." I burp hundred-year-old liquor fumes. "You know Adalla has a girlfriend? I know you do. Why didn't you tell me that part? I know you probably smelled them all over each other."

Wheytt lets out a sigh. "That's what this is about? You just want to get back at Adalla for moving on with her life?"

"I guess. Maybe. But I could have gotten back at her with Doka. I'm choosing to get back at her with you."

"I'm honored?"

"Well, you should be. You're a great catch, you know. You're really going places."

Wheytt seizes up. "I'm going places because of him." He points at Doka. "He's getting his mothers to petition on my behalf for a promotion. And now, I've betrayed him. He came to me, you know, worried about tonight. Asked me for advice."

"What advice did you give him?"

"To be gentle. Humble."

I take a long, hard sip of liquor. "Gentle, huh? That's what you think I like?"

He smiles bashfully, takes the bottle from me, and corks it up tight. He looks me in the eyes. "I think we've both had enough, and I really need to—"

My lips are nearly to his. They inch even closer.

His breath catches.

My stomach twists, turns. Finally, he makes a move just as I'm pulling back. I try to turn my head, but it's too late. Liquor expels from me with the force of a geyser. We're soaked in my vomit, head to toe. But we're laughing, the both of us, shushing each other, not wanting to risk waking Doka. We slip out of our filthy clothes, but before I can clean up, my head gets heavy. I nearly topple over, and Wheytt catches me in his arms. I lean into his chest, and he relaxes some, and then the world fades all away.

"TRAITOR! HOW COULD YOU DO THIS? WHERE IS YOUR LOYalty?"

The words slice through my head like an ax. It takes me a moment to leverage myself up from this stupor. I squint through the too-bright light, up at Doka.

"My mothers will hear of this, and your promotion . . . consider it gone. In fact, consider yourself no longer a part of the Accountancy Guard."

He goes on squealing for quite some time. Mostly threats and cusses aimed at Wheytt. Yes, I get that it looks bad, us lying together on the floor naked, Doka waking up next to a partially melted pile of puppet gel.

Wheytt manages to stand, the threat to his livelihood

sobering him up quickly. "Please, Doka, you have to understand. Nothing happened between Seske and me last night.
Not even a kiss."

"You think I'm a fool? I made you, Wheytt. I made you and
I will destroy you, too."

I look at Doka, but he won't meet my eyes. He's beyond
embarrassed, and I catch myself feeling sorry for him. He'd
probably dreamed of his wedding ever since he was a scrubby
little boy, and I'm sure he was the talk of his circles, future husband of the future matriarch. I'd chosen him. Then I'd let him
down. I'd crushed him.

"I'm sorry, Doka. I didn't mean for it to happen this way," I
say. He finally finds the strength to look at me. His patina is an
awful mess, smudged all over.

"We didn't mean it," Wheytt says.

"Well, what exactly did you mean to do? You think you're
so high and mighty, you think I should be honored to be your
husband," he says to me. "Well, let me tell you, *your* family
needs this more than mine does. You may be royalty, but I'm
the one who married down."

Rage swells within me, and any compassion I'd had evap-
orates out my ears. "Are you bad-talking my line?"

"I'm doing more than that! I'm having the marriage annulled. Matris won't be able to bounce back from this one."
He pokes his finger right in my chest, and Wheytt sets off like
he really is my honor guard.

"Touch her again and lose the finger," he says.

"You have no authority!" Doka wails. "I trusted you!" And
then he takes a swing, but we're all too hungover to have this
be anything but a slap fest.

There's a pounding at the door. Once, twice, then the
hinges give, and Sisterkin barges through, eyes red like they're

nearly aflame. She walks right up to me, not giving a glance toward the two mostly naked men now wrestling on the floor or the pile of gel in the bed with its eyes slid down to the sides of its face, mouth agape.

Sisterkin must have found out about the dissolution of her adoption. I brace myself for her fury, but before she gets a chance to yell at me, I say, "It's mine, Sisterkin. The throne is rightfully mine, and you should be ashamed of yourself for trying to snatch it away from me! Your adoption is history now, you have no name. You might as well scrub the naxshi off your face right now, because there's nothing you can do about it!"

Her eyes go wide, like this is the first she's heard of it.

"Seske . . ." she says, her mouth screwing up, mind churning.

"I don't want to hear it!" I yell at her. There's no apology authentic enough to undo what she tried to do to me.

She shakes her head, bottom lip atremble. "Matris is dead."

I SMELL OF BITTER TAR AND CANDLE WAX. IN TRUE FORM, EVEN Matris's funeral hadn't gone without incident. The embalmers had been too generous with the cleansing oils, or maybe the sickness had caused a change in her skin. Either way, her body wouldn't take to the spirit wall. Nearly slid right off, but the bearers caught her in time, and tar was applied to make her stick. I'd tried my best to keep focused, to bear the robes that had been bestowed upon me, but I heard the whispers, that even our ancestors must not have thought she belonged among them. This is the line I've been dealt.

Back in the throne room, it's quiet. Too quiet. I'm lost among my thoughts—thoughts of a matriarch. I wield this power but have done nothing with it. Decisions need to be made. There's no time to mourn, not when so much was left unsettled. I hadn't given much consideration to what kind of Matris I wanted to be. The title had felt like it was still decades away, plenty of time to plan. Now, I barely have time to react.

"Truce?" comes Sisterkin's voice. She's hurting, too, maybe more since she had been carried in Matris's womb and had always been her favorite.

I don't look back. She could be armed. Here to do me in for good, this time. I deserve it.

"I can help," she says. "I know it's a lot. I don't expect you to trust me, but with Matris leaving so suddenly, there are a lot of things that need tending to. Mourn another day or two, then we'll try to piece this back together. Doka says he won't go through with the annulment. At least not right now."

I'm sure he wouldn't. Not with his new title. Everything has changed. Everyone is treating me differently. My responsibilities have increased tenfold, and my vulnerabilities have become eyesores. With just Doka and me, our line needs strengthening desperately. My stomach churns at the thought, and the inevitability of me taking up a female suitor as soon as this mourning period has passed.

"Reports are coming in from all over," Sisterkin persists. "All seven extinction markers have surfaced. We'll have to consider premature exodus."

"Maim another beast?" I imagine myself giving the order I've been so eagerly waiting to give for years. But now all I feel is defeat. I've already witnessed the baby beast dying before my eyes, and I won't be complicit in continuing the tradition of murder.

More important, though, I know another way. I grapple with the tactical system, a blend of our best technology and acute sensory mapping algorithms linked directly to the beast's brain. I stand firm as I manipulate the sensors, sliding my fingers over a honeycomb input pad, projecting confidence despite the miniscule amount of training I've had.

At first nothing happens, and the screen above shows only a vast waste of emptiness, but then I close my eyes and remember the celestial patterns the baby beast had shown me. They crystalize in my mind, and just as the baby beast had taught me how to dance, I now realize she'd given me a much bigger gift.

I try again, and the honeycomb pad races under my fingertips, zooming over, zooming in, until a small blue dot appears among the blackness of space. It's a planet. The same planet the beast had shown me. It really does exist, and is within seven years' travel from here.

"There's another way," I say, swallowing my pride so I can focus on selling this idea. "We should consider—"

Sisterkin hand-waves the image away, and I almost banish her from the throne room then and there.

"There are millions of planets out there, Seske," Sisterkin says, "each with possibilities and risks. But beast life is all the life we know now. Even if you can find a planet, and even if you can convince our people to journey there, how will you convince the others?"

"Other who?"

Sisterkin buries her head in her hands, then sighs heavily. "The people on the other beasts, Seske. The other worlds? There are seven ships now, worlds just like ours, but the people are different. The customs are different. But we all need the same thing to survive, and with the herd diminishing . . ."

My head starts spinning. "What? What aren't you telling me?"

"There were two ships that went after this beast. A battle ensued. Only one survived."

"Matris killed them? An entire ship? With people on it?"

"Thousands. Tens of thousands. It was either us or them."

My heart sinks, but I push it back up. Another of Matris's past mistakes I vow to never make. "All the more reason for us to go for the planet. I want to talk to them, the matriarchs of all the ships!"

Sisterkin laughs particularly cruelly at this, like she's amazed at the depths of my ineptness, then shakes her head. "Mothers' mercy, we're as good as dead."

In the past, that laugh would have put me in my place, made me doubt myself, but no longer. I stamp my foot down. "If you have a critique of my plan, you will ask to give it, and if I feel like entertaining it, you will give it without insult, or you're going to find yourself jettisoned out of the nearest orifice. Understand?"

Even after all she's lost, Sisterkin has the audacity to sneer at me.

I don't let it unnerve me but, instead, let her animosity brew, right out there in the open. I stand my ground. And as if on cue, two of my guards come to stand at my flanks, hands on their weapons.

I look at Sisterkin, my gaze unwavering.

She withers under my glare. "I understand, Matris."

"Good," I say. "Now tell me everything I need to know."

SESKE

Of Higher Learning and Lowered Expectations

I run my hands over the weeping wounds on Adalla's back. The lace pattern is beautiful, the most beautiful thing I've ever seen. "Do they burn much?" I ask.

"Not as much as my heart has burned for you," Adalla says, big fat grin on her face, like the one she used to have when we were still just kids. Before things got complicated.

"You forgive me, don't you? Matris would have had you thrown from the beast!"

"Well, who told Matris in the first place?" Adalla spits back at me.

"*Well*," I mimic, "I couldn't just let you go on destroying our way of life! I wouldn't let Matris kill you, though. I couldn't bear for that to happen either. What was I supposed to do?"

Adalla takes my hands in hers. "Of course, Seske. It was a

tough choice, Seske, but you did the right thing. You saved my life, Seske! Seske—"

"Seske!" Doka screams at me. I startle awake, one eye clenched. Face pressed into a puddle of drool. I close my eyes tighter, trying to force myself back into that dream, as if my slumbering fantasies could patch the very real ache in my heart, but it's too late. And it wouldn't work anyway.

Reality calls. I answer. And Adalla is still missing from my life.

I sit up, notice the drool stain upon the Texts. Then I'm fully awake.

"Oh no. Oh no!" I say as Doka hands me a kerchief and I blot the mess up. It does the trick, mostly, just another slight discoloration that I hope will dry clear. No ink is smudged this time. "The answers must be here, in our histories, but the harder I try, the less I can concentrate, and it all just jumbles up on me."

"Would you like my help? Are you looking for something in particular?" Doka asks.

My head races. "Yes! You know all about how politics work on the ship. Any insight on how they've worked between civilizations—those other ships? How do we figure out who we're dealing with?"

Doka smiles and scoots close to me, moving the Texts so that it's perfectly between us. He flips pages toward the beginning of the book, then points his finger to a chapter when he finds it. "We can start here." He begins reading, talking about the original twenty ships and their vision, but my mind is already wandering. He sees that and shuts the book.

"Wait, no, I'm listening!" I plead. "Don't give up on me! This is too important."

"I'm not giving up on you," he says. "You just need a different approach." He takes my hand, and then we're off.

"Where are we going?" I ask.

"To the Muirabuko Emporium."

"The store? We don't have time to shop." I keep grumbling, but he keeps dragging me, and soon we're there. He orders all the customers out, wielding his new title like he's borne it his whole life. The place clears.

"How can I help you, Matris?" the shop owner asks with curiosity and perhaps a little nervousness.

But Doka is already in a zone, grabbing marbles and other small toys from the shelves, and running back to us, depositing them at our feet before running out to get more. And more. Finally, he comes back and starts assembling little figurines bound together with puppet gel. He'd looked at me with a trace of hurt in his eyes when he opened the first pack of gel, but whatever crushed feelings he was having, they were fleeting, and now his eccentricity is back. Thirty spaceship replicas sit before me, each made from an assortment of toys.

"So you know about Earth?" he asks me as he rolls a big blue-and-green ball behind the ships.

"Of course!" I say confidently. "What kind of question is that?"

"Sorry," he says. "Just making sure. So you know how there were lots of different countries, lots of different cultures and races?"

"Yes . . ." I say, less sure now. I'd fumbled my way through so many of my pai's lessons, grasping what I could about the history of our ships and the beasts we've called home. But his lessons on Earth were so odd, they were mostly incomprehensible. All those people, clinging to a dead rock, slinging themselves around and around a star, had seemed far-fetched at best, but I *need* it to make sense now. "I mean, I guess there would be, but I hadn't really given it much thought. I just assumed they all looked like us."

"Well, more or less. But there were differences. When the Great Cruelty came, thirty generational ships were commissioned to save what they could of humanity. Countries pooled their resources and knowledge to do the impossible. The Great Cruelty spread quickly through the Western Hemisphere. Their ships were constructed, some generational, some utilizing stasis, but some of the engineers had contracted the Cruelty, causing them to sabotage their programs. Ships exploded in their space docks before they could ever launch." Doka stomps hard on ten of the thirty ships, squishing them to pieces. Gel flies everywhere. The store's matron flinches at the mess but dares not say anything.

Then Doka animates the puppet gel of the remaining twenty, and they start undulating their way across the floor. "The others launched successfully, with a goal of finding another planet in a nearby star system. It was a three-hundred-year journey."

And then he's quiet for a long while. Nearly a minute drags on, and I just sit there, watching the ships do their little undulations together, working their way by inches. Less than inches. "Um, is that it?" I ask.

"No, just wanted to give you an idea of the timescale we're working with. It was slow, Seske. Really slow. Cultures were different when they started, and they got even more different with the isolation between ships. There was some trade at first, but the ships became more self-sufficient and more insular. We shut off from one another. And when the planet turned out to be a bust, several of the generational ships went on to a second-choice planet, only fifty years away now with advancements in travel speeds." Doka slaps six of the twenty ships, and they take off fast in a different direction. Fourteen are left. "The stasis pods were starting to give out on these other ships. Lives were being lost. They wouldn't make it another fifty years and needed another solution. They'd documented a herd of spacefaring beasts on their way, only a few years' travel back the way they'd come." Doka's eyes light up. He goes over to the bucket of marbles and dumps them all out. They go rolling everywhere. "Good news, they figured out a way to hitch the ships to the beasts, tapping into their life force to sustain their ships' power systems. Bad news, they killed a lot of beasts in the process of figuring out how to do it most effectively." Doka kicks the marbles hard, until the herd is severely thinned.

"Excuse me!" the shop owner says, finally irritated enough to speak out about the mess Doka has made of the place.

"You're excused," he says to her, a severe look on his face that instantly puts the shop owner in her place. All my life, I've known only one person who wielded such power with a single glare. Matris.

"Soon," Doka continues seamlessly, "someone figured out it was better to just modify the beast directly, and they figured out a way for us to live inside them. People were taken out of stasis. Communities established. Sanctions on family size were temporarily lifted. Finally, we had something we could call a real life. But the beasts didn't last forever. At first each ship needed a new beast every two years." He kicks more marbles. "Then every five years." Kicks more marbles. "Then every ten or so. We've gotten better over time. But we are still killing them faster than they can reproduce. It takes nearly a decade for a baby to gestate. Someone did the math and figured out that the beasts would be extinct in five hundred years. Cooperation turned to competition almost overnight. That was about six hundred fifty years ago."

"So their estimates were off?" I ask.

"Their estimates were for fourteen ships. There are just seven now."

I nod. Matris had destroyed a whole ship at her own will, and obviously there had been more, and *this* was the beast they'd fought over? The competition for resources, for life, had been a deadly one, and apparently, it still is.

"So you can see, there's a lot of animosity and distrust you're dealing with. It's not going to be an easy conversation to have."

"How many beasts are left?" I ask.

"One hundred twelve adults, sixteen juveniles, and a young one, still suckling at its mother's side." His eyes tear up a bit, then move to my stomach. "The stakes are high, Seske. I think we work well together."

"I do, too—"

"I think we can make real change," he continues, as if he hadn't heard me, "but we also need to protect our own line. We need to make an heir, one way or another. One we can teach our values to and move past this way of life. We can't risk the Matriarchy falling into the hands of someone who will drive us into dust." His hand is on my stomach now, right where my womb is. I feel my insides clench up.

"The last thing this city needs is another life to leech resources," I say. "And the last thing I want is some alien thing inside me, doing the same."

"But, Seske . . ." He grabs, pulls me in tight. "Our marriage. Our honor."

"Our marriage and honor are fine just where they are," I say, tugging away. "We work well together. Let's not complicate things emotionally, physically. Thank you for the lesson."

"It's just that my mothers are pressuring us to consu—"

"I swear to every single heart-father of memory's past, if you say the word *consummate* I'm going to have you strung up by your thumbs."

Doka laughs a nervous laugh, then swallows it back when he sees I'm serious. "Sorry, Seske," he says. "I won't bring it up again."

One of the remaining ships undulates its way up to my foot. I stoop down to pick it up and squint at the front shield, like I can see the little people inside. "This was good. Now I need you to tell me exactly who it is we're dealing with."

I WATCH, RAPT, AS A HOLOGRAM OF THE PLANET SPINS ABOVE us in the doldrums—the only open space on this beast large enough to accommodate tens of thousands. I'd had the technicians make the hologram as big as possible, big enough that a very tall person could reach up and touch the very tips of its highest mountaintops. The blues of the ocean are amazing. Such rich green land. In the history books, it's never been so grand.

"Earth," I say to the crowd spread out before me, Contour class to my left, beastworkers to my right. "We are one people from many nations. We have many pasts. But we have one future."

The image of Earth fades and is replaced by a slightly smaller planet. The blues are deeper, the greens lusher. I'd taken some liberties with the surface details, tweaking it so that it looked like a complete paradise. Our sensors weren't that precise at a distance so far, but they'd been able to determine the composition of the atmosphere and extrapolate from there based on some astrosciences I didn't dare ask the technicians to explain.

"This is the planet I would like you to settle with me, to break this cycle of killing we pretend to ignore. Our technicians are still doing the research, of course, but preliminary results look promising. The air is breathable. The temperatures are stable. There's enough room for each of the other ships to settle, enough room and resources for us all, but before I speak with those ships, I wanted to speak with you. I want you in on this with me. I want your trust. Our people can thrive on this planet, not just subsist. We can build a future for many generations to come, not doomed by some ticking clock. I can lead you there, and we can prosper.

"Who will come with me?"

I stare at the group. They stare at the planet. No one moves. No one says a thing.

"Who will be the first?" I shout. "Who will help me lead the way?"

Finally, eyes fall upon me. Full of distrust. Whether it's a distrust of my line or me, I guess it doesn't matter, but if no one steps up, we're all dead.

"I'll come," says a voice closing in on me. Sisterkin. "We can't keep looking to our past to solve our problems. We have to be forward-thinking."

"I'll come too." It's Chief Auditor Abacca. Apparently the dissolution of their adoption has not dissolved the loyalty between them.

But it makes a difference. Slowly, others step forward, and momentum gains until it looks like we have a slight majority.

"One people, one future," Sisterkin calls out, and suddenly they're all chanting. My nerves are steeled.

"One people, one future," I say back to them. The crowd erupts into applause. I let loose a sigh, lock eyes with Sisterkin.

I don't know what she's up to, but for now, I'm grateful this idea didn't die where it stood.

And she's still at my side when the calls go through. She arranges videoconferences with the leaders of the other six ships. One by one, their faces pop up on the screen, and I get to see what five hundred years of social isolation really looks like.

I can't stop staring at the men. Four of them. I can't imagine how their people could find the trust to allow a male to lead an entire civilization, but perhaps they've come around to realizing the value of equality faster than we have. One is a woman, and the other is concealed so heavily in furs that I can't tell either way.

"Thank you for agreeing to speak with me," I say. My voice barely trembles. At least that's what I'm telling myself. "I am Seske Kaleigh, true daughter of mothers, matriarch of this ship?" I hadn't meant for it to come out as a question, but here we are.

"You?" says one of the men, so pale-faced, he's nearly white. It's as if I'm staring into the face of a spirit. A shudder runs through me. "Little darkling child, we're expected to believe you are the leader of your people?"

Two of the other feeds immediately cut out.

"I assure you, I am completely fit to lead my people." I take a deep breath. At least some of them are still listening. There's a chance they might help to sway the others later. "We are a people of many nations, we have many pasts, but together, we can have one future. There's not enough out here for us. We can see the end approaching, and yet we continue to speed toward it. We need to talk of another way."

"Of conservation?" the woman asks. "We would be interested in a trade of technologies." I notice how gaunt she is, how much desperation there is in her eyes.

"Conservation is good, but I think we're beyond that now. I think we are more desperate than that. I think we need to consider taking a new stand: setting up a new life on a new planet." I nod for the tactician to send them specs of the planet. Their eyes all fall slightly away from camera. Two more feeds cut out. Only the woman and the pale, pale man remain. I try not to let nerves overcome me. I'll win over two now, worry about the others later. Later.

"There is enough land for the three of us, and much more, should the others decide to join us."

"Darkling child," the pale man says.

"Seske. It's Seske Kaleigh, true daughter of mothers. You can call me Matris, if you'd prefer."

"I will do no such thing! Have you no men to lead you?"

"Have you no women to lead you?" I mouth back.

Doka elbows me in the ribs. "Diplomacy," he mutters under his breath.

I cringe, trying to remember what's at stake, then put on my best serious face.

"We are willing to talk trade, but not if *he* is a part of it," the woman says, the ire in her voice churning the pit of my stomach.

"Still hard feelings, Klang? It's been nearly fifty years since our trade agreement."

"We have parents alive who still weep. We will not forget," the woman says, indignant.

"We will hear your plan, darkling child. We are also willing to trade," says the pale man. "The Klang have nothing of value. Trust me on that one." He gives me an awful grin.

"Do business with the Serrata and you will regret it for generations," the woman says.

It is clear this meeting cannot go on with the both of them.

I must choose. They stare. I can't wait too long, or I'll lose them both. The woman seems more desperate, like she'll end up taking more than giving. The man, there's some opulence there. His clothes are nicer. Face full, like he's eating well. "You, Commander Chubahl. What do you have to offer?" I ask.

He holds a fist up, then releases his grip. Several coins fall to the table in front of him, slowly, almost like they're sinking to the bottom of a bog. They land. "Titanium," he says. "Lots of it."

Titanium. Other than the copper distilled from the beast's blood, metal is so rare. I look to Doka. He nods. It's not what I wanted, but a trade would help with everything. We could repair our ship or construct exploratory vessels.

"We will do business with you, Commander Chubahl," I say.

The woman scowls at me. "May you live to regret this decision," she says, then her feed flicks out.

"I invite you aboard our ship," I say to Commander Chubahl, "so that we may discuss our proposition in person."

When he sees the big hologram, that'll really sell the idea. I'll give him first pick of territories. Anything to get him to agree.

"We will have you and your darkling crew aboard our beast," he counters.

"And what will you require of us? We have amazing spices and tea, some technology, or, if you're interested, we also have—"

"Girls," he says flatly. "We want a hundred of your girls."

"YOU CAN'T ACTUALLY BE CONSIDERING DEALING WITH THEM," Sisterkin says as I pore over the information on the ledger before me. There's not much of it. The Serrata have mostly kept to themselves outside of a few skirmishes. I do find the record of the so-called trade agreement the Klang commander had referred to. Fifty-seven girls had been stolen from their ship. She'd petitioned our Matris at the time, my grandmatris, for help, for retaliation, but we'd declined involvement. They weren't our children. They weren't our problem.

"Why do they have so much metal?"

"Their ship. They've scrapped their entire ship," my tactician says. "We've taken everything we could from ours but haven't completely dismantled it. We need the ship. For exodus."

We all look at one another. "How long have they been living in that beast?"

Sisterkin looks through the records. "At least a hundred and ninety years. Records are spotty before that. There were so many beasts then, nobody really bothered to keep track of such things."

"Then they've found a way to reach equilibrium with the ship," I say, overwhelmed by the possibility. "They coexist peacefully, taking only what they need from the beast and giving back whatever they can."

"Stealing fifty-seven girls isn't peaceful, Seske," Doka says. "We can't risk it. We just need to go the course without them."

I shake my head. "If we can get that information from them, about how they've reached symbiosis, we can pass it on to the others. Even if they don't agree to come with us to the planet, it'll give the rest of the beasts out there a fighting chance."

"Why should we care about *them*? They're just beasts," says Sisterkin.

"Each of those adults has been alive longer than our people have been spacefaring. We've destroyed them. We're not taking another single life!"

"And our daughters are collateral?"

I shake my head. "We don't have to give up our daughters. We've still got the grisette embryos, right? Thousands of them." I'm shocked at the words that come out of my mouth. But how do you weigh the lives of a hundred unborn souls against the survival of our people? "We'll send the embryos over with a few incubators. They've got to consider that a fair trade. And while we're over there, getting the titanium, we'll also pry from them how they keep their beast running. Did you notice how those coins dropped? They've got less gravity for sure. Maybe a third of what we've got. Maybe that has something to do with it."

"Seske!" Sisterkin says. "Please, let's take time and talk with Chief Abacca about strategies—"

"Let's make it happen," I demand with the ire learned from Matris, and the entire room scatters, except for Doka, who stands next to me, ever the dutiful husband.

"You're really going to go over there, onto that ship?" Doka takes my hand in his, holds it like he never intends to let go.

"I really am. And I want you to come with me."

"Me? I'm just—"

"You're not just anything. You're my husband, and I need you by my side. We work well together. Think of this as another of our adventures, sneaking around, only this time we're doing it for honorable reasons."

"I don't know, Seske. We can't afford for something to happen to you, but if it did, wouldn't it be better if I were here? Someone left to lead the ship without a turnover in line? I don't think we could survive that right now."

He looks small. Scared. I'm not going to go out and call Doka a coward, but Daidi's bells, I want to. "It's okay. I'll find someone else," I say. "Stay here, protect the line." He relaxes and smiles.

I still need someone I trust. Preferably a man, since I get the feeling Commander Chubahl would be more receptive to a little testosterone amid our proceedings. My mind goes straight to Wheytt. I trust him more than anyone on this ship. Plus, he's got the observational skills we need. And I owe him. I owe him big. But if Doka finds out I'm consorting with Wheytt again, he'll throw a fit. I need Doka out of the way for a while, and his mothers, too, with all their prying. I think about how preoccupied they all were in planning our wedding. Mothers forgive me, only one thing will come close to consuming them like that again.

"When I get back, I think we should do it. I think we should start our family." I want to vomit so hard right now, but this lie is for the entire ship. Our entire existence. "I know what I said before, but . . . maybe start thinking of some names? How we could decorate the nursery? Oh, and please don't tell your mothers just yet. You know how they get."

"Of course, Seske," he says. Leans in for a big kiss. I turn and take it on the cheek. And he's off, eyes glistening, smile spread across his face. His mothers will know in exactly twelve and a half minutes.

Then I'm off, heading to Wheytt's quarters. I knock at the door. His heart-mother answers. She stares at me something fierce. "Is Wheytt home?" I ask.

"He's got company." Aiee, the venom in her voice . . . and I deserve it too.

"I know he lost his job because of me, and I'm so sorry for that, but I need his help. It's urgent. Life or death."

"He lost more than his job. He lost his dream. You stole that from him! You stained our entire line! He never wants to see you again."

"Ama," comes Wheytt's soft voice from right behind her. "You're talking to our Matris. Please, it's okay to let her in."

I swear I can see the fumes coming out of his ama's ears. She steps aside. She wasn't lying, though. They do have company. A homely woman and her heart-mothers. I look at Wheytt.

"Seske, this is Talby and her mothers. You all know our Matris, of course." They all look like they're conflicted, seeing their leader and object of such scorn standing before them. They decide to offer me halfhearted bows.

"We are pleased to meet you." That's when I see the nuptial ledger, spread out and tallying the favors between families, six generations back. That's why only heart-parents are present.

"You're getting married!" I say to Wheytt.

He nods but doesn't smile. He's not marrying for love. He'd lost his job and reputation because of me, and now he'll need a woman to support him.

"Um, can I talk to you in private?" I ask him.

"No!" the heart-parents all say in unison.

"Come in, Seske. Sit. If it is this important, we should all talk about it," Wheytt says, biting his lip. Biting back a lifetime's worth of aim and focus, only to end up right where he was running from. I've seen him differently since our time with the baby beast. We pretend that our intimacy had never happened, but his emotions are transparent to me now.

He takes a seat next to Talby, pulling her hand into his so I won't miss the clues. He is to be a househusband to this nervous, fidgety woman. Her eyes are full of mistrust. I would have hoped someone as wonderful as he is would have fetched the attention of a less cruel-looking woman, but perhaps I've ruined those chances for him as well.

"You've all heard the announcement about the planet?" I say. "It's within our reach, but we need more knowledge and resources to ensure that we get there safely. We're set to trade with the Serrata. I have reason to believe that they've found

symbiosis with their beast, and while we're over there negoti-
ating trade, if I had someone to look around, to notice things,
then maybe we could bring some of those secrets back."

"You want me to be your spy?" he says.

"With the Serrata? I haven't heard anything good about
them!" says one of Talby's heart-mothers, flushing. "Talby will
not allow it, especially now when the relationship is still so
tender."

Talby opens her mouth, but I guess Wheytt is too stubborn
to let a woman speak for him. "I won't go," he says. "There are
plenty of others who could do the task."

"Not like you," I plead, "and you know it. You're the best,
and I trust you."

"I trusted you too. Look where it got me." He gestures
limply at Talby. She snatches her hand away, and we all notice
the look of disgust on Wheytt's face. He forces it into a smile,
but it's too late.

"*Where* has it gotten you?" Talby demands. "Stuck here?
With me?" She pouts her lips. "I'm an actress, you know! And I
played the bells in the reenactments of the Yoriden Exodus for
three straight years! You couldn't get better than this if your
mothers tripled your dowry!"

"My dowry?" His eyes shoot to his mothers. "You paid
them off?"

"Dowries are a part of our culture, Wheytt. It isn't un-
heard of."

"A hundred years ago, maybe. No family of our status
would offer such a thing. We have our lines—" He stops.

Had I ruined his name so badly? Had I set them back a century in the prestige they'd earned?

"How much?" he demands. Wheytt's mothers try to stare
off, and I wish I could slink out of this uncomfortable mess as

well, but then he screams again, so loud, my feet become fixed
to the floor. "How much? Tell me!"

"Six thousand chits . . ." his ama says calmly, ". . . a month."

His eyes light up. "Six thousand a month, and *this* is all you
could get me?"

He gestures at Talby's whole family this time. They all gasp
in offense.

"Daidi's bells, give it a rest," he says to them. "She's in the
pit of her career, and it's not going back up any time soon!"

Talby and her mothers all rise and leave in a huff. Wheytt's
mothers stare at him. He stares right back.

"I don't want this, Ama. I don't want to be a househusband. I don't want to see this beast sink lower and lower, and
our people with it. I want to find a way out of this. I *need* to find
a way out of this, and if Seske thinks she's found something, I
want to help her the best I can."

"You leave out that door, you never come back," his ama says.

"Do what you have to," he says. "But what use is a pristine
line when there's no future?"

My mouth stays a tight line—how could it not with all the
tension in the room right now? But inside I'm smiling, and I
know Wheytt will catch the small tells of my happiness: the
tiny sigh of relief, the slight crinkle at the edges of my eyes.

He doesn't bother to pack, doesn't bother to say goodbye.
The air becomes heavy. He's putting his fate wholly in my
hands. Maybe he sees me as more of a leader than I really am.

"So while we're on the Serrata ship," I say to him as we're
heading back to the throne room, "I'm going to need you to
take in as much as you can. I'll try to push for a tour of their
beast and take note of how each of the structures differs from
what we're doing."

"I'm good at noticing things, but I don't know enough

about the beasts' systems to figure out how they work. I think we'll need a—"

He bites his tongue, seeing the blush I feel already brightening my naxshi.

"No," he warns me.

"We'll need a beastworker, is what you're saying?"

"I am, but there are hundreds to choose from, Seske. Thousands."

"True. But I already know just the one."

ADALLA
Of Unborn Souls and Unanswered Questions

L aisze and I enter the throne room silently, like we intend on haunting the place. A holographic image of the beast takes up an entire corner. Not our beastie, I can tell right off, but a big, beautiful beast, full of spirit. I want to get closer to get a better look and see exactly what we'll be dealing with, but Laisze tugs me back, keeps me close. She'd sassed me the whole way here, reminding me to keep my guard up and that we'd be among the enemy.

She hadn't been talking about the Serrata, betcha.

Seske's tactician starts to introduce us, but Laisze pins her with a stare and she quiets.

"They're definitely spinning a lot slower," Seske says, still unaware of us. "And see how there're shimmering rings around the gills? There are ten times the number the other ships have.

Our tacticians estimate they've been aboard this beast two hundred and ten years, and there are no signs of necrosis either. They'll probably have at least two hundred more."

"Slower spinning is less stressful for the ship," Sisterkin says.

"You're probably right," Seske says. "I'll have the tacticians run some simulations."

"No, I'm not speculating. It's a proven fact. We've known this for quite some time. But the cost was too much to implement. Our infrastructures would have to change. Completely."

"A change in infrastructure for hundreds of years on a beast!" Seske shouts. "We should have done that centuries ago."

Sisterkin shakes her head. "Slowing the beast would double the time at most, not three hundred years' worth. There are a lot more factors at—"

Sisterkin locks eyes with me, my stare just as hard as hers is. The entire room goes stiff when they notice us too. Laisze and I have covered ourselves with too-thin shifts, more like a suggestion of fabric. Seske had told me to come fully clothed. She hadn't told me to come alone.

Seske walks toward us, hands outstretched for a moment, like she's caught in some memory from our past, one where we'd be happy to see each other. But then she remembers and puts her arms down at her sides.

"Thanks so much for coming to see Adalla off," Seske says to Laisze.

"Haven't come to see Adalla off. I've come to make sure she stays safe."

"I will guarantee her safety," Seske says, reaching for my hand.

"I can handle a knife ten times better than either of you," I say, swatting Seske away. "Laisze's coming because we need her.

She's been around longer than any of us. She's worked seven different organs."

"Sounds like she can't keep a steady job," Seske hisses.

"Sounds like you can't keep a steady relationship," Laisze snaps back.

Seske withdraws into herself so quickly. Up until now, even with all Sisterkin had put her through, with what Matris had put her through, I'd never seen such hatred on Seske's face. Nevertheless, she steps aside and allows both Laisze and me to pass. I have no idea how we're going to fit all these egos into a little shuttle, but we attempt it anyway. Seske sits up front with Sisterkin. Laisze, me, and the lash counter bunch into the back seat. Seske engages the autopilot, and suddenly we're on our way.

As the black sky opens all around us, I realize just how small we are and how small our beast looks among the stars. It's sickly, though, skin dulled, with great swaths of it frostbitten. Whatever natural protection it had against exposure to naked space is gone. It spins, eyes dead, mouth agape, tentacles dragging limply along. Weapons jut out unnaturally from its body, and I catch early signs of infection settling in around them.

Then the Serrata beast comes into view, a nice, safe distance out of our firing range. The differences are obvious. This is a well-cared-for, well-groomed beast. Its tentacles still move independently, hundreds of them. Some are as thick as this shuttle, some as thin as my arm. There are weapons, too— strange protuberances that can't be mistaken for anything else—but they look organically grown. Its only flaw is a garish scar along its side. From battle, likely.

We dock without incident, and Seske pulls us into a huddle. "We'll negotiate and then I'll try to get us a tour of the beast.

Keep your eyes and ears open. They're barbarians, primitive and ruthless, so don't turn your backs on them."

The air lock gives way, and the cold hits us almost immediately . . . as well as the smell.

Sisterkin draws her arms over her chest and starts shivering. "For the love of all mothers, haven't they figured out how to trick the beast into heating itself?"

"Fever pitch." Seske nods. "Another of the ways we abuse the beast, making it think it's constantly under attack from viruses so that it keeps the insides balmy. Cutting back could buy us forty years on a healthy specimen, maybe a few years on ours."

"You expect us to live in near freezing temperatures?" Sisterkin demands. "How are we supposed to do that?"

Then the answers stand before us, seven tall and burly men, bigger than any I've ever seen by at least a foot. Pale faces with pale eyes staring out from layer upon layer of felted swamp moss. That explains the smell. Commander Chubahl, the leader, steps forward, looks us all over. "Darkling children, all of you?" He laughs. "I suppose we seem strange to you as well." He pays particular attention to Laisze and me. "Get these women robes!" he yells, and moss garments appear. They sling them over our shoulders.

"I decline," Laisze says, shrugging off the robe. "Is there something about the shape of my body that offends you?" she challenges. I can already tell we're going to have a problem if this deal isn't over and done quick.

"We are sorry if we have offended," says Chubahl. "We just thought you might be cold."

"You thought wrong," Laisze says.

"I like this one," he says. "Feisty. On the older side, but we might be able to squeeze a few sons out of her yet." Chubahl is about to touch Laisze's hair . . . which will leave him short three fingers in a matter of seconds.

"Wait!" Seske says. "Let's talk details about the deal. We've come with a hundred em—"

"We will talk business later," Chubahl says. "Now it is time for us to get to know each other better. Do you drink?" he asks Wheytt. "Gin?"

The lash counter stammers, but before he can get his words out, Chubahl gestures at two of his men. "Haineem. Walles. Show the women around the ship while we're chatting."

Seske and Wheytt whisper something to each other, just out of earshot, and after that, Seske, Sisterkin, Laisze, and I are being ushered out the door.

I'M COLD, LIGHT-HEADED, AND MY MUSCLES ARE CRYING FOR A break from this weak gravity, but I press on ahead, trying to keep ten steps in front of Seske. I can't stand to look at her. She'd sent her messengers to our block, asking me to come, then begging, and then when I'd refused, she'd *commanded* me to come. So here I am, on another beast . . . and that part, that's amazing. They guide us quickly through their beast and I soak up as much as I can. The organs here are modified, but only very slightly. Sometimes I'm only aware of the changes when they're pointed out to me. Like instead of harvesting the four chemicals we use inside ley lights, they've got these little sails strung around the doldrums that capture energy for lighting and all sorts of uses. For the most part, it looks like the Serrata haven't even settled here at all.

Except they have. There are small houses, built from bricks of gall fiber, it looks like, not bone. Faces peek out at us as we pass. All male. All older, the youngest ones as old as Sonovan.

No children. They've found a balance with the beast, but as far as I can tell, they haven't found a balance with their own nature.

"Slow down, 'Dalla," Laisze says, a hand on my shoulder pulling me back. I'm so glad she agreed to join me. Truth is, I don't think there was a way to stop her from coming. She's taking it all in too.

"Can't slow down," I say, risking a glance back at Seske. She's busy arguing with Sisterkin, so she doesn't notice me looking, which I'm glad of, because I'm pretty sure the look on my face isn't the angry one I wish were on it. I sigh, then slow down and press my toe against one of the bulbous blooms lining our path. When I touch it, it leaks liquid, a viscous pool of honey-colored opalescence. I'm so used to seeing its wilted counterparts on our ship that it takes me a moment to realize what it is: a mucous gland at the base of the shafts that lead out to the beast's hide.

"Ones on our beast don't leak like that," says Laisze.

"They draw too much ichor, so we reroute the supply away from them, first thing. They're low priority."

"They're beautiful." She picks one of the blooms and presses it into my hair. I blush.

Our guides look like they're about to reprimand us, but I take the offensive and say, "I'd like for us to go to the heart next."

The two older men, gray twisted through their beards, act like they're afraid of us. They look at me, then at each other, speaking in low, deep voices.

"We can't," one of them says, not bothering to look me in the eye.

"Why? We're so close, just a few minutes away." I feel the heart's beat, stronger than any beat I've ever known. How do they live with such a strong, steady thing? "Please?"

They keep not-staring at me and say nothing.

"What? Have you never talked to women before?" I ask, growing annoyed.

"No," they say in unison. "We have not."

This gets my attention. "Don't you have women at all? We haven't seen any."

"We have women," one says nervously. "Several. The Great Queens." This earns him an elbow in the ribs from the other. They both look so scared that I'll ask what Great Queens are that he blurts out, "I can take you to the heart. But only one of you."

"I'll go," I say, stepping forward.

"I won't let you go alone," says Laisze.

"I'm afraid—" the man starts, but Seske is upon us suddenly, standing between Laisze and me.

"I'll go with her. It is my duty." Seske points at Laisze, finger pressed to her chest like it alone is enough to topple her. "You stay with Sisterkin. Keep an eye on her."

Laisze's entire body seizes up into a tense knot. She'd be leaving me alone with the woman who so mercilessly scarred her back. Who scarred *my* back. She'd be leaving me with the woman who could have so easily had my heart. I'm not sure which woman Laisze is more afraid of. She takes my hand in hers. "Is this okay, because if it's not . . ."

"I'll be fine, Laisze," I say, sure is sure.

"If she tries anything, call for me," she whispers into my ear, her cheek grazing mine as she pulls back. Her finger touches my collarbone; the back of her hand swipes my abdomen. *Be careful,* she says in our language. There is much danger to be avoided in the heart, but I know that it is not what she means.

The old man agrees to Seske's terms, and we are off, the climb quick under the low gravity. Arm over arm, we rise, until we are at the knot of it all. All the while I marvel at the depth and steadiness of the beat. It's so hypnotic, it completely pushes the three minutes thirty-seven and a half seconds out of my mind. Or was it forty-seven seconds? It no longer matters as we enter the mountainous organ through a thin tuck in ventricle seven.

The chamber gleams. The pools of ichor at my ankles are warm and thick, and the smell is so sweet. So pure.

"Amazing, let's go a little deeper," Seske says, the way she used to when we were on our adventures, and we were just kids, kids who knew nothing about the world and everything about each other. I almost fall back there with her, to that time of innocence, but the burns on my back cry out, and suddenly I'm back here, hating her for what she's put me through. What she's putting me through.

"I want to go back," I say, the furthest thing from the truth I've ever spoken. "I've seen enough."

"Please, Adalla. I need your help. Getting to this planet might be our only chance." Her voice lowers. "I haven't really told anyone this, but the beast, it showed me a place where we can thrive as a people. It's giving us this gift, despite all we've done to it. We can move forward, and maybe on this new world, we can strive to have the sort of open and honest communication these beasts—" Her eyes drift up and a smile crosses her face.

"Adalla, look," Seske says as she points at a small flock of heart murmurs just ahead. They don't even cull the murmurs. "Do you have a heartworker we could speak to?" she asks the old man. "Someone who could answer a few questions?"

He nods and walks a few dozen paces, talking to a heartworker up toward the valve, a huge guy armed with a whistle instead of a knife. If their men are all this large, I'd hate to see how big their Queens are.

And like that, Seske and I are more or less alone.

"This is so amazing," she says in that saccharine voice again. "Get your questions ready. We need to figure out a way to restore our heart and use some of their methods for managing it."

"I'm not going any farther, just so you know," I say, squirming as I cross my arms over my chest. The fabric of my shift was uncomfortable before, but now the added weight of the moss cover-up is causing me to have trouble breathing. Either that, or Seske's gotten so much better at sucking the life out of me. "If you want to go on an adventure, you can do it by yourself."

"You're still mad about the lace," she says. "I get it. But if I'd let Matris hand down your sentence, you and all of your friends would be frozen in space right now."

"You think that's why I'm mad?" I say, nearly foaming at the mouth. "I'm mad because you *left* me, Seske. You abandoned our friendship. You abandoned me when I was hurting the most, when I needed you the most." I've got tears in my eyes, and when I wipe them away, Parton's ghost is standing right behind Seske. The scars hidden inside me break wide open, and I lose it. "All those lives. All those babies born motherless, forced into bondage, then killed off when their bodies were no longer needed."

"The embryos?" Seske asks, confused. "Sisterkin is against it too, but what other choice do we have? We have nothing to trade but patinas and puppet gel."

"What?" I say, looking up at Seske. "What do you mean, embryos?"

"The ones that make grisettes. Isn't that what you were talking about?"

"Yes, but . . ." I shake my head. "Is that what was in the cargo area of the shuttle? Embryos?"

"I thought you knew," Seske says, indignant.

"How in Daidi's hairy bells would I know, Seske?" There's hurt in my voice. So much hurt. "The last time I saw you, you were meting out your 'justice' on my back. And now you're flexing your power again, except you're trading lives. Lives for what? So we can live a little more comfortably? Scratch that. So the Contour class can live a little more comfortably."

"I'm trading these 'lives' so that our beast doesn't die on us. So that our people can live on. Matris didn't let on how bad things are, but they're bad, Adalla, and they're not getting better. You and your friends know that better than anyone. The Accountancy Guard says we've got two years, tops, before our beast gives out. I think that's if we're lucky. And I'm not killing another one. I refuse. I'll drive us all into the spirit wall before that happens."

I don't know what gets in me. Probably the way she said "lives," like they really didn't matter. Like Parton's death hadn't snatched away my sanity. Like any one of those bartered souls couldn't be another of my sisters. So I do what I can. I grab her hair and pull her head until I've got her in a choke hold. And then we're fighting, and the men rush over, trying to separate us, pull us apart, but we're kicking and screaming and biting. Seske digs her elbow into my neck. I twist and buck her off me, then climb on top of her and pull hair until I feel it rip from her scalp. She shrieks, punches me in the eye, and my world goes white for a moment.

When I come to we're staring at each other like wild beasts. Chests heaving. Blood dripping. My vision in one eye clouding up. My mouth trembles like I want to yell at her some more, but I've already said everything there is to say. And then my whole body is trembling. She has the audacity to wrap me up in her arms, trying to calm me, saying she doesn't want to hurt me, that she never wanted to hurt me, but that's all she's done.

After a moment, I stop struggling, stop fighting. I stare up into her face and tell her the truth.

"You can't give them those embryos, Seske. Those are people. Our people. One of them could be my sister." I feel her body flinch against mine at the word, but I keep going. "Each of those embryos you brought here, they're someone to somebody."

"Adalla," Seske heaves, "Adalla, I'm so sorry. Of course. Whatever you say, we'll do it. We'll go home right now if you want. We'll figure this out, you and me, okay?"

I nod. And then she's staring down at me, like she wants to say something to me, and I know what that something is. And once she says it, I'm going to have to forgive her, even if my brain says that I shouldn't. Even if Laisze says I shouldn't. Even if every aching bone in my body says I shouldn't.

"Adalla . . ." Seske says, in that voice that's like a key to turning everything wrong inside me right again.

"Yeah, Seske?"

I'm trembling even more now.

And then there's a blur, a shriek, and Laisze is coming to my rescue, knocking Seske off me and straight into the wall with a big thud. And then it's her and Seske struggling, and both men and me trying to separate them, and I'm telling Laisze to stop. "We weren't fighting anymore!" I scream at her.

Laisze takes one more desperate swing, socking Seske in the stomach before she looks up at me and says, "I know."

And then the fighting is done, and they're both staring at me now, like I have the answers to anything.

"What do you want to do?" Seske says, bloody and huffing. "Go back?"

Go back to the ship? Go back to the way things were? I'd do both, if I could. But I can't.

"There is no going back," Laisze says. "Only forward." She

extends her hand to me, her body open to me, as close to a thing as I can call home. But I don't reach for her either.

The backflow of ichor swishes at my ankles, a sign of the impending beat. The heartworker breaks from his distracted thoughts as well.

"We have to leave right now," he says, and then we're all running toward the slit, the last of us slipping through when the beat bears down. Then there's another beat, louder, stronger. It shakes the entire beast. But it wasn't a heartbeat. It sounded more like a knock from the outside.

Like from explosives.

Seske sits up, eyes wide open, then looks at Laisze. "Where's Sisterkin?"

"I don't know, I—"

"You were supposed to be watching her!"

"I heard 'Dalla screaming and—"

Then another thud hits the ship, and seconds later, Commander Chubahl's voice echoes through the beast, telling its people that the Serrata is under attack.

SESKE

Of Open Space and Closed Hearts

We need to get back to our ship!" I yell at Commander Chubahl. The whole lot of them are bustling about, ignoring us. Most of the men are steaming drunk, including Wheytt.

"Get these deceitful darklings out of here!" he screams back at me. "You made us vulnerable so you could attack us!"

"No, this is on you," I say. "My sister, she was supposed to be with us. Why did you let her go?" Keep your friends close, your enemies closer . . . and never let your sister out of your sight. Especially when she's got a lot to gain from killing you.

"She said there was an emergency. She took your shuttle back."

I scream into my clenched teeth. "I assure you she is not acting on behalf of our people. She's a traitor!"

"Fire back at their ship!" Commander Chubahl orders.

"No, wait!" I scream. "You can't destroy our ship. Lend us

a shuttle. You have my word we'll bring it back. I'll squash her little coup within ten minutes."

"We have no shuttles," Commander Chubahl says. "Haven't for a long time."

"What do you mean? You boarded the Klang ship, didn't you? Stole their children!"

"We took only what was promised us. The Klang are liars. Their word is worth less than all the nothingness between stars. There's nothing worse than going against your word!" He scowls at me, and his men are all still nervous. I can tell they want us off their ship as much as we want off. "There is a way . . ." he says, then snaps his fingers. A large tub of honey-colored gel is placed in front of us. I recognize the smell immediately . . . it's got to be from those bulbous mucous glands we saw near the heart. If the secretions protect the beast from the harshness of the void, I guess it makes sense that it could protect us, too. They usher us to the doldrums, with an array of colorful sails flapping overhead, and high above that . . . the gills. "We'll get you close enough to skip over. Close enough so you can reach your ship on a lungful of air, and then we're gone."

"You want us to *jump* out of the ship?" I ask, incredulous.

"It's that or we throw you out—*without* protection. Either way, you're leaving."

I stare at him.

"It's easy. Just take aim at your beast's gills and kick off."

"Yeah, that sounds easy," I say, resisting the urge to roll my eyes.

"Okay, not easy, but it's your only option. Make your decision now, because we won't stick around much longer."

Another hit rocks the ship. We have to act, fast. But then I see the way Adalla is still seething at me. Arms crossed, like she's ready to make a stand. I can't leave the embryos here. Not if I ever want to speak to her again. Commander Chubahl won't be happy with this.

"Okay," I say, "but we'll need the embryos back. We're taking them with us."

His white face flushes red, a neat trick, if it weren't so intimidating. "You promised us girls! You cannot break that promise!"

"We promised you girls in exchange for the titanium. Keep your metal."

Then the desperation on his face becomes clear, and for the first time, I can really see him. They're not cruel, not barbarians—no more than we are, I guess. They're people like us who've made a different set of bad decisions, and if we can help them, we should. An idea hits me. "Keep the incubator. We'll send instructions for how to harvest embryos from your Queens. We'll send you everything we know. You'll have direct access to our best doctors. You have my word."

"We know what your word is worth!" he spits back at me.

"I'm sorry. I made a deal I had no right to make. These embryos do not belong to me. I will not send them off to be among strangers." But Commander Chubahl will not listen to reason, especially from the likes of me.

The ship shakes again. "Just let it go," Wheytt says to me. "We're not getting off this ship without their help. Deals here are done over drinks. They don't even know another way."

"We can't leave," I say. "I won't."

Adalla softens toward me, ever so slightly.

"I'll drink you for them," Laisze says to Commander Chubahl. "Challenge you to a contest. Most ale down wins the embryos."

"Ha!" he says. "You?" He looks Laisze over, top to bottom.

Sure, she is large, but she has nothing on these behemoths. So in the midst of battle, two flagons are brought forth, foaming with piss-yellow ale.

Laisze slams hers back like it's water and she's been thirsty for days. The room trembles from another blast, but not a single drop is wasted. Commander Chubahl raises an impressed brow, then does the same, letting out a belch that rattles us nearly as much as the blast had. The smell . . . it's otherworldly, all right.

"Warm-up's over," Commander Chubahl says, face suddenly stern and focused. "Let's see what you've really got."

A dozen flagons are set out on the table between Laisze and Commander Chubahl. They pound them back, one after another. And sure enough, the commander begins to sway in his chair. Laisze sits bolt upright, staring him down. His hand twitches for another ale, but then he relinquishes. "Fine. The embryos are yours. Just go . . ." he says, waving us away. "At the gills, disrobe and spread this over your bodies. It's important that you don't miss a spot."

Adalla dips her hand into the mucous, then draws it back, shakes her finger like it's burned. But then she's stripping down, and all the men are averting their eyes in a rush to exit. Except Wheytt, sipping on coffee, trying to sober up quick.

And then all of a sudden, Adalla and Laisze are naked and rubbing the gel all over themselves, over each other. I'm trying not to stare, but Laisze just keeps baiting me with that awful sideways grin. No—I've got a beast to save. This is no time to be getting jealous. I focus on covering myself, seizing up at the heat it sends into my skin, nearly burning. When I'm done covering myself, I help Wheytt, hitting all the patches he's missed, ignoring those ones he'll have to attend to himself. The gel starts to constrict as it dries, forming a protective sleeve that

Commander Chubahl promises will shield us from the rapid depressurization. Then it's only a matter of minutes before we're all set.

"Follow my lead," I say, then take several deep breaths, peel back the edge of the gills, then launch myself toward our beast.

Sixty-eight seconds. It's the longest I've ever held my breath. It seems like a long time, sure, but try adding the cold of space pressing against your skin. It bites, even through the heat of the gel, like hungry teeth.

A sadness washes over me, as we near our beast, seeing the full extent of what we've done to it—soft in places where bone had been harvested, hide raw and exposed in the places we'd stripped it for leather. Tentacles drooping like it's given up. But I do see some movement . . .

Weapons swing our way, aiming right at us. I wait for our ship to fire upon us, but nothing happens. Who knows what Sisterkin had told the tacticians when she got back to our ship. Maybe that we were dead, that the Serrata crew had murdered us, and she'd gotten away by the skin of her teeth. But even if Sisterkin had made it back and manipulated them into firing upon the ship, there's no way they would fire directly upon me. At least, that's what I hope.

I dare to look back and see Laisze and Wheytt and, finally, Adalla, clutching the embryo case to her chest. We're right on track. But something's wrong with Adalla. She's in pain. I mean, she's not screaming out in pain, because one breath out here would be the end of her, but something's not right. Then I see it, the frozen patch growing on her shoulder where her gel must have been too thin. There's no helping her, though, no way but forward. I spread my arms and hands when a gill is within reach. My body slams into it, hard, but I'm glad to be home. I peel the flap back so it'll be ready to shove Adalla through, and we can get her some treatment before the tissue on her shoulder becomes unsalvageable. Laisze hits first, and Adalla is heading our way, but she's panicking now, a lazy spin tumbling her all around. She tries to brace herself, but she hits side-on, with her bad shoulder. The embryo case breaks free from her grip; her eyes alight. She reaches for it, but I push her inside, then push Laisze inside, and leave the gill wide for Wheytt, who's nearly here. Then when he touches down, I reach for the embryo case, drifting farther and farther away.

My lungs are beating, but I'm. So. Close. And I can't deny, it'll be nice to bring the case back to Adalla in one piece. I hook my foot beneath the flap of the gill and stretch to my full height. My fingers touch it, just barely, but it's enough, and I'm able to pull it back into my grip.

Then the beast trembles and quakes. I'm tossed away, toward the void, but I keep the box clutched tight while reaching out to grab on to a dangling tendril. That's when I stop, out of air, and suddenly I'm staring the beast down, eye to enormous eye. She's looking right at me. I'm fading. I can tell she's fading too.

A punch to my shoulder awakens me, just enough sense left in my head to see Laisze looming over me. She'd climbed all this way? I won't make the climb back, that's for sure. She looks at me, touches my collarbone, drags her finger halfway down my breast, taps my elbow with the back of her hand, caresses my neck with the inside of her wrist; then her mouth is upon mine, over my nose, and she blows, mouthful of air, releasing my thoughts and reigniting my self-preservation. Both of our gels have faded down to nearly nothing. The cold bites so hard now. A second later, she tosses me, right toward the gills. I hit head-on, and Wheytt's pulling me in, and then we're watching Laisze, clawing her way back, slower, slower, until her grip on the tendrils releases, and she goes stiff, adrift at the side of the beast.

Wheytt tightens down the seal, and then air refills the room, and finally we can breathe. Finally, we can cry.

"Wheytt," I command. "Go have Sisterkin arrested. When I'm done with her, it'll be like she never existed."

"But I'm not an accountancy guard anymore. What authority do I have?"

"My authority. As Matris of this beast, I appoint you my chief auditor."

He looks down at himself, naked and smeared with gel. "But who would believe me?"

"Make them believe. This is the job you were born for."

"Where's Laisze?" Adalla demands. She's delirious and in so much pain, looking around but not seeing whom she needs to right now. Wheytt flashes me a compassionate smile, then leaves us alone. The void between Adalla and me intensifies.

"Gone," I say, my voice hitching in my throat. "I went to save the embryos. She came to save me. She didn't make it."

"Fuck the embryos!" Adalla screams. "Fuck them all." And then she's crying, big, painful heaves into my shoulder, and I press my hand to her back, but the ridges of her lace scars prickle my fingertips, and then I'm crying too. For all the pain I've caused her.

"I'll get her," I say. "I'll get her and bring her to the spirit wall. She'll rest with our ancestors."

Adalla pulls back, looks at me harder than she's ever looked at me. Beastworkers don't get interred in the spirit wall, especially boneworkers.

"I'll do it," I swear to her. "Even if it takes an act of the Senate, but I will see to it. She saved me. She saved these." I press the embryo case into her hands.

"Thank you," she rasps.

Then after a long, difficult silence, I say, "She wrote a note. On my skin. A message."

"How did it go?" Her eyes are wide, expectant. I bear her lover's final words, priceless words. I try my best to remember, then slowly trace them upon her skin. When I am done, she just sits there, eyes vacant.

"I did it right? It made sense?"

She nods.

"What did she say?"

"Nothing. Nothing important." She rubs her frozen shoulder, wincing at the pain. "I'd better go get this looked at."

"I'll hail my doctor for you, and—"

"No," Adalla says. "I've already got someone who can take care of it."

part IV

. . . .

exodus

Like the babe who cannot forever stay in her mother's womb, time will come again and again for the great exodus. Beware those who press back against this force, for theirs is a fight to press back against nature.

—MATRIS PALETOBA,
831 YEARS AFTER EXODUS

ADALLA
Of Hard Plating and Soft Lies

I bite down on a strap of beast hide as Sonovan peels frostbit-ten flesh from my shoulder. Tears blur my vision, and for a long moment, everything goes white, but then he's wiping me with a soothing salve and patching me with gauze.

"You need to talk to your mothers," he whispers to me.

I shake my head. I can't deal with them, 'specially Ama. "Please, don't tell them I was here. I don't want to be here. I just didn't have anywhere else to go."

He picks at one of the bone pieces entwined in my hair, sighs. "You always have a place here, Adalla. Nothing you could do will ever change that. Please, promise me you'll talk to your mothers before you go."

"How often should I change this wrap?" I ask, poking at the gauze covering my wound. Sonovan says I should be grate-ful the burn hadn't gone any deeper. Might have lost the whole arm. But I don't see it that way. I keep wishing the great dark had cut me deep, carved me up until there was nothing left. Like it did with Laisze.

Sonovan keeps talking, giving instructions for how to care for the wound, I guess. I'm nodding along, but my mind is elsewhere: on Laisze's last words, the ones Seske had traced across my skin. I wonder how long I can go on pretending they weren't true, wishing they weren't true. Sonovan's midsentence when I grab the salve he's holding out and kiss him on the forehead, and then I'm out of there, and he's whispering at me:

"Talk to your mothers, Adalla. Please!"

But I'm weaving through the pods of the surrounding families, making my way back to the heart. I need to put my mind to something useful. I cut straight for the ventricles, where all semblance of order is lost. Medical staff sits at the ready, a couple of them already treating an ichor-soaked worker still gasping for breath. It's so chaotic, they don't even notice me at first, a bare-chested, bone-haired, big-knifed bitch about to blast what they know about the beast's heart to bits.

Finally, someone notices. "You can't be here," Uridan says to me.

I don't meet her eyes. She's weak. Slow. Not worth my time. She approaches me, and I punch her in the throat. She goes down with a gurgle, trying to warn the others, but it's too late.

"We need to reinforce the valves on ventricles nine, seven, and three," I say. "And reshape the cardiac muscle with inch-thick bone strips around all the weak spots. I'll need three teams of eight."

"Who do you think you—"

Another throat punch ensures there are no more interruptions. "Matris Kaleigh sent me. I am here on her order to restore the heart as close to its original state as we can."

"But—" A hand raises, held up by a worker with scared eyes. I nod. "The heart is too erratic for that kind of major work. Lives will certainly be lost."

"Then let them be lost. The only life that matters now is the beast's. If she dies, we all die."

"But—"

I raise my fist again, and groups break off, bone plating is fetched. The beat comes, a hard beat, but not hard enough. When it's done, the groups start forward, ready to get to work, but I hold my hand up. "Wait!" I scream.

A lightness pierces through me, I can't quite describe it . . . like falling but from all directions at once. Twelve seconds later, a second beat comes, one that would have killed all twenty-four of us without a thought.

All eyes look at me, desperate to know if it's safe now. Or as safe as it's going to get. I nod, then we run, make the slits, and shove thin bone strips behind flaccid walls, bringing them closer to their original shape. Two minutes later, we're out again, leaving a large margin for error. The beat is late this time. So late, we could have installed at least a half dozen more strips, but we cannot rush this. The next beat comes, full of force. The others look to me and then we're off again.

Eighteen more runs, and the heart has steadied some . . . not the exact three minutes forty-seven and a half seconds we were used to, but it's only off by seconds now, not minutes. The other workers are exhausted and rest, but excited by the work and that no one has died. While they catch their breath, I slip into ventricle nine unnoticed.

I immediately see how red the flesh is, how inflamed. How *thin* the flesh is. Bet my knife would make it all the way through to the other side if I stabbed hard enough. I can't help but think of how much our accomplishments have cost us. Of the sacrifices we've made, only to commit the worst atrocities in return. I know this beast. I know we could fix it if we really wanted to. We could repair things, make things right, but do we even deserve that after all we've done? I press my knife into the flesh. Ichor dribbles around the shallow divot. I press harder.

Adalla would have chosen you . . .

Laisze's last words, I feel them upon my skin where Seske had written them. A message not for me but for Seske. There, on that Serrata ship, forced to choose between the woman I loved and the one who'd skewered my heart, Laisze thought I would have left her, abandoned her at a chance to be hurt by Seske once more, twice more, a dozen times . . . My knife inches deeper.

She's right. And I hate myself for it.

No one else could ever hurt me like Seske had. But what if human hearts could be mended, just like beast hearts? My knife retracts.

"Make the slit," Parton says. She's standing right next to me, watching the ichor dribble. "Make the cut. End all of this."

I startle. Not at her ghost. She's haunted me enough that I'm used to her presence, but she's never been so forceful, so adamant about anything. And she's so *corporeal.* Like if I reached out, I'm sure I would touch her.

"You know you want to," she says. "And you're right. We've messed this up. We will continue to mess it up. Best to just end things right now. There's nothing for you but more hurt."

I bite my bottom lip, try to shake the schematics from my head. It's never been that we "can't" . . . it's just that we love the little conveniences of life too much.

"There's no such thing as harmony, no such thing as symbiosis. Only struggle!"

"Why are you shouting at me?" I say to Parton's ghost. My knife is aimed at her now. "What do you care what happens to us anyway? You're dead!"

"She's gotten to you again, hasn't she? Worming her way back into your heart?"

"Who are you? Parton would never speak to me this way!" I turn to run, but there's a wall of people in front of me now. A wall of ghosts. It takes me a while to recognize their faces, but they're all there. The original ancestral mothers. All twelve of them. I must have gone completely mad.

"Make the cut, Adalla," they say. "Cut deeply, cut quickly. Free us from this torture. Free yourselves."

"No!" I scream. "I don't believe in ghosts."

"Well, I believe in you," says a new voice, a lone voice. My ama's voice. She steps through the crowd of ancestral mothers, as much of a gauzy wisp as the rest of them. "I always have. You've got the steadiest hand I've ever seen. Use it here, daughter. Use it now."

"Ama . . ." I gurgle. I shake my head. "You're not—"

"Dead? But I am. Caught by a rogue beat. It didn't hurt."

"No! Sonovan would have told me!"

"He's your tin uncle. He had no right to bear such news. That right belongs to your mothers. You refused to see them. I think it's because you knew in your heart."

My hand is shaking, barely able to hold on to the knife.

"Here," Ama says, pointing to a section of ventricle wall. "It's thinnest here. Won't take much effort. The heart will rupture after three beats. It will be quick for everyone involved."

My eyes flick to the ancestral mothers. Stately, graceful, put together. They are everything Seske is not. But maybe, judging where the mothers have landed us, that's a good thing. Seske is the leader we need. Maybe I'll never trust her with my heart, but I do trust her with this beast. She has her own visions, her own ideas. I have to at least give her a chance.

Then I hear a whimper. Down the shaft, I see a lone murmur, and I'm struck by the markings on its back. It's Bepok, my sweet pet, still as thin as the last time she'd curled up at my feet. Couldn't be anything else. But how? I'd left her behind with the last beast. She cries out to me. My tears well up in my eyes and I'm running to her. But I must have spooked her, because she's burrowing into the flesh. Hiding. I hush, whisper to her. "Come out, Bepok. It's me." I press the tip of my knife to where she'd gone below. Gently, gently, careful not to cut too deep. I can excise her if I'm quick enough, steady enough ... My knife goes still.

She calls out to me again, a deep purring from within the wall.

Something in my soul catches. The beat. I've lost all track of time, but I know it's coming. Parton, even the ancestral mothers, I could pass off as ghosts, or deficiencies in my mind, but not this. Something else is scripting my delusions. Something that wants me dead. Wants all of us dead.

I sheathe my knife. The mothers howl.

"You are nothing but a virus," my ama says to me.

"Deadly to everything you touch," Parton agrees.

"A plague upon the galaxy, this one and the next!" the ancestral mothers intone.

I turn tail and run through them all, get through the exit right as the tremble comes, so strong, it nearly rattles the teeth out of my head.

The beast wants us dead, so much so that it'll sacrifice itself in the process. The other workers pile around me, asking what had been done. Didn't I know that it was a restricted area? But I'm a blubbering mess.

"Look at what your girl has done," someone cries.

"Explain yourself," come my ama's words. I look up through my tears. She's standing there, in the flesh. I fling myself into her arms, make a million apologies into her shoulder. She hugs me tight, looks me over, then shakes her head. "Girl, you've worried us sick. Why didn't you come back home? What's happened to you?"

"The beast," I say. "It's speaking to me. Lying to me. It told me you were dead. This beast hates us with a fury I can't describe," I tell her.

"We must get you to bed, to rest," Ama says, looking at me worriedly, like I'm delirious.

I shake my head. "The beast has spoken to Seske. It was the one that told Seske of the planet. If the beast is capable of lying, she needs to know right now."

I pull myself from my mother's grip, and then I'm running, a dozen ghosts nipping at my heels.

SESKE

Of Shoddy Lists and Perfect Planets

I hold the list in my hand, looking it over for places to squeeze in last-minute additions. But for every person I add, another has to come off, and that person will be put into a stasis pod and have exactly four ounces of poison injected into their sleep balm. Death will come within fifty seconds, my tacticians assure me. They're sequestered. All of them. If news gets out, there will be pandemonium, and all hope will be lost.

I shuffle two more names and have to hold back the bile in my throat. "Here," I say, handing the list off. "It's done."

My tactician takes it from me. Her name is not on there. I don't even know her name.

"Set a course," I say. Culling our population by two-thirds will buy us eight years, just enough time to make it to the planet.

Eight years at war with our ship. Eight years fighting this sickness. Eight years of limping along through space in a

wounded ship, hoping that sacrificing all these souls will be
potent enough a medicine.

"We will get there," Wheytt says. "We'll mourn and praise
them when we do."

I nod.

There's a commotion outside the throne room, and I hear
Adalla's shouts among them. I run to her, find her coughing
and wheezing, body darkened by dried patches of ichor.

"Seske! Seske, the beast . . . it lies. It lied to me, and I
think . . . I think it's lied to you about the planet."

"What are you talking about? I saw it with my own eyes,
Adalla. And our preliminary scans confirm the presence of
liquid water and of a breathable atmosphere. It might not be
perfect, but it's as close as we're going to get."

Adalla shakes her head, then grabs me by the shoulders.
"The beast has no reason to help us. It wants us dead. Wants us
dead so badly that it's willing to sacrifice itself. What it showed
you was a lie! Have your tacticians scan it again."

I give the command, and then Adalla and I just stare at
each other. I want to confess to her. She is on the list—not just
because of what she means to me but because of her skill. The
list skews young, but her ama is on it, and Sonovan too—the
knowledge between those two combined is that of a dozen
beastworkers. But her other mothers and her will-father . . .

"Adalla, I have to tell you something—" I start to say, but
her words overlap mine, and suddenly, again we are at an im-
passe. "You go—"

She looks down at her toes. "Back at the Serrata ship, when
you were demanding that I choose . . ." She swallows. "It's just
that I couldn't, because my mind was telling me one thing
and—"

"Matris," the tactician interrupts. "All of our scans are confirmed. The planet is fine. Better than fine. It's near perfect."

"See," I say to Adalla. "I'm not saying it will be easy, but we can do this. This—this will be my legacy."

"Of course it's perfect. But what are the chances of that? All these years, searching for a suitable planet, and all of a sudden one falls into our lap?" Adalla shakes her head. "Your instrumentation, it's all hooked through the beast?"

"Of course," the tactician says.

"Then the beast could feed you whatever information it wanted. Use the ship, the *Parados I*. Scan it with something that has no connection to the beast whatsoever."

"Do as she says," I command the tacticians, and they scurry off to the ship with Adalla and me running behind them. "If you're right, Adalla," I say, "we're doomed."

"I think we could heal the ship if we really, really tried. We can't go out like this. We can't let this be all there is of our story. We've sacrificed too much to give up now."

The way she's looking at me, I can't tell if she's talking about me and her, or the entirety of our people. Maybe it's the same story.

"Matris," the tactician says to us. "We've found something . . ."

"What? Is it the planet?"

"No, the planet is fine. Everything you were promised." Her voice should be more relieved, but there's only tension behind her words.

"But . . . ?" I ask.

"It's the primary star that's the problem. Scans came through fine on the beast . . . but here, it looks like it's got a thousand years of life left. Two thousand, max."

There is a long silence.

A thousand years. I look at the planet. A thousand years is more than we could hope for out here, but to the beast . . . a thousand years is a blip. A joke. A lie. An act of betrayal. The view of the planet fades and is replaced by that of just over a hundred tentacled creatures, swimming through the blackest of ponds.

Finally, one of the tacticians dares to speak. "We've brought the beast herd up on sensors. They haven't gotten far," she says timidly. "They're all strong and fast. Any of them would make a suitable target. Should we ready the harpoons?"

I bite down so hard my jaws ache. They are not beasts. Calling them that will not make the slaughter any more palatable. The life-form we dwell upon, it's sentient. It's intelligent. It's manipulative.

It's trying to kill us.

"We are at war," I declare. "A war we started. And I will put an end to it. In the meantime, move all critical systems to the *Parados I*. All communication will happen in person. Wheytt!"

"Yes, Matris?"

"Let's draw up a set of demands and concessions . . ."

"For what, Matris?"

"For the beast."

"IN THERE?" I ASK WHEYTT.

"In there," he says, then turns his back.

The womb, it's destroyed, but Wheytt thinks I can communicate with the beast the way the Queens do on the Serrata, by giving themselves to this orifice. Commander Chubahl had taken him to see them in a room near the beast's liver, kept in a weird state between dream and wakefulness. The Queens were able to pacify the ship, to feel where it was hurting, to guide healing. Only women could do it. They'd tried men, but the results had been disastrous.

The orifice puckers at me. I swear it's watching me.

If this is what I must do to bring an end to a war we caused, I have to do it. But how do we come to terms with the atrocities we've committed? How do we make amends? What do we do if our promises are not enough? What if the beast never tires of taking our blood?

I peel away my clothes and slip my head into the orifice. Tentacles slither over me, tasting me like long, thin tongues. But nothing *happens*. I press forward, until I'm in to my hips, knees. Flesh ripples against me, but not the rough pull of suction Wheytt had warned me about. I'm not being tethered. It's not working.

I back out, slimy and wet and disappointed. Wheytt's still cowering in a corner. "For the sake of all mothers, Wheytt, it's just skin. Turn around."

He does, but his eyes come nowhere near me.

"If you're going to be my chief auditor, you're going to have to learn how to look at me and stop making things so awkward."

His eyes finally meet mine. "Sorry. I'll do better. But in all fairness, you were the one who kissed me first."

I flush, remembering that time so long ago, halfway wishing that we'd just gone through with our fraudulent engagement. An ache hangs in my gut just thinking about those times, when I thought I was a woman but had no idea of what that really meant.

"I don't know why it's not working," he says, stepping closer, and the mouth starts sucking and slobbering after him.

"Careful," I say to him. But no sooner than those words are spoken, a tendril juts out of the orifice, thick like a tongue and long as an arm. It grabs Wheytt and he's pulled inside, lips of the orifice devouring him up to his ankles. The undulations are immediate and mesmerizing, and soon, all the other orifices are sucking and grappling to the beat. I go to pull him out, but tendrils from the next orifice wrap around my fingers and tug me away. Some slip up into my nostrils, and I'm instantly put at ease, lulled into a calming gratification I can't turn away from, even as I try to fight it. The rim of the orifice widens enough to accommodate my head, my shoulders, and then all the outside world disappears completely.

This time, I'm in space, the emptiness lapping coolly over my skin—not frigid and biting, like we'd experienced before, but nice, like a dip in the springs. With an eye on each side of my head, I can see the entire sky at once, tendrils whipping in and out of my vision, mouth bared open, skimming traces of gases wading through the void, my ass end shooting out the same, propelling me faster, faster, toward a beast.

But it doesn't seem like a beast, it . . . *she* seems like a friend. I slip up next to her, our tentacles briefly knotting together in a complex greeting, and then we're staring eye to eye. I see immediately it is Wheytt behind that lens. How I know this, I am not sure, but there is a draw within me. And suddenly we're dancing, a dance I feel in my bones, bones that are older than the entire existence of humanity. It is a dance, and a song, and a story, all three together, telling of the rich history of these so-called beasts. And when we are done, I know that it is only one small section of one dance, one song, one story of millions. It'd take my entire lifetime to tell half a dozen of them.

I suddenly feel the weight of each culled beast in my gut, of the baby beast that had died before my eyes. I'm crying, tears evaporating off my lenses, but I know they're tears, and I now know that these majestic creatures do cry. How many tears have we caused?

I try to turn my thoughts to the beast, toward negotiations, toward reparations, toward making things right the best I can, but I'm seized again by the thought of the creature that is Wheytt. More and more of our tentacles tangle, until a breath couldn't pass between us. We pirouette together, synchronized.

The pleasure shared between us is of such an intensity that all the stars dim. Our two mouths undulate together, widening, widening, as if we were in a competition to swallow each other whole. More tendrils erupt like a thousand tongues, each finding its mate. They twirl, entangling, until there is one left, unmated. One of mine. It lengthens, flows deeper and deeper into his mouth. Wheytt shudders so hard, but the other tendrils, they hold tight. Such tender, tender flesh must not be exposed to the vacuum of space. Then the tip of my tendril touches something hard and round. An ovispore—the word slips into my head, like I've always known what it is. And like I've always known how *precious* it is. The tendril wraps it up, over and over, until the ovispore is safe in a cocoon. I reel it back, and it disappears inside me. The deed, it is done, and yet Wheytt and I, we remain entangled, watching the sky spin, watching stars go nova. The feeling of lust eases into one of familiarity, of a bond that stretches back eons, but it also rings of something hollow, of hurt.

Like this is not a vision, but a memory.

Sometime in our history, we'd taken the beast's mate. Then we'd taken its unborn child. I shake so hard, the connection fades. I suddenly become all too aware of the tendrils linked into me, all of me, no place left uncompromised. I vomit up the ones in my throat, barely able to pull the ones from my nostrils. The ones in my tear ducts suck up my tears, so many of them that tears will never reach my cheeks. I buck and writhe until they let me go, and I spill out onto the floor.

After I catch my breath, I run to Wheytt's orifice, now quiet and unassuming. I pry the mouth of it open and reach in. I can't feel anything. I'm shoulder-deep, reaching farther. The flesh stands still. Nothing grabs at me, tempts me in.

"No," I scream. "Wheytt!"

I call for help, but I know in the pit of my stomach that he is gone. That he's become our penance for taking the lives of her loved ones. But I don't stop digging. I can't.

I won't.

SESKE

Of Full Plates and Empty Wombs

At the interment ceremony, gossip spreads faster than prayers to the ancestors. The turnout is good at least, but the classes repel from one another like oil and water. In one corner, boneworkers gorge themselves on delicacies and ale, while the entirety of Wheytt's former accountancy crew are here, sobbing like they hadn't nearly harassed his dream out of him. And the Contour class looks down upon them all, sipping on their fancy teas, judging everyone's every move.

Adalla and I stand, dressed in layers and layers of bereavement gowns, fingers twined. Her face has been stoic, not a tear, even when Laisze's body was pressed into the spirit wall. Not even when several Contour class men fainted at the sight. Wheytt's family didn't show, so I stood in their stead. He was a friend. A true friend, maybe something more, whom I wish I'd treated better. If I were to list out every bratty thing I'd said or done to him, I wouldn't be any better than the accountancy guards who'd harassed him. But I stand for him now. And Doka is here, the dutiful husband, at my side in my time of need. Finally, when the crowd settles and condolences are mostly doled out, I send him off to fetch us another round of battered wood lice and gravied biscuits.

"How are you doing?" I ask Adalla when he's gone, her eyes still forward upon the wall.

"Okay," she says. "Sure is sure. You?"

"The wall still makes me nervous. But I'm glad you're by my side." I squeeze her hand. "If you knew this was how it was going to end when you first met Laisze, would you still have become friends?"

"Absolutely," she says without hesitation. She must have noticed that I started at her sureness, because she backpedals. "I do believe that, sure is sure is sure. And I know because I've already given it a lot of thought, and if I felt otherwise, none of us would be standing here right now. It's worth it, Seske. The price is high, and the price, it will change you. But the winner of life isn't the one who gets through with the least number of scars."

I wince at her words and the many scars I'd put upon her back. "How do we win, then? At life?"

She looks directly at me for the first time today. "We as in . . ."

"We as in us, as a people. The people of *Parados I*. Humanity."

Adalla nods, relaxes some. "We *humans* have a lot of scars. And some scars just don't heal no matter what you do. But most will, given enough time."

"Time is not something we have a lot of." They'll let me mourn for a few days, but then they'll need their Matris to lead. Only problem is, I have no idea of where to lead them. We can't cull another ship. We can't go off to a planet with a star that'll scorch everything we build. We can't keep going down the path of ignorance, hoping things will get better as the beast continues to take from us what we've taken from her.

My stomach grumbles. I set my eyes, trying to find where Doka is with our food, and then I see him coming with plates piled with a dozen delicacies, and behind him strut his heart-mothers. I groan. Adalla tries to let go of my hand to avoid confrontation, but I hold it tight. His amas notice but pay us no mind. They are too excited to care. Excited amas are never a good thing.

Ama Roszet pinches my cheeks, like I am a mere child and not the ruler of our people. In the whole of our history, there has never been a frown to hang so heavily upon someone's face as the one on mine. "Please do not touch me," I say. On instinct, I turn to Wheytt to give him our silent signal that I'm uncomfortable, but it is another accountancy guard who stands watch over me now. I sigh. Shake off the thought.

"Matris, you are so radiant," Ama Roszet coos, unoffended by my demand. "Oh, how you honor the fallen with your glow. And soon it will be time to celebrate new life, no?"

"No," I say, suddenly remembering the promise of a grand-child I'd made to get them off my back long enough to sneak off with Wheytt to meet with the Serrata. "No new life coming any time soon, I'm afraid."

Ama Linpur nods at me knowingly, then nudges me in the side for good measure. "Still too soon to speak of it? Won't be long now, not with the way Doka says you're piling down food." And then her hands are on my stomach, fingers rounded out to either side, with her thumbs right upon my navel. Fury grips me so hard. "Don't worry," she whispers. "We've already started compiling will-mother candidates and have a dozen heart and head families ready to join. Your entire family unit will all be arranged quietly before the little one arrives, so she'll get the best guidance from all of her parents."

I grit my teeth and ball my fists, ready to give her a harsh and fast lesson on disrespecting me, but fortunately, my guard finally notices my frustration and moves Ama Linpur out of striking range before I can connect.

I growl and grab the plate from Doka, stress eating biscuit after biscuit, then dipping the wood lice in the leftover gravy and sucking them down by twos. Doka reaches for one of those perfectly golden battered balls, and I fix him in place with a ferocious stare.

"Seske! Come on," Adalla says, wiping a smudge of gravy from my chin. "Let's take a little break away from here . . ." Adalla tugs my elbow, and I don't resist. I need to get away from these people.

We run, so fast, so hard, over to the gall fields. It's quiet here, the quiet I need, but Adalla keeps leading me, deeper, deeper. A mountain of old husks stands before us, and she pushes me up into one of them. She follows me in, then turns on a dusty ley light that washes the whole place in a warm red glow.

It's a nice, peaceful spot where we won't be interrupted. We both struggle to get comfortable in the swath of our raiment. We're a mess, the both of us, flipping and flopping in our skirts, and then we're both giggling, nervous painful laughs that do their best to lighten the mood. But then I'm crying into her shoulder, stuffing pastries into my face, unsure if I'll be able to hold myself together, much less an entire people.

She pulls me in closer, arms wrapped around me, but she startles as her hand touches my side.

"Seske . . . what you said about children back there, you're sure you're not pregnant?"

"Of *course* I'm sure. Why do you ask?"

"I . . . just felt something. Inside you. Move."

"It's just gas. I've got awful gas. I've eaten so much this morning." I shove another pastry into my mouth, not bothering to catch the crumbs. Both of her hands are on my stomach now, though. She brings mine down as well, and together we stare. There definitely seems to be more of me down there. In a fury, I'm unhitching and unwrapping all my skirts until I'm just in my silk slip. There's a pooch. A definite pooch. And Adalla is right. It's not just gas.

"It's Doka's," she whispers, as if the softer she says it, the less chance she has of it being true.

I shake my head. "No . . . we've left our marriage in an open state, despite his pleadings."

"Wheytt's . . ." she mumbles even softer.

"No, we've never . . ." I catch myself. We *have* been intimate. We were beasts in some kind of shared memory, but it was us. What if? No. It's not possible. And yet . . .

What if taking Wheytt from me was only part of the penance? Was the beast giving me this child, just to snatch it away and hurt me again?

"Oh, Adalla, what am I going to do?" My heart won't stop racing. I'm not ready to be a mother. I'm not ready to be the leader of this ship either. And yet, here I am.

"I'm here for you," she says, bringing our foreheads together. "Whatever you need, I'll help you with."

"The last thing my line needs is another scandal."

"Don't worry about them. Worry about you. What do *you* need?"

"Space," I say flatly. Adalla backs up. "Not from you. I just need a little more time to figure out who I am. I need to process. I've had so much thrown upon my shoulders. I can't balance all of this. No one could. Not all at once. I know I can do this. I just need people to give me room to be myself, to accept me for who I am."

"You can have all the space you need here," Adalla says. "And you know I'll always accept you for who you are. I'd never want to change you."

So we sit together, the soft nest of both our dresses beneath us. She tells me about Parton, tells me about the fight with her mother, tells me about Laisze. I catch her up with my escapades, bare my scars, hoping it will offer an explanation for the woman I've become. Our bodies have found comfortable places against each other, and we just . . . fit. All the world that exists is confined by the walls of this gall, and that's okay with me.

The ley light flickers out, but no one moves to shake it back up, and we're just two bodies caught together in the dark.

"Seske?"

"Yes, Adalla?"

"I'm thinking about kissing you."

"I was thinking the same thing." I can do this. No matter what scars the future may hold, I want this moment. This one moment. I put everything out of my mind and concentrate on the sound of her voice, on the smell of her skin.

"But I'm worried I shouldn't," Adalla whispers.

"I'm not trying to replace Laisze," I say. "I know how special she was to you. I know I can't compare."

Adalla laughs, but it's clipped off by a painful silence. "She always thought the same about you. Like I'm some sort of prize."

"You're some sort of something wonderful."

"Maybe I was, once. What I am now is just hopeful. Mostly hoping that I can kiss you without something weird happening. I'm hoping I can. I'm worried that I can't."

"Well, if you kissed me and something weird *did* happen, would you regret the kiss?"

"Not at all."

"Well, there's your answer."

"Well, there it is," Adalla says. She presses closer and I start tingling all over. Her body against mine. Thigh between mine. Breath hot and so close to my lips. She stops half an inch before our mouths meet. "Seske," she says. "I think something weird is happening."

"Nothing weird is happening."

"You're wet. Down there."

"I think that's pretty normal."

"Like *really* wet."

"And that's good, right?"

"Seske?"

"Yes, Adalla?"

"There's some kind of tentacle thing curling around my thigh."

Daidi's bells.

ADALLA

Of Damp Slips and Dry Buckets

'm sorry, I'm sorry," I say. I shake the ley light with all my might until our space brightens, even though I'm scared of what I'll see. I start getting dizzy-headed, but I keep my eyes locked on Seske's, ignoring the dozen black tentacles erupting from her humble bits.

"Why are *you* apologizing?" Seske asks, swatting the tips of the tentacles away like they're merely bothersome flies.

"I don't know. I don't know. All that talk about accepting you for who you are . . ." I bite my lip and oh, blessed mothers I could have dealt with it being Wheytt's baby, but this? "How are you so calm?"

"Because I think I understand what's happening, and I know how to make things right with the beast. She needs our help." A tentacle curls lovingly around Seske's pinkie finger. She strokes it softly with the tip of her thumb. "I have to deposit this egg into one of the other beasts for her. When

Wheytt and I were in the beast's orifices, when we were, you know . . . we were intimate, connected to a memory or something. It felt so real . . ."

"This sounds like information you might have volunteered earlier, Seske. You've lost your honor to an alien."

"I think I might have been given a chance to regain my honor. A chance to fix it all." Seske pulls down the hem of her dampened silk slip, then proceeds to wrap herself back into her raiment. At least the tentacle things are out of view.

I take a deep breath. I have to get that thing out of her, but it won't be easy. "We'd best get you to the doctor. Just to have a look."

"There's no need to look." Her hands cradle her belly, plump and firm as a gall bud beneath her dress now. "Everything is fine. Right on schedule."

I shake my head, fearful of what other tricks beastie is using to get its way. But whatever is inside Seske, it's growing fast. If it keeps up this rate, she's going to be in a whole lot of trouble.

"For me, Seske. Please, come with me," I say.

She shakes her head now. "I need to get to a shuttle. Probably quickly." She descends down the hole in the gall, barely fitting through, a noticeable waddle to her step once she's out. "I need to know now, whose side are you on?"

"Me? I'm on your side!" I say, scurrying after her.

"That was a trick question. There's only one side! What's good for the beast is good for us. What's bad for the beast . . . likewise. I need you to understand this is what has to be done."

"I'm not letting you go out there alone." I wring my fingers. Doubt floods my mind, but I've never heard Seske speak so surely, so confidently, about anything. I know that it is her and not the beast, but there's no way anyone else will believe it. "But we can't just go demanding a shuttle so we can impregnate another beast. The Accountancy Guard will have you locked up so fast. They'll smell you coming. Daidi's bells, the smell, Seske." It's not entirely unpleasant, but it is *unhuman.*

"I'm the Matris of this ship. All shuttles are at my disposal."

"They won't see you as Matris anymore. They're willing to put up with a lot of things, betcha, but tentacle-cooch isn't one of them."

Seske aims a mischievous grin my way. "We have to risk it," she says. "This egg is too precious. You remember how you felt about those embryos? Well, this is my thing I need to protect."

"What if . . . what if we found another way?"

Seske turns around, faces me. "What other way?"

"That gel, the one that let us travel through space. We can use that."

"I thought our beast didn't secrete that stuff."

"It doesn't. But I can get it to." I bite my lip. "I'm sure of it," I add, but mostly to convince myself.

Seske shakes her head. "We are too far away from the beasts. It would never work."

"We will need to get closer, then. We've—"

"What?"

"We've got to trigger an emergency exodus. Make them think we need to cull another one."

Seske flinches, visibly hurt by the idea.

"We won't, of course. It's just so we're close enough to fly."

"We?"

"I'm not leaving your side. I'm going to help you deliver that . . . that . . ."

"Zenzee . . ." Seske says confidently. Whatever happened

between her and beastie must go deeper than I thought. "That's what their kind is called. How do we trigger exodus?"

I hand her my knife. "*You're* going to trigger exodus. Now listen carefully ..."

WHILE SESKE GOES TO MAKE THE SLIT, I GO TO GET THE ICHOR supply to the mucous gland rerouted. I try to recall exactly the configuration I'd seen on the Serrata ship. I feel naked without my knife, but I trust Seske with it. Me, I make do with sharpened bone scraps, filing the edges so fine like Laisze used to do. I find a nice, thick artery, cut carefully, and reroute the flow to the wilted gland. It puffs up some, but it still looks nothing like the glowing, magnificent organ I'd seen on that other ship. I massage the organ, helping the flow of ichor fill it. It purrs against me, so I massage harder. Finally, the first drop of golden gel drips from the puckered orifice. I place a bucket beneath, continuing to milk the gland. My arms are aching, and yet the bucket is an inch deep, only enough to cover a pair of legs.

A tremor comes, deep and long. An expected tremor. Lasts longer than any we've ever felt. Then the air starts to change. A doldrums breech, venting mad vapors right into the living quarters. If Seske followed directions, the Accountancy Guard should be detecting the effects of a leak. Irreparable. Fatal. The cutting of the doldrums' branch nerves should *also* give that reading, but it's reversible. At least if we repair them in time.

Alarms ring, calling for emergency exodus. There is sheer panic all around me, everyone running around like they're being chased by vengeful spirits, but I keep beating the organ, three inches in the bucket now, enough for Seske at least, with nothing left over for me. I beat harder.

Finally, Seske's by my side, holding a couple re-breathers. She looks in the bucket and strips before I get the chance to tell her.

"They're probably looking for you," I say.

"Let them look. If I can't trust them to orchestrate exodus, then we're as good as finished anyway."

I stop beating the gland and stare at her. She's radiant, the swell of her stomach something close to perfect. Even the tentacles seem fitting now. She applies the gel to her skin, and all I know is that I've got to make enough of this for me too, because there's no way I'm letting her out there alone. I close my eyes and punch my hand up the orifice, hard as I can, deep as I can, and then I feel it, the hunk of atrophied muscle that should be doing all the work. I squeeze it once, twice, again, and all of a sudden, the flow floods down, and there's enough gel for me and half a dozen more people.

And then we're at the gills. Sure enough, the herd is in sight. My breath catches in my throat as I watch them, a handful of precious jewels strung among the stars. We have to time this just right. Hand in hand, we wait for the herd to swing back around into view, and we launch. Seske looks over at me, smiles. I smile back. She points us to one of the beasts—the Zenzee, I guess I should call it—a big, beautiful creature, the lights on its hide strobing in a mesmerizing pattern like it's trying to speak to us. Somehow, instead of feeling miniscule and insignificant aside its vastness, I feel honored and welcome. We land near its underside, and we crawl our way toward the patch of black tentacles surrounding an open maw. A large expanse of pale-purple flesh greets us inside, and when we pry open the lips, we're able to pull ourselves in. A whole ecosystem is spread out before us, swampy with drifts of fog floating past. The plant life gets denser the farther we venture in, as diverse as species in the woodward canopies.

I stop to caress the petals of a black flower. It curls up at my touch and disappears into the moist ground with what sounds like an aggravated harrumph.

"We've still got a bit of a hike," Seske says, huffing and wheezing.

"You look like you need to rest."

She shakes her head. "The egg is pressing up on my lungs. We need to get it out. Soon." She hands my knife back to me. "If things go badly, do what you have to. Don't worry about me. Just get that egg to the ovispore. Promise me."

"Seske!"

"*Promise me!*"

"Okay, okay. Let's just hurry, okay?"

We move faster then, swatting away the flies and curious buggies wandering about us, the invaders. The ovispore is just ahead.

"There," I say.

"It's just like in our vision," Seske says. "We've made it. Thank you."

A light flickers. A light that didn't come from the lamps on our re-breathers. I turn slowly and see a set of pincers, each the size of a woman, attached to a phosphorescent creature with a face so ferocious it could stop a heart cold. Nearly does, mine, betcha. But I can't die, because Seske needs protecting, and our world needs saving, and neither of those things is going to happen if I let this creature get the best of me. I swallow back my fear, push Seske toward the ovispore, and pull out my knife.

SESKE

Of Infinite Pain and Null Gravity

I fly toward the ovispore, hands out, and orchestrate a perfect landing. There's fighting going on not far—Adalla fighting ... something—but I can't let those worries distract me. She's tough. She'll protect me and I'll protect this egg.

Relax, I tell myself. The ovispore is a nest of fine hairs, and I lie upon them. The tentacles are excited. I grab a patch of hair in each of my fists to steady myself against the pressure mounting within me. I bear down, trying to help the process, hoping I'm not too late. Everything from my ribs down is a flame of pain, as if I'm being split apart. I'm there like that for five minutes, maybe ten, maybe an eternity, my screams blending with Adalla's.

Finally, she's at my side, covered in neon-green blood, literally glowing with the life force of some poor creature. Flecks of its carapace cling to her skin. Deep scratches cross her face.

They'll make good scars and a good story if we get out of this alive.

"You're doing just fine," she whispers as she wipes the sweat from my forehead. "Where do you want me?"

"Close," I moan. "Behind me."

She quickly slips behind me. Whatever's going on down there, she doesn't want to be a witness to it. Neither do I. But with her touch, my resolve redoubles, and I press harder, press until I'm about to pass out, and then there it is . . . a moment of lightness, of freedom, and I gasp. The egg has slipped out. The tentacles draw it into a deep divot, then the hairs start to press down neatly over it. Adalla scrambles to pull us out of the way before it drags us down with it.

She hugs me close for a long, long time. The fog of my mind clears, the hormone-induced euphoria ending so abruptly that I puke on the spot. Horror strikes next as I start to process what my body has just been through. Phantom tentacles whip across my thighs, and I remember the feeling of that alien thing stretching my womb thin, wrecking my insides, leaving little bits and pieces of itself tied to me.

I try not to panic.

"You did it. You were amazing," Adalla says, holding me tight. "We can rest here for a while, but we need to lie low. There are more of those beetles grazing about." She's being flippant. When she's flippant, there's more bad news to be had. Worse than woman-eating scarabs.

"Adalla. What's wrong?"

"You mean besides everything that just happened? Well, there's that, for one thing." She shines a light up to the dome where we'd come in. It's no longer supple flesh but webbed concrete and barbs, similar to those that had protected the baby Zenzee, but on a much grander scale. It looks impenetrable. Depositing the egg must have triggered a hormonal reaction. "We're not getting out that way for sure."

"We're trapped here?" I ask.

"We'll find a way out. Just think of it as one of our old adventures," Adalla says.

Somehow, this fails to comfort me, but as soon as I can drift, we're floating toward the wall. Adalla sizes up the space, doing some sort of mental calculations in her head; then she makes a straight cut, effortlessly slicing through layers and layers of flesh. She goes in first, takes my hand and pulls me through. A couple more turns, and a swift trip through some sort of ooze-lined tube, and we're here, in the Zenzee's stomach. Pristine, like an unspoiled garden.

There's no gravity, and palm fronds light up the entire inside of the stomach, and I see for the first time what they look like in their natural state, not the oozing puddles to be stepped upon. Dallis ferns reach up so high, some of them touch their counterparts on the other side. And patches of day moss! It had grown so wildly on our last beast, and as children Adalla and I had adorned ourselves with them. They had medicinal uses as well. It should have been a sign that our current beast hadn't any. I pick up a handful of it, take in a smell like warm vanilla. I hold on to it as a specimen to take back.

Above, flocks of murmurs drift through the air. Adalla and I look at each other, and then kick off our perch to fly among them. They know no fear and accept us into the flock. We cut through them, playing with the large ones. Several small ones land upon Adalla's back, but she doesn't flinch. In fact, I've never seen her so happy. We should be looking for the exit. Our oxygen is running low in our re-breathers, but I don't dare cut into this moment. She deserves this little bit of happiness. Maybe I do too.

"We could stay here forever," Adalla whispers to me, and the way she says it, I know it's not a hypothetical wishing. She means it. We could. Just her and me. Live off the land, make a home out of a gall, spend our days free, beyond judgment and expectations.

"I wish we could," I say. But my mind slips back over that time when interspecies hormones made me say some weird things. Weird, but true. We cannot be on different sides— Adalla and me on one and the crew of the *Parados I* on the other. Or the Serrata and the other ships. We are all on the same side, the side of the Zenzee. If we cannot all make this work, then ultimately there's no hope for any of us. "But we have to get back," I say.

Adalla kisses the wings of a baby murmur, no larger than the span of her hand. "Why? Don't you love it here? Couldn't you live like this—"

The Zenzee shudders, then reels. The entire stomach goes quiet.

"That's why," I say.

They've started the culling already. We scramble back down and toward the gills.

"If they've hooked her already, then I've got an idea to get us back home," I say.

At the gills, we stare at the harpoon lodged into the Zenzee's side. We wince as it pulls against the beast, trying to reel it into submission. Several others are lodged in it too, but I choose the closest. I press the moss sample to my stomach. "You trust me?"

"Of course!" Adalla says.

"Press your body to mine and hold tight. We need to make sure all three of us make it back safe."

Adalla looks side-eyed at the little tentacled flowers, but says nothing and presses to me.

"How steady is that knife of yours?" I ask.

"As steady as they get."

"Good. Because we've got one chance to make this work. When I give the signal, cut."

There's no more time to explain. I wrap my arms around her as tight as I can, then we kick off toward the cable. It's mostly copper, but in between each section, there's a space about a fourth inch thick that's rubber. If Adalla can get her knife in there, she can cut it loose.

The cold is ripping at us so hard. Patches of the gel are already gone, the cold of space burning me badly. But we're almost there. Finally, she grips the rope with one hand. I nod at the section, and she swipes down, perfect cut, through and through. With the tension released, the cord slings back toward the ship, sending us careening with it. We hit the hull unceremoniously, then Adalla skillfully cuts us an entrance, moving at a shallow angle through the flesh so that the atmosphere won't vent.

We fall into a pile on the floor. Adalla is burned worse than I am, but she's the one fussing over my wounds, talking about whisking me off to the doctor. But there's no time to worry about our bodies—there's a larger body that needs us more. We need to stop the culling.

We race to the throne room, both of us covered in semitranslucent gel and looking a complete mess. The only good thing is that the halls are empty since everyone is filing into stasis pods in the ship's cargo holds. "Go patch up the severed nerve and get our Zenzee stabilized," I tell Adalla. "I'll fix things on this end."

In the throne room, Doka is in the command seat. With no heirs and no other wives, the position has fallen upon him in my absence. A strangeness washes over me, seeing a man in that chair, but I know he is ready for this.

He catches my eye, looks me over, then waves for his guards to clothe me. "Seske! Where have you been? What's happened to you?"

"I've been busy trying to save our asses. There's no void leak. We tricked the system. Adalla is fixing it right now. I impregnated the beast you're trying to cull, and now ours isn't mad at us anymore. We don't need to go through with exodus. We've still got a chance to fix everything we've broken. It's not too late!"

"What?" Doka asks. "Slow down. You're not being rational."

"There's no time for slow and there's no time for rational. You have to abort the culling."

"Me? Then you're not asking me to step down as Matris? I had a whole speech laid out about how I am more fit for this job than you'll ever be."

"I know that. And you're right—you're a better fit for the position than I could ever hope to be. I don't want to be Matris, and I don't want to be your wife either. But I do want us to work together to do what's best for us and what's best for our world. We're good at working together, remember?"

Doka laughs. "Yes, you're right about that. I'll hear you out."

And we talk. And he agrees. He's not so awful. And him being Matris will have the ancestral mothers rolling in the wall, and that gives me more than enough satisfaction.

I LOOK OUT OVER THE STASIS PODS CRAMMED INTO THE CARGO bay. There are thousands of them, filled with Contour class families, sleeping deeply. Doka made me promise that we'd let them out eventually, but even he's been happy to get a little break from his mothers. In the meantime, beastworkers are busy returning our Zenzee to her original state, or as close as we can get to it. Bones are being grafted. Organs are being repaired. Manicured gardens are being allowed to grow free.

And our Zenzee's fever has finally broken.

"Psst . . . Seske," comes Adalla's voice from behind me.

I turn and see her, dressed in several layers of flowing silks, bundled over with a practical felted shawl, and just a hint of ichor caught beneath her nails and in the crook of her ear. And a faint smudge along her collarbone.

"How's the heart?" I ask her.

"Strong. Steady. A nice solid beat every three minutes, forty-seven and a half seconds."

"Excellent. So does that mean you finally have a few moments to spare?"

"For you? Sure."

Our Zenzee's heart may be steady, but mine is aflutter as I take her by the hand.

"Keep your eyes closed," I say to Adalla as I lead her to the gardens, carefully guiding her through the new swamp right near where the Muirabuko Emporium had once stood. The spongy ground gives wherever we step, sometimes swallowing our legs up mid-calf. Critters scurry out of the way for the most part, but I've gotten used to the ones that like to nibble at our toes or slink their tendrils around our ankles.

Or at least that's what I tell myself.

"Okay, open them," I say, barely able to contain my smile.

Adalla looks down at the patch of day moss that's spread out, clusters of succulent pink and green leaves upturned like miniature teacups.

"Seske!" she says, her teeth chattering. We're still getting used to the chilly air nipping at us. "They're so beautiful!"

"You could say I'm a bit of an expert at spotting beauty," I say to her.

She blushes.

"Adalla?"

"Yes, Seske?"

"I'm going to kiss you and something weird is going to happen. But a nice weird. No tentacles, I promise."

Adalla's lips purse up into something almost unkissable. Almost. "Stop teasing, Seske."

And I pull her close, and our lips touch, and an instant later, the world stops spinning—no artificial gravity, the last of my demands to Doka. At least while our Zenzee heals. And just like that, we're drifting up, up. Adalla pulls me closer, like she hasn't even noticed. Like all there is of import in this life is within this space heated by our breath.

And I can't say she's wrong about that.

Acknowledgments

One of the things I'm most proud of in this life is keeping good people around me. Their encouragement feeds my soul, which in turn feeds my creativity and weirdness, which is how we end up with the word *tentacle-cooch* in a novel. So to my friends and family, my agent and editor, my readers and fans—from the bottom of my four-chambered heart, I thank you for going on this wondrously strange journey with me.

Experience all of Nicky Drayden's award-winning

and critically acclaimed worlds with excerpts

from *THE PREY OF GODS* and *TEMPER*!

THE
PREY
OF GODS

Chapter 3

SYDNEY

Sydney Mazwai cusses herself as the roundabout sucks her in like a soap bubble circling the drain. She gets no respect on this piece-of-crap moped—rusted handlebars, no rear fender, expired license plate. But there's no point in worrying about being street legal when she's doomed to spend eternity doing clockwise circles in the midst of Volvos, Land Rovers, and tricked-out bot taxis looking for an easy fare in the crowded streets of Port Elizabeth, South Africa.

Victorian-style buildings pass by again and again, like the backdrop of a 1930s gangster movie car chase. The blare of a tour bus horn sets Sydney's nerves on edge. She'd spent the bulk of her morning coaxing coffee residue out of an all too empty can, hoping to churn up enough black gold to get her through her commute. Now Sydney grits her teeth as she passes the eighth beanery on her way to work. Dropping forty rand on fancy coffee drinks isn't an option, though, not when the rent check is three days overdue. She'll settle for Ruby's tart brew at the nail salon. It tends to taste faintly of acetone, but it goes down smoothly enough. More importantly, it does its job: injecting caffeine into her bloodstream as quickly as possible without the aid of a hypodermic needle. And while, yes, it's supposed to be for customers only, everyone in the shop knows better than to get caught standing between this Zulu girl and her morning Joe.

Sydney holds her breath and leans, cutting sharply in front of a bot taxi. She glances over her shoulder and laughs as the mono-eye of its robot driver flashes red, road rage mechanical style. Her happiness is short-lived as a sea of brake lights greets her on Harrower Road. She can't be late if she's going to hit Ruby up for an advance on her paycheck. Reluctantly, Sydney lifts her index finger and draws upon a fragile force within, but then pushes it back down. The lights will turn green on their own soon enough. There's no sense in compounding caffeine withdrawal with a stomachache as well.

Sydney grits her teeth, hops the curb, and motors down the pavement while swerving past bustling pedestrians, a late-model alpha bot running odd errands for its master, and a dreadlocked street musician tooting on an old bamboo pan flute. His staccato song flutters Sydney's heart, and she puts her shoulder to the wheel, pushing her little 49cc engine to its limit. At last, she cuts down a series of familiar alleyways, dodging ornery dik-diks rummaging through the overspill from a restaurant's rubbish bin, and kicking past a stack of wooden pallets from the Emporium her salon shares an employee driveway with. Sydney props her moped up against the side of the brick building and takes her helmet inside with her. At least it has some value.

She stumbles in, beelines straight to the coffee carafe, and pours herself a tall cup. The earthy aroma puts her at ease, and the warmth of the cup pulls the morning chill from her bones. But before she can take a single sip, Ruby's right there, glaring with those eyes too wide for her face and an unlit cigarette dangling between her lips. "You're late," she says, hands propped on her hips. She juts her chin toward the reception area. "Mrs. Donovan is waiting. She's not happy."

Sydney glances down at her watch. She's three minutes early actually, but her clients expect nothing less of her than to bend space-time to accommodate their schedules. Especially Mrs. Donovan. Sydney rolls her eyes, grabs her alphie off its dock on the shelf, then puts on a smile that's somewhere south of sincerity but north of keeping her job.

"You appreciate me, don't you?" she says, clicking the alphie's on switch. The robot's screen yawns to life, and its spider legs extend down from its round silver body until they clink against the floor with the sound of a rat tap-dancing on a tin roof. Sydney strokes her hand over the smooth dome surface, and the alphie coos like a beloved pet—all preprogrammed, but it's nice to feel needed nonetheless.

"She's waiting!" Ruby's voice comes from out back as she snags a quick smoke.

Sydney grimaces, then slips into an apron. The alphie follows behind her obediently, its myriad of compartments containing all her nail supplies, color palettes, and doggie biscuits—staples of the job. Sydney tries not to let it go to her head, but she's the best nail artist Ruby's got. Ruby knows it, and the other ladies know it. They're shooting her scowls right now, in fact, but dare say nothing to her face.

They know better. She ignores them and lets her body settle

into the smooth beat of classic Mango Groove piping softly from her alphie's tin speakers. Her spirits lift as the jazz fusion instrumental loosens her nerves, and suddenly Sydney feels like she's capable of enduring whatever nonsense Mrs. Donovan intends on spouting at her today. Mrs. Donovan is an arrogant heifer of a woman, but she tips generously when she's in a good mood. Very generously. Maybe even enough for Sydney to get her landlady off her back for a few days.

Sydney leaves the alphie at her station, then wades through the menacing stares of her coworkers, especially Zinhle Mpande who used to do Mrs. Donovan's nails. Sydney smiles brightly at Zinhle, gives her a little wave with her fingertips, then broadens her chest to greet her most loathed customer.

"Mrs. Donovan! My heavens, you look radiant today," Sydney says in the most saccharine voice she can muster, then switches from English to Afrikaans to earn some extra brownie points. "Like you swallowed the brightest star in the sky."

Mrs. Donovan flushes, splotches of red on her paper-white skin. Her features are striking—sharp nose, brilliant green eyes, lips maybe a little too full for someone who claims pure Dutch descent—though she's hardly what anyone would call a beauty. Maybe she could have been, but she's full of vinegar, this one.

"Precious, you're too kind," Mrs. Donovan says, shoving her way past Sydney and walking swayback toward her station. "Though it'd be kinder if you didn't leave me waiting out there like yesterday's laundry. If it was up to me, Precious, I'd take my business elsewhere, but Sir Calvin van der Merwe just wuvs you sooo much!" Mrs. Donovan reaches down into an enormous A.V. Crowlins purse, pulls a sleepy Zed hybrid out, and aims his head at Sydney's cheek.

"Good morning, Sir Calvin," Sydney sings, trying not to cringe as his reptilian tongue creeps along the side of her face. The best Sydney can guess is that he's a whippet/iguana cross with his lean legs and gray peach fuzz fur peeking between patches of scales, but of course it'd be impolite to ask, implying that his creation was something other than an act of God.

Sir Calvin smacks his rubbery iguana lips, then immediately begins barking, which sounds more like something between a whistle and a sneeze. It's annoying as hell. Sydney fetches a doggie biscuit from one of her alphie's compartments and snaps it in half.

"May I?" she asks Mrs. Donovan. "They're from the Emporium, 100 percent organic ingredients." Which of course is a lie, but it makes rich folk like Mrs. Donovan feel better. Sydney doesn't blame her. If she'd dropped half a million rand on a designer pet, she wouldn't want her Zed hybrid eating stale grocery-brand biscuits either. Sir Calvin doesn't mind and snatches it out of her hand before Mrs. Donovan answers. He curls up into Mrs. Donovan's ample lap and chews greedily, giving Sydney a long moment to regain her wits.

"So it's a mani/pedi for you today?" Sydney asks, pulling a nail file from its sterilized packaging. "Special event this evening?"

"A fund-raiser for Councilman Stoker." The councilman's name practically oozes from her lips.

Sydney decides to pry. That's half the reason why she earns the fat tips she gets. She's a confidante to these ladies. Stuff they wouldn't tell their therapists or trust to put in their vid-diaries, they spill to her with ease. She's nobody to them, after all. Just a poor black girl stuck in a dead-end job, struggling to make ends meet. She doesn't swim in their circles, so who cares if she knows about their infidelities or indiscretions?

"He's handsome, that Stoker," Sydney says, buffing away at the ridges in Mrs. Donovan's nails. Working two jobs, Sydney normally doesn't have time to keep up with politics, but rumor has it that Stoker's about to throw his hat into the race for premier of the Eastern Cape. He's an Afrikaner, but he's as genuine as the boy next door, and the rampant rumors about his enormous endowment probably don't hurt his popularity either. Especially among those constituents of the feminine persuasion. "You know him? Personally, I mean?"

Mrs. Donovan fans herself with her free hand, rose splotches once again springing up on her cheeks. "The epitome of masculinity. Precious, if I weren't married . . ." She trails off, then takes a moment to compose herself. "Yes, we're good friends. Our families have been close for centuries."

Sir Calvin begins yapping again, and Sydney hastily shoves the other half of the biscuit in front of him.

"Centuries, you say?" Sounds like the perfect opportunity to hear a long and convoluted story about how Mrs. Donovan's family came to South Africa during the Anglo-Boer War with intentions of raping the country of its precious metals and gems. Not that Sydney needs a refresher history course since she'd actually lived through it nearly two hundred years ago, but it'll give her a chance to do the thing that's the other half of getting those fat tips. Sydney grabs a small bottle of organic botanical oils and squeezes a drop onto each cuticle, then she rubs as Mrs. Donovan drones on incessantly about her lineage. Warmth buds inside that empty space right behind Sydney's navel, and it travels up—prickling like the skitter of centipede legs—through her chest, over her shoulders, and down her arms, and then finally into the pads of her fingertips, which glow as subtly as the sun peeking through gray winter clouds.

Mrs. Donovan's nails lengthen, just a few centimeters—enough to notice, but not so much to raise suspicions. Sydney then rubs out all signs of imperfection and hangnails.

By the time she gets to the left hand, Sydney's stomach is cramping, but it's nothing a couple of aspirin won't take care of. When she's done, she reaches into her alphie's bottom compartment and pulls out a bottle of clear coat, keeping it palmed safely out of sight. The empty spot inside her grows as she reaches into Mrs. Donovan's rambling thoughts and pulls out the shade of the dress she'll be wearing tonight. Sydney clenches her fist, envisions a nice complementary color, and opens her hand to reveal a feisty shade of mauve.

"Oh, that's perfect," Mrs. Donovan says as the first coat goes on. "I swear, Precious, the colors you pick for me are always spot-on. Sometimes I think you can read my mind."

"With your skin tone, there's not a shade that wouldn't look lovely on you, Mrs. Donovan." Sydney winces at the burn in the pit of her stomach but manages to put on a convincing smile. It's a small price to pay to keep her more generous clients loyal. Plus it breaks up the monotony of the day, reminding Sydney of a time, centuries and centuries ago, when her powers weren't limited to quaint parlor tricks. Her smile becomes more genuine with the thought, but then Sir Calvin starts up with the yapping, and all at once her headache's back. Sydney goes for another doggie biscuit, but Mrs. Donovan shakes her head.

"Too much of a good thing," she says, then leans back into her chair, eyes closed and fingers splayed carefully apart. "Don't want to spoil his appetite."

Sydney tries to tune Sir Calvin out, but he's right there in her face as she gives Mrs. Donovan her pedicure, which is torture enough with those meaty bunions of hers and heels that make even the roughest emery boards envious. Sydney's already pushed herself too far this morning, but she draws anyway, rubbing her warm hand under Sir Calvin's throat. His bark mutes, though his mouth keeps moving, which angers him even more. He nips Sydney, soundlessly, but drawing blood. Sydney seethes and gives him the eye. There's no way this little monster is going to cost her her tip, not after all she's put into it.

"Oh, what a playful little boy," she coos at him, stroking his head, pushing thoughts of calmness into his mind. The emptiness presses up against her rib cage and threatens to break through. She forces it back, looking for any spare nook, enough to make this damned Zed hybrid go to sleep, but his will is too strong. Sydney promises her body that she'll give it time to heal, and she'll even feed tonight if she has to. A small cry of pain escapes her, but finally the Zed hybrid lies still in its master's lap. Sydney doubles forward, catching herself on the leg of Mrs. Donovan's chair.

She takes a quick glance around the salon, hoping her foolish antics have gone unnoticed, but Zinhle Mpande stares back at her fiercely, her thick jaw set, cheeks tight, eyes intense like they're filled with the knowledge of every single one of her Zulu ancestors. She grabs a stack of towels and stalks toward Sydney's station.

"Fresh towels," she says perkily in English, before slamming them down beside the alphie. She whispers in the Zulu tongue so that Mrs. Donovan can't understand. "Haw! I know what you are."

Sydney gulps, then moves her attention to Mrs. Donovan's heels, scrubbing feverishly at them with an emery paddle. "I don't know what you're talking about," she says sweetly in return.

Zinhle clucks her tongue. "*Umuthi omnyama*," she says, picking up a bit of biscuit, then crumbling it in her hand before storming off. Black *muti*, dark spirits conjured through doggie treats nonetheless. Great. Sydney closes her eyes and sighs to herself. She'll have to be more careful. If Zinhle thinks she's a witch, it's only a matter of time before the other ladies find out. Even if they don't believe it, rumors are enough to cast suspicious looks in Sydney's direction, making it harder to do those things she does.

A witch.

She laughs at the idea, wishing it were that simple.

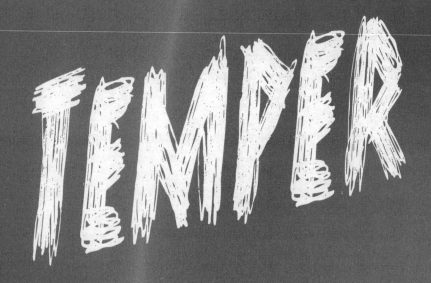

DOUBT

I feel like a drone in an ant colony," Kasim whispers to me as we follow the curve of a gravel pathway, weaving through swarms of students and passing the big brown mounds of school buildings set into the base of Grace Mountain. Knowing Kasim's fixation with bugs, he doesn't mean this as an insult, but I'm sure taking it that way. This is Gabadamosi? I'd expected something grand. Big glass buildings, daring feats of architecture, a place that exuded knowledge from every nook and cranny. This place looks so ancient, so tribal, and not in a good way. Doubt hits me like a punch to the ribs. What have I gotten us into?

My satchel hangs like a noose around my neck, holding the entire extent of the personal belongings we are allowed: two long-sleeved cikis and two short, all ruddy brown linen with orange jacquard embellishments around the collar and cuffs, with the school crest upon the right shoulder. Two matching sets of pants. A few pair of underwear. A sleep gown. Three note-books filled with twice-blessed paper. A set of defting sticks. A cup, a bowl, a spoon. One comfort item, and a note from home.

For my comfort item, I've chosen a pocket mirror, not to stoke my vainglory, but as a quick source of glass shards should the need arise. Kasim has picked a whole carton of individually wrapped Jak & Dee's dehydrated samp and beans. He eats them right out of the packet when he's stressed. And instead of a lov-ing note from our mother, we'd both gotten a slur of cusses, punctuated with "how could you?" and "I raised you better than this!" I wanted to explain to her why we had to leave, but how could we tell the woman who birthed us, who raised us the best she could, that her sons were beset by demons? And yet beyond her anger and disappointment, the way she looked at us, it was like she could *see* those monsters inside us as she slammed the door in our faces. Yes, it stings, but Kasim and I have to focus on figuring out a way to quiet our minds while wielding our powers. Then we can make it up to her.

We draw sharp stares from all directions. There is an un-spoken social order about things, the way students move in packs, the paths they take, who yields to whom when those paths intersect, but it is well beyond my grasp. We wear the clothes, but we definitely do not walk the walk. And I can barely stand to walk at all, the way these loafers pinch at my toes. Kasim stumbles along as well, scratching at his collar, like his grace has been left behind along with the rest of our possessions. He walks so close to me that our arms brush. The proximity is like a breath of fresh air. We may have next to nothing, but we have each other, and that's more than enough.

We near the administration building, another brown mound of old brick and thin panes of dingy glass, evoking im-ages of the simple wooden huts our ancestors once dwelled in.

Don't get me wrong, the place is immaculate, but the buildings cannot escape the burden of their age. We ascend a short set of stairs, our heads passing directly under a WELCOME TO GABADA-MOSI PREPARATORY banner. When I open the door, the dimly lit rotunda is abuzz with school staff scurrying across the packed dirt floor, flitting in and out of the glass doors of offices carrying stacks of precariously high paper and wearing impossibly wide smiles. That all grinds to a sudden halt as each and every eye falls upon us disappointedly. Whispers stir about as we pass, referring to us as *those boys* before we even get a chance to identify ourselves. Apparently, Uncle Yeboah had called in a huge favor from one of his welshing buddies who sat on the school board. Together they pushed through a Religioning Exchange Program that took poor secular kids from the comfy and immersed them in Grace's shadow for a quarter. He'd spent many multiples of the money he'd offered to us to pay our tuitions via "scholarship," bribe the proper officials at Gabadamosi, and keep his name from it all in any shape or form.

One quarter. Or what's left of it. Ten weeks is all the time we have to learn all we can, and hope that it's enough.

I place my hands on the front counter and nervously touch one of the pens held by a gilded cup bearing the school's crest— a bird-faced cheetah with a snake for a tail, wielding a long knife. "Hi. We're Auben and Kasim Mtuze. It's our first day."

The receptionist behind the desk forces a smile upon eir face, but would have had an easier time squeezing water from a rock. "Welcome, new students." The receptionist smacks eir lips like the words have left a disgusting aftertaste. "Munashe!" ey calls out, annoyed.

A smallish wooden door opens, which I'd thought was a maintenance closet, and out comes a young woman dressed in a high-quality yet ill-fitting blouse, neck adorned with a chunky kola nut necklace, and slacks with their cuffs skimming the floor. Her hair is pressed and fashionably unkempt, though I get the feeling that this was not her intent.

"Hello," she greets us, face aglow with the compassionate gaze of a child's doll. She looks a few years older than Kasim and me. "You must be Auben and Kasim. I'm Munashe, recent Gabadamosi alum, class of '09. They couldn't get rid of me, and now I'm a new student liaison. I can show you around and answer any of your questions. I'm at your beck and call."

We shake hands. She seems sincere enough, and her face doesn't have that look like we're polluting up the place, which makes me both trust her and feel immediately warier at the same time.

"You should get along with the tour, then," the receptionist says briskly. "We'll send all of the necessary paperwork over to your dormitory." Ey brushes me away with a finger flick, then sets about polishing the spot on the desk where I'd leaned . . . and tossing the pen I'd touched. The receptionist straightens the remaining pens, shuffles paperwork, neatens eir tight afro with a pat, waxes on a smile.

"Don't mind them," Munashe whispers to us. "I wish I could say they usually aren't quite this awful, but then I'd be a liar." She gives us an impish smile, then bids us to follow her to the exit. "It's just that everyone is a bit on edge. Gueye Okahim is paying a visit to Gabadamosi today. It's all very exciting. Rumor has it that he's seeking out an apprentice. Perhaps one of our students will catch his eye."

"Gueye Okahim?" Kasim asks.

Munashe stops so quickly, I run right into her back. "Seriously? You don't know who Gueye Okahim is? For the glory of Grace, this exchange program couldn't have been any more prudent. Gueye Okahim is the Man of Virtues at the Sanctuary.

The man who stands directly in Grace's shadow. Who has been thoroughly touched by those Hallowed Hands. Who speaks His word. Also a Gabadamosi alum, I have to add. Class of '71."

Munashe takes Kasim by the hand and eagerly bids us forth. "Come on. We don't want to be here when he arrives. I can't even imagine the extent of the school's embarrassment if his first visit in nearly five years involved a couple of sec-heads. No offense." Munashe pushes open the front door, and stiffens as she looks out. Coming up the stairs is a man clad in dark purple sequined robes that kiss the ground, his thin black thighs peeking from the slits upon either side. A collar of stiff pheasant feathers frames his head like a lion's mane. Hints of age dance lightly about his wizened eyes, though no evidence of his years exists anywhere else upon his chiseled face. His hair is shorn, except for a smooth bald band straight through the center, where the symbols of the seven virtues have been branded front to back. The one for grace overlaps onto his forehead.

Munashe immediately falls to her knees and makes the quick gesture we have seen our uncle do enough times. Kasim and I exchange a worried glance, and in the instantaneous language shared by twins, decide that we should at least make a minimal effort to fit in. We also go to our knees, but refrain from the religious gestures.

It soon becomes apparent to the three of us that we have chosen to show our respect right in the doorway to the building so that it is impossible for the Man of Virtues to pass. I slowly start to stand, but Munashe tugs me back down by the collar of my uniform. "We can't move until he's passed," she rasps to us. "Or until he's addressed us to do so." Unless the Man of Virtues intends to step over us, it will have to be the latter. He will have to speak directly to Kasim and me, and we have no idea what to do or how to respond. "Don't look at anything besides his feet. Say nothing other than 'Yes, Amawusiakaraseiya.'"

Say *what?*

My eyes stay fixed upon glimpses of bare feet peeking from beneath Gueye Okahim's robe. The feet stop inches away from us. I hear the amused smirk on his face as he says, "Arise, my children," in a voice full of intonation and power.

We comply thoughtlessly, like puppets pulled by strings.

The scurrying of many feet fills the rotunda behind us. I dare to part my glance from Gueye Okahim's feet to see the small army of school administrators with horrified faces.

"Amawusiakaraseiya," Munashe says, a quivering mess. "I am incredibly sorry you have been inconvenienced by these students. Please—"

"There is no inconvenience. I am here to be among the students and to witness how the Hallowed Hands have touched the minds and souls of our young ones. You," Gueye Okahim says, lifting my chin up with one of his ageless fingers. "I trust this fine institution is seeing to your religioning in an adequate manner?"

"Yes—" I try to get my mouth around the title, but the syllables refuse to cohere. I do the next best thing I can think of "—sir."

I swear I hear Munashe gritting her teeth at me.

"And you." Kasim's chin is lifted as well. "Do you feel your time here has brought you closer to Grace?"

Kasim grimaces, his mind churning over one of his sideways truths. "It certainly hasn't brought me any farther away, Amawusiekeseiya." The word slips effortlessly over his lips.

The air in the room is sucked thin by a collective gasp.

Kasim flushes. "What? I said that right, didn't I?" he whispers to Munashe.

Her mouth gapes, then opens and closes like a dying fish.

"I throw myself upon your mercy, Amawusiakaraseiya. It is my fault. These students here do not know any better. They are exchange students sent over from a secular school in a nearby comfy. They do not mean any offense."

"None is received. It is a good thing for His hands to reach into the hearts that need Him the most. It is good to meet you both. I am called Gueye Okahim by birth, Amawusiakaraseiya by His hands. You may call me Gueye if it is easier for you." He presses both of his hands around mine.

"I'm Auben, Gueye. Auben Mtuze. It is an honor to meet you."

"Likewise," he says with a major helping of humility.

"I'm Kasim Mtuze," Kasim says. "We're brothers. Twins." He stands next to me, his arm pressed against mine. It is like we are a united front in Gueye Okahim's presence, and together we might get through this unscathed.

"Kasim? It is interesting that parents raising a child in the secular way would give him such a highly religious name. *Controller of temper* it means in ancient Sylla."

"There were a dozen *Kasims* at our former school," Kasim says with a shrug. "I think it was a popular name at the time."

Munashe stands tight-lipped, her wide eyes drilling into Kasim's. I think a "Yes, Amawusiakaraseiya" was meant to go there. Sweat beads prickle upon her forehead, and I'm sure she's stopped breathing.

Gueye Okahim looks us over intently. We have caught his eye, and definitely not in a good way. "Yes, perhaps," he says with a short bow. "May Grace walk with the both of you."

And then he takes his leave. As soon as he is out of sight, Munashe hyperventilates. She attempts to speak at us between her quick and desperate breaths, but all that comes out is a broken string of indistinguishable consonants and airy vowels.

"That was an absolute disaster," she finally wheezes. "But it's all my fault. It's always my fault. Sorry, boys. I've got a mess to repair. Here are your class schedules." She shoves crest-embossed folders into each of our hands. "There's a map tucked inside. Come to me if you have any questions . . . just not today!"

About the Author

Nicky Drayden is a systems analyst living in Austin, Texas, and when she's not debugging code, she's detangling plotlines and mixing metaphors. Her award-winning debut novel, *The Prey of Gods*, is set in a futuristic South Africa brimming with demigods, robots, and hallucinogenic high jinks. Drayden's sophomore novel, *Temper*, is touted as an exciting blend of Afrofuturism and New Weird. Her travels to South Africa as a college student influenced both of these works, and she enjoys blurring the lines between mythology, science fiction, fantasy, horror, and dark humor. See more of her work at nickydrayden.com or catch her on Twitter at @nickydrayden.

MORE FROM NICKY DRAYDEN

In the tradition of Lauren Beukes, Ian McDonald, and Nnedi Okorafor comes a fantastic, boundary-challenging tale, set in a South African locale both familiar and yet utterly new, which braids elements of science fiction, fantasy, horror, and dark humor.

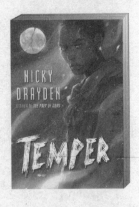

A *Publishers Weekly* Best Book of 2018!

A Vulture Best Sci-Fi and Fantasy Book of 2018!

In a land similar to South Africa, twin brothers are beset by powerful forces beyond their understanding or control. Two brothers. Seven vices. One demonic possession. Can this relationship survive?

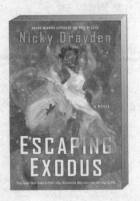

Rave reviews from
The *New York Times*, Bustle, and BookRiot

From Compton Crook award-winning author Nicky Drayden, a stand-alone novel that weaves her trademark blend of science fiction and dark humor into a dazzling story where society lives in the belly of the beast—quite literally—and one idealistic young woman will assume a yoke of power she's unprepared for and ultimately determine the fate of humanity.